A PLUME BOOK

SWAPPING LIVES

JANE GREEN is the author of eight bestselling novels, including *The Other Woman*, *To Have and to Hold*, and *Jemima J*. She
lives in Connecticut and London with her family.

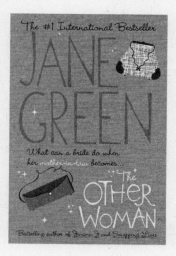

"Well-written and engaging."   —*Marie Claire*

"A sparkling comedy-drama."   —*Connecticut Post*

"Green's writing is deliciously witty and her heroines authentic. This is a charming book that demands, 'Read me in one
sitting!' "   —*People*

"A perfect summer read . . . funny, poignant."   —*Toronto Sun*

"Green skewers Connecticut suburbia with gleeful relish, and she hits the right marks with sympathetic Londoner Vicky, a quirky, imperfect heroine." —*Kirkus Reviews*

"Hard to put down . . . thanks to affable leading characters and interesting commentary on the cross-Atlantic cultural gap." —*Publishers Weekly*

Swapping Lives

JANE GREEN

*To Name,
With best Wishes,*

Ⓟ

A PLUME BOOK

Jane Green.

PLUME
Published by Penguin Group
Penguin Group (USA) Inc., 375 Hudson Street, New York, New York 10014, U.S.A. • Penguin
Group (Canada), 90 Eglinton Avenue East, Suite 700, Toronto, Ontario, Canada M4P 2Y3
(a division of Pearson Penguin Canada Inc.) • Penguin Books Ltd., 80 Strand, London WC2R
0RL, England • Penguin Ireland, 25 St. Stephen's Green, Dublin 2, Ireland (a division of Penguin
Books Ltd.) • Penguin Group (Australia), 250 Camberwell Road, Camberwell, Victoria 3124,
Australia (a division of Pearson Australia Group Pty. Ltd.) • Penguin Books India Pvt. Ltd.,
11 Community Centre, Panchsheel Park, New Delhi – 110 017, India • Penguin Group (NZ),
67 Apollo Drive, Rosedale, North Shore 0745, New Zealand (a division of Pearson New Zealand
Ltd.) • Penguin Books (South Africa) (Pty.) Ltd., 24 Sturdee Avenue, Rosebank, Johannesburg
2196, South Africa

Penguin Books Ltd., Registered Offices: 80 Strand, London WC2R 0RL, England

Published by Plume, a member of Penguin Group (USA) Inc. Previously published in a Viking
edition.

First Plume Printing, June 2007
10 9 8 7 6 5 4 3 2 1

Copyright © Jane Green, 2005
All rights reserved

Except for this work's original UK title, *Life Swap,* this work is not associated or affiliated with any
work entitled or with any person or entity publishing any books or other materials under that title.

Ⓟ REGISTERED TRADEMARK—MARCA REGISTRADA

The Library of Congress has catalogued the Viking edition as follows:
Green, Jane, 1968–
    Swapping Lives / Jane Green.
        p.   cm.
    ISBN 0-670-03480-0 (hc.)
    ISBN 978-0-452-28850-8 (pbk.)
    1. Periodical editors—England—London—Fiction.   2. Housewives—Connecticut—Fiction.
3. Single women—Fiction.   I. Title.

PR6057.R3443L54 2006
823'.914—dc22   2005058478

Printed in the United States of America
Original hardcover design by Daniel Lagin

PUBLISHER'S NOTE
This is a work of fiction. Names, characters, places, and incidents are either the product of the author's imagination or are used fictitiously, and any resemblance to actual persons, living or dead,
business establishments, events, or locales is entirely coincidental.

Acknowledgments

With gratitude and thanks as ever to all at Penguin, Anthony Goff, Vicky Harper, *Red* magazine, Peconic Baking Company, John Roch and Gary Chase, Alisa Messer, Nancy Laner, Dixie O'Brien, and of course my family, not forgetting the wonderful Fishy.

Chapter One

This is not a straightforward story of romance. Which is not to say there are no happy ever afters, but that you ought not to open this book knowing that the Prince and Princess disappear hand in hand into a glorious sunset.

In many ways, the story I'm about to tell you is not about romance at all. If anything, it is a story of real life. Of how each of us may think we know exactly what we need to make us happy, what will be good for us, what will ensure we have our happy ending, but that life rarely works out in the way we expect, and that our happy ending may have all sorts of unexpected twists and turns, be shaped in all sorts of unexpected ways.

And our own personal paradise may be someone else's version of hell. Or indeed vice versa . . .

Take Victoria Townsley, for instance. At thirty-five she is wonderfully, fantastically successful. She is features director of *Poise!* magazine—a magazine so stylish, so hip, so glossy and perfect, Victoria is, as she should be, the very embodiment of what the *Poise!* reader strives to be. Tall and on a good day slim-ish, she uses Aveda on her glossy hair, Eve Lom on her peachy skin, and Bliss lemon scrubs on her not-so-toned-except-you'd-only-know-that-if-you-saw-her-with-her-clothes-off body. In short, she uses exactly what the beauty director of *Poise!* prescribes as the latest and greatest of all beauty products, guaranteed to give you youth, dewiness, and to prolong your life by thirty years.

Victoria—Vicky to her colleagues and friends—lives in a beautiful flat off Marylebone High Street, decorated in Heal's best neutral shades, accented by rich chocolate-brown leather accessories, Balinese bamboo bowls picked up on a travel junket last year, and a touch of oh-so-trendy chinoiserie in the form of Chinese dressers that were found one Saturday morning down at Portobello Road.

The fridge is stocked with bottles of white wine, two cans of Diet Coke, and a couple of low-fat yogurts. In the butter compartment is a half-eaten bar of Cadbury's Milk Chocolate, but Vicky has forgotten it is there, and it is now three months past its sell-by date, although on Wednesday, two days before Vicky's period starts, she won't very much care about that.

Vicky's cat, Eartha, is curled up on her bed, lazily rolling over to stretch a paw out to claim her domain, happily looking forward to Vicky's arrival home from work, when she will jump on her lap purring, thrilled to be the most important person in Vicky's life, thrilled, in fact, to be the only one to sleep in Vicky's bed on a regular basis.

Because while you and I might look in awe at everything that Vicky has, at how she has built a career up from nothing to become one of the most successful female journalists in London, how she has no responsibilities, is able to go to glamorous parties and book launches and preview shows every night, and sleep in until nine in the morning, Vicky is not happy.

At thirty-five, Vicky is stunned that she is still single. Stunned that each of her friends has slowly been picked off, that she has been bridesmaid more times than she cares to think of, but that no one has ever chosen her.

And it's not even as if she has come close. She never worried about it in her twenties, when her longest relationship was six months, when she was far too busy making a name for herself in journalism, jumping from the *Liverpool Echo* down to London as a staff writer on *Cosmo*, switching to *Poise!* a few years later. When she hit thirty she vaguely thought that now she ought to start thinking about settling down, but by the time she came up for air, at around thirty-two, she realized that all the good men had been taken, and all of a sudden her prospects didn't look too good.

On her thirty-fifth birthday Vicky stayed home and got drunk. She replayed all the movies she'd loved when she was single and hopeful—*An Officer and a Gentleman, Baby Boom, When Harry Met Sally*—and she forced a few tears as she thought about how lonely she was and how much she wanted a husband and children, how much she wanted the life that her brother, Andy, had.

Andy, three years younger than her, had married his girlfriend from university, Kate. They had three children—Luke, Polly, and Sophie; two huge lurchers; and had moved out of central London a few years previously to bring up their children with fields and green and ponies.

It was, in short, everything that Vicky ever wanted. She adored Kate, always described herself as having the best sister-in-law in the world; in fact, she thought of Kate as the sister she always wanted, and she loved her nieces and nephew more than anyone in the whole world.

Vicky thought she was going to die when they all moved

out of London, but she hops on the train down to Somerset at least twice a month, and spends happy weekends sitting around the scrubbed pine table in the Aga-heated kitchen, bemoaning her single status as Kate rolls her eyes, attempts to shake off a Polly who's clinging to her leg and shrieking with glee as Kate drags her across the kitchen floor, and says she'd kill to be in Vicky's shoes, that Vicky doesn't know how wonderful her life is.

Vicky does know how wonderful her life is, it just isn't the kind of wonderful she wants. She wants the kind of wonderful that Kate has. The kind of wonderful that involves children shrieking with laughter, giant dogs draped over squishy sofas. A kind, loving husband who worships your every move.

At that point Kate was the one shrieking with laughter. "Does Andy worship my every move, then?" she said.

"Well, no," Vicky grunted. "But you know what I mean."

"Actually, no. I don't," Kate said firmly. "Your problem is you're a complete romantic. You keep thinking that marriage and children are going to come along and give you this wonderful life when first of all your life is pretty damn wonderful anyway, and second of all I don't know where you got it into your head that a life with marriage and children is so great in the first place."

Vicky looked at Kate in shock. "It's not?"

"It's not that it's not." Kate sighed. "It's just that it's not this perfect romantic idyll that you seem to think it is. Not that I'd expect much less from a girl whose favorite film is, what was it again? *Pretty Woman*?"

"No. *Baby Boom*," Vicky said reluctantly. "But for God's sake don't tell anyone. It's my secret shame. I'm always going on dates and telling them it's a Louis Malle, or some fabulous French art-house movie that actually I found spectacularly boring."

"Is *Baby Boom* the one with the vet?"

Vicky did a mock swoon. "Sam Shepard. You see? Why can't I find a vet like that? Why doesn't someone leave me a gorgeous cottage in the country?"

Kate rolled her eyes yet again. "If you think life is so wonderful in the country, why don't you sell the flat and buy something? It doesn't have to be Somerset. You could buy in Oxfordshire somewhere and commute."

"Don't be silly," said Vicky. "Then I'd never find a man."

"What about that Daniel?" Kate said. "Aren't you still seeing him?"

"I'm not seeing him," Vicky sighed. "It's just an arrangement we have. He's my neighborhood shag. As long as we're both single and we live so close, we just get together from time to time."

"Sounds very odd to me," Kate said. "Couldn't it develop into something more?"

"God, no." Vicky shuddered. "He's great in bed but not husband material in the slightest."

On the other side of the Atlantic Ocean lives Amber Winslow. She too looks, on the surface, to have everything she's ever wanted. Married to Richard, a trader at Godfrey Hamilton Saltz, a large Wall Street investment bank, they have much the life that Vicky craves, only with more money and less mess.

When Amber met Richard she had struggled up from her humble beginnings in Hoboken, New Jersey, joining a midtown law firm straight from college. She had worked her way up, met Richard, and was about to be made partner when she discovered she was pregnant.

Amber considered getting a full-time nanny and going back to work, but in the end she decided to go with the nanny and forget the work.

After a couple of years of squeezing Jared into a bedroom that was only slightly bigger than a cupboard in their apartment on West Sixty-eighth, they decided to take the plunge and move out of the city. Richard was doing better and better, and although they couldn't afford much more than a badly decorated tiny sixties colonial in the much-coveted town of Highfield, Connecticut, it was on a plot of two acres, and after a couple of years they decided to build an addition.

There was only one architect in town to work with— Jackson Phillips—and although he was the most expensive— some might even call him a rip-off merchant—he was the one all the in people used, and Amber knew how important it was to impress her newfound friends in the Highfield League of Young Ladies, and so they duly signed contracts with Jackson Phillips and off to work they went.

Their initial plans for a one-bedroom addition and family room swiftly became a two-bedroom addition and family room. While they were at it, Jackson suggested, why not turn the garage into a playroom, and build on a new garage? It wouldn't be too much work.

Amber and Richard thought it was a wonderful idea. A couple of weeks later they thought, why not add a new master bedroom on top of the garage? And thus began the spiraling out of control.

Just as they had finished the initial ideas, were about to

start construction drawings, and had already spent fortunes with Jackson Phillips, Amber realized what was bothering her all along about the work they were doing.

"It's the roof," she said to Richard. "As long as we have that shallow pitched roof everyone will know our house was a sixties colonial. All the new houses have steep roofs with dormers in them. We need to put a new roof on."

Months later the sixties colonial, the house that Amber was adamant she didn't want to knock down because she loved its charm, was knocked down, and Amber's dream McMansion was built in its place.

It took twice as long as the builder had said, and cost them three times the price. Jackson Phillips's bill was so huge they spent the next few years warning off anyone they spoke to who was looking to do the same thing, but at the end of two years Amber knew it was worth it.

She had the most beautiful house on her street. Possibly even in the town. A stone and clapboard colonial that impressed way before you opened the front door to take in the marble floors and sweeping curved staircase.

Amber had a house that *begged* her to host Highfield League of Young Ladies' coffee mornings, *ached* for her to hold trunk shows displaying beautiful children's clothes from a young designer she'd just discovered, *insisted* she invite the girls around for girls' nights in, pretending it wasn't just to show off her house.

Of course, what these girls don't realize as they ooh and aah over her galleried great room, her huge marble bathroom with Victorian-style claw-footed tub, is that Amber, Amber resplendent in her Prada clothes and Hermès bags, Amber with the perfect husband and gorgeous children, with her golden retriever who had been sent off to doggy boot camp to learn how to be a dog, is not as to the manner born as she so desperately wants others to think.

Amber Collins, as she was before she met Richard, was a fighter. She was brought up in a run-down trailer park backing on to the railroad from which her father left to get cigarettes when she was two years old, and never returned. Her mother had a succession of boyfriends after that, men who would supply her with cigarettes and sometimes money to pay the rent, and Amber was left in the care of neighbors, becoming as self-sufficient as any child who doesn't have parents around to take care of her.

Amber put herself through college. As a teenager she watched her friends get pregnant by loser boyfriends, saw them repeating the patterns of their parents, and she vowed her life would be different. She would make something of herself. She would leave all this behind.

She was lucky because she was clever. And luckier still because she was driven, had the motivation to work hard, to have a number of jobs throughout school, to save enough money to put herself through college.

At her state university, Amber was careful to study people from different backgrounds, the girls from the middle classes, the girls who had a confidence, a sense of entitlement that was entirely new to Amber.

She listened to the way they spoke, noted how their speech was far softer than her strong New Jersey accent, and she changed her voice accordingly. She watched how they dressed, not in the skimpy mini-skirts and revealing tops of her friends, but in pants and loafers, chic simple clothes, cable-knit sweaters and flat ballet pumps.

She grew out her perm, learned to wear her hair in a sleek shoulder-length bob, redid her makeup so it was natural and understated, and when she went home for the summer after her first year at the university, no one recognized her. She was delighted.

She met Richard at a dinner party hosted by some friends who were the perfect embodiment of the people Amber aspired to be. By this time Amber was a lawyer, and she and Richard immediately bonded over their professional aspirations.

But mostly she was drawn to Richard because he had grown up with everything she'd never had. Originally from Brookline, Massachusetts, close to Boston, he had been brought up in a house that looked like a palace from the outside, and inside appeared to be falling apart. Old, old patrician money. Money so old that it had in fact disappeared. There was still the family compound, and an ancient valet who looked after the family, there just wasn't the money to maintain it.

Richard's mother, Ethel, but known to everyone as Icy, was, as her nickname suggests, a cool blond in the Grace Kelly mold. Their Christmas cards were always family photos—the parents, five children, and three dogs—snapped unawares at their grandparents' summer house on Martha's Vineyard.

Richard didn't have the money, but he had the background and he had the name. As soon as she heard it—Richard Winslow—she knew he was of *the* Winslows, and Amber was determined to make him fall in love with her.

It wasn't easy. Despite her glossy hair and simple chic clothes, Amber knew that Richard had women falling at his feet. And so she played hard to get. She sat next to him at dinner and ignored him, professing to be fascinated by the terribly boring man on her left.

When he attempted to speak to her she was cool and un-interested, and the couple of times after dinner when she caught him looking at her with a puzzled expression, she just looked away.

She played it perfectly. Richard wasn't used to women not responding to his charm and boy-next-door grin, wasn't used to women not responding to the very fact that he was Richard Winslow of, yes, those Winslows.

So although Amber wasn't quite his usual type—brainless models and bimbettes of varying hair colors and heights—he was intrigued, and when he got her phone number from the host of the party and phoned, and she acted as if she couldn't remember meeting him, he was all the more interested.

It was the hardest thing Amber ever had to do. Harder even than reinventing herself and hiding her background. For this was something she wanted more than she had wanted anything in her life. This was her opportunity to be truly accepted. If she could get Richard to marry her she'd never have to worry about anything ever again.

When Richard phoned, Amber would pretend to be out. She'd sit in the living room biting her nails as her answering machine picked up. She only relaxed when she could see it was working, when caller ID showed that he kept phoning. One Saturday evening he phoned every ten minutes until one in the morning when she eventually picked up.

"Where have you been?" he asked in his little-boy-lost voice.

"Just out with a friend," she said lightly. "No one you

know." When in fact she had eaten cold pizza alone in her apartment, worked a few hours, then watched a couple of videos.

Amber developed an air of mystery that Richard couldn't penetrate.

"I don't know what it is about her," he said to Hal, his best friend, "but she's different. I've never felt this way about anyone before."

They were married at the family compound in Brookline, and it truly was the happiest day of Amber's life. Before you think this was all too premeditated, too cold, know that Amber had fallen deeply in love with Richard. Yes, she had decided he would be hers, and for all the wrong reasons, but the more she saw him, the more he made her laugh and made her relax, the more she realized that she loved him.

In fact, when she wasn't trying so hard to be something that she wasn't, Amber found that she was able to relax with Richard in a way she hadn't ever been able to before.

But those days, those early carefree days of their marriage, seem like a long time ago now. Richard's career is going better and better—so well, in fact, that Amber hardly ever sees him—and although she loves their house in Highfield, adores her children, Jared and Grace, there is something about the old days that she misses.

Her house may be beautiful, but often it feels as if it's not her own. There is the constant presence of Lavinia, the nanny, not to mention the cleaning team that comes in three times a week to thoroughly clean.

Sometimes she gets back from meeting friends for lunch and tries to enjoy a quiet coffee in the kitchen, then Lavinia will come in and start emptying the dishwasher, or Jared and Grace will get back from school and jump around her, climbing onto her lap, desperate for her attention regardless of whether she's in the middle of something important.

And there's the ever-present guilt. She knows she's a better mother when she's able to spend quality time with her children, when she's able to give them to Lavinia when they're tired and clingy and whining, and yet she always feels guilty about not spending enough time with them.

But her life is so busy. It's not that she ever wishes she didn't have children—God forbid that thought should even cross her mind—it's just that sometimes she wishes life were a bit simpler. And mostly she wishes that Richard were home more, although she knows this isn't likely to change, and after all, look at all she has, look at her beautiful house, beautiful clothes. If Richard didn't work the hours he does she'd never be able to have all this.

Oh, how far she has come.

Chapter Two

"Damn, damn, bugger, and damn!" Vicky checks her watch as she grabs her coat and starts to run toward the lift, shouting instructions to her assistant, Ruth.

"Can you just make sure the copy for that story on anorexia is given to Janelle tonight? I'm so sorry but I've got to go—I'm already going to be late for this bloody dinner party."

"Another setup?" Ruth grins as Vicky is about to disappear out of the door.

"Not even." Vicky rolls her eyes. "This time they asked me to bring a date and I completely forgot. Don't forget that copy!" And she steps into the lift.

Until she hit her early thirties, the vast majority of Vicky's friends were single. There was the core group of hard-bitten journalists, most of whom had worked together at one time or another. Jackie had been the other staff writer on *Poise!* when Vicky had first started, although now she had moved on to producing on Radio 4, regularly relying on Vicky to come on and be a talking head when the issue of the day was anything vaguely concerning women. The same age as Vicky, Jackie had married two years previously and had created a bohemian love nest in Islington. No children as yet. Jan had been Vicky's first features editor. A decade older than Vicky, she had married young, had two children, then got divorced and rediscovered her career. She now lived with Mike, an editor on *The Times*.

Georgia was the only one left who was still in the same boat as Vicky, but Georgia didn't seem to mind in the slightest, which Vicky never quite understood. Like Vicky, she too had a couple of lovers she could call up when necessary, but unlike Vicky, she didn't crave more than the odd night of intimacy.

Georgia never let her "friends" stay the night. "Are you crazy?" she once said to Vicky, who always insisted Daniel sleep over. "I want to stretch out and sleep diagonally on my bed if I feel like it. Plus I'm a horror first thing in the morning and I don't want to see anyone, never mind let anyone see me."

"But don't you miss the cuddling?" Vicky said.

"Are you kidding? I can't bear anyone to touch me when I'm sleeping." Georgia shuddered. "Frankly, as soon as they've done the dirty deed they can leave."

Vicky laughed. "I'll never understand you," she said. "You make it all sound so clinical."

And Georgia shrugged. "I guess it is, but that suits me. No point confusing sex with anything else. And really, at the end of the day, that's all it's about—sex. No strings attached. That's your problem with that Daniel. You think it's just about sex, but how can it be when you want him to stay the night and wrap you up in those big manly strong arms of his?"

"Oh shut up," Vicky said. But she had a point.

* * *

Ah, Daniel. Wouldn't he be the perfect guest to this dinner party tonight? The dinner party held by Deborah, the final member of the core group, who had not only dropped out first but had dropped out quicker and more absolutely than any of the others had dared.

Deborah and Dick. And their three gorgeous towheaded children. Deborah who had left her staff job on the *Daily Mail* when her second child came along, and now did the odd freelance job working from home. Deborah who was never happier than when standing outside the school gates of her eldest son's exclusive Hampstead prep school, chatting to the other mothers about what exactly they would do to solve this bullying problem everyone was talking about.

Tonight was Deborah's attempt to blend some of her new friends with some of her old. The friends from school were Lisa and Christopher, Chris and Vanessa—old friends of Dick's, Jackie and Pete, and Vicky plus one. She did think about trying to find an appropriate single man for Vicky, but really, who has the time?

As for Vicky, the only reason she had accepted was because Jackie was going—she never gets to see her socially these days—but why, oh why hadn't she remembered she was supposed to bring a date?

Single men are not an easy thing to find when you're thirty-five years old and you've got precisely one hour to catch the Tube home, jump into the shower, make yourself presentable, then turn up to a dinner party with a gift under one arm, trying not to look utterly frazzled.

But Daniel would be perfect. Hurrying to the Tube, Vicky calls him on her mobile.

" 'Lo?"

"Daniel? It's Vicky."

"Hey, Vicky! How are you?"

"I'm great, Daniel, but listen, I know this is short notice, but I've got to go to this dinner party tonight and I've only just found out I was supposed to bring a date. Please, *please* tell me you're free."

There's a pause. "Oh Vix, I wish I'd known earlier, but I can't. I've got a dinner myself."

"Oh please get out of it. Can't you?" Vicky lowers her voice seductively. "I'll make it worth your while."

"Vix, I really couldn't, but seeing as you've made such a strong case, how about I come over later? Say, around eleven-thirty?"

"Oh forget it," Vicky snaps. "I'm not your bloody sex toy," and with a sigh of irritation she clicks her phone shut.

It is only when Vicky walks into the living room that she remembers quite how much she detests being the only single person at events such as this.

Jackie and Pete are not here yet, and perched on sofas are women Vicky doesn't know, and even though Deborah sweeps her over and introduces her, it is clear from the outset that these are not people with whom she will have much in common.

Oh stop it, Vicky admonishes herself for these habits of old. I will not feel inferior to these people just because I am single. I am features director of *Poise!*, for God's sake. I am just as good as they are. Hell no, I am better.

But from the very first second Vicky knows she won't be accepted. It's the way the woman introduced to her as Vanessa glances at her boho chic outfit, so very different from Vanessa's own Joseph trousers, Jimmy Choo boots, and chic little cashmere cardigan.

"These are Maloles!" Vicky is tempted to shout, proffering her gorgeous new shoes. "Yes that's right, too trendy for you to even have heard of them in your uniform of Joseph and Jimmy Choo! I'm trendier than you. Ha!" But of course that voice in Vicky's head is only attempting to drown out the slightly stronger voice that tells Vicky she's not quite good enough, she doesn't fit in, she doesn't have the uniform.

Or indeed the husband.

"I was just telling Deborah that my daughter is finally potty-trained," Vanessa says warmly, and the voices in Vicky's head start to recede. "She's the last girl in her class, which is just so mortifying."

"Oh?" Vicky has no idea what to say to this. "How old is she?"

"Nearly two and a half. Can you imagine? How many kids do you have?"

"I don't." Vicky shrugs. "Just me."

"Ah." Vanessa doesn't seem to know quite how to continue. "So, is your husband coming straight from work? I couldn't believe Chris actually got home in time."

Vicky grins. "I don't have a husband. Just me, I'm afraid."

Deborah reappears with a glass of wine for Vicky, and puts her arm around her. "I know, isn't Vicky lucky? Can you even remember what it was like having no husband and kids?"

"To be honest, the only thing I desperately miss is my sleep. Especially on the weekends. I adore my daughter, but I wish she'd sleep beyond six o'clock on a Sunday."

The other pretty blond woman that Vicky doesn't know comes over and introduces herself. "I couldn't help overhearing. My son's started having bad dreams so now he climbs into bed with us every night. You try sleeping with two men in your bed, both of them snoring and kicking you all night."

"I was going to say that was one of my fantasies," Vicky says, "until you got to the snoring and kicking bit."

"Used to be one of mine." Vanessa laughs. "Now my fantasies involve earplugs and feather beds."

The men, congregating on the other side of the living room, come over. "Couldn't help hearing something about fantasies," says the man who turns out to be Vanessa's husband, Chris. "Thought now was the time to come over and join you."

Vanessa rolls her eyes. "Trust me, it wasn't anything for you to get excited about."

"Hello, I'm Christopher." Another man shakes Vicky's hand. "I belong to Lisa. Where's your other half?"

Oh for God's sake, Vicky thinks. Is it really so alien that I should not have an "other half" . . .

She shrugs. "He had an accident this morning and had to have his nose and left ear removed. I'm going to see him at the hospital later."

Christopher stands stock-still and stares at her. He has absolutely no idea what to do.

"Oh, I'm only joking." Vicky attempts a smile. "I don't actually have a husband. And if I did and he had to have a nose and left ear removed, trust me, I'd be sitting at the hospital with him."

"Right," says Christopher, who quickly moves to the other side of the group.

It wasn't until dessert that Vicky realized what was so strange. Nobody had asked her what she did. They had spent the evening talking about films they had seen, books they had read, indulging in the odd celebrity gossip story involving Kate and Jude and Sadie that Jackie swore came from an excellent source and was undoubtedly true.

And a large part of Vicky's evening had been spent listening to them share their concerns about whoever the current au pair or nanny was. Deborah's nanny, apparently, was lovely but ate like a horse.

"I couldn't believe it," Deborah said. "When she came she was, well, not skinny but slim, and I swear to you, six months later, she's now an elephant. She just doesn't stop eating."

"Well, what does she eat?" Lisa asked.

"She comes down in the morning and pours herself a mountain of cornflakes," Deborah said, as Dick started to laugh.

"I have to admit," Dick said, "even I was somewhat surprised."

"Then after the cornflakes she has two slices of toast with about an inch of peanut butter and jelly on them, and recently she's started making herself fried eggs as well. I wouldn't mind, but I keep going to the fridge or larder to get something to eat and it's all bloody well gone."

"See, that's what drives me mad," Dick added. "I don't care so much about what she eats, but she'll put back an empty box." The others around the table started laughing. "No, seriously," Dick pleaded, "who does that? Why doesn't she just throw it away? I'll go to pour myself some Rice Krispies and there are three Rice Krispie grains at the bottom of the box. Throw the damn box away!"

"My au pair's just dopey," Vanessa said. "Lovely, sweet girl, but wouldn't know initiative if it came up and hit her on the head. I came home the other night at quarter to seven and the kids had had no bath, and were running around the kitchen on a total sugar high. Guess what she'd made them for dinner . . ." Vanessa paused dramatically. "Apple strudel."

"No!" came the shocked response from the rest of the women in the room.

"I'm serious. I phoned and told her that I wouldn't be back to make dinner so could she make something, but instead of sticking some fish fingers under the grill she took me at my word and made the only thing she knows how to make. Apple bloody strudel."

"Your kids must have been happy." Deborah grinned.

"Happy? They were delirious. It took me about four hours to calm them down enough to get them to actually lie down."

"Well, at least you didn't have the pornmeister," said Christopher, exchanging grins with Lisa.

"Oh God, that was unbelievable," said Lisa. "Tell them what happened."

"We had this fantastic nanny, Lucia. She'd been with us for two years and then her boyfriend came to visit and he stayed with us. A few days became a month, and then our cable bill arrived. He'd been going into the spare room every night at midnight and ordering porn films on cable, and watching them all night. Our cable bill was hundreds and hundreds of pounds."

Lisa shuddered. "Not to mention the fact that this was a man helping Lucia look after our children."

"You don't think . . ." Vanessa said, not wanting to speak the unspeakable.

"No. My kids were old enough for me to quiz them, and I know they would have told me if anything untoward had happened. Still, it was awful."

And Vicky decided to speak up. "We did an article last

month about porn addiction, particularly on the Internet. It's becoming more and more of a problem, and one of the main findings is that the more you watch the more desensitized you become, and therefore the more you need to watch in order to get turned on."

"What do you do?" Vanessa broke the silence. It clearly hadn't occurred to anyone, other than Jackie and Deborah who knew, that Vicky might have a job, let alone something that might actually be interesting.

"Vicky is features director of *Poise!*," Deborah announced proudly on Vicky's behalf, and Vicky then spent the rest of the evening—short though it was—answering envious questions about her life, the magazine world, what celebrities she had met, and how incredible her life must be.

Finally they took notice of Vicky. Even though she didn't have a husband.

"I'm sorry for shouting at you." Vicky is contrite as she lies in the bath and picks up the phone.

"Does that mean you want me to come over?" Daniel's smile is audible down the phone line.

"Am I really that obvious?"

"When you phone me at eleven at night then I pretty much know it's not just for a chat."

"Well, I'm in the bath now. How soon could you be here?"

"Don't move," Daniel says. "I'm on my way."

Daniel, Daniel, Daniel. Why can't I fall in love with you? Vicky thinks as she watches him sit naked on the edge of the bed as he checks his e-mail on his BlackBerry, then turns it off for the night.

"You're lovely," she says, reaching out and stroking his back, and he turns and smiles at her before climbing under the covers.

"You're not so bad yourself," he says. "Wanna spoon?" And Vicky snuggles against him, loving the warmth and intimacy of being cradled in another body.

He's kind, funny, intelligent, but the only time Daniel ever makes her heart beat faster is just as she's about to have an orgasm. And even then it's entirely predictable. Daniel is just the quintessential boy next door, and Vicky believes he'd settle down with her in a heartbeat.

Although she's not entirely right. There's no question that Daniel does adore her, but Daniel has never been much good at exclusive relationships. He loves the ease of this arrangement, it suits him just as well as it suits her, and he'd be happy if they were to see each other more, but he's not ready to give up the others. Not by a long shot. And one of the reasons he adores Vicky is that he thinks she knows that.

Vicky may be his regular neighborhood shag, but that doesn't stop him from going out with other women. So far there's been no reason to stop seeing Vicky; after all, there don't seem to be any rules about sleeping with more than one woman, just as long as you always wear a condom.

This evening, for instance, he had a date with Maya. He noticed her first because of her hair—a rich, burnished copper—and since he's always had something of a thing for redheads he was happy to see that her face was just as striking as her hair.

Daniel had discovered that the greenroom at work seemed to be an excellent hunting ground for the producer of a sought-after evening chat show. Every Friday night the room was filled with gorgeous girls, most of whom dreamed of somehow getting on television, none of them particularly worried about casting-couch associations. And anyway, Daniel was no slouch in the looks department, so it wasn't as if they had to lie back and think of *Heat* magazine.

Maya was the PR for the winner of *Celebrity Survivor*—an ex–glamour model with enormous breasts that covered a heart of gold. Daniel had introduced himself to both of them, but while he had found himself completely unattracted to the ex–glamour model (who incidentally wasn't interested in Daniel but was perturbed that he didn't appear to be interested in her), there was a definite frisson with the gorgeous redhead.

On his way home that night she had texted him. Flirtatious, funny, bold, it was exactly what he liked. Thank God, Daniel had been born when he had. Too lazy to make much of an effort himself, he adored these new women who seemed to do everything that was once presumed exclusive male territory. They phoned him, texted him, left messages for him. He couldn't even remember the last time he had to work to get someone, the last time he felt the thrill of the chase.

Even his date with Maya was easy. He may have booked the table—the Wolseley, which was suitably impressive for a first date—but she was the one who phoned him and suggested they have dinner, and this was after a series of late-night flirtatious phone calls, when Maya inevitably called Daniel.

Daniel was what his friends called a serial shagger. "It's by default," he always shrugged. "I'm not doing anything! I can't help it if women find me irresistible." And his friends would always splutter with laughter, except the ones who were married, and they tended to be both envious and patronizing—nothing's as good as finding the woman you want to spend the rest of your life with, they'd say, at the same time begging for details and shaking their heads in wonder at how Daniel managed to pull it off.

At thirty-eight years of age, Daniel's charms didn't appear to be waning. If anything they were growing stronger, and the fact that he was still able to date a full spectrum of women aged anything from eighteen upwards was reason enough not to settle down.

Of course, there were the women who tried to change him. Who thought that the only reason he hadn't settled down was that he hadn't found the right woman and that *she,* whoever the *she* of the month happened to be, would be the one to make him change his mind.

But they soon realized their mistake. It was one of the things he loved about Vicky. She didn't have any other expectations of him. It was a mutually compatible arrangement that suited them both perfectly. Even tonight when she'd invited him along as her date, he knew it wasn't with any other motivations in mind.

Meanwhile, tonight had been a wonderful taster of what was to come. He'd had dinner with Maya, the conversation growing more and more flirtatious as the wine flowed. They'd jumped into a cab outside the restaurant and had ended up kissing passionately on the backseat as they'd pulled up to her flat in Muswell Hill. She hadn't invited him in, which surprised him, but meant there was even more to look forward to next time.

So he was very happy to come home to the phone call from Vicky. Far better to join her for the night than go to bed alone with a hard-on.

And he does stay the night, which is no great hardship

given her bed is a huge comfortable king-size. And he does fall asleep wrapped around Vicky, which is no great hardship given she's warm and soft, and it is so unbelievably comforting, falling asleep entwined with someone else. And he does think, just for a moment when they wake up in the morning, that it must be quite nice to have this every day. To have someone to chat to as you're getting dressed, to have this kind of ease with another person, to be able to share everything with a partner for life.

But then he remembers Maya. Her copper hair. Her quick tongue. The curve of her breasts that he traced outside her sweater on the backseat of the taxi. So many women. So little time.

Chapter Three

Amber groans as she rolls over and hits the alarm clock, sinking back into the pillows as she tries to force herself awake. Not that she should be tired, last night wasn't, after all, a late night, but every morning it seems to be harder and harder to rouse herself from the cocooning comfort of her bed.

In the old days Jared would come in and wake her. She'd be woken by a little hand on her shoulder, or a whispered, "Mommy? Are you awake?" And she'd throw back the covers for Jared to climb in and snuggle up next to her, stroking her face and relishing this alone time with Mommy.

Jared—Jar—was her first, and the one great love of her life. When she became pregnant with Grace, she spent months carrying a secret fear that she would never be able to love another child as much as Jared, that however fond she would be of this second child, Jared would always have her heart.

And it's true, it did take her a long time to bond with Grace, far longer than with Jared, although the fact that she handed Grace over to a nanny two weeks after the maternity nurse left may have had something to do with it.

The nanny, Lavinia, used to bring Grace in for cuddles with Amber, who would hold her for a while, breathing a sigh of relief when Jared would demand her attention so she could hand Grace back.

Yet now she finds she adores Grace, is quite as much in love with her as she is with Jared, albeit in a different way. Jared was her gentle child, sweet, sensitive; she and Richard smugly prided themselves on never having experienced the terrible twos with Jared because they were obviously such wonderful parents.

All that changed with Grace. Grace who is stubborn, willful, strong. Grace who is absolutely sure of what she wants and has no fear whatsoever. Grace who suffered such terrible twos there were times when Amber wanted to just sit down and cry or, failing that, send her back for a new, improved model.

But Grace is also funny. She makes faces and puts on voices and has an imagination so extraordinary that Amber and Richard constantly look at her in amazement that they created such an incredible little girl. She has sweetness and charm, and the ability to wrap anyone she wants around her little finger. And she is cuddly in a way Jared never was; passing Amber in the kitchen Grace will often just lean her head on Amber's back, kiss her on the knee, climb onto her lap and fold into her body.

Amber finally forces herself out of bed, knowing that, if nothing else, she will have to battle with Grace soon to get her dressed for school. At only three years old, Grace already refuses to wear anything Amber picks out for her. Naturally, because Amber didn't grow up wearing beautiful clothes, never had the money for them, she now spends hours browsing European children's clothes, flicking through the more upmarket catalogs.

Grace's wardrobe is chock-full of Bonpoint and Tartine et

Chocolat, Jacadi, and Petit Bateau. Stunning French clothes with elaborate smocking, piqué Peter Pan collars, beautiful Liberty-print dresses, with classic black patent Mary Jane shoes.

Grace refuses to wear any of it. No subtle colors or clothes for Grace. No plums, nor peaches, nor soft cornflower blues. Grace is all about *pink*. Pink clothes, preferably sparkly, and if there are transfers so much the better.

Her current favorites are hot-pink velour tracksuit bottoms—she has one pair with a stripe down the side, and one without. The tantrums that ensue should Amber try to force her into something else have become not worth Amber's while. Although she can't help but wince when Grace teams the tracksuit bottoms with pink Disney sweatshirts, or polyester T-shirts with shiny pictures of princesses all over them.

Not that Amber would ever buy Grace anything like that. Unfortunately her mother does. Amber barely sees her mother now, but Richard has met her and she was at the wedding, much to Amber's distress, although she managed to sit her out of the way; anyway, by that time it didn't really matter what Richard's family thought of her as it was ever so slightly too late.

Amber's mother is longing to get to know her grandchildren. She knows she wasn't the best mother she could have been, but also knows she was the best mother under the circumstances. "Thank God, you'll never know what it was like," she said to Amber at Amber's wedding, shocked into speechlessness by the family, and the money, that Amber was marrying into.

Sue, Amber's mother, phones from time to time, and from time to time great big packages arrive, gifts for Jared and

Grace. Amber made the mistake of admitting that Grace had loved a particularly disgusting Lurex hoodie Sue had sent, and since then the clothes have got progressively louder and more sparkly. And Grace is in heaven.

It's only preschool, Amber tells herself. It doesn't really matter what anyone thinks, she adds, although she doesn't even believe that herself, but she doesn't have the energy to fight anymore.

Grace isn't in her bedroom, and as Amber walks down the corridor toward the back staircase she hears the sound of laughter drifting up from the kitchen. At least, she thinks, they've woken up in a good mood.

Lavinia is always in the kitchen preparing breakfast at seven. Recently there have been times when Amber has been about to come downstairs and she has heard shouting, or crying, or whining coming from the kitchen. After hesitating at the top of the stairs, she is ashamed to admit that she has very quietly turned around and tiptoed back to bed.

"Mommy!" Both kids turn as she walks through the doorway and climb down from their chairs, flinging their arms around her.

"Hello, darlings," she says, giving them big kisses. "Morning, Lavinia. Did Richard leave already?"

Lavinia turns from where she's making French toast, and nods. "Off to the gym before work, he said. Coffee?"

"Mmm. Lovely." Amber sits down at the table as a high-pitched whine escapes from Grace.

"No, Mom, sit next to me!"

"No!" Jared shouts, pushing Grace off the chair she's attempting to climb up. "Mommy's going to sit next to me."

"No!" Grace shrieks, and hits Jared hard on the head; he immediately starts wailing.

Amber grits her teeth and prays for patience. "Stop it, both of you!" she snaps. "Grace, no hitting. And Jared, stop pushing Grace. I'm going to sit in the middle so you can both sit next to me, okay?"

Peace is restored as Lavinia brings the French toast over to the table and places a much-needed strong cup of coffee in front of Amber.

At ten o'clock the kids are in school—Jared at kindergarten, Grace at the little preschool down the road—Lavinia is busy doing the laundry, and Amber is busy whizzing around the house cleaning up before the cleaning team arrives. Yes, she's paying them to clean, but they also clean the houses of several of the big names in the Ladies League—how do you think Amber found them?—and she doesn't want anyone gossiping that she keeps her house a pigsty.

Not to mention that Julian and Aidan are coming this morning. They're the decorators everyone in town is talking about. Recently moved to Highfield from Manhattan, they've been the subject of various editorials in the *Highfield Gazette*, not to mention much speculation as to who will be their first clients.

Amber knew exactly who they were. She may live out in the suburbs but she still subscribes to *Architectural Digest* and *Vogue*. She knows which pop stars' homes they did, which fashion editors they're friendly with, even where they went on holiday last year ("Phuket, and isn't it *so* dreadful about the tsunami . . .").

Nobody expected Julian and Aidan, or Amberley Jacks as they are known professionally, to move out to "the boondocks." "Darling," as one society matron had said to them when she ran into them a few months before at Da Silvanos, "if you're that desperate for the country get a summer house in the Litchfield Hills, for God's sake. Don't leave us permanently." But Julian and Aidan were ready to settle down. Aidan missed living near the water, plus Lincoln, their schnauzer, needed more room to run.

They bought a beach shack, which naturally they "did up" in super-quick time, and after the *Gazette* ran a double-page spread celebrating their arrival in Highfield and featuring their "stunning new home," everyone who was anyone, or who indeed wanted to be anyone, tried to take them on.

But Amberley Jacks is hardly desperate for business. They can afford to be choosy, don't like taking on more than a handful of clients at any one time, and certainly don't want to work for just anyone.

The call from Amber Winslow, though, they just had to take. "Do you think it's *that* Winslow?" Aidan had said to Julian, who, although born in Ireland, had taken to America and all things American like a duck to water.

They made a few calls, found out that indeed Amber Winslow was married to Richard Winslow of the known Winslow family, and so she was one of the lucky few they called back. They had heard that she had come from nothing, that no one knew what her background was; the rumor said the mother was—gasp—a cleaner from Long Island.

Whatever the truth, Julian and Aidan loved nothing more than a good story, and so Amber Winslow was one of the few people they set up a meeting with.

"We like to interview potential clients first," said Aidan during that initial phone call, as Amber's heart fluttered with fear and all her inadequacies rose to the surface.

"Good Lord, that sounds scary," she managed. "What if I fail?"

Aidan had laughed. "Oh we're not scary at all. It's just that we only tend to work with people we really like, and this is just to make sure we get on. But don't worry, I can tell already that we're going to like you."

Amber relaxed. But only a little.

She has bought beautiful flower arrangements and placed them in every room, hidden the TV guides under piles of *Architectural Digest*, and put away the odd vase that she suspects will not pass muster.

Her clothes have been planned two weeks in advance. In fact, the minute she put down the phone to Aidan she sat in her wardrobe and planned what she would wear to make the very best impression. She didn't want to wear her daily uniform of Gap pants and sneakers, nor the smart little Chanel suits she wears for Richard's work do's or the rare occasions they go up to Brookline for family get-togethers.

In the end she decided on a pair of chocolate-brown pants with a soft pink cashmere sweater, and flat brown suede Prada pumps. Classic, elegant, with a slightly trendy twist thanks to the shoes, she'd team it with a huge chunky diamond and rose quartz ring that had cost several thousand dollars but that she hadn't been able to resist.

The very fact that she was able to go into a store and walk out less than five minutes later with a diamond ring, without having to think about it, still managed to amaze her. She knew by now she ought to be used to it, and in many ways she was, but this not having to think about how much she spent, nor about what she spent it on, still, even after all these years, felt slightly odd.

And Richard had always encouraged her. "You deserve it," he'd say as she showed him the fur scarf she'd just bought, or the Balenciaga bag, or the Loro Piana shawl. "I know you never had any of this before, and what's money for if not to spend?" His generosity was one of the things she loved most about him. She couldn't bear to be married to one of those men who questioned everything, who gave their wives a strict budget and expected to be consulted on everything outside the budget.

Recently Richard had been slightly less generous, slightly more questioning about the amounts she spent, but he had a point. The market wasn't as good as it had been, and wouldn't it be better to set aside savings for a rainy day, and really, didn't she already have everything she needed?

Still, she hadn't shown him the ring yet. She'd bought it just last month when she'd been in the city for the day. She'd walked past a jeweler on Madison and had stopped when she'd seen this ring in the window.

"It's a fun piece," the sales assistant had said as she fetched it. Fun for the women on the Upper East Side. Fun if you consider several thousand dollars on a precious stone to be fun.

"It's gorgeous." Amber had held her breath as she slipped the ring on her finger. It was gorgeous. And it fitted her. Perfectly.

"I think this must be fate." The sales assistant had smiled, and really, who could argue with a statement like that?

Amber left the shop five minutes later, the ring on her finger, the amount having been split between two credit cards and a check.

"Don't worry," the sales assistant had said, "lots of our

ladies do this all the time. One of our regular ladies keeps buying pieces from the same collection and she tells her husband she picked them up on eBay for fifty bucks apiece."

Amber had smiled, hadn't given anything away, although she hoped the assistant wouldn't recognize the Winslow name, wouldn't gossip to anyone about how she couldn't tell her husband how much she was spending.

Although she was sure Richard wouldn't mind. She was just trying to prove to him that she could be responsible with money. That she didn't have to immediately and automatically buy everything she fell in love with, without thinking about the cost.

Amber has just finished spritzing herself with perfume when the doorbell rings. She reaches the door at the same time as Lavinia, waves Lavinia away with a smile, and opens the door to find Julian and Aidan standing on the doorstep.

"What a wonderful position," the taller of the two, Aidan, says as he introduces himself and walks inside, looking up and down and around the foyer before turning back to Amber.

"I love that you're on the top of this hill," Julian says. "We were just saying how jealous we are of your views."

"But you've got that divine beach house right on the water." Amber smiles, leading them in and taking them into the formal living room. "The article in the *Gazette* had the most wonderful photographs. Isn't the balcony off your bedroom right over the water?"

"Well, yes," Julian admits. "It is rather wonderful. But what do you want us to do for you?"

Amber shrugs, because the truth is she hadn't really even thought of employing a decorator until everyone in the

League started talking about Amberley Jacks and how they were coming to town and how desperate everyone was to use them.

Amber had always done the house herself. She and Richard used to go to estate sales to pick up pieces—a nineteenth-century armoire that stood in the family room, some beautiful French needlepoint rugs that in fact they are standing on now.

She had kept the house fairly neutral, and had always been happy with it, but when Nadine, one of the League's queen bees, had turned to her and said, "Of course you must be getting Amberley Jacks in to see you," Amber had nodded and said, "Of course."

And now here they are, examining her living room. "I just thought maybe you could give me some ideas," Amber starts vaguely. "I quite like this room, although maybe it could do with some curtains. Yes. I'd love your help with the curtains."

Julian and Aidan both stand up and turn slowly around, each of them echoing the other with their hands held softly beneath their chins in a silent prayer.

"Are you thinking what I'm thinking?" Julian takes a deep breath and looks excitedly at Aidan.

"I am." Aidan smiles.

"We're thinking . . ." Julian pauses as a slow smile spreads on his face. "Lavender!" he announces with a flourish.

"Yes! Lavender!" Aidan says. "It would be fabulous in here."

"A gorgeous soft lavender on the walls, and then we need to bring this whole look up to date."

"What about my sofa?" Amber asks meekly. "Would this go with lavender?"

"Ugh no." Aidan looks at the sofa with horror. "But I'm

thinking a wonderful rich-plum sofa. Very modern. It would make this room very fun. Very *now.*"

"Oh yes." Julian claps his hands together with excitement. "Plum is my favorite. And then bookshelves. You need some detail." He turns back to Amber. "Mrs. Winslow, can I be honest?"

"Call me Amber, and yes, you can be honest."

"These new houses, while wonderful, are boring, boring, boring."

"Yes," echoes Aidan. "Dull, dull, dull."

"And our job is to bring in some character. You don't want to live in a big boxy house that's like everyone else's, filled with"—Julian gestures at one of Amber's favorite pieces, an old cherry sideboard that held all her silver photographs—"tacky pieces of junk."

"Oh. Right. Of course." Amber's face falls. She loves that sideboard.

"Not that Julian is saying your furniture is junk," Aidan says quickly, noting her face.

"*Oh no!*" Julian feigns horror. "Our job is to bring beauty and grace to your home. We can rearrange your furniture so that it looks like new. We'll bring in wonderful pieces that we find on our antique-buying trips. Amber," he leans in to her and drops his voice, "we will make your home the envy of all your neighbors and friends."

"Well, how's a girl expected to say no after that?" Amber laughs, and with that she takes them on a tour of the house.

"But they're really talented," Amber pleads with Richard later that evening, having cooked him a huge fat juicy steak to try and soften the blow.

"I just don't understand why suddenly you want a decorator. You've always said you never understood why people used decorators in the first place. Didn't you go on that house tour last year and say every home looked like a show house? Isn't it you who's always saying you love your house so much precisely because you and I chose everything in it?"

"Ah, well. Yes. I suppose I did say that. But I think that was just because I hadn't found the right decorators. Honestly, Richard, I really didn't know how talented the really good ones are, and Amberley Jacks are the best. They do everyone."

"Everyone? Who's everyone?"

Amber reels off the list of celebrities and society people whose lives Amberley Jacks have transformed.

"I still don't get it. And lavender in the formal living room? Are you absolutely sure?"

"Yes, I'm absolutely sure, and you'll love it, Richard. Honestly. And anyway, they're really not that expensive."

"Uh oh. Here we go. How much is not that expensive?"

"They're two hundred dollars an hour, plus everything we buy through them is practically wholesale."

Richard thinks for a while. "But how many hours does it take? Can we put a ceiling on it? What do they expect it to be?"

"I don't know but I'll find out!" Amber throws her arms around Richard and kisses him, knowing she's won. "I love you, Richard! And I'll call them tomorrow and ask. I'm sure it's not going to be that expensive. How many hours can it take?"

Chapter Four

J anelle Salinger, esteemed editor of *Poise!*, regular guest on shows like *Through the Keyhole*, glamorous, gorgeous, and still as giggly as a girl, casts her shimmering smile around the room at her "girls."

"Okay." She claps her hands together. "Everybody got coffee? Everybody ready?" Her team of editors smile as they lean forward slightly, getting ready to throw their ideas out for the next issue of *Poise!*.

Although it's December, they're already working on their huge spring issue, preparing their readers for the beginnings of summer. The fashion department is strewn with bikinis, elaborately embroidered and beaded kaftans, thongs so studded and bejeweled they are almost works of art in themselves.

The editors all know what spring and early summer means to the women who buy the magazine—sun, sea, sand, and sex, even to their thirty-something young mums who are up to their eyes in baby food and nappies. "A girl has to dream," Janelle always says, although, despite having her own child, it's hard to imagine that Janelle was ever up to her eyes in anything other than Crème de la Mer.

"My Yummy Mummies," Janelle calls their readers, referring, as she so often does, to their demographic of women in their thirties with successful careers, loving husbands, beautiful children, stylish homes, fantastic friends, and wonderful wardrobes. And if they don't already have all that, the *Poise!* readers definitely want it.

"Of course we can have it all," Janelle often laughs. "Look at me." And looking at her you would certainly think she has it all. Married to Stephen Golding since the year dot, they have one daughter, Diaz (shortened to Dee, rather than the far more common Di), a palatial home in Holland Park that Janelle redecorates, or rather asks her friend Tricia Guild of Designer's Guild to redecorate, every three years.

Currently the house is super-minimalist chic, which means that all the interior stories in the magazine for the past few months have been super-minimalist chic. Every Christmas, Janelle and Stephen host a staff party, and although Vicky thought the house was certainly . . . dramatic . . . she wouldn't want to live there, couldn't believe that anyone could, in fact, live there.

The floorboards, three years ago stripped back when Janelle was going through her country phase, have subsequently been painted gloss white. The original Georgian fireplaces were thrown out to make way for clean holes in the white wall, with a heavy slab of black soapstone above. There are two pieces of furniture in the enormous double drawing room where all the parties are held: a giant chunk of driftwood from Bali that serves as a coffee table, although God forbid you should ever attempt to balance a cup of coffee on the uneven surface, and an oversized sofa, low-slung and hard, in a color Vicky always thinks of as "dreige."

On the walls are three huge canvases—vibrant splashes of

color that Janelle bought from the Saatchis and were written up in every newspaper as being one of the most expensive art transactions of the year.

"Don't you love it?" Janelle asked excitedly when everyone arrived for the party. "It's now truly my haven," and she'd breathed deeply, stretching out her arms so her gauzy white cotton djellaba lifted up to show her bare feet and toe rings.

That had been Janelle getting back to nature, and like all her phases it hadn't lasted long. Now, in this conference, she was back in a full, patterned Prada skirt, flat alligator pumps on her feet, and a Michael Kors fur shrug around her shoulders.

"For this June issue . . ." Janelle pauses dramatically, "I'm thinking . . ." another dramatic pause, ". . . Africa!"

There is a round of excited applause from the fashion girls, while everyone else tries not to laugh.

"Gorgeous beaded necklaces," Janelle continues, her voice loud with excitement, "color, vibrancy, animal prints. I'm thinking fashion shots on the Masai Mara, profiles of Peter Beard. Think *Gorillas in the Mist, White Mischief.* Think 'I had a farm in Africa.' British colonial, Jamaica Inn . . ." Vicky catches the eye of the assistant editor and quickly suppresses a snort of laughter, for Janelle has a tendency to do this. Her mind works so quickly it frequently goes off on tangents, and what, after all, did Jamaica Inn have to do with Africa, other than being decorated in a British colonial style?

But Janelle isn't paid a disgusting amount of money for nothing, hasn't been the editor of *Poise!* for about a decade without there being good reason. She has vision and foresight, and immaculate taste, even though she has sometimes fallen off the wagon for a while. She knows what her readers aspire to, whether they can afford it or not, and she knows how to give it to them in a way that has driven their circulation up and up until *Poise!* ranks among the top three women's glossy magazines.

"Right." Janelle finishes her directive and looks eagerly around the room. "What have we got? Let's start with . . . fashion. Stella?"

Stella, the poor beleaguered fashion editor, quickly reshuffles her notes, moving all her story ideas out of the way, because she, poor woman, had been thinking boats. Yachting. Navy and white, splashes of orange. Classic, traditional, she'd been planning a huge nautical theme, plus of course the obligatory article on flattering swimsuits, and a lookbook pull-out of the greatest accessories of the summer.

But Stella has worked with Janelle forever, knows how mercurial she is, and is well used to thinking on her feet.

"Africa is a wonderful idea," she stalls for time slightly. "Prada has these incredible saris, and I'm thinking lions, Virginia what's-her-name with the lions—"

"McKenna," Vicky adds.

"Yes, thank you, Vicky. I'm thinking about *her,* a classic blond beauty, very Grace Kelly in colonial clothes. Sexy cargos and Michael Kors striped tops. Love the shrug by the way, Janelle, one of the highlights of his collection."

"Oh, thank you." Janelle beams, always happy to be complimented on her sartorial choices.

"And . . ." Stella thinks quickly, "I'm also thinking Africa, South Africa . . . Morocco!" Her eyes light up with inspiration. "I'm thinking Talitha Getty on the rooftop, hippy chic in Africa, wonderful embroidered seventies-inspired flowing clothes; I'm thinking Allegra Hicks kaftans, Louboutin beaded thongs. Long hair, candlelight, smoking joints on a beach at midnight . . ." Stella's voice grows slightly wistful as she pauses to remember her youth.

"I *love* it!" Janelle shrieks. "Just what I was thinking! It's going to be fabulous!" They all turn as the door of the office opens and Leona, the features editor, the woman to whom Vicky is closest at work, rushes in.

"Oh God, I'm so sorry," she says, taking her place at the table and throwing a grateful smile at Vicky who has already placed a cappuccino in front of her empty seat. "I just completely overslept, slept right through the alarm clock."

"Late night last night?" Janelle smiles, for despite her reputation she is not difficult to work for, does not, as do some other editors, terrorize her staff for not doing things the way she wants them done.

Janelle's staff may make fun of her, but they are fiercely loyal and they love her. They love her because she treats them like her family. She is firm when she needs to be, and always fair even when she is hopelessly inconsistent. Others may look at her and think her grand, but in fact Janelle has always strived to be on an equal footing with her staff, and knows that the best way to get the best results is to create an atmosphere of fun and friendship.

Leona lets out a barking laugh. "If you're suggesting what I think you're suggesting, you must be crazy."

"You do have that just-been-shagged look, actually." Stella looks over at her with a smile.

"Now I know you're crazy." Leona unbuttons her coat and lets it fall back on the chair. "I have a two-year-old, a six-year-old, and a career. The last time I had a late night because of sex was probably my wedding night. Nowadays the shorter it is the better, as far as I'm concerned."

Becky, the lifestyle editor, starts to laugh. "I'm having a competition with myself. Last Saturday I actually managed to get it down to eight minutes."

"Eight minutes?" Vicky splutters, horrified. "That's terrible! You mean sex lasted eight minutes?"

"Yup," Becky says with a wide grin. "And that was from foreplay to closure."

"Good for you." Leona rolls her eyes. "I'm still at fifteen, and let me tell you, that's an effort."

"Speed sex!" Janelle shouts, clapping her hands. "I love it! We have to do a story on speed sex! Vicky, you and Leona need to talk about this."

"I can't believe we're actually going to do a story about wanting sex to be over as quickly as possible. God, maybe I don't want to get married after all."

"It's what I keep telling you." Leona turns to her. "You keep thinking marriage is the happy ever after, but baby, it's just the beginning, and it ain't all hearts and flowers."

"Far from it," Becky concurs. "I used to be a romantic too, Vicky. And then I got married and was dragged into the real world."

Vicky shrugs. "I can't help it. I just want to wear that white meringue down the aisle."

"God forbid." Janelle puts her hand on her heart and raises her eyes to the ceiling. "No employee of *Poise!* is ever going to get married in a white meringue, not when Matthew Williamson can make you something fabulous."

"Well, I'll let you know when to contact him," Vicky snorts, "but I'm warning you: don't hold your breath."

"And in the meantime you just enjoy those marathon sex sessions while you're still getting them," Leona says.

"Right, back to features," Janelle interrupts. "Much as I'd

like to hear about your sex lives all day, we've got a magazine to get out."

Every now and then a story comes out that captures the media's imagination, and speed sex ends up being one of those stories. The spring issue hits the newsstands at the end of February, and almost immediately the features desks of newspapers pick up the story, followed quickly by radio and TV.

Vicky had given the story to Deborah to write, figuring that as a married mother of three Deborah would presumably be well versed in speed sex, and even if she wasn't she was an experienced-enough journalist to be able to pull it off.

Deborah had filled the copy with quotes, and three case studies of married couples who thought speed sex was the answer to their prayers, and only indulged in anything longer on the occasional times when they were on holiday without the children, which didn't happen very often.

The case studies had agreed to be photographed in the magazine, and had already appeared on *This Morning* and *GMTV*. Deborah was flattered that her career picked up again instantly, with magazines and newspapers she hadn't heard from for years suddenly getting in touch with her and asking her to do features.

Vicky has just got back to her desk after an extended lunch break in the local park, where she and Leona had ignored the fact that this was London and they were surrounded by office workers eating sandwich lunches, and had subsequently stripped down to bra and knickers (that were actually shorts) to take advantage of the unseasonally hot day.

Ruth buzzes her. "Deborah's on the phone," she says. "She wants to talk to you about some radio show she can't do. Do you want to take it?"

"Of course," Vicky says, and picks up the phone. "Hi, Deb. Still enjoying your newfound celebrity? Did I hear you were on the *Wright Stuff* the other day?"

"I know!" Deborah giggles. "My kids are thrilled. They keep telling everyone their mum's famous. Did you see it?"

"No. Sorry. How was it?"

"It was great, but I looked terrible. I was enormous."

Vicky shakes her head silently. Deborah can't have been enormous. Inarticulate? Possibly. Nervous? Probably. But enormous? "How can you have been enormous when you're, what, a size six?"

"Actually I'm an eight, but that's not the point. Just as we were going on air they zoomed in on me and I saw myself on this bloody monitor, and I swear I'm all chin. I never even realized I had a double chin and now all I see when I look in the mirror is chin."

Vicky laughs. "That's ridiculous. You're slim and beautiful, and you absolutely do not have a double chin."

"Well, if you ever decide to do an article on removing your double chin, I'll be the guinea pig."

Vicky laughs again.

"I'm serious," Deborah says earnestly. "I'm seriously thinking about it. Can't I do a piece for you about it? Apparently they do it with liposuction and there's no scarring, nobody would ever know. They just go in behind your ears and one tiny incision under your chin and suck all the excess chin out."

"Oh my God. You're serious. You've looked into this.

Deborah, for Christ's sake, you do not have a double chin! What does Dick think about this?"

"He thinks I'm being ridiculous and says there's no way he's going to pay for me to have a nonexistent chin removed, which is why I'm trying to get someone to do a piece on it, then I won't have to pay, and if I wait until Dick goes on his next business trip, he won't even have to know."

"You're nuts," Vicky says as Deborah sighs. "So what's this about a radio show?"

"Oh yes. I've got a christening in the country this weekend but Radio Two wants me to be a guest on some evening show talking about, you guessed it, speed sex. I can't do it so I thought maybe you could."

"When is it?"

"Saturday night."

"Oh great. How do you know I haven't got a fantastically hot date on Saturday night?"

"Have you?"

"Wishful bloody thinking," sighs Vicky, because for the last few months her dating life has been disastrous, or, as she likes to say to Leona, "What dating life? I have no dates and no life."

Throughout her twenties Vicky had an incredible time. As a young staff writer she was constantly meeting eligible men, bedding them if she felt like it, having relationships if she chose, or affairs if that was what was on offer. She was, as the saying goes, footloose and fancy-free, never worrying about the future because it was assumed that sometime around thirty Prince Charming would show himself and she would then go on to live the life that her brother appears to have stolen from her, which is all the more irritating because he's younger, and really, what right did a thirty-two-year-old have to have everything she was supposed to have?

Unlike some of her friends, Vicky had been dying to turn thirty, knowing that thirty was when it would all happen, when her happy ever after would start. It never occurred to her that it wouldn't happen, that five years on she would still be exactly where she was ten years ago, except with a better wardrobe, a bigger flat, and fewer prospects.

At twenty-five there were men everywhere. Tall men. Short men. Funny men. Ugly men. Nevertheless, men. So many men, so little time, she would say then, when elderly aunts would ask why she didn't have a boyfriend.

Now, at thirty-five, the good men have slowly dropped out of the dating pool, leaving the weakest specimens behind, and Vicky is well aware that the older she gets, the harder it's going to be.

"There are always the divorcees," Kate said to her recently, but Vicky has always shuddered at the thought of inheriting someone else's baggage.

"What if they have children?" she said. "I don't want to be involved with someone else's children, plus it means the ex-wife is going to be in your life forever. Thank you very much, but no. I need to find a single man, not a divorcee."

"But that's ridiculous," Kate said. "Anyone thirty-five and upwards is going to have baggage anyway, and frankly, I think there's something deeply suspicious about someone in their late thirties or forties who's never been married. The last thing you want to do is fall in love with a commitaphobe."

"I don't buy that stuff about it being odd when men are single in their thirties. Look at Daniel. He's not odd."

"So why aren't you having a proper relationship with him instead of just the occasional shag?"

"God, no. He's not my type."

"But you like him and you fancy him enough to have sex with him?"

"Yes," Vicky admitted reluctantly.

"Then I bet there's something wrong with him and you're just not telling me."

"Okay, you got me. There is something wrong with him. His penis is orange."

"Oh ha ha. I just don't want you to keep thinking your life is going to start when you get married."

"Thanks a lot," Vicky grunted. "I think my life already has started. Some people would kill to have my life."

"Just as long as you remember that," Kate said. "Does that mean you're going to stop banging on about wanting my life?"

"No. I do want your life. But how am I supposed to have a husband, kids, dogs, an Aga, and a house in the country without a man?"

"You could start with the Aga and the house in the country."

"I would, except I think I'd die of loneliness."

"God, there's no winning with you, is there? You're just too bloody clever by half."

"How do you think I got to be features director of *Poise!*?" Vicky grinned.

But she wasn't feeling quite so good about it at night. Lately, when she'd taken her makeup off, she had been shocked to notice that tiny lines had started appearing around her eyes, lines that she'd swear hadn't been there a month ago.

And speaking of her eyes, the skin underneath suddenly seemed very thin. Now when she had late nights, no amount of Touche Eclat managed to conceal it, and her skin seemed to show every drink, every odd cigarette, every vice that had managed to go unnoticed in her twenties.

During her twenties her weight had gone up and down like a yo-yo. If ever she felt her jeans were becoming ever so slightly tight, she would cut back for a couple of days and lose five pounds in the process.

Now those five pounds seem to be permanently attached to her stomach. She's been cutting back for a month, and she's only lost a pound and a half. At exactly what point in her life did diets stop working and, more to the point, why?

Everyone seemed younger at work. Not, obviously, Janelle, who was truly ageless—the joke being she had a portrait of herself locked away on the top floor of the office that was aging far more mercilessly than that of Dorian Gray—and not Stella or Leona, who were slightly older than Vicky, but every freelancer seemed to be getting younger and younger, and the fashion assistants who came and went with every season were practically still in kindergarten.

Vicky was forever getting phone calls from freelancers pitching ideas, and as soon as she heard their bright, young, eager voices, she wanted to tell them to go away and come back in ten years, when they had a bit more life experience and actually understood the demographic of their readers.

Some of them even had good ideas, but it was all about execution, and the brightest twenty-four-year-old in the world couldn't understand what buggy envy was really like— that feeling when you were pushing your secondhand Peg Perego down the high street thinking it was pretty damn hot all things considered, only to pass three Bugaboos that you could swear were sneering at your instantly inferior Peg Perego.

Admittedly, Vicky doesn't quite understand that one either, but luckily Leona is around to take care of any commissions that Vicky can't quite get her head around—age being less of an issue than children, or Vicky's lack thereof.

She swore she would never say that even the policemen seemed like children, but she thought it all the time. Just the other day a policeman had stopped her and spoken to her sharply for driving the wrong way down a one-way street (she had been genuinely lost and hadn't known it was one-way), and she had to physically stop herself from echoing her mother and saying something like, "Show a bit of respect, young man," for he truly did look twelve years old. I'm old enough to be his mother, she thought, as she drove off fuming, and then with a start she realized she really was.

The problem is that Vicky doesn't particularly feel any older. She may have the lines, the lack of energy, the dearth of decent men, but she still thinks of herself as twenty-five. She still listens to Kiss FM, still wears all the latest trends, still thinks of herself as looking just like the fashion assistants.

When they talk about clubbing in Soho, holidays in Ibiza, Vicky wants to join in, feels entitled to join in, even though she has become increasingly aware that they look at her strangely, that they do not see her as one of them, that they think of her in a similar vein to the way they think of their mothers, and that's despite her Chloe trousers and ever-so-pointed Jimmy Choo boots.

"I was there when Manumission first started," she wants to shout. "I used to go to Bar Italia for cappuccinos at five in the morning when you were still in nappies." But now she doesn't. Now she realizes that the slightly embarrassed silences she gets when she tries to join in, tries to prove she is just like them, are just that: slightly embarrassing, and mostly for her.

Vicky has never had a problem fitting in. But now she finds that she does not have a place in the world. Or at least not the place she wants.

Chapter **Five**

The Highfield League of Young Ladies was established in the 1940s, at a time when all the women in Highfield were housewives and stay-at-home moms. The League gave them an excuse to dress up, get together, and all in the name of charity, for the money they raised from their various events went to local good causes.

During the eighties the League suffered somewhat. It was a time when the young wives and mothers of Highfield were too busy commuting into the city and concentrating on their careers to focus fully on charitable concerns; but the powers that be are grateful that now, in 2005, life has come full circle, as it always does, and it is once again fashionable for women to stay at home and join the League.

And join the League they do. Ask most of the committee members the reason why they are involved, and they will tell you it feels wonderful to give something back. They will say that once upon a time they had busy, important careers, and they gave them up to raise their children, but now that their children are in school, raising money for the homeless and impoverished is quite as fulfilling as their careers once were.

Where *are* the homeless in Highfield, Amber had wondered, at an introductory meeting when they first moved to

Highfield, because Highfield seemed to have changed enormously from the small artists' community it had been famous for in the twenties and thirties.

Thanks to the arrival of a couple of celebrities—who live discreetly and quietly and don't seem to involve themselves much in what there is of a Highfield scene—Highfield has become a place to live, particularly for the aspirational widow of Wall Street, the woman whose husband is constantly working, who knows that all she needs in order to be happy is a mansion, a nanny, and a Hermès bag.

Young, successful, she is this millennium's soccer mom, except she doesn't sit around at soccer matches waiting for her children—she's far too busy for that, and what, after all, does she pay the nanny for? (Not to mention the nanny has her own Land Rover, cell phone, en suite bedroom, and various perks including inheriting gorgeous, barely worn designer clothes from her walk-in luxury closet wardrobe that she never gets around to wearing.)

Nor is she, like the eponymous popular television series, a desperate housewife. There's nothing desperate about this girl, and if she relates to anyone on *Desperate Housewives* it's less the frazzled mother of three (Good Lord, why didn't she hang on to that nanny all those episodes ago?), and more the sexy single Teri Hatcher mom, and only because she'd kill to look as good in her Seven bootleg jeans.

If she's anything at all she's a Charity Chick, or a Manolo Mom. A woman who refuses to be defined by her children alone, who keeps herself busy with various philanthropic and charitable concerns, who ensures she always looks her best at all times. Her mornings are filled working on herself: hairdresser, nail salon, and, most important, gym, because although she has a fully stocked mirror-clad gym in the finished walk-out basement of her giant and brand-new house, exercise just isn't the same when it doesn't involve chatting with your friend on the Elliptical next to you, and it's definitely not the same when you don't meet the girls afterward for a smoothie in the café of the new sports club.

Everyone is a member of the new sports club. For just as the women who are moving to Highfield are changing, so the town is having to change to accommodate them. The sleepy, country Connecticut town, just over an hour outside Manhattan, is having to expand, to cope with the daily teardowns of pretty, antique houses to make way for the ten-thousand-foot-plus new builds to take their place. It's having to cope with the ubiquitous Starbucks, and not one but four opened in the past year, so now wherever you are in town you are able to hop out and grab a skinny grande latte.

Main Street was once filled with little boutiques, artisan shops, pretty cafés, but the chain stores have moved in, and now the women in town spend their days in Gap workout gear, much like women in the rest of America.

Apart from the women in the League. They may occasionally wear Gap, but heaven forbid they should wear it to one of their monthly meetings, which are rapidly turning into unofficial fashion shows.

Amber, bless her, was completely unaware of this in the beginning. In fact, if she remembers correctly, which she tries very hard not to do given how mortified she still feels about it, she turned up to one of the early meetings in jeans, a black zip-up fleece (there was a chill in the air), and flat loafers.

Not that she would ever have been seen dead in clothes

like that in Manhattan, but Amber has always been something of a chameleon, and so unsure of who the real Amber is that she'll morph herself into whoever she thinks she needs to be at any given moment.

And she had taken her cues from the women at preschool, who she quickly realized were not the same crowd who got involved with the League. Admittedly, there was some crossover, but the women from school turned out to be doing this for purely charitable reasons—to do some good in the world—and not because they cared what they looked like, and thus they were relegated to the out crowd in the League, easily spotted by their everyday school uniforms of fleeces, clogs, and shapeless jeans.

But Amber hadn't known this then, had indeed heard about the League from one of the women at school, and had slowly moved her more glamorous Manhattan clothes to the back of her wardrobe as she had tried to fit in with the other moms by wearing what they wore.

At that first League meeting Amber had climbed out of her car and turned as she was halfway down the path toward the front door of the house at which the meeting was being held, because she had heard footsteps behind her.

Tip tap, tip tap, tip tap. A short blond woman in tight flared suede pants, super-high super-pointed boots, a fringed tweed jacket with a mink collar, and the Luella bag—the very one Amber had been lusting after for a few months now—was walking up the path.

And Amber, Amber who had battled her way out of her blue-collar background, who had been a successful lawyer, who had had to fight more than any woman she had known, had been overcome with shame and inadequacy.

She had felt like a failure in her fleece and loafers, her understated makeup, and she'd wanted to turn around and go home, but it was too late.

She had stood at the back of the kitchen allowing the other women, most of whom knew one another, to mingle, while she attempted to make herself invisible, all the while making mental notes about what to wear next time.

It seemed that tight trousers with high heels were the thing, little fitted jackets, lots of fur. Perfect hair, perfect makeup, and a great bag. Admittedly, not all the women looked quite like that, but even the ones who didn't looked like they were trying. Even at her first meeting, from her vantage point by the Sub-Zero, Amber could sense the social game playing and the hierarchies that existed in the room.

On the other side of the island stood a woman Amber had heard called Suzy. Suzy was clearly one of the queen bees. She was head to toe in Gucci, bag to match, and was icily blond, which, although clearly highlighted, made Amber sure that this woman would rather die than let her roots show.

The other women had buzzed around Suzy like little worker bees. All trying to attract her attention, all trying to get as close as possible.

"Oh I love that suit," Amber had heard one girl say. "I was looking at it in Rakers last week but then I bought it in lilac instead. But it looks so great on you I'm going to have to go back and get it in black and white."

Amber had allowed herself a secret smile, for of course she knew what the girl was saying: you're not better than me even though you think you are. Even though you're in Gucci I can afford it too. I'm just as good as you are.

"God," whispered an English voice next to her. "Isn't this awful?"

Amber had turned to see a woman dressed much like herself, the same lack of makeup, the same hair pulled back into a ponytail.

"It is a little overwhelming." Amber had smiled. "I'm Amber."

"Nice to meet you, Amber. I'm Deborah. So let me guess. You're new to town and everyone told you that you just had to join the League, because that's where you make all your friends and it's all for a great cause."

Amber had laughed. "Pretty much. How about you?"

"My husband, Spencer, and I moved over from London about a year ago, and I thought it was about time I saw what everyone was talking about, although looking at these women I'm not sure it's for me." She'd sighed. "But then again it is for a good cause, and I do want to do something. I'm just never going to be one of these super-chic women," and she'd gestured down at herself.

Amber, who had already decided that she would be coming back except next time she would out-fabulous even Suzy in her choice of outfit, had shrugged. "I feel ridiculous standing here in these old clothes, but nobody told me you had to dress."

"You don't," Deborah had said. "Unless of course you're trying to prove something."

"Well, I can tell you, next time I'm going to make more of an effort."

"And I thought you looked so normal."

Amber had laughed. "I may look normal on the outside, but inside there's a desperate social climber itching to get out."

"You go, girl." Deborah had laughed too. "At least you're honest about it."

Amber had been joking. But not really. She did feel inadequate, and although she had the name Winslow (which, incidentally, she was tempted to shout from the rooftops: "By
the way, all you snotty women who are ignoring me because
I don't look good enough in my fleece and loafers, I'm Amber Winslow. Yes, one of *those* Winslows. Oh, now you're interested. So sorry, I'm busy with my new friend, Deborah,
who's not good enough for you either"), like most of the
women who had stood around her in the kitchen that day,
money was quite new to her.

And although she hadn't understood the rules of that first
Highfield League of Young Ladies meeting, she did understand how money could protect you, how clothes and jewelry could be used as armor, making you feel just as good as
those around you, even while inside you knew you weren't.

Amber knew exactly what her mother-in-law would have
said if she were to have stepped into that house and seen
those women. Her mother-in-law in her centuries-old cashmere sweaters and Ferragamo shoes, still quality despite
being bought back when the family had money. Her mother-
in-law with her ubiquitous string of pearls, her aristocratic
gray/blond hair scraped back in a soigné chignon, her
mother-in-law who didn't have to carry a bag that shouted
Chanel, or a diamond ring that was so heavy she could barely
lift her hand in order to prove that she had money, that she
was good enough.

"New money," Amber could hear her mother-in-law sniff
dismissively. "How very déclassé," she would say, yet Amber
knew that deep down Icy Winslow would be ever-so-slightly
jealous. Not because she wanted to be déclassé, but because
although she had the name and the prestige that went with
the name, she didn't have the money to go with it.

Amber had thought, when she first married Richard, that with the name and the money to go with it, she would have everything in life. She would feel good enough for the first time in her life, would be able to hold her head up high no matter who she was with, would never have to feel inadequate again. But she had found that whatever she had, wherever she went, she brought herself with her, and there seemed to be no escaping the baggage that she had collected throughout her life.

Of course there were times when she felt good enough, but every time a League meeting approached Amber would start to feel *less than,* and so she started going to Rakers—the one designer store in town—once a month to ensure she had an outfit good enough for the meeting, one that would make her the envy of the rest of the girls.

She hasn't admitted this to anyone. Not even to Deborah, who has become one of her closest friends, largely because Deborah is as real as she first appeared at that meeting, and she is the kindest, greatest friend Amber has ever known.

But she can't admit it, has trouble at times even admitting it to herself because it just feels so damn childish. There are times in these meetings when she knows they've all regressed back to high school.

Times when Suzy's fallen out with Heidi, or Elizabeth and Patty have decided they think Jennifer is weird, or Nadine didn't pull her weight when she chaired the Arts Festival.

Amber has tried to stay out of the bitchiness, but it's hard to avoid with groups of women, and anyway, she's on a mission—the same mission she had when she was in high school: to be queen bee. Suzy Bartlow may be the current queen of the League, but Amber is quietly pulling her troops around her and preparing for a takeover. She has the name, she has the house, and thanks to Rakers she has the clothes. Now it's just a matter of time.

"Hi, Judy!" Amber finds her sales assistant in Rakers and they kiss hello—one of the benefits of being a regular and high-spending customer at the most expensive store in town.

"How are you, Amber! Don't tell me it's that time of the month already?" Judy is in on her secret, knows that Amber comes in to buy an outfit just for the meeting, usually has already picked out a few choices that generally Amber will love, Judy now having worked with her long enough to be able to anticipate her likes and dislikes.

"I know! Can you believe it? Do you have any ideas?"

"I do. I've already been through the new collections and I pulled some things out for you. There are some wonderful Michael Kors pants, a jacket from Escada, and some Cavalli tops that may be a bit dressy but they're absolutely stunning."

"And you're sure no one else has bought them?"

Judy nods. "I've checked the computer. Nobody else has them." Yet another benefit of an upmarket store in a small town is that everyone knows everyone, and because most of the women in the League buy their clothes at Rakers (although Suzy has recently started going to the city, which Amber is going to have to start doing herself very soon), the women can ask the staff to ensure that no one else has bought the same thing, thereby avoiding the humiliation of turning up to a meeting or, far worse, an event, in the same outfit as another committee member.

Amber tries on the trousers—perfect, and gasps as she puts on one of the Cavalli blouses. Judy was absolutely right. It is on the dressy side, a light gauzy chiffon with a loose tie at the neck, but somehow teamed with the tweedy trousers it looks perfect, and Judy nods in approval when Amber comes out of the fitting room.

"And," Judy lowers her voice, "it's the only one we got in so you'll definitely stand out in the crowd."

"I love it." Amber breathes in, admiring herself as she turns and examines herself from every angle in the mirror. "It's perfect."

Judy disappears for a couple of minutes, then reemerges holding a pair of high satin pumps with a crocodile toe. "These just came in from Prada. Aren't they *darling*? And wouldn't they be perfect?"

"Oh God," Amber groans. "Richard's going to kill me."

"No he won't," Judy snaps, used to comments like this from her wealthiest customers, and frankly she never knows why they complain, given the amount they spend so regularly and so unthinkingly. "We'll put it on the house account as usual, and by the time the bill comes at the end of the year he won't even think about it."

"Okay." Amber grins. "Judy, you're amazing. Thank you!"

"It's my pleasure." Judy smiles, and given how much and how regularly Amber spends, of course it is.

Amber throws her Rakers bags into the back of her Toyota Sequoia and shudders with pleasure as she anticipates the meeting next week. Next week, for the first time, it's at her house, and Amber has already phoned the caterers and ordered tiny, delicious French pastries, exquisite fruit tarts, mini éclairs stuffed with fresh cream.

She has bought a selection of the finest teas in the world, has stocked the fridge in the butler's pantry with every soda imaginable, determined that hers will be the meeting that everyone will remember.

Of course some of the girls have been to her house, and her only regret is that the influence of Amberley Jacks will not be seen for a few more weeks—why does it take so long to order a sofa, for heaven's sake, and why is their painter fully booked for another month?—but in the meantime Amber knows the girls will be studying the noticeboard in her kitchen, and so she has pinned the letter from Amberley Jacks slap bang in the middle of it, just to be sure they all know.

Amber only knows this because Deborah told her that everyone was talking about the meeting two months ago when Heidi had an invitation on her noticeboard to Elyse's daughter's birthday party, and Patty had seen it and been upset because Patty's son and Elyse's daughter occasionally had playdates, but Patty's son hadn't been invited. Patty in fact didn't even know Elyse was having a birthday party because Elyse had decided she had gone off Patty and didn't want to invite her, and had told all her friends not to tell Patty about it.

And who would have thought that Heidi would be so stupid as to keep the invitation on the noticeboard when she was holding the meeting at her house, and everyone knows that everyone else studies the noticeboard in the kitchen, just to make sure they're not missing out on anything.

So now nobody's talking to Heidi either, who has no idea what she's done wrong, and the phones are buzzing around Highfield about this latest brouhaha, although, as Deborah said, it will all be forgotten about in a week and then something new will blow up. "We are, after all, back in high school again," she said with a roll of her eyes, and Amber laughed.

Amber drives off along Route 1, turning the radio on and singing along to a Billy Joel classic, feeling great as she pictures herself in her new outfit, three inches taller and ten pounds thinner, because after all, isn't that what fantasies are for?

She passes CVS, and jams on the brakes, suddenly remembering the prescription she was supposed to pick up. "Oh hell," she curses, unable to do a U-turn, and too lazy to turn around. She picks up her cell phone and presses quick dial to Lavinia.

"Lavinia?"

"Hang on," Lavinia yells, as Amber hears screaming in Lavinia's background.

"What's going on?" Amber says.

"Sorry," Lavinia comes back on again. "Jared just took Gracie's cookie so she's having a fit. No, Jared, give it back. Grace, don't hit him. Grace! Grace! Stop that! Sorry, Amber. Is everything okay?"

"Yes, fine. I just remembered, though, I have a prescription at CVS, would you mind picking it up for me?"

"Sure," says Lavinia, who is on the other side of town, with two overtired and fractious children, dinner to cook, and a pile of laundry to get through tonight as she watches television in her room, with just the ironing board and Ginger, the golden retriever, for company.

"Thanks, Lavinia, you're an angel," says Amber, who suddenly spies a parking space next to the new French furnishing shop in town, one that she'd been meaning to go to since it opened three weeks ago. Perfect, she thinks, as she expertly maneuvers the car into the spot, then checks her watch. Just enough time to see what everyone's talking about before going home and getting ready for dinner tonight with Richard.

* * *

By the time Amber gets home the kids have eaten and are quietly watching *Madagascar* for the 149th time.

"Lavinia!" Amber shouts as she walks into the mud room, greeting Ginger, then pushing him away so he doesn't get dog hair all over her black coat.

"I'm just clearing up the dishes. Do you need some help?"

"Oh yes, please!" Amber unbuttons her coat, throws it over the banisters from where she knows Lavinia will retrieve it later to hang it up in the coat closet where it belongs, and walks into the kitchen where she collapses on a chair. "I've got a load of shopping in the car. Would you mind bringing it in?"

"Sure," says Lavinia, who truly is an angel for she sees that Amber walked in empty-handed and doesn't resent being asked in the slightest because she loves the children, loves living here, and thinks that Amber and Richard are incredibly nice, if a little spoiled. But she is now part of the family, so much so that Amber regularly sits in the kitchen and chats to Lavinia, has even shared with Lavinia the secrets of her background, so while Lavinia sees that Amber is a little spoiled, she understands why, and she forgives her for it.

Chapter Six

It may only be a BBC radio show where no one is going to see her, but as Vicky pulls on a skirt and flat pumps, shakes her hair out to give it some more body, checks her makeup in the bathroom mirror, she thinks of her mother and smiles to herself.

"You never know who you might meet," her mother always says, and while, on the whole, Vicky tends not to listen to her mother, these words have been drummed into her so often it is now second nature to ensure she looks if not her best then certainly acceptable before she leaves the house. Because her mother, she hates to admit it, is right. You just never know.

There was the time when she was driving her Beetle along Chalk Farm Road and she had spotted a parking meter and zipped over, jumping out to find the car behind had also pulled over. She had looked at the driver strangely, wondering if he had something to say to her, but he hadn't said anything and she had shrugged and walked off, only to return to find a note on her car asking her for a drink.

That drink had turned into a five-month relationship.

There was the time when, again driving her Beetle along Park Lane on the way to a club, she had passed a Triumph Stag, the roof down, crammed with laughing men, one of whom had jumped out and climbed into her car at the traffic light. She slept with him a week later.

There was the time she had taken the train to see some friends in Manchester, and had started talking to the man who had come to sit opposite her, even though the rest of the carriage was practically empty. She hadn't fancied him in the slightest, but he had become a good friend, and was now married to a girl Vicky had introduced him to.

So her mother was right, you just never knew, although those times, those spontaneous, exhilarating meetings, hadn't happened for a while, and every now and then Vicky worried that they'd never happen again, that you are supposed to have adventures when you are in your twenties, but by the time you reach your mid-thirties the adventures stop happening: you are supposed to be settling down and growing up.

Vicky drives herself to the BBC studios in Portland Place and parks the car. She's early, so she sits in the car listening to the show for a while before going in to collect her pass and wait outside the studio.

"Next on the show," says the voice of Lisa Diamond, one of the presenters of the show, "we're going to be talking about . . . wait for it, Jamie . . . speed sex. Yup, speed sex is apparently the answer to all my problems."

"*Any* sex is the answer to my problems," says a male voice with a soft Irish accent, one that Vicky recognizes and struggles to place as Lisa laughs.

"Typical," she says, "although according to the papers you haven't had a lot of problems in that area lately."

"Didn't anyone ever tell you not to believe everything you read in the papers? Although in this case I would say believe everything. Particularly the story about me and Paris Hilton—"

Lisa's slightly sardonic voice interrupts him, "So, coming up after this we'll be talking about speed sex between Jamie Donnelly and Paris Hilton, oh and we'll have the features director of *Poise!* on to tell us why we're all raving about speedy sex, although I'm sure Jamie will do a perfect job all by himself."

"Careful, you'll get me sued," Vicky hears Jamie's voice in the background as Damien Rice's haunting tones fill her car, and she quickly checks herself in the mirror before getting out. Shit. Jamie Donnelly. She had no idea he'd be on the show, and all of a sudden she starts to feel slightly nervous. Jamie Donnelly! The star of *Dodgy*, a comedy sketch show that started small on BBC2, swept the boards at the British Comedy Awards, and is now the show that everyone's talking about, phrases being repeated in pubs all over the country, amid much laughter.

All it takes is a raised eyebrow and a "Not in my backyard, missus" for a roomful of people to start cracking up. Or an "Is that your dog or are you just pleased to see me?"

Jamie Donnelly: Irish, twinkly, usually made to look horrendously ugly in most of the sketches, his teeth blacked out, or dressed as a baby, or a homeless man with a luxury home in the doorway of WH Smith's on the Strand, has become an overnight star, not least because he is also the writer and producer.

A regular guest on various radio and TV shows, Vicky never understood what all the fuss was about until she switched on the TV one night and happened to catch Jamie Donnelly being interviewed by Jonathan Ross, and all at once she got it. She sat in her living room, all by herself, shrieking with laughter until her face actually hurt.

Jamie Donnelly hadn't been in her consciousness at all until that night, but since then she had seen his name everywhere. He'd been linked with every gorgeous single woman in London, and a couple from overseas who had just been visiting, including, allegedly, Paris Hilton, from whose hotel he had been spotted emerging in the early hours of the morning.

But what had really done it for Vicky, what had sealed the deal as it were, in turning Jamie Donnelly into her number one crush, was when Deborah had phoned her at work one day and offered her an interview she had done with Jamie Donnelly.

"I can't believe you interviewed Jamie Donnelly," Vicky had said. "I love him! I wanted to interview him."

"Sorry," Deborah said. "But I managed to get him on his own at a film do last week and he gave me half an hour. I've got some great quotes about being single, the womanizing, what he really wants out of life. A lot of stuff he's never talked about before. I was going to give it to the *Mail*, but I thought *Poise!* would pay more . . ." They both laughed, knowing that no one paid more than the *Mail*, but also knowing that half the time the *Mail* never actually printed the story, and Deborah wanted her byline in print more than she wanted the money.

"So what was he like?" Vicky asked. "I have to tell you I'm deeply jealous. I really do think he's gorgeous."

"The funny thing is I didn't think he was gorgeous before I met him, but he does that thing where he completely focuses on you and makes you feel like the only person in the room, and he kind of nods earnestly at everything you say, and I have to be honest, I do understand why all these women fall head over heels. He's also kind of flirty, which is always nice. If I wasn't happily married . . ."

Vicky sighed. "Oh God. Stop. Be still, my beating heart."

"Well, he does say in the interview he's ready to settle down."

"Okay, now you got me. Send it over now and I'll have a look. Maybe we can set up a photo shoot to go with the piece and I'll go along to style it. Christ, I've got to be able to meet him somewhere, I'm features director of *Poise!*, for heaven's sake, I meet celebrities all day every day."

"And I thought you were jaded by now."

"Oh I am, I am. Just not when it comes to Jamie Donnelly."

But what had really affected Vicky, turned her minor silly crush into a series of full-on fantasies, had been the interview itself. Jamie had said that despite his reputation for being a womanizer, what he really wanted was to settle down. He dreamed, he said, of a house in the country, with children and big dogs everywhere, of finding the one woman who would make him happy for the rest of his life.

So Vicky decided she would be that woman. He was, after all, the same age as her, and even if he did tend to be photographed with young bimbettes, that didn't necessarily sound like what he wanted. No, surely what he *really* wanted, *really* needed, was a thirty-five-year-old successful, intelligent features director of a magazine; someone who wasn't all that great at cooking but who would be willing to learn; someone who shared his dreams, who would bring him cups of tea while he sat in his office off the kitchen writing wonderful comedy scripts.

And thus began a series of fantasies: Vicky and Jamie

(even the pairing of their names sounding perfect), their children Lola and Milo, their deerhounds Fitzroy and McHairy, their friends, their profiles in *Hello!* with photographs of the happy couple in their cozy country home.

Meanwhile, Vicky hadn't ever met him, hadn't even come close to meeting him, and her fantasies of a perfect happy ever after with Jamie Donnelly had slowly faded to fantasies of a perfect happy ever after with a tall, faceless stranger.

And now here he was, a guest on the radio show that she wasn't even supposed to have been on. Could this, she thinks, as she tries to swallow her nerves, finally be fate working in her favor at long last?

Vicky is ushered into the studio during a song. Lisa smiles and waves from her position on the other side of the console, and Jamie Donnelly—Jamie Donnelly!—leans over and shakes her hand. And Vicky thinks she is going to be sick.

Thankfully she gathers herself enough to be ready when the song finishes and Lisa gaily announces, "My next guest's dream night of passionate sex lasts roughly eight minutes, and she says that most married women agree with her. Vicky Townsley, welcome to the *Lisa Diamond Show.*"

Vicky's mouth drops open as a deep flush covers her cheeks. It has just been announced on national radio that she enjoys sex for eight minutes, which is a complete lie, there has been no mention of the fact that this was work, that she's from *Poise!*, and meanwhile Jamie Donnelly is sitting next to her watching her mortification and is cracking up laughing.

"So, Vicky, tell us why speed sex is such a fantastic thing, and what the rest of us who are spending a good hour on foreplay are missing out on."

Jesus. Could this get worse? Vicky takes a deep breath and

manages to compose herself. "Lisa, thanks for having me on the show, and can I start by saying I'm features director of *Poise!*, and this was a feature that we ran after we noticed the number of married women, particularly those with children, talking about sex and how quickies were all they had the energy for."

"I think what she's trying to say is that her shags last longer," Jamie laughs.

"I'm not actually married," Vicky smiles, "so my shags are not up for discussion."

"Oh go on." Jamie raises an eyebrow. "You're here, we're talking about sex. I'll tell you mine if you tell me yours."

Vicky just stares at him. Is he flirting with her? Is she imagining this? And more to the point, what kind of conversation is this to be having on national radio, even if it is a hip, late-night show that gets away with practically everything. Her mother could be listening to this, for God's sake.

"My mother could be listening to this, for God's sake," she says, shaking a finger at him. "And I'm not here to talk about my sex life. Although if you want to reveal a few details about Paris Hilton," at this point she raises an eyebrow back at him, "please, be my guest."

"Er, excuse me?" Lisa interrupts. "But you're both my guests, and I want to hear a bit more about speed sex. Vicky, ignore Jamie, and tell us about what *Poise!* magazine found during research for the article."

To Vicky's immense surprise she manages to be articulate, quick-thinking, and even quite funny. The chemistry between the three of them works better than the producer has expected, and quips and puns fly back and forth throughout the show.

At nine-thirty Vicky and Jamie are led out of the studio by the delighted producer, leaving Lisa to finish her show.

"Guys, that was fantastic," he says. "Honestly, that was one of the best shows we've had in weeks. I could tell Lisa was having a great time too. Jamie, you were hilarious. Just hilarious. I love the show, man," and Vicky winces as she feels it coming. Please don't say it, she thinks, please don't say it, but sure enough the producer closes one eye and with a grin says, "Not in my backyard, missus," then shoves Jamie playfully on the arm as Jamie nods and says, "Great. Glad you like it. Thanks again," before turning to Vicky and surreptitiously rolling his eyes.

They walk over to the lift and as the doors shut Vicky's heart starts pounding. What is she going to say? She's in the lift with her number one crush who has definitely been flirting with her this evening, although that doesn't necessarily mean anything because he does seem to flirt with everyone, and all of a sudden she feels like a teenage girl and doesn't know what to say.

"So?" Jamie turns to her as he leans back against the wall. "You were pretty funny."

"You weren't so bad yourself." Vicky smiles.

"It's a tough job but somebody's gotta do it," he says, looking at his watch. "It's still early. Do you want to come and have a drink?"

Oh thank you, God, Vicky silently prays, trying not to beam like a lovestruck teenager. "Sure," she says coolly, as the fantasies, those fantasies that had disappeared for the last few months, come back with a bang.

"Do you mind if we go to Soho House?" he says. "If we go anywhere else I just get hassled all the time, and without wanting to sound ungrateful, every bloke thinks he's the first one to quote, and they all think it's hysterical, and they all want me to think it's hysterical, and sometimes I just want to shoot them."

"Nothing like a bit of honesty," Vicky says. "Soho House is fine. I haven't been there for ages," she lies, having been there just the other night for a screening.

Vicky feels like a queen walking into the club with Jamie Donnelly. Everyone turns to stare at him, all of them pretending not to be impressed with his celebrity, but all of them impressed nonetheless. Those people already in the celebrity club, which includes a pop star, a couple of major actors, one comedian, and one girl famous for being famous, all immediately come over to say hello, and with a sinking heart Vicky realizes that this isn't going to be the cozy, romantic drink of her dreams, but that they are going to be surrounded by people all night, and even if they manage to get a table somewhere, just the two of them, people will be coming over all night to congratulate Jamie on his win at the British Comedy Awards.

"Come on," Jamie says, after he gets the drinks, "let's go upstairs where it's quieter. I asked them to get me a table out of the way so we can talk properly." And he takes her hand to lead her out of the room and up the stairs.

I'm thirty-five, Vicky tells herself. I'm not some kid impressed by celebrity, even though Jamie Donnelly is holding my hand, which is growing horribly sweatier by the second. I will make this work, she thinks, as they pass a girl who looks her up and down, checking out who Jamie Donnelly is picking up this time. I will make him fall in love with me.

"I have a question for you," Vicky asks as they sit down.

"As long as it isn't what was Paris Hilton *really* like in bed, I'll answer anything."

"It wasn't actually." Vicky smiles, that's exactly what she was going to ask. "Do you like the way your life has changed since the success of *Dodgy*?"

"Blimey," Jamie sits back in his chair and grins at her over the top of his glass, "I forgot you're a journalist. Are you going to be interviewing me all night?"

"I hadn't thought what I was going to do with you all night, actually." It comes out in a far more flirtatious voice than Vicky had planned, and Jamie raises an eyebrow.

"Promises, promises," he winks, and Vicky quickly takes a sip of her drink and changes the subject, determined not to be just another easy lay, another notch on his bedpost, a pretty journalist to be forgotten about by tomorrow evening when he'll doubtless be here with yet another girl, unless of course she manages to play her cards right.

"I've got a question for *you*." He leans forward. "How come a successful, clever, attractive woman like you hasn't been snapped up yet?"

Vicky groans. "Now you sound like my grandma."

"That doesn't sound like your grandma," Jamie grins, "that's *my* grandma."

"Her name isn't Sylvia by any chance, is it? Blue rinse? Airedale terrier called Charlie? Addicted to Tunnocks caramel wafers?"

Jamie laughs. "Close. Mine's Phyllis. Purple hair. Black-and-white cat called, rather bizarrely, Sylvia. Addicted to butterscotch."

"Phew. Just checking we're not one another's long-lost secret brother and sister."

"Nice idea," Jamie says thoughtfully, taking out a piece of

paper and scribbling something on it. "I could get a good sketch out of that."

"See!" Vicky says delightedly, thrilled that she might have inspired a sketch in *Dodgy*. "I knew there was a reason we met. Maybe I'm supposed to be your muse! I've always fancied being someone's muse. I could lie on a chaise longue eating chocolates all day while I give you great ideas for your next hit comedy show."

"Only if you promise to lie naked," Jamie says slowly. And Vicky blushes.

I will not sleep with him, Vicky tells herself, as they continue drinking, leaning closer and closer toward each other, the flirting growing more intense, the rest of the room, the club, the world having disappeared.

I am old enough and have been around enough to know that sleeping with someone you might very well want to marry is not the way to generate their interest on a long-term basis, she thinks, as she looks down at Jamie's hand resting on the table, and suppresses an almost overwhelming urge to pick it up and place a soft kiss on his palm.

And oh God, he is so perfect. So perfect for her. He is just as funny as she had thought when she watched him with Jonathan Ross, although in a quieter and calmer way, not having to switch himself "on" when not on television, not appearing in a public place.

I will be cool and hard to get, she thinks, watching the streams of young women walk past their table, trying desperately to get his attention, although thankfully he is, as Deborah has said, entirely focused on her, and doesn't even look around.

But it is very hard to play hard to get when you are taken

unawares by a soft kiss behind your ear. When you are sitting quietly, minding your own business, lost in a world of fantasies, waiting for your companion to come back from the gents, when said companion silently glides up behind you and places his lips just behind your ear, in a place that sends shivers down to your toes.

When you turn, shaken and surprised, and before you even have a chance to say anything his lips are on yours, but so softly and so fleetingly that when he sits down again, when you have a chance to catch your breath, you think you may have just imagined it.

"Sorry," he grins like a naughty little boy. "It's just I've been wanting to do that all night."

And there isn't anything that you can think of to say.

Later that night, when you are lying in your bed, the phone rings and you quickly reach over and answer it. Who would be calling you at two in the morning? But of course you know exactly who would be calling, the only person who ever calls you at two in the morning.

"I can't talk now, Daniel," you whisper. "It's too late." And you put the phone down and turn to see if it woke Jamie Donnelly up. And it did, and Jamie Donnelly—Jamie Donnelly!—reaches out his arms and pulls you down to him, and you snuggle up tight, and just as you fall asleep you think how you never realized how wonderful it felt to have your dreams come true.

You wake up in the morning thinking it was a dream. There is, after all, no one beside you in the bed, but then you turn as Jamie walks out of the bathroom, and you think, shit. Why did I do that? Why didn't I play hard to get?

Chapter Seven

Amber, chameleonlike today in her own school uniform of jeans and T-shirt (oh if only the women in the League could see her now . . .), sits on the bench in the playground in school watching Grace hold hands with Molly as they both squeeze together on the slide.

"How sweet are they," says Deborah, plonking herself down on the bench next to Amber, cardboard cup of coffee in hand. "And how nice to see you today. Where's Lavinia?"

"She's at home waiting for Jared's bus. I thought it would be nice to pick Gracie up myself, plus we have . . ." she pauses, unsure of whether or not Deborah has been invited to Hunter's birthday party, "um . . ."

"Hunter's birthday party?" Deborah laughs. "Don't worry, the whole basketball class is going."

Amber had learned the rules of suburban socializing quickly, and one of them was never mention where you are going in case the person to whom you are talking has not been invited.

Admittedly not everyone followed these rules. The more gauche or desperately upwardly mobile, including of course the competitive women in the League, tended to tell everyone where they were going, or post it on their noticeboards, just so everyone knew they had been included too, irrespective of who else might have been excluded, but Amber tried to be careful, tried not to hurt anyone's feelings.

And even though Deborah was her closest friend, there were times when she turned up at dinner parties and there was Deborah, to whom she had spoken less than an hour before, when neither had mentioned they were off to the house of a mutual friend.

Deborah tended to be pragmatic about it. "You can't invite everyone to everything," she always said, but Amber knew that the few times she had been excluded, she had taken it personally and had wondered why not her, what was wrong with her that she hadn't been invited, was it perhaps that they thought her not good enough?

Poor Amber. Still so self-conscious, despite being married to a Winslow, still worried that if the girls whom she seeks to impress were aware of her humble beginnings, they might sneer at her, might ostracize her from the in crowd.

Of course Amber never stops to think of their own backgrounds. Never questions their own overwhelming need to impress with labels, ostentation, name-dropping.

Although Deborah has noticed. "God, they're all so nouveau," she said, just last night, to her husband, Spencer, putting on a Brahmin Boston accent. "Half these girls were brought up with nothing, but to look at them today you'd think they were born in Buckingham bloody Palace."

Spencer shrugged. "What about your friend Amber? If you don't like it, how come you see so much of *her*?"

"Amber's different," Deborah said. "Deep down she's a good person."

"But still, you always say she's just as desperate to keep up with the Joneses."

Deborah nodded sadly. "I know, you're right, but here's

the difference: she doesn't judge me because we don't have what she has, whereas the others, that Suzy for example, probably wouldn't even set foot in our house."

"What's the matter with our house?" Spencer was genuinely bemused, and Deborah laughed and sat on his lap, putting her arms around him.

"That's why I love you," she grinned. "You haven't even noticed that our entire house could fit into Amber's kitchen."

Spencer frowned. "But you like it, don't you? Not that we could afford more, but would you want to live in something bigger?"

"Would I want to? Sure. In a dream world I'd love to have a big, beautiful house, but in the real world the only thing I want, other than my darling husband, is a finished basement so the kids have somewhere to play."

"I know, I know. Hopefully I'll get a bonus at the end of the year and I promise that will be a priority, that's what we'll spend the money on."

Deborah snuggled up to him. "I don't care that we're poor," she said. "We have each other. And the kids."

"We're not poor," Spencer insisted. "We're just not rich."

"Same difference when you live in this area." Deborah laughed. "But still, I don't care. At least we have our priorities in the right place, which is more than can be said for some people."

"Including your friend Amber?"

"Oh give the girl a break. She's a good friend to me and I love her."

Today, after school, is Suzy's son Hunter's birthday party. It's being held at Gymini Stars, the local kids' play space, which opened only six months ago and has rapidly become the in place for birthday parties.

Initially the parties were all the same. You would open the same invitation from Gymini Stars, have the same allotted time on the gym equipment, play the same games during circle time, eat the same pizza and birthday cake, and receive the same balloons tied to your loot bags on the way out.

Lately, though, Amber has noticed a change. Now some of the invitations are not the generic invitations from Gymini Stars, but have been specially ordered from Sarah Belmont, who has opened a stationery business from her home. And the parties are changing. In the last six weeks Amber has been to children's birthday parties that had face painters, clowns, and an inflatable bouncy castle in the parking lot.

"What can we do?" shrugs David, the amenable, consistently cheerful owner of Gymini Stars. "Everyone wants to outdo everyone else."

Just last week Amber picked up Jared from Henry's birthday party, where they had flown in a karate teacher from Los Angeles to give the kids customized karate lessons. It was over the top, but got worse when Jared got in the car after the party and ripped open the wrapping paper on his party favor to find it was a Transformer—a fire truck that turns into a robot, which made Amber feel sick with shame because it was exactly what they had given Henry as his actual birthday present, and she drove home in a cloud of humiliation that she had spent the same amount of money on the birthday gift as the parents had for party favors—thirty-two of them.

This time she isn't going to make the same mistake for Hunter. Even though he is only three years old, Amber has bought him a building block castle that, when assembled, is the size of a playhouse. It has cost a fortune, but is worth it to know that she won't have to suffer the same humiliation.

Oh God. It is so exhausting, this constant competition. Sometimes Amber longs for a simpler life. Not that she'd ever want to go back to where she came from, but sometimes she thinks about her life in Manhattan, before she met Richard, or in those early days when they were married, before children, when they just had fun. No responsibilities, no children to worry about, nothing to get up for on the weekends, life had been so carefree and easy.

Not that she'd want to change her children; she does, after all, adore them, even though she doesn't spend very much time with them, but life seems to have become so busy, so harried, and there are times when she disappears into her office and goes to realtor.com, when she looks at farms in Montana, cottages by the water in Vermont, places where there are no Joneses with whom to keep up, places where money doesn't matter and happiness is not about who is the best dressed or has the most expensive handbag.

But of course that's just a dream. How can they possibly leave Highfield when Richard commutes in to Wall Street every day, and even if they moved to a different town, would it really be any different? She has friends in Westport, friends in New Canaan, friends in Rye, friends in Englewood, and all of them seem to have similar issues. As long as Richard is working in the city Amber knows they have to stay within the commuter belt, and as long as they stay in the commuter belt, Amber will have to play the game, and as long as she is going to play the game, why not win? Or at least make an attempt. Remember, Amber didn't get to where she is today without a thread of steel running through her.

* * *

Oh what the hell, Amber laughs as she pulls off her Manolo boots and follows Gracie onto the jungle gym, clambering awkwardly up the rope ladder to the jumbo swirly slide as Jared and Gracie shriek with laughter and excitement, unable to believe that their mother is the only mother who is playing up there with them.

"Yay, Mom!" Jared whoops. "Come on the slide with me!"

"Can I come on your lap?" Gracie shouts, pushing Jared aside.

"Come on, guys," Amber laughs, opening her legs so Jared can sit in the middle as she pulls Gracie onto her lap and the three of them tumble down the slide, coming out the other side to a gaggle of women, heads together, talking intently.

Suzy looks up to see Amber and shakes her head. "Amber Winslow, I cannot believe what I am seeing. Are you crazy?"

Amber forces a laugh. "Just trying to keep my kids happy," and she rolls her eyes as if she'd rather be anywhere else than barefoot on a jungle gym, although the truth is she'd far rather be on the jungle gym than sitting on the benches by the side, gossiping with the other women.

Twenty minutes later Amber has no choice but to join the women. She's exhausted, and despite Gracie clinging to her and begging her to come on the trampoline, she has to sit down.

"Oh boy," she says, collapsing on a bench next to Deborah. "I am exhausted. I thought my workouts were bad but that is something else."

"How do you think Lavinia manages to stay so thin?" Deborah grins. "I've seen her up there running after your children."

Amber shoots Deborah a sharp look. "Please tell me

you're not trying to make me feel guilty about not spending enough time with my children. . . ."

"Are you kidding? I'd kill for a full-time nanny. If Spencer's bonus comes through he thinks we're going to be finishing the basement, but frankly, I'd rather spend the money on a baby-sitter. I'm exhausted every night, the television is the only baby-sitter I've got so my kids are watching about two hours a day, which I hate, but God knows I need a break by then, and it's all I can do to stay up to say hello to my husband before collapsing into bed. Not to mention the fact that by the time the witching hour comes along I've turned into a screaming harridan. My poor kids have forgotten that it's even possible for me to talk in a normal voice."

"At least you've got an excuse," says Amber. "I fall into bed every night at eight-thirty and I've got Lavinia. Why the hell am I so exhausted? What happened to my energy, my zest for life?"

Deborah shrugs. "I suppose it's just being a mother and having a busy life and being thirty-five. And it's not as if you're sitting around doing nothing all day. You're at the gym, you're doing all the charity stuff, the League stuff. With all your running around you're bound to be just as tired."

"You're probably right. I just felt that we hibernated all last winter. Richard went crazy not going out, and I promised that in the summer we'd be back to socializing, and I'd have people over all the time, and we'd be barbecuing every night, and meanwhile it's now almost the end of March, the weather's unseasonably beautiful and do you think we've entertained once?"

"We came over last weekend. That's entertaining."

"Nope. It doesn't count if the kids are there. I mean proper grown-up entertaining. Richard wants us to have a party this summer, cocktails around the pool, grown-up music, that kind of thing."

Deborah shrugs. "Richard needs to accept that he's a family man now. It's different once you have kids."

"But it wasn't," Amber pleads. "Up until about a year ago we used to go out all the time, we always had energy. Now when we're out for dinner I start having an anxiety attack as nine o'clock approaches because I'm not home and in my bed."

Deborah starts to laugh. "We went to Jerry and Stacey's house for dinner last week, and they asked us to get there at six-thirty, so we found a baby-sitter and thought great, it will be an early night."

"What night of the week?"

"Thursday." Amber raises an eyebrow to which Deborah nods, "Exactly! So we turned up and sat around the kitchen table talking and Stacey kept saying she was going to cook, and she really ought to start cooking, and meanwhile she didn't even start chopping onions until half past eight."

"You're kidding!" Amber gasps in horror.

"I kid you not. So we sit down for dinner at quarter to ten, by which time I'm so exhausted I can barely keep my eyes open, and we don't get out of there until midnight."

"God, how selfish." Amber grins. "Don't they have children the same age? How are they able to do it?"

"I know. That's what we were saying. Who the hell stays up that late with young children? On a Thursday! So, if Jerry and Stacey ever invite you over, make sure you say no."

"Good advice. So have you figured out what you're going to wear to the gala?"

Deborah shakes her head. "Not yet. I've got a black dress that I wore to a wedding a couple of years ago, which I'll probably wear. But how about you? I bet you've bought something fabulous."

Well of *course* Amber has bought something fabulous. This gala isn't any old gala, it's the high point of the Highfield social calendar, the sparkling society ball where everyone dresses to see and be seen.

This year it's at Sweeping Views, the town country club, and although those on the committee, Amber included, claim to view it as the biggest fund-raiser of the year (which it is), it's caused many a near–nervous breakdown among women planning their wardrobes.

Amber didn't even bother with Rakers this year. She didn't want anyone to have seen her outfit. It was straight into Bergdorf's for Amber, and straight upstairs for a delicate, feathered, Oscar de la Renta cocktail dress that Amber had already earmarked in last month's *Vogue*.

Months had been spent planning the gala. Local businesses had been approached to make donations to the silent auction, and anyone with connections was asked to try and finagle something special.

Highfield being Highfield, among the items being offered this year were a week on Necker Island, traveling back and forth in Virgin Upper Class; a guest cameo appearance on *Will and Grace*; and the opportunity to work as a roadie on Maroon 5's upcoming tour (this was the pièce de résistance, the husband of one of the women on the committee having a best friend who was a music promoter, and would prove to be hotly bid for by parents of hip teenage girls with crushes on the lead singer).

Amber herself had gone to Uncle Bobby—Robert Winslow III, the only member of the Winslow family, other than

Richard, who still has money, even though it is self-made—and requested he donate some time on his yacht. Naturally he had complied, and Amber was thrilled to have a page donated to a free sail around the Hamptons for a long weekend this summer, donated by Amber and Richard Winslow.

Let Suzy put that in her pipe and smoke it.

Suzy and her husband had donated a case of rare wine. She had talked for months about their house in the Bahamas, and how they were going to donate that, but it seemed that it had suffered damage during the recent hurricanes, and she was so upset but it wouldn't be ready in time.

In truth, the damage suffered consisted of two missing roof tiles, but Suzy was no fool. She wanted her friends to know they had a place in the Bahamas, she just didn't want them to know it was a minuscule one-bedroom condo that was on the wrong side of the tracks, and a twenty-minute drive to the beach.

"What are you two talking about?" Suzy approaches with an approximation of a gracious smile and sits down with Amber and Deborah.

"We were just talking about what we're going to wear to the gala." Deborah smiles innocently. "What about you, do you have your outfit?"

"Oh yes." Suzy nods. "I picked up this adorable little dress the last time I was in the city." The city. Codespeak for expensive. "I was just looking at Dolce and Gabbana and I really didn't think I'd find anything, and it's so expensive, but then I fell in love and I tried it on, and I just had to have it. My husband went crazy, so I don't think I'm going to be allowed to buy anything else for the rest of the season!" She trills with laughter, pretending to poke fun at herself. "How about you, Amber?" she says. "Do you have your outfit?" Deborah grins to herself, knowing that Suzy would never bother asking her, Deborah being no competition whatsoever.

"Yes," Amber smiles. "I've got a lovely dress."

"Oh?" Suzy waits for more information. There's none forthcoming. "From Rakers?"

"No." Amber shakes her head with a smile and decides to leave her hanging. There's an awkward silence that Amber is tempted to fill, but she decides not to.

"Well, I'm sure you'll look beautiful," Suzy says eventually. "Oh and by the way, thank you again for that yacht trip, I think that's going to be a big winner at the auction. We had a last-minute addition this week, did you hear about Amberley Jacks?"

"No."

"Well, we got so lucky. I managed to get them to donate a full house makeover. Obviously, whoever wins will have to pay for the furniture, but they're donating their time for free. Isn't that extraordinary? I was so lucky to even get hold of them, apparently they don't even return eighty percent of their calls, and they only take on a handful of clients at a time."

Deborah nudges Amber. "See? You should have waited. Richard's already having a fit about how much money they're costing."

There's a pause. "Oh." Suzy raises an eyebrow. "You're using Amberley Jacks?"

Amber shrugs apologetically.

"Well!" She sniffs in an attempt to hide her jealousy. "You're very lucky to have got them, I must say. You're going to be the envy of all the town. Girls, I have to go and socialize, excuse me, but help yourself to Diet Coke."

* * *

"You are *so* bad!" Amber turns to Deborah, who flashes an evil grin.

"I know!" she chuckles. "But I couldn't help it. God, she's such a desperate social climber. Dolce and bleedin' Gabbana. Who does she think she is? I'm surprised she didn't tell us exactly how much her outfit cost."

"I'm sure she would have if we'd shown a bit of interest," Amber laughs.

"Did you see her face when I told her you were using Amberley Jacks?" Deborah rubs her hands together. "Talk about ruining her birthday party." Deborah turns around and sees Suzy talking closely to three other women, all of them looking over at Amber. Deborah gives them a small wave and turns back to Amber. "Don't look now but I think you'll find the whole room's going to know about Amberley Jacks any second."

"Oh God," Amber groans, suddenly tired of trying to keep up. She turns to Deborah with a sigh. "Can't we just give it all up and go and live in Vermont? Don't you get tired of all this?"

"Nope. I love it," Deborah says lightly. "But that's because I don't get involved. Actually I *can't* get involved. Haven't got the money, and that's probably why I enjoy it so much. Look, you've got to admit it's ridiculous. Someone should write a book about it. Social Climbers in Suburbia. Bet that would be a bestseller."

"I wish I could be more like you." Amber sighs. "Sometimes I can look at it and see how awful it is, but other times I feel so insecure, and it's as if the clothes and the jewels and all that superficial stuff is like armor, it protects me, makes me pretend I'm as good as all of them."

"But you *are* as good as all of them." Deborah's voice is suddenly serious. "In fact, no, Amber, you're much better. I know you feel insecure with them, but life isn't a competition, you know that, and you're a real person, which is more than can be said for Suzy. You have a wonderful husband, two gorgeous children, and a fantastic best friend." She grins. "The trick is to surround yourself with the good people and not to get involved in all the crap, other than for anthropological reasons, of course."

"You know, you're right," Amber says firmly, standing up as she prepares to lead Jared and Gracie in for the requisite birthday pizza and cake. "After this gala, that's it. I'm done. No more charities. No more mixing with people who care about stuff like that. I'm going to change my life."

"That's it!" Deborah says, clapping her hands. "See? You can do it."

"But . . ." And Amber turns to her with a worried look. "Do you really think it's possible to get away from all of that in a town like Highfield?"

Deborah shrugs. "I manage," she smiles. "And if not, there's always Vermont."

Chapter Eight

Vicky got back into bed after the third session with Jamie and, smiling, went to sleep. They'd had breakfast, read the papers together—oh what bliss, wasn't this what she had always wanted?—and gone back to bed.

Jamie has been everything she thought he would be, and when he leaves, saying he'll call her later, she immediately phones Deborah to tell her the good news.

"Swear you won't tell anyone," she starts, as Deborah yawns down the phone.

"Let me guess. You've just shagged Jamie Donnelly."

Vicky is shocked into silence. "What?" she says finally. "How did you know?"

Now it's Deborah's turn to be shocked. "You're joking!" she says, suddenly wide awake. "I was joking. Now I'm confused. You didn't really shag Jamie Donnelly, did you?"

"You have to swear you won't tell anyone," Vicky pleads.

"I swear I won't tell anyone. How in the hell did this happen?" Deborah takes her cordless phone over to the sofa and curls up for a long one, and Vicky tells her everything.

"So what do you think?" Vicky says when she's finished. "I mean, you actually know him."

"What do you mean, what do I think?"

"I mean, do you think he likes me? Do you think he'll call?"

Deborah takes a deep breath. "If he likes you, then he'll call."

"But from what I've told you, do you think he likes me?"

"Vicky, here's a question for you . . ."

"Yes?" An eager voice.

"How old are you exactly?"

"I know," she moans. "I sound like I'm twelve. But that's about how I feel. I've fancied him for ages and we had this amazing night, and now I'm sitting here like a lovestruck teenager wondering exactly what he's doing today and whether he's thinking about me and whether he's going to call, and if he is, then when."

"Okay, here's some advice," Deborah says. "First, get out of the house and do something, and that's an order. Do not, under any circumstances, stay in the house and wait for him to call. The worst thing you could do is be available to him anyway, so if he does call, you want to be out and busy, and if you're not out and busy at least pretend to be out and busy."

"So can I stay home and pretend to be busy?"

"No you bloody well can't. Why don't you go and see Kate and Andy? When was the last time you went to see them in the country anyway? That will take your mind off Jamie Donnelly for a few hours."

"You know what? That's a great idea. Even though I'd rather sit by the phone, I take your point. I'll ring them now. Thanks, Deborah."

"My pleasure, and don't bore them stupid with Jamie Donnelly."

* * *

"I can't believe you slept with Jamie Donnelly!" Kate's sitting at the kitchen table as Vicky recounts every second of the night before. "God, he's gorgeous! Tell me again that bit about how he first kissed you."

But just as Vicky starts talking again, the back door slams and the noisy sounds of children and dogs echo through the corridor.

"No, Luke!" Vicky's brother, Andy, calls. "Take your wellies off before you go into the kitchen. Polly! Sophie! Pick your coats up and hang them up. No, not drape them over the chair, hang them on hooks. Polly, stop pushing your sister! *Kate!*" he yells. "Can you come and help me!"

Kate looks at Vicky and rolls her eyes as the two dogs come rushing through the hallway and into the kitchen, jumping up excitedly on Vicky.

"Aaargh, get off," she yells, trying to push them off, because both of them are the size of small ponies, and they're filthy dirty. "Oh Christ," she says, looking down at her now mud-splattered sweater. She looks over at Kate. "Tell me why I'm wearing cashmere to come and see you in the country?"

Kate shrugs. "God knows, Vix. You of all people know it's impossible to stay clean within four minutes of walking into this house. I keep telling you to dress down, absolutely no reason to wear cashmere in deepest darkest Somerset, particularly not with Herk and Hogie over there," and she gestures over to where Hercules and Hogan, the lurchers, are now sniffing around the counters, trying to gauge whether it's worth the effort of standing on their hind legs to see if there's any food worth stealing, although in the eyes of a lurcher, if it's food and it's on a counter, it's worth stealing.

"Go on, Herkie, come on, Hogie," Kate says, beckoning them outside to the kids. "Let's go and help Daddy."

"Vix? Is that you?" Andy calls out from the hallway.

"Yup. I thought I'd come down and see everyone," Vicky says, standing up and brushing herself off as the children come running in.

"Auntie Vix!" they yell, all leaping up into her arms, each one just as enthusiastic and energetic as the dogs, but perhaps a little bit cleaner, and Vicky welcomes them, giggling as they smother her with kisses and immediately take her hand to drag her upstairs to their bedrooms.

"Come and see my dollhouse," Sophie says, pulling her toward the stairs.

"No, come and see the play I did for Mummy and Daddy," says Polly, pulling her back toward the kitchen.

"Auntie Vix, Auntie Vix, will you come and see my spy binoculars?" Luke asks gravely, standing patiently at the bottom of the stairs.

Vicky throws her hands up in the air. "Okay, okay. One at a time. Why don't I sit in the kitchen and Luke, you bring me your binoculars, Polly can perform her play, and when you're done I'll come and see your dollhouse, Sophie. You lucky girl, when did you get such a lovely present?"

"Daddy made it," Sophie says, running upstairs. "And Mummy helped make some furniture."

Vicky turns to Andy. "You made a dollhouse? Since when have you been that handy with a saw?"

Kate starts laughing. "Wait," she says. "It's not exactly a deluxe version. More the nine-old-shoe-boxes-stuck-together-with-Pritt-Stick version."

"I thought it sounded a bit too complicated for my brother." Vicky grins as Andy shakes his head.

"As it happens I've become pretty damn good at DIY, haven't I, Kate? Tell Vicky who made the chicken run."

"You didn't!" Vicky starts to laugh. "And what chicken run? Since when do you have chickens?"

"We thought it would be a good idea for the kids to get fresh eggs," Kate says.

"But won't the dogs eat the chickens?" Vicky looks dubious.

"Ah yes." Andy looks pointedly at Kate. "I have tried to tell her that we'll be lucky if the chickens last the week."

"And that's why you've built such a strong run." Kate returns the look. "The dogs won't be able to get in, will they, Andy?"

"Hopefully not," he says. "Anyway, the chickens don't arrive for another three weeks, so we'll have to let you know."

"Oh God," Vicky moans. "I'm so jealous."

"Jealous? Of what?"

"You just have the perfect life here. Chickens. Children. Dogs. It's not fair."

"Oh stop it," Kate says, refusing to let Vicky give in to an ounce of self-pity. "I'd kill to have a bit of your glamorous life for a while, as would all the women around here. Most of them would gladly swap lives with you in a heartbeat. *I'd* gladly swap lives with you in a heartbeat."

"Oh yeuch," Vicky grimaces. "That means I'd have to be my brother's wife. That's disgusting."

"Oh don't be so ridiculous. I'm only joking, but I'm just saying that you'd be a damn sight happier if you enjoyed your life, because plenty of other people would kill for it." She lowers her voice and checks that Andy is out of earshot. "Don't you think I'm longing for an adventure like the one you had last night with Jamie Donnelly? Look, I adore Andy and would never be unfaithful, but I miss the fun, and the dating, and the excitement of not knowing whether they're going to call or not."

Vicky nods as she listens, and after a pause she looks up at Kate. "So what do you think?" She grins. "Do you think he's going to call?"

Vicky spends the rest of the afternoon playing with the kids in the garden, soaking up the sun, and drinking copious amounts of tea before they stick the kids in front of *Shrek 2* and make a pitcher of Pimms.

Andy goes off for a while to see Bill, the chicken man, who is advising him on all things chicken-related, and brings Bill back to inspect the run, while Vicky and Kate stand on the sidelines nudging each other and giggling as Bill pretends to be impressed.

"Oh come on, Bill," Kate whispers as they walk off, "seriously, is it any good? Shouldn't I get a carpenter to come and check it out?"

Bill grins. "Nope, it's absolutely fine. My first chicken run wasn't nearly as good as this, and you'll be okay. I'm more worried about the foxes than the dogs anyway, but Andy put the wire underneath the ground so they shouldn't be able to get in."

Andy's chest visibly puffs with pride. "And you don't think your husband's up to much," he says.

"All right, all right. I'm wrong. Well done, darling. You're a chicken-run genius."

"Do you want to join us for supper, Bill?" Kate says, as Vicky moves behind him and shakes her head violently. The last thing she wants is to be set up with a chicken man.

"Can't tonight, but thanks, Kate. The kids are with their mum and they should be back soon. I promised them McDonald's and you know what happens when you break a promise."

"Especially when it involves McDonald's," Kate laughs.

"I'll call you during the week," Bill says to Andy, waving good-bye to all as he climbs up into his truck.

"Such a nice man," Kate says as they take their drinks inside and start getting supper ready. "And sheer fluke we found him. Andy was in the pub last week talking about chickens and someone overheard him and put him in touch with Bill who seems to be the expert, and we'd never even heard of him before. And he's attractive too, don't you think?"

"He's okay." Vicky shrugs. "But how come you didn't know him? I thought you knew everyone in the village."

"So did we!" Kate laughs. "But evidently not. He had a weekend cottage in Sherborne but bought a farm down here a couple of years ago, and now he's here permanently." She looks at Vicky pensively. "I wonder if he sold his cottage? That would suit you perfectly, a cottage to come down to on the weekends. I should ring him and ask."

"Thanks, but no thanks," Vicky says firmly. "As long as I'm coming down to this neck of the woods I want to stay with you and my gorgeous nieces and nephew. And anyway, my *Poise!* salary probably wouldn't stretch to a cottage in the country, although it's a nice idea."

"Something to think about," Kate says, starting to peel potatoes. "Everyone's got to have a dream."

"Now if you could find a cottage with a dreamy husband attached, that might be something worth thinking about."

"I thought you were going to marry Jamie Donnelly."

96

"Oh bugger," Vicky says, looking sadly at her silent mobile phone. "Why didn't I give him my mobile?"

Vicky stays the night in Somerset, then takes the early train to Waterloo, going straight to the office. She never figured out how to pick up her messages from her answerphone at home, and now, as frustrating as it is, she's pleased, because by the time she gets home tonight Jamie Donnelly will surely have called. Who knows, if she's very lucky he may have called two or three times.

The light is blinking as she finally walks through the door, and she rushes over, pressing play, her heart sinking lower and lower as she listens to the messages. Deborah phoning to see if Jamie Donnelly has called. Her mother just phoning to say hello. Kate to tell her she'd left her entire makeup bag in the bathroom and she'd be sending it registered so hopefully Vicky would have it on Tuesday, and her accountant wanting her to call and make an appointment.

No Jamie Donnelly. And it's now Monday night. But he's probably been busy taping the new season of *Dodgy*, and he doesn't want to appear too keen anyway, and just because he hasn't called yet doesn't mean anything because he'll almost certainly call tonight. Even if he doesn't she'll give it until Thursday. That's a reasonable time to wait. Even if you really liked someone you'd want to wait until Thursday, wouldn't you? Just so you don't appear too keen.

Vicky replays every event of Saturday night. The flirtatious comments, the way he kissed her, the way he cuddled her after they had sex. And he didn't run away immediately, he read the papers with her—okay, not the whole papers but he read the Style section and flicked through Culture—and he kissed her good-bye and surely he wouldn't have stayed if he didn't like her, I mean, who would do that? What kind of a man would lead a girl on in that way unless he was really interested?

By Thursday morning Vicky still has a shred of hope. Jamie Donnelly knows she works at *Poise!*—he could call her at work, you never know. She lowers her voice to a sultry purr every time she picks up the phone, and each time it is not him.

At lunchtime she takes the tabloids down to the café on the corner, grabs a sandwich, and attempts to drown her misery in a Perrier as she flicks through the papers, keeping up with what's going on in the entertainment world, what the women's desks are writing about, hoping for inspiration, looking for ideas.

She turns to the showbiz section of the *Sun* and her heart stops. There, in the center of the page, is a huge picture of Jamie Donnelly and Denise Van Outen. Kissing. Actually, not quite kissing. More like snogging. Vicky puts her sandwich down and swallows the wave of nausea rising up before reading the text, praying that this is an old photo, that it doesn't mean anything.

At last night's afterparty for the new smash film *Forgotten Mountains*, hot new couple Jamie Donnelly and Denise Van Outen show why they're so sizzling. As they disappeared into his flat, he said, "I've fancied Denise for ages." All we can say to Jamie is: Is that your dog or are you just pleased to see her!!

Why does this always happen to me? Vicky thinks, blinking back the tears. It's not as if Jamie Donnelly is the love of her life, but he represented a dream, and every time Vicky's dreams threaten to become reality, something always happens, and she always ends up alone.

Self-pity washes over her as she sinks her head in her hands, pushing her food away, wanting to just get away from all this pain.

"Vicky? Whatever is the matter?" Vicky looks up to see the concerned face of Janelle Salinger, a rarity only because Janelle usually goes out for lunch, rarely goes to the local sandwich shops or cafés herself. On the odd occasion she has a craving for a KitKat or a grilled chicken sandwich, she will send her assistant over, although today her assistant is off sick, and she's spent the last hour dreaming of sour cream and onion crisps, which are now nestling at the bottom of her green ostrich Prada bag.

"Oh nothing." Vicky attempts a bright smile, closing the paper so Janelle doesn't see, because of course Vicky couldn't keep it to herself—it was Jamie Donnelly, for heaven's sake, how was she supposed to keep a pull like that to herself? She'd started off vowing to just tell Leona, but then she'd ended up confessing to Stella, and before she knew it assistants she barely knew were standing admiringly at her desk and asking if it was true that she was going out with Jamie Donnelly.

I wish, she had thought, but instead she had smiled serenely and said, "Oh, I wouldn't say that. We're just seeing each other."

And now clearly he is seeing Denise Van Outen.

"I heard about you and Jamie Donnelly," Janelle says in a sympathetic voice, sitting down and noting exactly what Vicky had been reading and why she closed the paper. "You just saw the picture, didn't you?"

At this show of sympathy Vicky's voice finally breaks. "Oh God," she says, looking pleadingly at Janelle. "It wasn't as if he was the love of my life, for God's sake. It's just that I'm thirty-five and it isn't getting any easier and I hate being single and why the hell does this keep happening to me?"

Janelle nods in sympathy, then places her hand on Vicky's. "Vicky," she says. "I didn't get married until I was forty. I was exactly where you are now. I never thought I'd find anyone, but once I met Stephen it was just so right, and then I understood why none of the others had worked out."

But I don't want to wait until I'm forty, Vicky thinks. I can't wait another five years, and who's to say it will even happen?

"You will meet someone," Janelle continues. "Trust me."

"When?" Vicky blurts out. "And how do you know? I don't think I ever will. I'm going to end up with Eartha, pushing a bloody shopping trolley."

"Who's Eartha?"

"My cat," Vicky sniffs.

"Oh. Maybe you're romanticizing too much. Do you think perhaps that might have something to do with it? Because it's not all a bed of roses. I think the problem with all you young girls today is you expect marriage to be like something out of a movie, and the minute it becomes boring, or bland, the minute your heart stops beating faster, you're all running to the divorce court. Honestly, Vicky, you have a wonderful life being single, why don't you just try and enjoy it, because once you start really enjoying it Mr. Right will come along, and there are plenty of women who'd leave their husbands in a heartbeat to be single and have a fabulously glamorous life as the features director of *Poise!*."

Vicky looks at Janelle in amazement, because Janelle is

more romantic than the rest of the staff put together. She's the one who comes in every Valentine's Day spouting on and on about the benefits of sharing rose-petal baths with your partner, and how she and Stephen are still—yawn—as blissfully happy as the day they met.

"That's what my sister-in-law always says," Vicky admits eventually. "She says she'd swap with me in a heartbeat. I'd take her up on it except then I'd have to sleep with my brother." Vicky attempts a grin, but Janelle doesn't smile. Her eyes have that faraway look in them that means she's got an idea brewing.

"Swap with a married woman," she says slowly. "What a brilliant idea! Not your sister-in-law—but it's true, plenty of married women *would* want your job. We could run an ad in the magazine looking for a married woman who would swap, then," she flashes a brilliant smile at Vicky, "you could go off and see what it would really be like to be married."

"You mean like *Wife Swap* on TV?" Vicky says dubiously.

"Yes, but we'd take it further." Janelle's voice quickens as she grows more excited.

"You mean I'd have to sleep with the husband?" Vicky is confused.

"No, don't be ridiculous. Not unless you fancied him. But I mean swap lives. Swap wardrobes, swap everything. Wear her clothes, go out with her friends. See if you could really experience what it would mean for you, a single girl, to be married with children, and see if a married woman could go back to being single. It's brilliant. We always think the grass is greener on the other side, and this would be a real opportunity to find out."

"But why would a married woman leave her husband and children to do it?"

"Because she's bored, unfulfilled, would love to work for *Poise!*. Who knows why, a myriad of reasons, but I bet you if we advertise we'll get hundreds of replies. Maybe even thousands . . ." She sits silently for a few seconds, staring into space. "Swapping Lives!" she announces loudly with a flourish. "We'll call it Swapping Lives, and if we hurry we can probably get it in the June issue. Oh Vicky," she leans over and gives Vicky a hug, "this is a genius idea. Well done. Quite brilliant."

"It's a pleasure," says Vicky, leaning back, trying to figure out what just happened as Janelle disappears off in a flurry of Prada. Oh God, she thinks, standing up wearily as she puts the *Sun* in the bin. Did I really just agree to swap lives? Am I out of my tiny mind?

But maybe it won't be so bad, she decides, getting into the lift. After all, given this most recent Jamie Donnelly fiasco, could her life really get any worse?

Chapter Nine

Richard Winslow has a Sunday-morning routine. Leaving Amber asleep in bed, he dresses the kids, piles them and the dog into the car, picks up doughnuts, muffins, orange juice, and coffee, and heads down to the beach in the neighboring town of Westport.

They start with breakfast at one of the picnic tables, Jared and Gracie ending up feeding the remains of the food to Ginger, the retriever, who spends the entire meal begging hopefully before happily devouring the leftovers. Amber keeps quizzing Richard as to why Ginger is so enormous given that he is walked every day by Lavinia and that he is not allowed to eat food from the table, but that of course is only when Amber is around, and Amber is so often not around for the children's mealtimes, so often not around to see how the children delight in throwing food on the kitchen floor to be eagerly lapped up by a grateful Ginger.

Sunday is Richard's time with the children. During the week he leaves the house too early and gets home too late to have any real quality time with them, and although he sometimes wishes he had just a bit of downtime to himself on the weekends, the idea of being with his children is so wonderful—occasionally far more wonderful than the reality, when they're both screaming and fighting—that he sacrifices what little time he might have for himself and spends it with the kids.

They walk Ginger along the beach, then leave him tied to a bench as Jared and Gracie spend a good couple of hours climbing on the playground. Richard has now come to know the Sunday-morning playground regulars—the other fathers who don't see their kids during the week, who bring them down to the playground as an excuse for themselves to bond with the other dads.

And the children have become friends too. They have formed a big pack, the older boys and the younger ones who struggle to keep up, leaping off the huge slide, pretending not to be scared even as their little jaws wobble with fear.

"Hey, Rich!" A tall man in a baseball cap, cradling a Starbucks coffee, waves to Richard from across the playground. "How's it going?" He wanders up, shaking Richard by the hand.

"Hey, Steve, how's the world of hedge funds?"

"Great. Beats the Street. No commuting, no hassle, and what a market. We're up ten plus year-to-date. How 'bout that KKD trade?"

"Not bad." Richard starts looking around for the kids.

"Come on," Steve grins. "You guys must have made boatloads. What did you take on that—five bucks?"

"Well . . ." Richard shrugs.

"More than that?" Steve raises an eyebrow. "Come on, how much did they hit you for?"

"I don't kiss and tell," Richard says. "Listen, I've got to go find the kids," and with a wave he quickly leaves.

* * *

Richard can't stop worrying about money. Mostly, he tries to keep these worries to himself, but when he does mention his concerns to Amber, she teases him, tells him not to be so ridiculous, he is a Winslow after all, not to mention the most successful Winslow of this past generation.

He's trying to relax, but every month his Platinum American Express bills arrive, and every month he gives Amber a pep talk, explains that she has to curb her spending, that she can't buy everything she wants just because she wants it, and that next month he expects the bill to be lower, and the next month the bill is even higher.

"But it's the League gala coming up," she had crooned to him one night, after his anger had dispersed somewhat. "I can't wear Gap to the gala. I'm on the committee. I have to look good," she'd said, kissing his neck in a way usually guaranteed to make him forget all his worries.

"Several thousand dollars?" he had gasped, attempting to push her away.

"It's Oscar de la Renta," she'd whispered, straddling his lap in a way she didn't tend to do much these days. "It's a classic," she'd whispered again, reaching down with her right hand, and soon he hadn't thought about anything much at all.

It had been so different when they met. In the beginning, those heady, early days, he had loved that Amber wasn't a gold digger. He was so used to the high-maintenance Manhattan socialites that Amber was a breath of fresh air. She may have looked high-maintenance, but he quickly discovered that she painted her own nails, dyed her own hair in the bathroom sink, and bought her exquisitely tailored clothes at huge discounts from Loehmann's.

He'd never met anyone that resourceful before, never met anyone so seemingly uninterested in finding Mr. Right, or Mr. Rich, to keep them in a manner to which they had always been accustomed—Park Avenue and Prada.

He would go to parties all the time and meet these gorgeous girls, each one thinner, blonder, and prettier than the next, and at the mention of his name—Richard Winslow III—he would see their eyes widen slightly in recognition, notice that suddenly they were placing a hand on his arm rather more often than was altogether necessary, leaning in and laughing as they flicked their hair around, even if what he was saying wasn't the slightest bit funny.

Amber had been different. Where the others were flirtatious, she was cool. Where they were keen, she was diffident. Where they were eager, she was nonchalant. In the beginning she was a challenge. After all, who was this woman who didn't want him? She wasn't as thin, as blond, or as pretty as everyone else, and yet *they* all wanted him. She intrigued him, and part of that intrigue was her background, the fact that she didn't come from money, didn't need money, didn't even seem to particularly want money.

When they had started living together they lived like every other couple on the Upper West Side. Sunday brunches at Sarabeth's, strolling through the park in sweats and sneakers, both of them in matching baseball caps.

Jared had been born at Mount Sinai. They had subsequently turned the dining room in the one-bedroom apartment into a makeshift nursery, then moved ten floors down to a two-bedroom apartment in the same building, and then, when Amber discovered she was pregnant again, they had decided to look farther afield.

They had looked at Westchester, but neither of them felt

particularly at home there. The *New York Times* had recently run a piece saying Highfield, Connecticut, was the hottest place for young families and Wall Street hotshots, and both of them had immediately sped up there, had strolled down pretty Main Street for an ice cream at the old-fashioned ice-cream parlor, and had decided, by the time they reached the other end, that Highfield was home.

At first glance Highfield appeared to have country charm galore, to be the quintessential New England town, with just a touch of city sophistication. There were art galleries dotted along Main Street, proving the old stories that Highfield had started as a small creative community of artists and writers.

They had walked into a Realtor's office, Jared in his stroller, and before they knew it were looking at properties, and compared to Manhattan real estate prices this seemed to be a bargain.

Within six months they had packed up their apartment and bought the house that was to become the house of their dreams. Richard's bonus had been a small fortune that year, and they were able to build exactly what they wanted, no compromise.

If only he'd known then what he knew now.

At first it had felt that they had more of a simpler life, it had felt quieter, more peaceful, more real than Manhattan. Richard would commute on the train every day, and as they passed from New York into Connecticut he would feel able to breathe again, as if all the tensions and stresses of the day were leaving him as he crossed the state line.

He had loved looking out of the window and seeing tree-tops. Waking up in the morning to see a herd of deer grazing at the hostas in their front yard, which he knew would send Amber into a fury, but was nonetheless magical.

And he had loved their house, both the sixties colonial they had torn down and the huge house they had built from scratch in its place. Their huge, brand-new house that a jealous person might describe as a "McMansion," but which was exactly the sort of house Richard had always dreamed of living in.

The house had everything Richard could possibly want. A cherry-paneled library, a gas Viking barbecue next to the swimming pool, room for a tennis court should he so desire, and a fully decked-out screening room in the basement.

He had loved everything about their house, but particularly that everything was brand, spanking new. And it had been so much fun, spending money! Walking into Rakers and dropping a few thousand on some suits, hitting Circuit City for the latest and greatest plasma flat-screen television for the family room.

Amber and Richard had spent and spent and spent—how different from the way Richard grew up, and how much fun to be able to see something you wanted, and just pull out a credit card and buy it without thinking twice.

The Winslows had always been cautious about money, had felt the pressure to keep up appearances despite having nothing. Richard's mother had a wardrobe of Chanel—albeit thirty years old. His father wore the same sports coat at seventy that he had been wearing for almost fifty years. The more the coat frayed, the more time he would spend cutting off the fraying edges.

Richard had of course offered, if not to support them, then at least to buy his father a new coat, to treat his mother to some new clothes, but his parents were far too proud to accept a gift of money from their son, and this is the way they had always lived, it was far too late to change those habits now.

The irony, Richard now realizes, is that growing up, he and his siblings were always told they ought to pretend to have no money. Heaven forbid any of them would be so déclassé or nouveau as to display their wealth with ostentatious jewelry or the latest sports cars.

Richard had thus assumed that they did have money, but that people like the Winslows just pretended not to have any. It didn't occur to him that if they had actually had money, their home, Templeton Hill, might have been heated once in a while. That Richard wouldn't have gone to school in all his older brother's cast-offs, even when they were well past their sell-by date and flapping around his ankles, Richard being by far the tallest in the family.

Through school—Exeter followed by Brown, the one indulgence paid for by Richard's wealthy uncle—Richard had continued to assume that the Winslow family money was tied up somewhere, in trusts or funds or something, and it was only when he started working that he finally realized there wasn't anything left.

Nothing other than Templeton Hill, the vast, rambling, crumbling family estate on the shores of a pond in Brookline, Massachusetts, a house that required more maintenance than the Winslows had been able to provide since the 1930s, a house that was slowly rotting away.

Templeton Hill, or Templeton, as the family referred to it, had been one of the great eastern estates. Even now, if you should come across a book on famous American architecture, or great estates on the East Coast, or perhaps in a bored moment if you should decide to Google the subject, you will find Templeton foremost among all the houses listed.

The photographs of Templeton you will see show the house in its former glory. Set far back from the road, at the end of a driveway three-quarters of a mile long and lined with linden trees that are supposed to have been pruned to perfection but have long since become overgrown and diseased, lies the sprawling white clapboard prettiness of Templeton.

Because Templeton is pretty. It alludes less to grandeur and more to elegance. It is a gracious, low-slung Georgian clapboard house, perfectly symmetrical with two wings flanking a large gravel courtyard, now mostly green with the weeds pushing their way aggressively and persistently through the small sand-colored stones.

From a distance, as you round the driveway and see the house nestled at the end like a pearl in an oyster, she is breathtaking. And yet, drawing closer, you will see the paint peeling from the clapboard, the wooden balustrades that have almost rotted away, the window frames that are splintered and raw.

Richard always thought Templeton Hill was the most beautiful house he had ever seen, the most beautiful house he would ever see, but now, now that he lives in his palace of granite and marble and polished wooden floors, Templeton seems like Miss Havisham. Longing for better days, longing to be rescued and delivered back to her former glory, cloaked in tattered, decaying splendor that still manages to give the visitor a glimpse of what she once was.

In her heyday Templeton Hill had been glorious, and the parties held there by Richard's grandparents, and great-grandparents before that, were legendary. In summer the parties were held on the sweeping lawns that led down to the water, past the gazebo that always served as a meeting place for secret liaisons between lovers.

All of Boston's high society, the crème de la crème, gathered on those lawns, the Forbes and Cabot families among them, resplendent in tuxedos and elegant ball gowns, all toasting one another their beauty, their riches, their very *wonderfulness*.

Everything had been wonderful. Everyone who lived at Templeton led charmed lives until the stock market crash of 1929. Everything the Winslows had was there one day, gone the next. Everything, that is, except for Templeton, which they managed to cling to, despite not having the funds to maintain it.

The staff had to go, most of the good furniture had to go. Richard's grandfather became a salesman, traveling door to door selling cigarette boxes, making just enough money to feed his family and to hang on to Templeton until Richard's father, Richard Winslow II, inherited it.

Templeton had originally had 360 acres, but Richard II managed to hold on to it by gradually selling off the land. Now Templeton has a mere 15 acres, enough for the family to retain a vestige of the privacy they once had, to avoid seeing the new developments that have sprung up around them during the boom years of the eighties and nineties.

In many ways, Richard's childhood had been idyllic. He remembered always being outside with his brothers and sisters, canoeing down the river, crawling to the top of the dusty old barn during games of hide and seek.

He wanted the same thing for his children. He had visions of taking Jared and Gracie boating, teaching them to fish, to sail. Playing baseball with Jared in a large green field. He wanted them to experience what he had experienced when he was a child: fields and green and trees. It was why they were so keen to move out of Manhattan; what he thought he was getting when he moved to Highfield.

It's only now that he realizes his mistake. Perhaps it's just that Amber has fallen into the wrong crowd, but everywhere they go she knows people. They walk into restaurants and immaculately groomed women, women who would not look the slightest bit out of place on Madison Avenue, look Amber up and down before deciding whether or not to say hello.

Richard is strong enough in himself to resist this. He's a Winslow after all, has generations of the family name to bolster his security, but he sees how Amber has changed, how she is trying to compete, how all this stuff she surrounds herself with is just Amber getting caught up in keeping up with the Joneses.

"It doesn't matter," he said to her, just last week, when they were sitting down to a quiet dinner in the kitchen after the kids had gone to bed. "None of this stuff matters," he said. "What's important is family, and having each other. Who cares what they think? That isn't why we moved here, and I hate the way you seem to change when you're around them, how inadequate you seem to feel."

Amber puffed herself up. "I don't feel inadequate," she protested. "You just don't understand what it's like. I have to look a certain way here."

"But why? What's wrong with dressing to please yourself? Do you really care so much about all these damn labels? You barely even knew what Prada was when we met, and now you can practically reel off this season's collection."

Amber grimaced. "I know. It's a bit disgusting, isn't it?"

"It *is* disgusting. These aren't the things that matter. Why do they suddenly matter to you so much?"

Amber sighed. "They don't really. I suppose I just get caught up in it. I do look back at the days before we moved here and think that life would be so much easier if it were simpler, if we didn't live in a place where everyone was so competitive."

"We could move," Richard said, hopefully.

"But we love our house." Amber shrugged. "And the schools here are wonderful, and in some ways we have wonderful friends. Why rock the boat when most of what we have here is so good?"

Richard didn't say anything. Amber is right. In many ways they are very happy here, and the kids adore their schools. Why rock the boat indeed?

After the playground Richard whisks the kids up to Borders, the fathers' play destination of choice on the weekend if rain clouds threaten to strike. He plants the children firmly in the children's section, then wanders over to the magazine rack to browse. He flicks through the *Robb Report*, *Forbes*, and *Newsweek*, then idly picks up a selection for Amber. The women's glossies are mixed in with imports, and he ends up with this week's *US Weekly*, *People* magazine, *American Marie Claire*, and the June edition of the UK import, *Poise!*.

If only he knew, standing in line on this beautiful May day, waiting to pay, what he was doing, he would turn around and put *Poise!* back on those shelves in a heartbeat. Richard didn't notice the cover headline: SWAPPING LIVES!!! And even if he had, how on earth could a magazine cover make the slightest bit of difference to his life?

Oh, if only he knew.

Chapter Ten

"Are you completely mad?" Kate's voice is giggling on the end of the phone. "I was in the newsagent's, and I picked up *Poise!*, and I've just finished reading your spread on Swapping Lives. I'm in shock. Are you seriously going to do this?"

"I don't know why you're so surprised," Vicky says in a huff. "After all, it was your idea."

"What do you mean it was my idea?"

"You said that thousands of women would love to swap lives with me, that the grass was always greener."

"Well, yes, but I didn't expect you to actually go ahead and do it! Who do you think will respond anyway? I'd never do something like that. Would anyone *normal* do something like that?"

"For God's sake, Kate!" Vicky practically shouts. "You were the one saying you'd give your eyeteeth to have my life."

"Yes, but I was just *saying* it. I wasn't actually planning on *doing* it! Although I have to give credit to myself—it is a brilliant idea. Unless of course you get complete nutcases answering, in which case it could be a bit dangerous. But I'm dying to find out what kind of women write in. Have you had any letters yet?"

"Truth?" Vicky smiles.

"Truth."

"So far the issue's been out a week and we've had two hundred and fourteen e-mails, and sixty-two letters."

"No!"

"Yes!"

"But who are they?"

"Well, that's the interesting thing. Mostly they're exactly what you'd expect. Regular women who are a bit bored, who are looking to shake their lives up a bit, or who feel there must be something more out there and think this might give them the push they've been waiting for."

"So have you been in touch with any of them yet?"

"You're joking! We're still sorting them out into the yes, no, and maybe piles, and God knows how many more letters we'll get."

"Any of them sound like nutcases yet?"

"Yup. Hang on . . ." Vicky clicks on her e-mail, opening up the absolutely not folder. "Here, listen to this one: Dear Vicky Townsley, I was reading the current issue of *Poise!* when I came across your fascinating feature, and I thought you might be very interested in hearing about my current situation. Although I know you are looking to swap lives with a married woman with children, I am currently a man in the process of undergoing an operation to fully transform myself into a woman. I thought that following me through the process, particularly with regard to how it affects my wife and three teenage children, would make a fascinating story for *Poise!*. I look forward to hearing from you. Warmest regards, Elisabeth (Bert) Parkinson."

"Well at least he's got balls," Kate says.

"But not for much longer, apparently."

"Did he attach a picture?"

"Yes, and all I can say is it's going to be pretty hard to pass yourself off as a woman when you're six foot five and built like a rugger center forward."

"Poor bloke," Kate sighs. "Any more?"

"Far too many to mention," Vicky says.

"Well, make sure you keep some of the choice ones for when you come down, which I expect to happen soon. The chickens are here, and the kids are dying for you to see them."

"Are they tiny and fluffy?"

"Yes, and the sweetest things I've ever seen, although Hogie and Herk are doing lots of lurking around the pen, eyeing them hungrily. Thank God Bill-the-chicken-man came back to do some reinforcing. It turns out your brilliant brother hadn't done such a brilliant job after all. Still, bless him for at least trying."

"I should be down this weekend," Vicky says. "I'll probably come straight from work on Friday, how does that sound?"

"Sounds perfect. And by the way, did you ever hear from that creep Jamie Donnelly?"

"That fuckwit? Nope. I hope he rots in hell with Denise Van Outen."

"I read he's already moved on. I think this week's catch is Rachel Stevens."

Vicky sighs. "Oh God. I suppose I ought to be flattered that he appeared to even fancy me at all. At least I'm in good company."

"Exactly. He just doesn't know what he's missing."

"Kate, have I ever told you that I love you?"

"Yes. You tell me all the time. And you know I love you too. You're much more like my sister than sister-in-law."

"Okay, okay. Enough sentimentality. I'll see you on Friday."

Janelle Salinger is delighted with the piece. Everyone on the advertising side is delighted with the piece. Everyone, that is, except Vicky, who is now wondering what exactly she was thinking of. Living in another woman's house, looking after another woman's children, wearing another woman's clothes.

Because that is what they decided. It wouldn't be enough to just turn up to someone else's house, to someone else's life, bringing everything from your own life. Janelle had decided that if this was going to work, if the experiment was actually going to prove anything at all, both swapees had to immerse themselves as far as possible into the life of the other.

Which meant that Vicky was allowed to bring nothing but underwear. She would wear the married woman's clothes. Use her makeup. Shampoo her hair with the other woman's shampoo.

She would step into the married woman's social circle as if she had belonged there all her life. Whoever was the married woman's best friend would be expected to be Vicky's best friend. It wasn't enough to swap lives. The real interest lay in discovering whether it would be possible to truly inhabit the world of another person, to find out what her life was really like by *becoming* her, or becoming as near to her as was physically possible.

And in turn Vicky was giving over her life. Her clothes. Her makeup, which she had swiftly replaced, embarrassed by the crusting mascara that was three years old (even though her very own magazine regularly advised its readers to throw out their mascara after six months . . .). Her friends. Her own brother and sister-in-law. Luke, Polly, and Sophie would have to endure stories read to them by what she hoped would be a pale imitator of herself. They wouldn't be fooled.

If Vicky is honest with herself, she didn't expect this to go quite so far. When Janelle had hit upon the idea, Vicky had thought she would just go and live her dream lifestyle for a couple of weeks, probably find out that looking after someone else's children isn't nearly as much fun as looking after your own, and would come home again feeling much the same as she did when she left.

What she didn't expect was how far she would have to go, how much Janelle expected her to transform and, even more surprising, how many women would respond.

The letters keep coming. The e-mails are flooding in. And Vicky has already had to direct the magazine receptionist to request that people write in instead of phoning, because for the first three days after *Poise!* hit the stands, her phone rang off the hook, women thinking they were being clever in looking up her number, figuring they stood more of a chance if they spoke to her in person rather than simply writing in.

Who are these women?

Some have sent photographs. Quick snapshots attached to their e-mails, digital pictures of their children playing, their handsome husbands, their living rooms and gardens.

Some of the letters are short. Some go on for pages. All of the women claim to love their children, some of the women claim to love their husbands, and most of them feel that there is something missing, that if they are the one picked, they will find whatever it is that is causing them dissatisfaction.

A few are brutally honest. They don't like being married. Aren't happy. Are hoping that this will give them the courage to leave, to go back to a life that fills them simultaneously with envy and fear.

A handful of those have suggested they bring their children with them for the swap. Let Vicky come and live with their husbands while they hole up in Vicky's bachelorette flat with their children.

As if.

Vicky dumps those letters firmly on the no pile.

She sits back and rereads the small pile of potentials.

Dear Vicky,

What an amazing idea! I've been a reader of Poise! *for years, but this is the first time I've written in and I still can't quite believe I'm doing it, particularly when I have a wonderful life that is the envy of all my friends, two beautiful children, and a husband who is my best friend.*

My kids are Jack and William, aged six and four, and we live in a small but charming cottage on the outskirts of Oxford. Simon, my husband, works for a local law firm, which is lovely because he's always back by six to help with the kids' bathtime. (Have I tempted you yet???!!!)

Before I had children I was in advertising. I had just been promoted to account director when I fell pregnant with Jack. We were still living in London at the time, in a lovely flat in Putney, and I planned on taking three months' maternity leave and then going straight back to work, but of course I fell head over heels in love with Jack, and when the time came I couldn't do it.

We moved out to Oxford when William was conceived. It seemed like the right time, and I'd always wanted to bring my children up in the country, with fresh air and trees and animals. I love the fact that we have three acres with a stream at the bottom of the garden, and the boys spend hours down there fishing. Not that they ever seem to catch anything but it keeps them happy and, more importantly, quiet!!!

So, I stopped working, and now that the boys are that bit older and in school, part of me is desperate to work again, but the other part is really scared. I sat down with Simon and showed him the article, and we both thought it was a brilliant idea, and that as hard as it would be, being away from everyone for a month, it might give me the impetus I need. Plus I've always fancied myself as a bit of a writer, and I love the idea of working for Poise! *magazine, even if it is merely stepping into your shoes for a while.*

I know you're looking for someone who's the same size so you can swap wardrobes too. On a good day I'm a size six, and on a bad day an eight. On a terrible day it's a ten, but luckily I haven't had any terrible days for the last year!! Oh, and I'm a six and a half shoe. I'd love to tell you that my wardrobe is filled with glamorous stuff like Armani shirts and Manolo shoes, but actually it's far more likely to be Jigsaw sweaters for best, Oasis, and Nine West shoes. Sorry! (Although I'm hoping to take advantage of your wardrobe, which looks pretty fantastic from the photo in the piece. I think those strappy lilac Jimmy Choos are the sexiest things I've ever seen!)

I probably ought to stop banging on about clothes now, other than to say that I think you'd really enjoy it here. You said your dream was a house in the country, children, an Aga, and big dogs. Well, we've got the house in the country, we've got the children, we don't have an Aga (am hoping Simon might accommodate me for my thirty-fifth birthday!), and we've got two West Highland terriers.

And my husband is also fantastic. I've enclosed photographs of everyone for you to see, but he's funny, and clever, and a huge help with the children. But you're not allowed to sleep with him!!!

(I'm assuming you're not planning on jumping into bed with the husband. . . .)

I hope I hear from you. I'm around most of the time. And if you decide to choose someone else, good luck—I still think it's a brilliant idea.
Best wishes,
Sarah Evans

Dear Vicky Townsley,
I'm a thirty-eight-year-old wife, mother, cleaner, launderer, dog-walker, chauffeur, cook, bartender, hostess, and chief-cake-maker at 745 Station Road, Chislehurst.
And I'm bloody tired.
Please take me away from all this for a few weeks.
Yours gratefully,
Sally Lonsdale

That one only made it onto the potential pile because it made Vicky laugh. And then there were the letters that Vicky didn't have the heart to put on the no pile. The letters that almost brought her to tears, that made her want to help, to be a part of the solution.

Dear Vicky,
Well, I suppose I ought to start by being honest and saying that my husband would probably kill me if he knew I was doing this, although don't let that put you off—if you pick me I'll make sure I explain it to him in a way that he decides to spare me my life and take me back once the month is over.
The truth is that I'm not very happy. Actually, we're not very happy, which is probably not what you want to hear, but I thought I may as well be honest. I have some of what you're looking for in

*your perfect life—a lovely house in Bath that is incredibly beauti-
ful, and three children, and a cat that thinks it's a dog. And of
course my husband, Adam.*

*Adam and I were childhood sweethearts. I'm only thirty-two,
so we've managed to fit an awful lot in! We've been together since
we were fourteen, and a year ago if you'd asked me whether I was
happy, I would have said I was the happiest and luckiest woman
in the world.*

*Six months ago Adam came home and said he had something
to tell me. You probably know what I'm going to tell you. It seems
that everyone else always knows when something is going on, that
the wife is always the last to know, and sure enough he said he'd
been having an affair with someone at work, that it was over, that
he loved me and was sorry, it would never happen again, and the
only reason he'd decided to tell me was because he couldn't live
with the guilt, and he wanted to wipe the slate clean and start
again.*

I bloody well wish he'd kept that slate dirty.

*Adam's the only man I've ever been with. The only man I've
ever loved, and I never dreamed that he would do something like
this. I do know the girl he was involved with—I met her at the
office Christmas party and I never liked her, she was exactly
the type of woman you want to keep away from your husband.
The thing is, I do believe he loves me. And I do believe he probably won't do this again, that it was a terrible mistake and he has
learned his lesson. But the problem is, I can't seem to forgive him.*

*Every time he touches me I think of him touching her. (Oh
God, is that too much information for you?) Every time he tells
me he loves me I feel this rush of anger, and I keep thinking that
time is the great healer, that at some point I will feel the forgive-
ness, be able to carry on as we were before, but it only seems to be
getting worse.*

So when I read your article, I thought that it would be exactly what I need. What we need. I think I need something huge, momentous to happen. My friends keep saying I should leave him, but the truth is I don't want to leave him. Not permanently. If I believe that it won't happen again, then why would I leave when he's a good father, he's good to me, I know he loves us. But because I can't forgive him, I know I have to do something, so this seemed perfect. To leave him temporarily. To make him realize what it might be like if I left, to make him really realize what it is that he's got in me and his family.

Anyway, I didn't want to depress you, and actually I feel better now that I've got it out there in this letter. I'd love to be the person you swap lives with, and I hope you get in touch!
Yours sincerely,
Hope Nettleton

And finally this:

Dear Vicky,
I know you won't be expecting a letter from the other side of the pond, but our local bookstore carries magazines from England, and my husband bought me some magazines the other week, among which was the June issue of Poise!. *(Little did he know what he was letting himself in for . . . !)*

So, I read your article and have to confess I find it fascinating, particularly because I'm always saying that the grass is always greener, but have never actually put it to the test. And let me start by saying that my life, on the surface, appears to be perfect. Actually, in many ways, it is pretty perfect.

I'm married to Richard and we have two children, Jared, six, and Gracie, three. We live in a town called Highfield in Connecticut, which is about an hour outside Manhattan. It feels like the country, but every time I need my fix of the city, or Bergdorfs is calling, I can hop on a train and go in.

We have the requisite golden retriever, Ginger, who's horribly overweight; a lovely nanny, Lavinia; and although we don't have an Aga we do have the American equivalent, a Viking range, which I'm sure you'll find just as appealing!

I'm lucky enough to live in a huge house, with a swimming pool, about twenty minutes from the beach, and my days are filled with carpooling, playdates, and a huge amount of charity work for the Highfield League of Young Ladies. We're just planning our Summer Gala, which raised $1.8 million last year that we distributed to various local charities—it's a wonderful cause and keeps me busy!

I guess that a lot of the letters you will have had will be from women who are unhappy, and I have to start by saying I'm really not. My goodness, if you looked at my life (I've enclosed pictures of the family, the dog, the house, and our beautiful Main Street, which includes a proper old-fashioned ice-cream parlor to tempt you further . . .) you would think I have everything, and although I adore my kids and my husband, I just can't get rid of this feeling that there must be more to life than this.

I suppose at times I feel like a Desperate Housewife (I'd like to be the Teri Hatcher one but I'm far more like Felicity Huffman!)—that's kind of the life we live. For most of the women around here all this charitable work seems to be far more about social climbing, and even though that's not why I got involved, it's so hard not to get caught up in it.

Because this town is only an hour outside Manhattan, a lot of the people who have moved here work on Wall Street—at least the husbands do. Not that I should complain, Richard works on Wall Street and thank goodness! But it makes for a very competitive lifestyle—everyone's always trying to keep up with everyone

else: who has the biggest house, who has the most expensive car,
whose children got into the best private school.

And it's exhausting. I didn't grow up with anything, I came
from the wrong side of the tracks altogether, and I'm not sure
how much longer I have the energy to do this. So that's why I'm
writing. I'm sure I'm not what you're looking for, and I'm sure
you weren't expecting to hear from someone in America, but the
idea of having a break from keeping up with the Joneses is
hugely appealing.

Plus I thought you might just like the idea of finding out what
life really is like on Wisteria Lane (although in truth my road is
called Sugar Maple Lane!).
Yours,
Amber Winslow

Vicky slides the letters back into the potential file and checks
her watch. Damn. She's going to be late. She has a one
o'clock lunch meeting with a couple of people from Channel 4. They saw the magazine and phoned her, pitched her
about making a documentary about the swap, doing a fly-on-
the-wall, coming along with both women to see how they
fare.

Janelle almost cried with excitement when Vicky told her.
She had to tell her. Even though she couldn't think of anything worse than being on television as part of a fly-on-the-
wall documentary.

There was the not insignificant issue of television putting
on at least ten pounds for one thing. Plus the whole world
would be watching her, and Vicky hasn't wanted fame or
celebrity since she was six years old and wrote to Jimmy Sav-
ille to ask him if he could fix it for her to meet the Bay City
Rollers (he couldn't).

She's hoping that during this lunch meeting they will think her not interesting or charismatic enough to make a documentary about her, even though the premise is a good one. Janelle is joining them later, which is unfortunate, but hopefully Vicky can do enough damage before Janelle arrives and put them off for good.

Chapter Eleven

Amber stands once again in the corner of her new Amberley Jacks–designed living room, and smiles as she surveys the changes.

The walls are lavender now, just as they proposed, the sofa a rich plum, the armchairs reupholstered in a plum and chocolate-brown print. The curtains are a mocha and lavender check, and the pièce de résistance is the new antique Asian coffee table in the center of the room, dressed for today's committee meeting with silver platters of exquisite handmade cookies and pastries.

Amber comes into this room at least three times a day. She doesn't actually sit down on the sofa—doesn't let *anyone* sit down on the sofa—but she stands and admires how lovely it is, and thank goodness it managed to be ready for the final committee meeting before Friday's Gala for the League.

Julian and Aidan did a wonderful job, she tells anyone who asks. Now they are working on the family room, the library, and Amber is thinking of adding the master bedroom to the list, although she hasn't managed to tell Richard about adding a few more rooms, and he's been so difficult lately about money, it might be best not to mention it at all.

In fact she's even had to intercept the monthly bills from

Amberley Jacks and pay them herself from her own bank account. Richard was furious when he got their first bill. "Amber!" he had roared from his office as he was sorting out the bills. "Look at this!" He'd pushed the piece of paper at her and glared at her in an angry-father sort of way. "I thought they weren't going to be expensive," he'd said finally.

"Ah yes," Amber had said, because not only had the furniture they'd found cost far more than Amber had anticipated (everything had turned out to be "a piece," all of it genuine, all of it old, and all of it horrendously expensive), but they claimed to have put in thirty hours during the month of April, which came to $6,000.

"How can they possibly have spent thirty hours?" Richard had said. "I thought they only came to the house twice."

"They did." Amber had immediately jumped on the defensive. "But they were out buying for us."

"Thirty hours' worth of buying? How can that be? They only bought the coffee table, a couple of side tables, and a few lamps. How is that thirty hours?"

Amber had shaken her head. "I'm sorry, darling, I don't know, but if that's what they say it is, then that's what it is."

"I'm going to phone them and ask them," Richard had said, reaching for the phone.

"No!" Amber had gasped, already humiliated at the thought. "Don't do that. I'll speak to them. I'm the one with the relationship with them, so I ought to speak to them, don't you think?"

"Well, okay, but make sure you get them to detail the hours. I want to see a list of exactly where these thirty hours went, and Amber, this is it. We can't afford this sort of money on decorating. Now that the formal living room is done, that's it. Okay?"

"Okay, okay. I'll speak to them tomorrow." Amber had blown him a kiss, knowing that he would have forgotten about it by the next morning, and he was at work all day, he wouldn't even know if they carried on. She could always tell him she did it herself.

And although the lavender and plum living room isn't what Amber would ever have done herself, isn't even what she might have picked if she'd seen a picture in a magazine, it is pure Amberley Jacks, and she can't wait for the committee, especially for Suzy, to see her new room.

"Oh it's lovely," Nadine says, walking in and sitting on the sofa next to Suzy, admiring the coffee table and antique brass lamps. "Didn't they do a wonderful job?"

"I know," Amber says proudly. "They really are worth every penny. Help yourself to some pastries. I'm just going to get some fresh coffee. Can I bring you anything?"

"No thanks." The two girls smile sweetly and shake their heads. "We're good."

"Oh. My. God." Suzy turns to Nadine and mouths the words, her mouth hanging open, as Nadine starts to giggle.

"Oh stop it," she shoves Suzy playfully as they both look around the room. "What *is* this color? What does it remind me of? Oh I know!" She turns back to Suzy. "It's puke."

Suzy splutters with laughter. "I thought Amberley Jacks were supposed to be talented. This is the most disgusting thing I've ever seen. Look at this coffee table! How ugly is that?"

"And what about those curtains? Could they be any more revolting?" The two girls turn and giggle at the curtains, then stop abruptly as Deborah walks in.

"Hi!" She walks over and they all hug before Deborah turns to admire the room. "Well, this color is definitely unusual," she says, sitting down.

"Nadine thinks it looks like puke," Suzy whispers with an evil grin. "Oh my gosh, will you listen to me? I'm being so mean. Don't tell Amber, I think she loves it."

"Do you hate it?" Deborah returns the smile.

"We hate it," Suzy whispers.

"So I take it you won't be using Amberley Jacks, then?" Deborah's voice is all innocence.

"Well, they are supposed to be the best. Maybe they just screwed up here. For all we know Amber forced them to use the barf color."

"So you will use them, then? Even though you hate this room?"

"Um. Well. I don't know." Suzy is aware she has been trapped. "I haven't decided."

"I'm going to the kitchen." Deborah stands up and walks out of the room, shaking her head in disgust as she goes. "Bitches," she says under her breath, and walks straight into Amber.

"What did you say?"

"Oh nothing." Deborah apologizes. "Just Suzy and Nadine being as pleasant as always."

"They weren't being mean about me, were they?" The color drains from Amber's face.

"No. I think they're just jealous that you were the first to use Amberley Jacks. In fact, Suzy's so jealous she's practically turning green. I can't even stand to be around the pair of them. Let's go wait in the kitchen, and anyway, I could do with some of that incredible-looking cake."

* * *

Amber is as gracious a hostess as always, a skill she studied for years from her mother-in-law. When Amber met Richard her insecurity and lack of self-worth would come across to others as arrogance, or snobbishness. They didn't realize that the reason she was cool was because she felt so inadequate. Icy Winslow taught her the value of graciousness. Icy Winslow, despite her glacial looks and frosty nickname, is warm and inclusive to everyone she meets, almost to the point of gushing, and everyone loves her in return.

Icy Winslow doesn't have to be frosty, or supercilious, or pretend to be better than anyone because she knows exactly who she is, and has never had anything to prove. Amber still feels that she has lots to prove, that she is definitely less than the women sitting around her living room, and yet she has learned that she needn't let that show, that to be warm and friendly costs so much less than being rude.

When people talk about Icy Winslow they say she still has the unique gift that several great women have when they're talking to you, of making you feel that they would not be anywhere else at this current moment than standing right here, talking to you.

"Think Icy," Amber always says to herself when she feels insecurity strike. "What would Icy do?" and she flashes a wide Icy-style smile, makes sure she touches the people to whom she's talking a lot, and asks lots of questions. She may not feel like Icy, but has learned that acting as if she does can take her a hell of a long way.

And so now, during this committee meeting, Amber channels her mother-in-law. She hugs everyone who comes in, even the women she doesn't like. She makes sure the plates of goodies are passed, that people's coffee cups are refilled, that no one is left out in the cold.

So while Suzy and Nadine can say whatever they like about the Amberley Jacks living room, there is very little with which to find fault in Amber. Who could possibly not like Amber? Who could possibly not be taken in by her charm?

Chapter Twelve

Vicky arrives at the Wolseley fifteen minutes later than planned. She'd waited ages for a cab, and then got stuck in traffic, so she's slightly more flustered than she had planned as well.

The waitress leads her through the beautiful people, through the famous and wannabe famous, to a table where a thin, bespectacled man with a large smile immediately jumps up and extends his hand.

"You must be Vicky," he says. "I'm Hugh. We spoke on the phone."

"Nice to meet you." She shakes hands, then turns to his colleague, a small, pretty girl with blond hair and freckles who looks about twelve.

"Hi," she smiles as well. "I'm Elsa. I'm the director. It's so nice to meet you. I've been reading your magazine for years."

"Great," says Vicky, wondering how this child could possibly have been reading *Poise!* for years when she looks like she graduated from kindergarten a few weeks ago. "Our editor, Janelle Salinger, will be joining us as soon as she gets out of a meeting. I hope that's okay."

Hugh pulls out a chair for Vicky telling her it's fine, that Vicky is the one they're most interested in, and as he steps away from her chair he raises an encouraged and pleased eyebrow at Elsa. Vicky's perfect. Already, after two minutes, he can tell the camera's going to love her.

"Here," he says, sliding his card over the table. "Let's start with giving you my business card so you can get hold of me any time you want."

Vicky takes the card, studies it briefly, then looks up at Hugh in disbelief, a smile twitching around her lips.

"Hugh Janus?" she says finally, a giggle breaking out. "Is that really your name? Huge Anus?"

Hugh sighs his exasperated sigh because this happens every time. "No," he says slowly, "it's Janus. Pronounced Jan-us. Not Jayn-us. It's Hugh Jan-us."

"Oh come on." In her nerves Vicky feels on the brink of hysteria. "Seriously. That can't be your name."

"I know. It's horrific," he shrugs, with an apologetic grin. "But at least I'm not fourteen anymore."

"School must have been horrendous." Vicky is fascinated.

"Yup. You can't even imagine."

"Yes I can." Vicky grins. "Did they ask if you had a brother called Lar?"

"Large anus!" Elsa starts cracking up with laughter, and Vicky joins in, even though Hugh doesn't seem to find it particularly funny.

"And what about your cousin Sor?" Elsa says eventually, wiping the tears from her eyes.

There's a long silence as Vicky and Hugh look at a delighted Elsa. "Oddly enough," Hugh says in disbelief, shaking his head at Elsa's delighted smile, "no. No one ever asked if my cousin was called Sor Jaynus."

"Oh God," Elsa flushes. "How stupid am I?" And it sets off another round of laughter.

"Well this is very professional," Hugh says finally, when order is returned. "So much for a business lunch."

"How in the hell does anyone keep a straight face with your name?" Vicky asks. "Seriously, what were your parents thinking?"

"They didn't think, basically. My actual name is Hugo, which is fine. Hugo Janus doesn't elicit any kind of response whatsoever, other than people assuming I'm an upper-class twit . . ."

"Are you?" Vicky grins.

"Do I seem like it? Don't answer that!" he says. "But no, I'm neither upper class nor a twit, but once I got to secondary school everyone, not surprisingly, started calling me Hugh, and unfortunately it stuck, which caused endless mirth among the stars of the last reality show I did."

"Hang on," Vicky says, as the wheels of her memory start churning. "You're not the guy who did *The Robinsons,* are you?"

Hugh nods. "Yup. That's me."

"I loved that show!"

"I was the director on that too," Elsa interjects. "That's how we started working together."

"Didn't you win a Bafta for that?"

"It currently has pride of place in my loo. Every time the cleaner comes she moves it to the mantelpiece, and every time she leaves I put it back in the loo."

"But why? You ought to be proud of it."

"I am, just embarrassed for it to be out. It's the first thing everyone comments on when they come over, and it means a half-hour chat about whether the Robinsons were really as awful as they appeared."

"Were they?"

"Worse," he says with a smile, as the waitress comes over to see if they are ready to order.

Vicky hasn't done her research. Normally before a meeting such as this she would have, at the very least, Googled the person in question to find out who they are and what they have done. Had she not been so busy sorting through the responses to Swapping Lives, had she in fact found the time to Google Hugh Janus, here's what she would have found:

Hugh Janus is thirty-nine years old, a graduate of Bristol University where he studied English and Drama, before going straight into the London Daytime Television graduate training program.

After joining Channel 4 he became one of the leading lights in the new phenomenon of reality television. Initially copying successful American shows like *The Bachelor* and *Survivor*, Hugh Janus went on to make the biggest breakaway hit of last year, *The Robinsons*.

The Robinsons are a family who live on a council estate in Peckham, south London. The mother is a drug dealer, as is Wayne, the oldest son. Darren, the middle son, is in prison for grievous bodily harm. Warren, the youngest son, is in training to go into the family business, and Kylie, the fourteen-year-old, is trying to give up smoking and find a job as she looks after her baby daughter, Paris.

Hugh found the Robinsons after reading a newspaper article about them. They were dubbed the Family from Hell after all the neighbors had requested the council move them because of the constant noise, aggression, and threatening behavior from the Robinson family and their six pit bull terriers.

The *Daily Mail* had run a double-page spread on the family entitled "Neighbors from hell!," accompanied by a large color photo of the family staring belligerently into the camera, with other, smaller photos of frightened-looking neighbors alongside.

It had been Hugh's idea to follow the family for a year. "You don't get better television than this," he said. "We wouldn't have to do anything. Just plant the cameras and we've got gold." He got their phone number, but every time he phoned they told him to fuck off, and slammed the phone down.

Eventually he borrowed a mate's beaten-up Volvo—his own 1978 Alfa Romeo Spider was not a car he was going to take to this council estate in Peckham, no matter how desperate he was for the work—filled it with beer, cigarettes, and pigs' ears for the dogs, which Sheila Robinson, the mother, had referred to in the *Mail* as "her babies," and drove down to Peckham, turning up on their doorstep.

"Fuck off," Sheila said, attempting to slam the front door in his face as a baby wailed in the background.

"I'll pay you," he shouted as the door slammed. There was a long silence, then just as he was about to turn around and leave, the door opened again and Sheila blew a large cloud of smoke into Hugh's face.

"How much?" she scowled, and after Hugh mentioned the figure he'd agreed with Channel 4 in advance (he knew there would have to be money involved, why else would the Robinsons agree to do it? Kylie was the only one who might enjoy her fifteen minutes of fame, but there was no way the others would agree to something like this without being paid, particularly when the *Mail* had to fork out several thousand pounds just to get the photograph), Sheila stepped aside and gestured for Hugh to come in.

"Posh git," she called him from the first, but he figured it could have been a lot worse, and he suspected that after a while she actually grew quite fond of him. Hugh and the crew spent a year filming their every move, editing the hours and hours of footage into one-hour weekly slots that held the nation riveted for the best part of six months.

"Makes Wayne and Waynetta Slob look like Charles and Camilla," he later joked to the head honchos at Channel 4. Except he wasn't joking.

And this is what Vicky would not have found out about Hugh Janus, despite scrolling through the multiple pages:

He is the younger of two boys, was brought up in Gloucestershire, and owns one cat, called, rather unimaginatively, Cat. Cat sleeps on Hugh's side of the bed every night, curled up on his pillow, purring into his face.

He lives in a basement flat in Notting Hill with his girlfriend, Lara, who he has been with for seven years, and who he is planning on marrying, when he can find the time. Lara is also in television—they met when she was a researcher on one of his shows while still at London Daytime Television.

Lara is now head of factual programming at London

Daytime Television, and they joke about how powerful she is. Hugh has been approached many times to go corporate, but he loves the day-to-day producing, has no wish to be a *suit,* to commission others to do the work he so loves.

They have the perfect relationship. Or at least, perfect for them. They understand one another completely, do not feel the slightest hint of jealousy or insecurity if one or the other is spending the evening in the pub with the rest of the gang, and have successfully merged their friends to create a hip media crowd who live mostly in Notting Hill if successful, or in Kilburn and Queens Park if not quite up to the same level.

The only fly in the ointment, if it can be described as such, is that Lara has started talking about having children, and Hugh just isn't sure that he's ready. He likes their life. No, loves their life. Is very happy with Lara and Cat, and can't see how a child would fit into it.

His brother, Will, has three children whom Hugh adores, and every time he and Lara go up to Islington to see Will, Lara delights in seeing how Hugh plays with his niece and nephews: he leads them down to the woods at the bottom of the garden and creates secret clubhouses complete with passwords and magic doorways.

He spends entire afternoons sitting at the kitchen table with them, making pretend passports that will allow them entry into worlds of enchantment and surprise, weaving myths and fairy tales that leave the children breathless with excitement whenever they learn he is coming to see them.

"How can you not be ready for children?" Lara always asks when they leave. "Look at what an amazing uncle you are! You're going to be an incredible father, and I don't believe you're not ready. It's just an excuse. And anyway, when is anyone ever ready for children? If we all waited until we were ready there would never be any children born at all. We just need to *do* it, we'll worry about whether we were ready afterward."

For some time now Lara has thought about just getting pregnant, telling Hugh she didn't know how it happened. For the longest time they used condoms, and she actually thought about sticking a pin through the packet to try and fall pregnant; the only thing stopping her was the thought of Hugh seeing the hole and realizing what she had done.

Recently she switched to the pill, telling Hugh it's to balance her hormones, although her latest plan involves not taking the pill, and when she becomes pregnant telling Hugh that she had taken a course of antibiotics that negated the effects of the pill.

But she hasn't quite got the nerve to go through with it. Not yet. Last year she put it off until her work schedule became easier, only that never happened. This year she keeps telling herself, and her girlfriends, that she's going to go through with her plan, but although it seemed like a good idea at the time, the idea of the deception, the scale of the lie, is not something she's certain she can live with.

So in the meantime she's trying to persuade Hugh to change his mind. He would be a wonderful father, that much she's certain of, and surely it's just a matter of time.

* * *

"We think it would be a great documentary." Hugh leans forward and looks Vicky square in the eye. "It was only ever a matter of meeting you and seeing if you have what it takes, and then of course meeting your choice for Swapping Lives, but you're the first step and I'd say this is going pretty well."

"Oh?" Vicky raises an eyebrow and pauses, her fork halfway to her mouth. "Meaning?"

"Meaning if you'd been completely lacking in charisma and personality, then I would have had to think twice."

"And what if I'd been desperate to become famous? How would you have got out of it?"

"I would have come up with some excuse like the network had suddenly canceled on me."

"Wimp," Vicky says, and Hugh and Elsa both laugh.

"The only thing I'm nervous about is being recognized," Vicky says finally. "I'm not sure I can bear the thought of being famous just because I'm on television. It's not like I would be well known for having achieved anything. I haven't written a book, or invented a new kind of vacuum cleaner. I'm just being followed around by a camera crew."

Hugh nods and leans back. "I do see your point, Vicky," he says slowly, "but I'm not sure that would be the case. The fact is you're features director of *Poise!*, which is one of the most popular magazines in the country. We wouldn't be presenting you as Jo Schmo, just a woman on the street we're following. It would be very clear that you're doing this as a journalistic exercise, and the publicity for *Poise!* would be fantastic."

At that moment Vicky's cell phone rings and Janelle's voice comes through loud and clear as she apologizes profusely for being late. She claims to be stuck in a meeting, although the many junior hairdressers milling around Daniel

Galvin while Janelle sits under a hairdryer, her head covered with foil as her hair gently highlights, would beg to differ.

"I'm so sorry, darling," she croons to Vicky over the phone. "Do you mind handling it by yourself? Will you apologize for me?"

"Of course," Vicky says, unsurprised, as Janelle is known not only for her creative brilliance but for her unreliability and unfailing charm.

"As I was saying," Hugh continues, once Vicky has explained Janelle's absence, "it would be great publicity for *Poise!*, plus you mentioned it's not as if you've written a book, but I see no reason why you don't use this for a book. We could tie them in together. Now that really could be a ratings winner."

"Hmmm." Now it's Vicky's turn to sit back. "That is an interesting idea." Something catches her eye as she sits there, and she turns her head to see a familiar face whose eyes meet hers at exactly the same moment.

"Oh shit," she whispers, as Jamie Donnelly blinks, looks at who she's sitting with, then quickly starts making his way over to the table as Vicky feels a hot flush rising up her cheeks.

"Hugh!" Jamie Donnelly is standing there shaking hands with Hugh; the pair of them clearly know each other well.

"Jamie! How are you, mate?" Hugh grins as he turns to introduce Jamie, first to Elsa who seems suddenly tongue-tied, and then he turns to Vicky. "And this is Vicky Townsley, features director of *Poise!*."

"We know each other," Vicky mumbles, willing the flush to disappear from her cheeks, barely able to look Jamie Donnelly in the eye. What she wants to say is, "You bastard. How could you not call? How could you not be who you appeared to be? Who I wanted you to be? Bastard!"

But of course she doesn't say anything. Just looks at him and wishes she didn't think he was so handsome. Didn't remember how he tasted. How he looked when he had raised himself up on top of her and leaned down to kiss her with lust-glazed eyes, moving down her body, down to her stomach, down farther as she swooned with anticipation and passion.

Vicky Townsley stands in the middle of the Wolseley and again feels a shiver of excitement at the memory. Oh shit. This isn't supposed to happen.

"Vicky," Jamie says softly, moving forward and kissing her on the mouth, except at the last minute Vicky turns her head slightly so he just catches the corner of her lips.

"I'm going to have to assume you two know each other, then?" Hugh laughs, as Elsa bites her lip in envy.

"Oh yes," Jamie says, never taking his eyes off Vicky. "I've been meaning to call you, Vicky," he says, and despite herself, despite the pictures she's seen of Jamie Donnelly and Denise Van Outen, despite the fact he never called, Vicky feels her heart skip with hope.

"You know where I am," she finally manages, the coldness in her voice betraying her feelings. The feelings that haven't changed. The hope that still remains. That somehow the papers got it wrong. That he wasn't with those other women, that he's been desperately trying to track Vicky down, to tell her he wants to see her again, can't stop thinking about her.

"What are you doing after lunch?" he says, his eyes focused intently on hers.

"Back to work," she says, even though she doesn't want to.

Wants to cancel her afternoon, call in sick, something, just to follow Jamie Donnelly wherever he wants to take her.

"I'll call you later," he says, as Hugh raises his hands up in the air.

"Whoa, you two," he laughs. "Talk about serious chemistry. Should Elsa and I leave?"

"No, you're all right," Jamie says. "Vicky and I just have some unfinished business to take care of. Speaking of which, you and I never followed up on the meeting we had about that comedy show. I'd still love to work with you, Hugh. Loved *The Robinsons*. Really. Fantastic show."

"I'll call you," Hugh says. "Sorry I didn't get in touch after that meeting, but life's been crazy. Let's do lunch. Next week?"

"Sounds great. Nice to see you. And Vicky," he turns to Vicky and touches her lightly on the arm as a shiver goes through her, "I'll call you in an hour."

"So . . ." Hugh grins at Vicky.

"Okay," Elsa butts in. "Can I just say that if you've shagged Jamie Donnelly I may have to kill you."

"Ah," Vicky grimaces. "Am I allowed a final dessert?"

"I knew it!" Elsa says. "God, I am so jealous! Jamie Donnelly! I love him!"

"What's going on with you and Jamie Donnelly?" Hugh grins. "Because clearly something is."

Vicky shrugs and shakes her head. "To tell you the truth, I don't really know. Something did happen but it didn't seem to lead to anything."

"He's a nice guy," Hugh says, "but are you concerned about his reputation as a womanizer?"

"Womanizer? Who? Jamie Donnelly? No! You're not serious!" Vicky clutches her heart as if in shock.

"Okay, okay. Not that it's any of my business, but don't say I didn't warn you."

"I'm a big girl," Vicky says. "I can take care of myself."

"Just as long as you don't end up either getting married or having a broken heart before we start filming. The whole point of this exercise is that you're single."

"Hang on a minute. I haven't agreed to do it yet. There's a hell of a lot to think about. You have to give me some time. Plus we haven't even found the person we're going to swap with yet."

"What kind of people are on the short list?"

"The names themselves won't mean anything to you, but there's Sarah Evans, Sally Lonsdale, Hope Nettleton, and, funnily enough, a woman in America called Amber Winslow. I can e-mail details about them to you when I get back to the office."

"There's someone from America? You mean you'd actually go to America to do this? Okay. Well, I suppose we could find it in the budget to do that if that's what you decided, although if we did go ahead with the filming I think we ought to be in on the selection process. How would you feel about that?"

"Let me speak to Janelle. I know that at the moment she's most keen on the American woman because she's obsessed with the show *Desperate Housewives*, and Amber Winslow sounds like she's a real-life Desperate Housewife. She's out in the suburbs in an enormous house with a golden retriever, two kids, a four-wheel-drive and a husband she never seems to see. Janelle thinks it might be far more interesting to swap with her, but I'm trying to set up some meetings with the women here, and I've still got to get in touch with Amber Winslow."

"I think your editor may have a point. Real-life Desperate Housewives. That might be television gold. Just let me know as soon as you decide so we can set up a meeting with the swap. Vicky, let me tell you, I've got a really good feeling about this."

"I hope you're right," Vicky says as the waiter comes back to the table. "Because quite frankly I don't know what in the hell I was thinking."

Chapter Thirteen

"That goddamned Amber Winslow thinks she's better than me," hisses Suzy as she finishes pinning her hair up at the back.

"Well, she's not going to be better than me tonight," she says, snapping open the black velvet box on the bathroom counter and smiling as she surveys the diamond necklace she's wearing for the gala.

It's not actually hers. Lawrence, her husband, is a jeweler, which means that Suzy not only has the biggest and best jewelry in town, but whenever there is a special occasion she gets to wear jewels the others can only fantasize about. And who has to know she's only borrowing them? Whenever any of the girls comment on her "newest" ring, or bracelet, or, on this occasion, flower-drop necklace, she just smiles sweetly and gestures over at Lawrence, saying only that she's the luckiest girl in the whole world.

Tonight, as chairperson of the gala, Suzy is going all out. With her Dolce & Gabbana plunging dress, her strappy Manolos, her diamonds, and her beautiful bronzed skin courtesy of the tanning salon yesterday afternoon (she chose the spray, so much healthier although she did have to put up with smelling like a herd of camels until she was able to finally take a shower this morning), Suzy has no doubt that she will be the belle of the ball.

Whenever Suzy feels threatened, she tells herself that she is better than the others. She is prettier, thinner, and has more money, and up until Amber Winslow moved to town, she was leagues ahead of everyone else. But there's something about Amber. Amber doesn't seem to care that Suzy has bigger diamonds or, up until the Winslows built their house, the biggest house in town. And it pissed Suzy off that Amber got that decorating firm first, just because she's a Winslow.

And just because she's a Winslow, Amber seems to think she's special. But Suzy will show her tonight. As she twirls in front of the mirror in her diaphanous backless dress, the carats glittering around her neck and at her ears, Suzy grins to herself. Bring it on, Amber Winslow, she thinks, looking forward to outshining everyone. Bring it on because I'm ready and waiting.

"You look beautiful." Richard turns to look at Amber as she comes down the stairs. He's sitting with Jared and Gracie as they have supper, both of them behaving like angels given the rare treat of having Daddy home to have supper with them.

"Mommy, you look like a princess," Gracie says, smiling with delight at Amber's dress.

"You look sooooo pretty," Jared coos.

Even Lavinia comes back into the kitchen to see.

"Oh my goodness," she says, "you do look lovely."

Amber does a little twirl in her champagne dress, the ostrich feathers at the hem brushing her knees.

"I have to say I do feel like a princess." She grins. "All I need is a tiara."

"No, a crown," Gracie says, climbing down from the table.

"I'll give you a crown, Mommy." She skips out of the room, and reappears a few moments later bearing a plastic sparkly pink crown. "Here, Mommy," she says very seriously, as Amber bends down so Gracie can place it carefully on her head.

"How's that?" Amber stands slowly so the children can examine her crown, as Richard smiles at her lovingly.

"Perfect," he says. "Now, shall we go?"

"You really do look beautiful," he says again in the car, turning to smile at his lovely wife.

"You just forget how good I look when I clean up," Amber laughs, but she takes the compliment and allows it to warm her heart. And she does feel beautiful. She didn't want anything over the top. Knows there will be plenty of mutton dressed as lamb, of women who should have learned that plunging, backless chiffon in your late thirties and early forties doesn't do anyone any favors. She knows exactly what people have been buying at Rakers, and is so much happier in her simple, elegant dress, just the feathers adding a dash of exuberance, pretty pearl earrings at her ears, and her hair swept back in a sleek, simple chignon.

Suzy is standing at the door greeting everyone as they arrive. She sees Amber and feels the hatred well up. God, would you look at her? Boring old cream dress. Pearl earrings. Ha! Suzy has definitely outdone her.

"Amber!" She gives her a warm hug. "Look at you! You look beautiful!"

"Oh so do you," Amber lies perfectly. "I love your dress."

"Dolce," Suzy says, her hand rising to play with the diamond necklace, just to make sure Amber notices.

"Oh yes, I remember you saying. And what a beautiful necklace."

"Thank you. I really am the luckiest girl in the world, aren't I? My husband just spoils me rotten."

"God, isn't she awful?" Amber says pleadingly to Richard as they walk away.

"Is she?" Richard, like most of the husbands, is largely oblivious to the social interactions of the women in High-field. "But she seemed to be so nice to you," he says sarcastically, aware this time of the game that has just been played.

"You know it's all false," Amber says as she smiles at him. "But never mind. I'm not going to let her spoil my evening. Oh look! There're Deborah and Spencer. Come on, let's go and join them for a drink."

Given the amount of preparation, the amount of trepidation that has preceded this event, Amber is astonished to find she has a wonderful evening. It is by far the busiest and most successful gala thus far, and Amber found that a couple of Cosmopolitans were all she needed to ease the stress of such a serious social situation, and now she's positively having a blast.

She and Richard wander around the tables displaying the silent-auction items, and even Amber has to admit they did a wonderful job. There are Cartier watches on display, diamond earrings, the opportunity to visit the set of *Oprah*, plus have tea after the show with Oprah and Gail.

Amber manages to persuade Richard to write his bid down for a luxury cruise around the Caribbean. The value is $15,000. Richard's name is the fourth one down, and he writes $12,000, revisiting the table while Amber is in the ladies' room, relieved to see that six more people added their names after him so he's in the clear.

It seems the entire town of Highfield has turned out for the event—or at least the people who matter. The women are all checking one another out, seeing who has the best dress, the best jewels, and the men are grouped together over by the bar, catching up on work talk.

And Amber, standing there with a Cosmopolitan in hand, in her quietly elegant clothes, suddenly has an epiphany. As she watches the women jostle one another to have their photograph taken by the Highfield magazine social diary photographer, Amber suddenly realizes how ridiculous this lifestyle is.

She watches the whispers, the glances, the social smiles, and Amber sees how false it is, and as the photographer comes over to her and asks her to smile, she shakes her head and turns away.

I can't do this anymore, she thinks, as she heads over to Richard in a trance. This isn't who I am. This isn't what I want. She looks at Richard, standing awkwardly with a group of men, with them but not with them, not really joining in their conversation, and her heart goes out to him. It isn't Richard's scene either. What the hell are we doing? she thinks. Why has it mattered so much to keep up with these ridiculous people, this ridiculous lifestyle?

And all of a sudden Amber wants to be away from this. She wants to be at home, with her children, with her husband. Doesn't want to have to play this game any longer. Doesn't care about being queen bee, about doing this so-called charity work.

I want a simpler life, she thinks, as she slides next to

Richard and slips her hand into his, smiling up at him as he looks down in surprise. I want to get rid of all this stuff. She leans up and whispers in his ear, "Come on, darling, take me home."

"I really love you," Amber smiles, after they've made love and are lying in bed, looking into one another's eyes.

"I really love you," Richard says, unused to this spontaneous affection from his wife. It's a Friday night, and Sunday is always their "date night," and far be it from him to presume that he may be getting his oats at any time other than a Sunday night.

"No but I *really* love you." Amber snuggles into his arms.

"What's brought this on?" Richard pulls back and looks at her suspiciously. "Do you have something to tell me?"

"No, don't be silly. As if I'd have the time. It's just that at the gala tonight I suddenly realized how much I love my whole family. I feel like I've been so caught up in all the social stuff here, I haven't been focused on you all, and tonight I suppose I just realized that none of that material stuff matters."

Richard opens his eyes wide. "About time," he says.

Amber shrugs. "I guess tonight was just the pinnacle of everything that's wrong with Highfield. Even though I had a good time, it was partly because I felt detached from everything. For the first time I didn't feel inadequate, didn't feel I had to keep up with everyone, and I suppose it made me realize how superficial this all is."

"Well, we're always talking about moving to the Berkshires, or Vermont or somewhere. We could, you know,"

Richard says hopefully. "We could get a house on the water where the cost of living is way less."

Amber snorts. "And I guess you'd make a living as a fisherman? Oh darling, I know you still have to be within commuting distance of New York, and anyway, this realization doesn't mean I'm ready to change. Not yet. I just want to pull out of all this constant competition. I don't care anymore. Like having Amberley Jacks do the living room. God, I hate that living room."

Richard sits up. "You'd better be joking, given how much that cost."

Amber gulps. "Oh yes. I don't hate it. I just meant it wasn't what I expected, and I see what you mean about how unnecessarily expensive they are. I don't care about having Amberley Jacks do our house. I'm going to cancel them tomorrow."

"I thought you'd canceled them weeks ago?"

"Oh yes." Amber looks away, thinking fast. "Well, I left them a message but never heard anything. I'll just phone and absolutely confirm they understood."

"You know, if you were serious about wanting a simpler life, I could find something local. I don't have to work in the city. I could find a business to run, something small, something that would mean me being at home with the kids."

"In a dream world that would be ideal." Amber smiles. "But we're still consolidating; we spent so much money on this house. You're the one who's always saying we need to start saving rather than spending. We should put together something like a five-year plan, put some money away every year so we can have that as a goal to look forward to."

"You're the one who's always spending," Richard says bitterly.

"Darling, don't start a fight now," Amber soothes. "And I'm much better this month than I was. I'm really trying."

"You're a bit better," Richard says dubiously. "Not much."

"But I will be much better," Amber says firmly. "I'm going to resign from the League and I swear to you, I won't need any of those clothes or the jewelry once I resign. I only bought that stuff to keep up with them, and Suzy didn't even comment on my ring at the last meeting."

Richard furrows his brow. "What ring?"

"Oh—" shit—"my engagement ring," she says quickly.

"But she's seen that before, hasn't she?" Richard frowns.

"Not since I cleaned it. It's really sparkly now."

"Honey, I'm tired now." Richard leans over and kisses her on the lips before reaching over and turning off the light. "Sleep well. I love you."

"Yes, honey," she says, thankful he didn't realize she'd bought that ring recently. "I love you too."

Amber's sense of well-being continues through until breakfast on Monday. She feels so good about her decision to quit the League she even gives Lavinia the day off, after she's finished doing the laundry. Richard is just about to go to work when the phone rings, and since he's closest he picks up, after giving Amber a quizzical look, because who, after all, would call them at seven forty-five in the morning?

"It's for you," he holds out the phone, covering the mouthpiece. "Some English person called Vicky Townsley."

Amber frowns. *Vicky Townsley. Vicky Townsley.* The name is vaguely familiar but she can't think why. She takes the phone. "This is Amber Winslow."

"Amber? Hi! This is Vicky Townsley from *Poise!* magazine.

You wrote to us about Swapping Lives and I'd love to talk to you further."

Oh shit. Amber had completely forgotten about that. What on earth had she been thinking?

"So who's Vicky Townsley?" Richard's back in the kitchen, besuited with briefcase in hand, kissing the kids good-bye as he sets off to the train station.

"A journalist on a British magazine," Vicky says nonchalantly. "I'll explain later. Have a good day," and she kisses him good-bye, almost steering him through the mud-room door.

The next hour is spent on autopilot. Lavinia is busy upstairs with the laundry so Amber gets the children dressed and ready for school, so busy she doesn't have time to think about the conversation she's just had, what she must have been thinking when she sent that letter in to *Poise!*.

The truth is she never expected them to call her. She was intrigued by the article—who wouldn't be?—and just wrote the note on a whim. Now they've called and, worse, they want to fly over to meet her. What was she *thinking,* and more to the point, what in the hell is she going to tell Richard? "Darling, I love you and the kids more than life itself, but I'm just popping over to the other side of the Atlantic for a month. Cheerio!"

How do you explain to the people you love that it isn't about them? That you've done this, even though you didn't expect it to amount to anything, because it's about you. Because despite how perfect your life is, how you appear to have everything you have ever wanted or needed, you don't know who you are anymore.

Amber may no longer want this life—the charities, the

social climbing, the insecurities, and the constant exhaustion that comes with attempting to keep up with the Bartlows and everyone else in the League—but neither does she know quite what to do about it.

She's stuck. Too frightened to make a change, too frightened to stay still. And it isn't about Richard. Isn't about the children. Isn't anything to do with them. It's just that she needs to step outside her life for a bit. Remind herself of who she used to be, of what life was like when she didn't want or need a Viking range, when she hadn't heard of Amberley Jacks, when her wardrobe was half empty instead of bursting at the seams, and when the clothes inside came from Old Navy and Gap instead of Oscar de la Renta and Chanel.

She wants to remind herself of a simpler life. A simpler time when the things that mattered were friendships—real friendships, people who didn't judge her because of what her living room looks like or what handbag she's holding. When happiness was something real and attainable, not something she only catches a glimpse of these days, and even then only once in a while.

But how on earth is she going to tell Richard? How is she going to tell him that she did this without consulting him, and now, if they want her, she's going to go through with it, because despite her nervousness about his reaction, there's something stronger going on.

Excitement. And the overwhelming feeling that this could be exactly what she needs.

"Ow!" Jared whines as Gracie smirks and inches her foot back from kicking his shin. "*Mommy!* Gracie just kicked me."

"No! I did not!" Gracie scowls as Amber gives her a warning look from the kitchen sink where she's washing up the dishes, catching Grace's evil smile as her foot inches back toward Jared, causing Jared to start whining again.

"Oh stop it!" Amber shouts. "Jared! Stop whining! Gracie! Leave him alone!" God. She shakes her head as she tries to finish the dishes, finally wiping her hands furiously on a tea towel and running over to the table to wrench Gracie's leg away from Jared. How can a three-year-old be so much trouble? Why didn't anyone warn her about little girls?

As she makes her way back to the sink there's a sharp slap from the other side of the room and instantly Gracie starts screaming, Jared runs into the family room with a panicked look on his face. He'd finally been pushed too far and had retaliated, and as usual, even though Gracie started it, he can see he's going to get the blame.

"Oh for God's sake!" Amber shouts. "Both of you be *quiet*!" Her voice rises almost to a scream, and she turns the radio on at top volume to try and drown out the crying from both of them.

She hates herself when she's like this. Fully understands how people hit their children, not that she ever has, but boy is she tempted when they whine and scream like this, particularly first thing in the morning before she's even had time to have coffee.

Carrying Grace on her right hip and dragging Jared along with her left hand, she eventually manages to get them to the end of the driveway for the school bus. She hugs and kisses a tearful Jared—he's always been the sensitive one, always the one who finds it hardest when she shouts at him, and despite herself she finds she blames him more, expects more from him because he's older. Even though he's only six years old.

As soon as Jared goes and Gracie has Amber to herself, she's happy. She turns back into the gorgeous little girl that everyone at her preschool thinks she's like all of the time—oh if only they knew—and skips along next to Amber, holding her hand, singing, "Mommy, Mommy, Mommy. I love my mommy," and Amber's heart melts. Oh God. England. A month away from the children. A month away from this. Could she do it? Does she even want to do it?

And still a small voice says yes. Still the butterflies flutter with excitement in the pit of her stomach when she stops to think about waking up in a small apartment in—where did that article say Vicky Townsley lives?—Marylebone High Street? Yes that's it. Marylebone High Street.

Vicky puts Gracie in the car seat and turns on a Wiggles CD. You know things are bad, she thinks idly as she listens to the now all-too-familiar strains of *fruit salad, yummy, yummy,* when you're watching *The Wiggles* and wondering which one you'd sleep with if you absolutely had to. Just for the record, it's Anthony, and just in case you're a mother who hasn't learned each of their names by heart, he's the blue one.

And as she drives, she tries to remember the article that Vicky Townsley wrote, the collage of pictures documenting her life—her apartment, no, make that a *flat,* her wardrobe, pictures of her family, her friends. She does her grocery shopping at a supermarket called Waitrose, but buys fruit and produce from a market that sets up close to her on the weekend.

London. Wouldn't it be wonderful? "Hello, I'm Amber Winslow," Amber attempts in a British accent. "How lovely to make your acquaintance." She giggles to herself, thinking she really ought to practice.

"What?" Gracie shouts, leaning forward from the backseat. "What you say, Mommy?"

"Nothing, darling," Amber smiles. "I'm just talking to myself."

Amber has only been to London once. Up until she was in her mid-twenties she hadn't been anywhere at all, but as soon as she started making money as a lawyer she started traveling, although London wasn't until she met Richard.

He'd taken her there for a romantic weekend soon after they'd met. They had stayed at Claridge's, had shopped on Bond Street, taken a boat on the Serpentine in Hyde Park, strolled around Kensington Palace, and had, rather disappointingly, waited in line for two hours with all the other American tourists to get into Madame Tussauds. Not worth the wait.

But she had loved it. Had loved how the people spoke. How quaint and charming everything was. She had felt as if she had stepped into the movie *Four Weddings and a Funeral*. She kept expecting to turn a corner and find Hugh Grant standing there, although even if he had been she was probably too besotted with Richard to have even taken any notice of him.

Even Amber knew that London as a tourist and London as a Londoner were two very different things, and she was aware that as much as she had fallen in love with the city, she couldn't possibly know what it was really like unless she lived there. Not that she ever thought she would. But a month in London! She imagines herself striding over to the market, a basket over her arm, in Vicky Townsley's clothes, far trendier and more boho than anything she has in her own wardrobe.

She sees herself sitting in pubs, nursing a pint of beer, laughing delightedly with some of Vicky's cool journalist friends who, in these fantasies, immediately welcome Amber as one of their own, treating her like someone they've known their entire lives.

She could sleep in, she thinks, imagining herself waking

up to the sunlight streaming through the floor-to-ceiling picture windows in Vicky Townsley's bedroom, a cafetière of
fresh coffee waiting on the kitchen table, maybe a touch of
Diana Krall floating from the stereo.

She'd get to work for a magazine—how much fun would
that be? Going to work again! Being an adult! Being someone who doesn't have to have thirty-three conversations a
day about why it's impossible to find a nanny who stays with
you for longer than a year anymore, and why all the people in
Highfield are so snooty, even though many of the women
with whom she finds herself having those conversations are
considered by others to be the snootiest of all.

Think of the trendy restaurants, the bars, the clubs. Not
that Amber has the energy anymore, but maybe, without the
children, without any responsibilities other than getting to
work by ten a.m. every day, maybe she would *find* the energy.

Not that Amber's looking to meet anyone. Not in the
sense of having an affair, at any rate. No. She's perfectly
happy with Richard, and although she occasionally thinks, if
they were into wife-swapping, which of her friends' husbands she would want to sleep with—the truth is she isn't
actually attracted to any of them, but at an absolute push
she'd have to say Spencer because she's always had a bit of a
secret thing for men with long hair—she loves her husband,
and wouldn't be unfaithful. Not even when the likelihood
would be that he'd never find out.

The more Amber thinks about how single life in London
would be, the more excited she becomes, and the more
nervous she is about telling Richard. Because once she's
dropped Gracie at preschool, once she's arrived back home
and has opened up the magazine again to study the pictures,
reread the article, see if there's anything left to fantasize

about that she may have missed while in the car this morning, she knows that if she is the one *Poise!* ends up picking, there's no way she's going to say no.

When they say jump, Amber already knows her response: How high?

"What?" Richard sits across the table from her at the French restaurant opposite the train station and looks at her in disbelief. Surely he couldn't have heard what she just said. It doesn't make sense. Why would she be leaving him and the children for a month? Did she say England? What on earth is she talking about?

Amber slowly repeats the speech she has practiced with Deborah, in whom she confided earlier today. "I think you're completely mad," Deborah had said, placing two Starbucks grande skim lattes on the table in front of them, "and I'm deeply jealous. But what in the hell is Richard going to say?"

What indeed.

"What?" he says again, shaking his head in an attempt to clear the confusion of thoughts that have sprung up as Amber continues speaking. He watches her lips move but struggles to make sense of the actual words.

"Are you saying that you want to leave me and the kids and go to live in London for a month for some magazine article?" He pauses as Amber nods, hopefully.

"Are you out of your fucking mind?" he continues, his voice menacingly low.

"I know it seems crazy . . ." Amber starts, having already predicted his reaction, although she didn't expect to see quite this much anger in his eyes.

"Crazy? You're insane. I don't understand. You want to

leave us? What the hell are you talking about? Why would you want to leave?"

"Richard," she places a hand on his arm, "it's not that I want to leave you and the children. I don't. I love you, and you know I love the kids, it's just that I'm not happy, I haven't been happy for a while, and this isn't leaving, this is just a journalistic exercise for a magazine piece. I just need to go and find myself." She sighs, struggling to think of the right words to say. "Remember what life used to be like before we got caught up in all this Highfield crap? This doesn't have anything to do with you or the children. This is about me. And I'll be home in a month. It's not leaving you, this isn't a separation, nothing like that at all.

"Richard," she continues, seeing that there's no reaction from him at all. "I love you. Do you understand? I don't want to be with anyone else other than you. This isn't about you, okay? It's just something I have to do."

"So you've made up your mind?"

"Well . . . no. I don't even know that they'll choose me, but the journalist wants to come next week and meet us, see how we live and what we're like."

"And what if I say no? Absolutely not?"

"I'm hoping you won't," Amber says quietly. "Because this is something I really, really need to do. I'm hoping that you'll understand the reasons why I'm not happy, why I feel I'm stuck, and why I need to do this. If you love me you'll let me go."

Richard exhales. "I can't believe you're doing this to me."

"Doing what?" Amber says in exasperation. "I'm just going on vacation for a month. If you wanted to go away with the guys for a month I'd let you go."

"But that's the point. I wouldn't want to. I wouldn't want

to be away from you for a month, and anyway, this isn't the same thing at all. This isn't going to a spa or something with your girlfriends. If I understand you correctly you're telling me you want to be single again, to live a single life without a husband, without children, and even though you're saying it's only for a month, what the hell am I supposed to think that you're even considering this? That this is something you actually *want*?" Richard's voice rises with anger.

"If I hadn't read the magazine I would never have wanted this. I never want to be without you and Jared and Gracie, not permanently. I just need a break. It's not that I want to be single, I just want to remember what life used to be like. I feel as though I look in the mirror and I have no idea who I am anymore. What happened to the strong, successful, independent woman I used to be? How did I become a person whose sole topics of conversation involve what I bought at Rakers last week, or why no one can get good goddamned help anymore?

"Do you understand, Richard?" Now it's Amber's turn to raise her voice. "This isn't about you. This is about remembering who I am. It's about defining myself outside of this narrow suburban world. I've become a woman I don't recognize. I never used to care about keeping up with the women in the League, and now I've bought into all that crap, and I don't want to be that person. I don't want to be that insecure, bitchy person I feel I'm becoming.

"I just need a break," she says forcefully. "I just need to see life from a different perspective, and this is a once-in-a-lifetime opportunity and I have to do it."

"Do I have a choice?" Richard says, and Amber finds she can't look him in the eye.

Chapter Fourteen

Sarah Evans, whose letter is at the top of the possibles pile, is a real possibility for the first three minutes Vicky spends with her. She drives up to Oxford on a perfect June day—the sun is shining brightly, belying the coolness of the air outside, there is almost no traffic, and as she turns off the motorway and onto the country roads, she feels her heart swell just as it does every time she goes to see Kate and Andy.

"It must be because our ancestors were farmers," she has said to Andy, who doesn't quite feel the same pull. "I'm sure this passion for the country is genetic." But nevertheless, be it Somerset, the Cotswolds, or Oxfordshire, Vicky always has the same feeling of coming home.

Sarah Evans lives in a slightly messy Edwardian brick house, just as she described, on the outskirts of Oxford. Her two West Highland terriers scamper out to lavish Vicky with licks and jumps when she pulls slowly into the gravel drive-way, and Sarah, standing at the end of the path, hand in hand with her two towheaded children and a large smile on her face, looks just as lovely as she seemed in her letter.

"I'm Sarah," she says, disengaging for a second to shake hands. "And this is Jack. Say hello, Jack." She looks at Jack encouragingly, but he continues to scuff his foot along the gravel and refuses to look up. "Come on, Jack, say hello to Vicky. This is the lady I was telling you about. Just say hello, darling."

"No!" Jack says finally, and pushes his mother hard as he runs off around the corner.

Vicky watches him disappear with some disbelief. That was a hard push. She looks at Sarah expectantly, waiting for her to say something, tell him off in some way perhaps, but Sarah laughs nervously and apologizes. "He's going through a stage," she explains. "He's been pushing and smacking me, but I know it's just how he expresses his frustration."

"Right," nods Vicky. "How old is he again?"

"Six. I know, I know. Sometimes I think he's old enough to know better, but he's had these phases before and they don't last. Honestly, he's just a very clever little boy, and very much an individual, as you can see. Jack!" She turns and raises her voice ever so slightly as a rock comes flying from the place where Jack was last spotted. "Darling! What have I told you about the wall?

"Sorry, Vicky, what a terrible first impression. Just hang on. Come on, Will, let's go and see what Jack is doing," and dragging Will behind her she disappears round the corner, followed closely by Vicky who sees that Jack is in the process of demolishing a drystone wall. Clearly this is an ongoing process, one that has taken quite some time and dedication, and given the fact that this wall surrounds the garden, has a gate and arbor in the middle of it, trees and bushes all around, Vicky has the feeling that no one, other than Jack, is planning on taking this wall down.

For one corner has now disappeared. Several large stones are lying on the ground, others have been thrown, or attempts have been made to throw them, to greater distances, and Vicky watches as Jack clambers up on top of the pile of rocks that used to be part of the wall, and heaves a giant rock off it, kicking and pushing until he manages to topple it over.

"Jack!" Sarah says sternly. "Enough, I said! Right that's it. Stop!"

"I hate you!" Jack yells from the wall. "Shut up."

"Darling, don't say that," Sarah pleads. "It hurts Mummy's feelings when you say that."

"I don't care. It's true. I do hate you." Another stone comes flying.

"I'll let you watch *Power Rangers*," Sarah says finally.

"Yay!" Jack shouts, jumping off the wall and running inside.

"Thank God for television," Sarah smiles wearily. "It's the only thing that keeps me sane. Oh God, I shouldn't be telling you that, should I, not when I want to be the Swapping Lives person. It's not usually this chaotic, I promise."

"Don't worry," says Vicky, already wondering how soon she can leave. She can't think of anything worse than spending four weeks in Jack's company. As lovely as this house is, as picture-perfect as Sarah's life might appear, ten minutes with Jack and Vicky can see it would be a living hell.

The day goes from bad to worse. Jack is an expert in terrorizing Will, who has learned the best defense is screaming, and Sarah is too worn down to do anything to stop it other than shout herself.

Amid the chaos, the screaming, and the crying, Sarah keeps apologizing to Vicky, telling her it's not usually like this, that the boys didn't sleep well last night and that's the only reason Jack's behaving like this.

"What time do they go to bed?" Vicky asks curiously.

"Jack goes to bed around eleven," she says. "But we manage to get Will down by nine."

"Really?" Vicky's eyes are wide. "Eleven? Do you think he's getting enough sleep?"

"We've tried putting him down earlier but he refuses to sleep. And last night he was running around the house until one o'clock in the morning."

"Never mind him being tired, you must be exhausted," Vicky says sympathetically.

"Now you see why I want to swap lives with you." Sarah grins wryly. "I'd probably spend the entire four weeks sleeping."

At four o'clock Vicky sinks gratefully into the driver's seat of her car. "Peace!" she sighs to herself, waving a hearty good-bye to Sarah, Will, and the horror as she pulls out of the driveway and stops in a layby to phone Janelle.

"Absolutely not," she tells Janelle, who hoots with laughter when she hears about Jack. "I couldn't put up with that for a day, let alone four weeks."

"Not your dream lifestyle?"

"The house was lovely, the dogs gorgeous, but revolting kids. Never going to happen."

"Oh well." Janelle smiles. "Let's see what happens tomorrow. Remind me, who are you going to meet tomorrow?"

"Next up is Sally Lonsdale. I think she may be more promising. She's the one in Chislehurst who sounds very funny."

"Have you told the TV people today's a no?"

"Not yet. They're planning on coming up to meet everyone after me, but I'll phone Hugh and tell him not to bother with Sarah. Even if it makes great television I'm not putting myself through that kind of hell."

"Well, good luck tomorrow, then. And darling, don't forget to keep me posted. This is fun, isn't it!" Janelle trills as she puts down the phone.

Sally Lonsdale is exactly what Vicky had hoped she would be, only smaller. Too small, Vicky suspects from the first minute, ever to be a viable swap—her clothes wouldn't fit Vicky in a million years. With streaky blond hair and a strong cockney accent, she's as warm and clever and funny as she had seemed when Vicky had phoned her after receiving her letter.

"Don't get me wrong," she'd said on the phone. "I love my husband and I love my kids, but I'm bleedin' exhausted, and I know they all love me but they don't appreciate me. Best thing I could do is disappear for four weeks, although chances are they wouldn't even notice I'd gone. Still, all you have to do is drive the kids around, keep the fridge stocked with food, put the dinner on the table, and you'll be fine."

Sally's kids are older than Vicky had expected. Dave is sixteen, Daisy fourteen, and Pete eleven. They aren't around when Vicky pulls up outside 745 Station Road, and it takes a while for the door to be answered, although as soon as the bell rings a sharp yapping starts up inside the hallway, and after a minute Vicky hears a voice yell, "Shut up, Pixie! Quiet! Keep it down!"

The door opens to Sally, cradling a small white shih tzu dog, which pants excitedly as Sally gives Vicky a kiss on the cheek and invites her in. "Be careful, love," she says, stepping over the paint pots and bundled-up dust-rags in the hallway. "John, my husband, is doing up the house and you know what men are like—not exactly known for their tidiness!"

"Is he here?"

"Wish he were," she sighs. "That's the problem with having a builder for a husband. You think it's going to be fantastic, that you're going to save a fortune and live in a bleedin' palace, and then what happens is they take on too many jobs at once and you become the last priority on the list. Look at this," and she gestures to the living room, which has a gaping hole where a fireplace either once stood or is waiting to stand.

"He took out the old gas fire a year ago, and we've been waiting for a fireplace for over a year now. Meanwhile I've got to live with that great gaping hole. Wait till you see the kitchen." She rolls her eyes.

Ah yes. Wait indeed. Vicky winces as she walks in. Half the flooring has disappeared, exposing unfinished planks of wood. Several cupboard doors are off, and a couple of cupboards have actually been removed, so piles of plates and mugs are tottering precariously on the counter.

In the middle of the room, however, is a beautiful island, chunky maple topped with solid butcher block, it has pull-out rattan baskets, small hooks for hanging tea towels, and is far and away the nicest thing in the kitchen, if not the entire house.

"Ah yes. I see you're eyeing up my husband's pride and joy. What kind of man starts demolishing a kitchen," she gestures to the mess, "then stops halfway to make a butcher-block island? Not that I don't love the butcher-block island," she says, "but I'd be much happier if he finished off the rest of the bloody kitchen first."

"How do you live through this?" Vicky asks in horror, once she's determined that pretty much the whole house is in a similar state—every room appears to have been started, but not a single room has been finished. Piles of clothes, books, CDs are everywhere, nothing has a home, and nothing is where it's supposed to be.

"He keeps promising me he'll finish it, and when it's finished I know it will be gorgeous. Whoops, here comes Bob the builder now."

"Anyone home?" John, a giant at six-foot-four, twice the size of his wife, walks into the kitchen, puts his arms around Sally and lifts her up as he plants a kiss on her lips.

"Oh stop it," she bats him away, but laughs as she does so, and Vicky smiles at the demonstration of affection. This is why she puts up with it, she realizes. Because she loves him. Because it doesn't matter.

Vicky spends the entire day with them, meets the kids, then joins them for a drink at the local where she's introduced proudly as a big cheese from *Poise!* magazine. The Lonsdales are what Vicky would describe as salt of the earth, the very best people she could hope to have met, and she leaves with a huge smile on her face, yet she cannot think of anything worse for her than to live in that house.

She knows she would go crazy living in that dust and debris. And while she's trying to find nice people, it's more important that she finds people with whom she wants to swap. The point of the exercise, as she keeps reminding herself, is to discover whether the grass is in fact greener on the other side, and there's no point in swapping with someone whose grass is already dead, not to mention covered with dust.

No. As lovely as the Lonsdales are, Vicky doesn't want what they have. And with a sigh she realizes it's onwards and upwards, and tomorrow is the final possibility in England— Hope Nettleton.

* * *

"God, I hope this is worth it," she says when she phones Leona at the magazine for a chat on the drive down. As a London girl, Vicky hasn't spent this much time in the car since she was at university, and while it's lovely being out of the office and listening to Radio One during the daytime—a luxury she hasn't had since she was a student—she's beginning to find these long drives ever so slightly boring.

Thank God for mobile earpieces. So far today she's spoken to Jackie, Deborah, and now, as she's circling the outskirts of Bath looking for the right turning, she's talking to Leona.

"Oh. My. God," she breathes, as she turns into a sweeping driveway through large stone pillars topped with old stone finials. "This is beautiful!"

"What? What?" Leona says excitedly. "Are you there? What's it like?"

"It's enormous!" Vicky breathes out. "Christ! I'd kill to live in a house like this. Actually, it's not a house, it's a palace."

"No, seriously, describe it."

"I think it's Georgian. White, stucco, ivy or something climbing up the walls. Huge floor-to-ceiling windows. Planters of bay trees on either side of all the windows, and there's a, what do you call it—a parterre? Potager?"

"Describe it."

"One of those gardens that is a pattern made of low hedges."

"A parterre, I think."

"Well, one of those with little benches. Jesus. This is the most beautiful house I've ever seen. I feel as though I've just stepped into the pages of *World of Interiors*."

"And just think, you haven't even seen the interior," quips Leona.

"Okay, World of Exteriors, then. I want this Swapping Lives," groans Vicky, quickly saying good-bye as the front door opens and a tall, dark-haired woman glides out to greet her.

"You must be Vicky." Hope Nettleton smiles a nervous smile as Vicky gets out of the car and instantly feels inadequate. Not that Hope Nettleton is unfriendly, far from it, but she has the kind of natural beauty that women like Vicky can only ever hope to emulate, and even then with truckloads of beauty products and makeup. On a good day Vicky knows she would be described as pretty, on a spectacular day she may even make very pretty, but that's with an awful lot of artificial help, and first thing in the morning Vicky is the first to tell you she looks like a monster.

One glance at Hope Nettleton tells you she *never* looks like a monster. Has never known what it is to wake up with puffy eyes and a spotty forehead. Has never stood in front of a floor-length mirror and squeezed the flab on her thighs, bemoaning just how much can be squeezed between a finger and thumb.

Hope Nettleton has clearly never had a bad hair day in her life. She is one of those tall, slim, elegant beauties. Large brown eyes, a perfect button nose, high cheekbones, and when she smiles Vicky is further aghast to see she has a set of the whitest, straightest teeth Vicky has ever seen.

Her glossy chestnut hair is pulled back in a low ponytail that sits perfectly over the shoulder of her crisp white shirt. Her brown linen trousers fit her toned thighs perfectly, flaring ever so slightly over turquoise beaded sandals.

She has the kind of clothes-hanger body that can buy

clothes at Marks & Spencer and carry them off as if they were Armani. She is, in short, everything that Vicky is not, everything that Vicky has always wanted to be; and with a start Vicky remembers that Hope Nettleton is the woman who has an unfaithful husband. How could any man be unfaithful to this? How could any man want anything more perfect than Hope Nettleton?

It turns out, over the course of several cups of Earl Grey tea in the Mark Wilkinson–designed kitchen, which is exactly the kitchen that Vicky would have chosen if she had all the money in the world and lived in a house just like this one, that Adam Nettleton didn't want perfection.

Adam Nettleton, it seems to Vicky, seemed stifled by all this perfection, and the woman with whom he'd chosen to have the affair that has caused Hope Nettleton to write to Vicky in the first place is the very opposite of Hope Nettleton.

"That's what I couldn't ever understand," Hope keeps saying over the kitchen counter. "I could understand if she was gorgeous. If she was brighter than me, or prettier than me, or more fun than me, but I know this woman, I've met her several times at work do's, and Adam and I had always joked about how boring she was. Is."

They are interrupted by the crunch of a car on the gravel outside, and Hope's face lights up as she goes out to meet her children from school.

Vicky can see how much she adores her kids, and for the rest of the afternoon she bakes jam tarts with the girls in the kitchen, then goes with Hope and the kids for their riding lesson at the stables down the road.

Vicky finally has hope, in more ways than one. I could live

like this, she thinks, excitement fluttering in her stomach as she realizes that this is her dream life, that this could be the perfect swap.

Hope is upstairs giving the little one a bath while Vicky sits on the stone steps outside the front of the house, watching Sadie and Molly put on a play, when a large black BMW glides through the pillars.

"Daddy!" the girls shriek at the same time, and Vicky stands up, pushing her hair back, wishing she'd had a chance to blot the shine on her face and put on more lipstick, wanting to make a good impression because she's pretty damn certain that this is going to be it.

"Hello, girls." Adam steps out of the car and gives the girls an absentminded kiss, never taking his eyes off Vicky. "Where's Mummy and who's this pretty lady?"

Vicky looks at his raised eyebrow, his smile that, unless she's going completely mad, seems to be flirtatious, and she knows that the affair that Adam had confessed to was not his only one.

It is obvious in the way he shakes her hand, the way he looks her up and down, undresses her with his eyes, smiles approvingly when she tells him why she's there.

"So you're the woman who's going to be my wife for a month?" He grins, much like the cat that got the cream. "Excellent. I understand you'll be swapping clothes as well? I have to say I was rather dubious when Hope told me about writing to you, but now I've met you I'll have to make sure Hope leaves behind her sexiest underwear."

"Oh please," Vicky attempts, "your wife's tiny. I'm supposed to swap with someone the same size as me so we can wear each other's clothes. I don't think I'd even get her trousers past my ankles."

"Good. No reason for them to go any higher anyway. I've always liked a woman with a bottom," and he looks at Vicky admiringly as a shiver of horror goes through her.

"You do realize," she says tartly, "that if I were to choose Hope, one of the requirements is not to sleep with the husband."

"Not a requirement, sure. But a possibility?" He looks around to check that the girls are out of earshot, then leans closer to Vicky and lowers his voice. "If two people are mutually attracted to one another, why not? If no one will ever know? What's the harm? It's only sex, for heaven's sake."

Vicky shakes her head in disgust as Hope comes out of the house carrying the two-year-old, her face lighting up as she sees her husband.

"Hello, darling," she says, proffering her cheek for him to kiss, and Adam obliges, winking surreptitiously at Vicky as he goes inside.

"What did you think of Adam?" Hope says, as Vicky prepares to leave.

"He seems . . . charming," Vicky manages. A slimeball, she wants to say. Sleazy and a lech, and you deserve so very much better. So he's good-looking. So he makes a huge amount of money to keep you in this lavish lifestyle. He cannot keep his penis in his pants, she wants to say. Look at you and look at me. Look at how gorgeous you are and how ordinary I am, and still he wants to sleep with me, just because I'm not you, just because he can, because weaker women than I, women less secure than I, would be taken in by being flirted with by a man such as Adam.

I wish you would leave him, she wants to say, but instead she gives Hope a hug and says, "Take care. I'll be in touch," and she knows as she drives away that she couldn't stand spending four weeks fighting off Adam's advances, and that even the firmest of rebuffs would only inspire him more.

No. Hope Nettleton, for all the wonderful things she has, is not the person with whom Vicky is going to swap. The grass is not greener here, she has seen. Is it possible that this whole experiment will fail? That the only people she has found to have grass that is greener will remain her brother and sister-in-law, and swapping with her sister-in-law, however innocent, is too bizarre to even contemplate?

Oh well. There is still one more possibility, and Janelle Salinger's first choice all along. Amber Winslow.

Highfield, Connecticut, here I come . . .

Chapter **Fifteen**

Amber wakes up with a start. Oh my God, she realizes. Today's the day. Today, June 16, is the day Vicky Townsley flies in from London to see whether Amber is good enough to be the life swapee.

Poor Amber. This is not, for her, about Vicky. About Vicky choosing the person whose life she most would want. This is about Amber's life being good enough for someone else to choose, and she is filled with anxiety that somehow she won't make the cut. Last night she even took an Ambien to sleep, and she lies in bed for a while as the Xanax calls her from the top drawer in the bathroom, but in the end she decides not to take anything—surely better to be fully conscious than off in La La Land on Xanax—besides, there's an awful lot to do today.

The house is spotless but she has to buy fresh flowers, fill each room with armfuls of wonderful-smelling blooms. Hazelnut-scented coffee must be freshly brewed, cinnamon buns baking in the oven—every Realtor's dream, except Amber isn't selling her house, but using the same methods to sell her lifestyle, *herself.*

Gracie has a new dress just for today. A smocked, pink cotton dress, little ankle socks, and black patent Mary Janes. And Jared will be in a chambray shirt, navy chinos, and loafers, just a touch of hair gel to slick his hair back, make him look ever so handsome. They will look as if they stepped right out of the pages of a catalog. Amber stands in Gracie's bedroom admiring the new dress. How could anyone resist children as adorable as this?

Amber herself has decided to be low key. Chameleon that she is, today she is aiming for all-around good girl. Casual, warm, friendly. Nothing too intimidating, nothing that might put Vicky Townsley off. Stretchy khakis, a pink cable cashmere sweater, suede Tods on her feet, and her hair pulled back in a casual, girlish ponytail. She's aiming for Hope and Michael from *thirtysomething*. The perfect people with perfect lives. The family that everyone hopes one day to have, particularly the thirty-something single girl from London.

Richard, however, is the only fly in the ointment. Effortlessly charming, unfailingly well dressed, pleasant-enough-looking to still attract second glances that Amber notes with pride when they go out, he is still not happy, to put it mildly, about this journalist, about Amber writing in, about the increasingly real possibility that Amber will be disappearing for four weeks and a woman he doesn't know will be taking her place.

Richard has barely spoken to Amber since the night of the argument. They are communicating mostly through their children, and every time Amber tries to bring up the subject again, he refuses to speak about it.

And so last night, after Richard had fallen fast asleep, his back turned toward Amber, she crept out of bed and went down to the desk in the kitchen, pulled out some notepaper and started writing Richard a letter.

My darling Richard,

I want you to know that I love you today as much as I loved you when we took our wedding vows. If anything, I love you more. When I talked about making changes I didn't mean you, would never mean you, because you and the kids mean so much to me. I just meant that I have some questions, some issues in my life that I can't seem to resolve. It just feels that there must be more to life than this, and if I get picked for the swap (which, by the way, may not even happen . . .), I wouldn't be doing this because I want to get away from my family, I would be doing it because I need to step out of my life for a bit to try and figure out what it is that's missing. Maybe it's that I need to be working again. Maybe we do need to think about moving somewhere other than High-field. But right now my mind feels as if it's filled with squirrels, and the only way to stop them running is to take a break. If there was a way to take you and the kids with me, I would, but then if I did I suspect I wouldn't find the answers I'm looking for.

I love you more than life itself. I promise you this isn't about you, and it's not about hurting you. The last thing in the world I want to do is hurt you, and that's why I wrote in. To be honest, it was a spur of the moment thing, I never even dreamed I'd be one of the contenders. But the journalist, Vicky Townsley, is coming today. She'll be here when you get home . . .

I hate that we've hardly spoken the last few days. I hate that you turn away from me when we go to bed. I miss your laugh, your smile. I miss having a bath with you last thing at night when we tell one another about our days. I love you, love you, love you. Please try and understand!

Me xxxxx

As Amber polishes the stainless steel of the microwave for the fourth time that morning, Lavinia sailing past her with vases of flowers, Vicky presses the recline button on the plane seat and smiles to herself as she flicks through the movie channels waiting for the next film to start.

Not that she can particularly concentrate on the movie, not with so much to think about. She hasn't actually stopped smiling for the past week, has barely thought about this trip to meet Amber Winslow, because for the first time in her life Vicky thinks she may truly have found the one.

Okay, not quite the first time. In fact, if Vicky were to be entirely honest with herself, she has said this many times before. Despite being thirty-five and single, despite telling people she has hardened herself, she is strong, she thinks of herself as something of a ballbreaker, take a good-looking man with dimples in his cheeks, have him gaze into her eyes as he softly strokes her hair, allow him to sneak up behind her as she's making coffee in the morning and put his arms around her waist, burying his face in her hair, and the ballbreaker will turn to jelly.

Which is exactly what happened when Jamie Donnelly phoned.

Vicky abandons the movie altogether and gives herself up to the movie in her head, which stars Vicky Townsley and Jamie Donnelly.

He phones! And he doesn't just phone, he phones whispering that he is desperate to see her. That the papers lie, they always do. That he and Denise Van Outen are old friends, that nothing happened, and that they phoned one another the next day and roared with laughter about the ridiculousness of the thought of them sleeping together.

"Really?" Vicky asks hopefully, because although a journalist, she is a magazine journalist, which is quite a different thing from being a gossip journalist on a tabloid. And she says it hopefully because she so wants to believe. She doesn't want to be a cynic, to accuse him of lying, to ask why they aren't suing the paper, or at the very least demanding a retraction if the paper printed lies.

"Really," Jamie Donnelly confirms in his soft and oh-so-sexy Irish accent. "And I lost your phone number, and then I couldn't remember the magazine you worked on and I phoned *Cosmopolitan* and *Company*, and no one there knew you, and I didn't know how to find you."

Of course it is perfectly reasonable that he did lose her phone number. And possibly he did phone some other magazines. If he were that desperate it is perhaps slightly odd that he didn't just get on the Internet—surely anyone can find anyone, or anything, these days, but not everyone is as savvy as Vicky, and perhaps it just didn't occur to him.

"Well that is flattering," Vicky says. Flattered.

"I haven't stopped thinking about you. About that night we spent together. And then today, when I walked in and saw you sitting with Hugh I couldn't believe it. It feels like God was listening and he placed you there just for me."

And Vicky melts.

"So . . ." she says after recovering. "Do you want to get together?" Oh shit, she thinks. Shut up. Isn't it up to the man to suggest that?

"You took the words right out of my mouth," he says. "What about tonight? What are you doing tonight?"

Play hard to get, she thinks. Tell him you're busy until next week. Don't do it. Don't say yes.

"Not much," she says, her eagerness to see him overtaking any sane inclinations she may have had. And immediately her imagination starts working overtime—tonight. The Ivy, perhaps? Hakkasan? A romantic dinner for the two of them. She imagines them walking into the restaurant, everyone looking over at them for of course everyone knows who Jamie Donnelly is, and then looking at her, wondering who the lucky girl is who is holding Jamie Donnelly's hand, who he is gently guiding through the tables.

And perhaps the paparazzi will be waiting outside. She has seen them regularly at the restaurants she frequents for work. As she steps outside they are clustered around the doorway, looking up expectantly as soon as they hear the door, hoping for Cameron, or Jude, or Julia to finish eating and step outside. They will undoubtedly snap a picture of her and Jamie, and tomorrow it will be in the paper.

Oh how lovely if that happened. Think who might see it. That bastard Michael who dumped her for the brainless model. The other bastard Clive who professed to have fallen madly in love, then never called her again after she slept with him. *And* she didn't even sleep with him for six weeks because she didn't really fancy him. It took six weeks for her to decide she liked him so much as a friend that she'd sleep with him and see what happened, even though physically he wasn't her type at all. The bastard never called again.

And what about the gaggle of bitchy girls from school? Really, at thirty-five she ought not to have ever given them a second thought, but she recently Googled Catherine Enderley, just out of curiosity, to find out what happened to the queen bitch, and Catherine Enderley now works at a boring old law firm in Brighton. Please God, she thought, let Catherine Enderley see me in the paper with Jamie Donnelly. Please let Catherine Enderley, Rachel Myerson, and Tara Barking all see me looking thin, beautiful, and blissfully happy with the new love of my life, Jamie Donnelly.

"Wonderful!" Jamie says. "I'll come over. Around nine? I have a meeting at seven in town, so I'll probably make it over to you by nine."

"Do you remember my address?" Vicky quickly covers her disappointment. So okay, no paparazzi. No public outings tonight, but that will come. Think romantic dinner instead. A roaring fire—although it's not real but gas, which is almost as good and far less hot, given that it's summer—a wonderful dinner—oh God, what to cook? Nigella, come to my rescue, please, help me come up with a meal to make his mouth water, a meal to make him realize I could be a wonderful wife, he would never have to eat McDonald's again—chocolate-covered strawberries perhaps for dessert. They would feed each other in front of the fire, kiss during the meal, be unable to keep their hands off each other.

"I've been looking for you my whole life," Jamie Donnelly would say, and Vicky would just smile a secretive smile and not say anything at all, drive him wild with desire with just a cool gaze.

Tonight, she thinks cooly, I will be Angelina Jolie. I will be sexy, seductive, and super-cool. I will drive him wild with desire. I will make him fall in love with me.

"I remember your address," Jamie says.

"Should I make dinner?" Vicky says in a voice that she imagines Angelina would use.

"Nah, don't worry. I'll eat earlier. See you later, Vicky," and he's gone.

At nine o'clock Vicky is sitting on her sofa, cradling a glass of red wine. The fire is blazing, Diana Krall is crooning from the stereo, the lights are dim, and she is wearing a short blue linen dress, her favorite and sexiest lacy underwear underneath.

At nine-thirty she is pacing around the living room, worrying about where he might be, whether he might have forgotten or, worse, whether something might have happened to him.

At ten-thirty she is well and truly pissed off. And when a girl is well and truly pissed off because a man hasn't done what he has said he is going to do, the very best thing is a revenge fuck.

Not that the wrongdoer ever needs to know, but Vicky knows that sleep is no longer an option, that her body is so tense she feels ready to snap, and although she is now furious with Jamie Donnelly, she will phone Daniel, because he is around the corner, can be here in a heartbeat, and while he's not and never will be Mr. Right, he's certainly a better candidate for Mr. Right Now.

"Daniel? It's me. Vicky."

"Vixster! I haven't heard from you for ages! What a lovely surprise!" And it's true, for Daniel it is a lovely surprise. His fling with Maya the gorgeous redhead ended just last week. She'd announced a couple of weeks earlier that she wanted to date him exclusively, and although he agreed at the time—what's a man to do when put on the spot like that?—he found that his passion started waning straight away, and soon he wasn't calling, wasn't returning her calls, and she did exactly what he hoped—phoned him up and tearfully told him she deserved better.

"You're quite right," he agreed, attempting to sound contrite. "You're an amazing girl and you do deserve better. I'm sorry I'm not the one."

But Vicky? Now Vicky never demands anything more. There's no pretense about Vicky. She's just a bloody good neighborhood shag who never requests a relationship or asks why he hasn't invited her somewhere. Daniel looks at his watch. Ten forty-five. Couldn't be better.

"So Vixster," he says smoothly, smiling to himself, knowing there's only one reason Vicky would call at this time of night. "Your place or mine?"

Daniel rings the doorbell as a black cab pulls up and a tall man climbs out, paying the driver, then turning to look up at the building outside which Daniel is standing.

Jesus Christ, thinks Daniel, it's Jamie Donnelly. For a minute the temptation is to say one of the *Dodgy* catchphrases, or at the very least tell him how much Daniel loves the show, but no, that would be too naff. But he has to say something, can't let an opportunity like this pass him by.

"All right, mate?" Daniel says, nodding amiably just as Vicky buzzes him in. "Love the show," he finds the words involuntarily leaving his mouth. Damn.

"All right," Jamie nods back. "Hold the door, will you?" And they both walk in at the same time.

"Have you got a friend who lives here?" Daniel says, leading the way up the stairs.

"Depends on the definition of friend." Jamie grins and winks, as Daniel laughs knowingly, walking down the corridor toward Vicky's flat. How bizarre. Jamie Donnelly is following him. Must be the flat opposite Vicky's, for there are only two flats at this end of the corridor, and yet, isn't that a married couple with a baby? Maybe they moved. They must have moved.

And then they both come to a stop outside Vicky's door.

"Oh shit," Daniel says, as the light dawns on him.

Jamie grins and shrugs. Truth has always been stranger than fiction in his experience. "May the best man win," he says pleasantly, with the full knowledge that, given the choice between himself and pretty much any other man in London, he will win.

Vicky opens the door, wrapped in her bathrobe, all makeup off, and her hands fly to her face as she stands in front of Daniel and Jamie Donnelly.

"Oh my God!" she hisses, slamming the door shut again. "Wait there," she yells, flying down to the bathroom to retrieve her dress from where it is draped over the bath, pulling on her underwear, slapping on some makeup. Oh shit, she keeps whispering, running back down the hall and panting as she opens the door again to find the two men standing there, Jamie with a wide grin on his face, and Daniel looking ever so slightly uncomfortable.

"Jamie, I thought you weren't coming," she says, pulling him in. "And Daniel? Whatever are you doing here? It's a lovely surprise but a bit late, isn't it? I'll call you tomorrow," and she leans up to give him a kiss on the cheek, whispering, "Sorry, Dan, I'll explain tomorrow," and she practically pushes him out of the door as she goes back inside to wrap herself around Jamie Donnelly.

Daniel does not feel good. Not because she chose Jamie Donnelly. Christ, put him in the same position and he'd choose Jamie Donnelly too. But Vicky's never rejected him before. And she looked so cute in her bathrobe, no makeup on, all squeaky clean and cuddly. Oh God. Don't have him start falling for her now.

"Where were you?" Vicky breaks away from Jamie and goes to sit on the sofa. "It's eleven o'clock. I thought you were coming at nine?" She hears the whine in her voice and quickly corrects herself.

"I feel awful," Jamie says, taking both her hands in his and looking deep into her eyes. "The meeting went on for hours and I couldn't get away. The only thing that kept me going was that I was going to see you later. I'm so sorry. I promise you it will never happen again. Will you forgive me?" And he takes her face in his hands and kisses her ever so gently.

"You're forgiven," she says when he pulls away. What choice does she have?

And lying here on her Virgin flight, Vicky alternately smiles dreamily and shivers with lust as she replays every moment of the night. They made love—and for Vicky it was making love, so much more than a shag, than just sex—three times, and each was better than the last. But more than the sex, he cuddled her again. She went to sleep in his arms and they had breakfast together and the intimacy and warmth between them was not, could not, have been something she imagined.

And the way he looked at her, the way he touched her, the way he stroked her hair was not the way you treat someone who is merely a quick screw. She knows this is different. Knows this has real potential. So can you blame her for barely giving work a second thought, for bringing along all the notes she has taken during her now numerous phone calls with Amber Winslow, but not even glancing at them, not when Jamie Donnelly is taking up all the space in her head.

By the time she lands at Kennedy Airport it's lunchtime, and the long line of people snaking slowly through immigration brings her back to reality. Here she is. In America. About to meet her potential Swapping Lives partner, because frankly, if not Amber Winslow, then who? The only other possibility after meeting the others was the lovely Sally Lonsdale, but as much as Amber liked her, liked her family, Sally Lonsdale's life is not, has never been, the one Vicky would choose for herself.

The car service drives her up the Hutchison River Parkway, through Westchester, and finally past a sign saying WELCOME TO CONNECTICUT. Vicky spends the time reading her notes, blotting out the bags under her eyes with Touche Eclat— thank God for freebies on the magazine—and admiring the scenery.

For it is beautiful. Even from the highway Vicky can see numerous picture-perfect clapboard houses, swimming pools in the garden, trees and greenery everywhere. And soon they come to the exit for Highfield, off the ramp, twisting left and right, along tree-lined country roads until the woods open out to flat green meadows, huge mansions sitting at the end of each driveway. Turning into Sugar Maple Lane, the sleek black town car finally grinds to a halt outside a large, beautiful mansion, white clapboard and stone, with black shutters, an asphalt driveway, a full-size professional-looking basketball hoop.

A vastly overweight golden retriever barks lazily as Vicky opens the door, then ambles over to greet her as the front door opens and Amber Winslow runs down the front steps to shake Vicky's hand warmly.

"Oh I can't believe you're here!" she says. "I can't believe you came all the way to the States to meet me, and I'm so excited, there's so much to show you. Oh, I should stop talking. Come in, come in. Come in and make yourself at home."

And Vicky steps into the foyer of what is looking increasingly likely to be her new home.

Chapter Sixteen

"It's amazing," Vicky whispers to Janelle on the phone, tucked away in the Amberley Jacks living room.

"What do you mean? What's Amber like?" Janelle says, rifling through the papers on her desk until she finds the photos that Vicky left for her before she went away.

"She's lovely, but more to the point the house is incredible! I swear to you, Janelle, I would kill to live like this. I want her life. I want this house. It's huge and there's a swimming pool and the beach is a couple of towns over, and even though it's June it's almost eighty degrees! I want to stay here forever."

"Well, thank God, is all I can say." Janelle breathes a sigh of relief. "Because really I don't know what we would have done if this hadn't worked out. And what about the whole *Desperate Housewives* angle? Is she a Desperate Housewife?"

Vicky drops her voice even lower. "Well, she's completely perfect. She has those perfect, even, huge, gleaming American teeth. Her body looks as if she works out in the gym at least once a day, and I'd say she'd give that Bree a pretty good run for her money."

"I love it!" squeals Janelle. "And what about her family?"

"I haven't met them yet. I only just got here, just wanted

189

to let you know I'd arrived safely, and you asked me to give you first impressions. I'll e-mail you as soon as I've got more to tell you."

Vicky replaces the phone and walks back to the kitchen, a kitchen, incidentally, that is pretty much the same size as Vicky's flat, to find Amber busy putting out a plate of delicious-looking muffins.

"I've made some coffee," Amber says, pouring out a cup. "And please have something to eat."

Vicky polishes off a muffin before Amber even has a chance to sit down.

"Are you not having anything?" she says to Amber, sliding the plate toward her.

"Oh no!" Amber says in horror. "I don't eat refined sugar and I'm currently restricting my carbs. My trainer worked out this new diet for me, and muffins unfortunately aren't on my food plan."

"Oh." Vicky suddenly feels enormous.

"But don't feel bad," Amber smiles. "Have another one. Please."

"Oh no. No. I'm fine. Well, I suppose at least that explains your amazing figure."

"I have to work pretty hard at it." Amber grins. "Hence the gym in the basement. Do you want me to give you a tour of the house? The kids are up in the playroom with Lavinia so we can go in and see them too."

"I'd love it," says Vicky, who's been dying to see the rest of the house since she arrived, so off they go.

There's a family room off the kitchen, a Great Room—the American equivalent of a living room only ten times the size—with the highest ceilings Vicky has ever seen in a private house; a formal living room—the room in which Vicky made her phone call; a dining room that could happily seat twenty people; a walk-in pantry that's the size of Vicky's bedroom; a guest bedroom and bathroom; and his and her offices, cherry-paneled with French doors onto the wraparound porch.

And that's just the ground floor.

Upstairs are mile-long corridors, with bedrooms off, a master at one end with a bathroom that's the size of the bedroom, two enormous dressing rooms, and its own sitting room.

It's only after Vicky has seen all six bedrooms, all of them with ensuite bathrooms and walk-in closets, that she realizes there's still no sign of the children.

"We'll go to the playroom last," Amber says. "Let's do the basement first."

"I've never seen anything like it," Vicky says, trying not to gape at the basement complete with gym, wine cellar, and a media room made to look like an authentic 1920s cinema, with plush red-velvet seats and a popcorn machine in the corner.

Vicky knows that everything is supposed to be bigger and better in America, but this is ridiculous. No one she knows lives like this. No one except perhaps the Queen and the Beckhams, and they don't really count.

Because, really, who lives in houses like this other than royalty and celebrities? Who could possibly afford to maintain a house this size, never mind have an actual cinema, albeit a small one, in their own home! A cinema! With popcorn!

"I just have to ask you something." Vicky turns to Amber,

who is showing her around as if it's completely normal, as if her house is nothing out of the ordinary, nothing special. "Are you fantastically rich? I know that's rude. I'm sorry. I shouldn't have asked."

"No, that's okay," Amber says. "And no. We're not—how did you say it?—*fantastically* rich. My husband is a trader, and I'd say he does fine, but there are loads of people in Fairfield County who have far more money. Why do you ask?"

"This house," Vicky gasps. "It's just spectacular. It's enormous. I've never seen anything like it."

Amber pauses, wondering how much to tell Vicky. Oh what the hell. "You probably won't believe me," she smiles, "but I grew up in a trailer."

"What do you mean, a trailer? You mean like a caravan?"

"Basically, yes. I grew up in a trailer park with a single mother and nothing. Literally, nothing. My clothes were all hand-me-downs from friends and neighbors. If you'd told me that one day I would live in something like this I would have known you would need to be certified."

Vicky gasps again. "But how in the hell did you go from that to this?"

"With a lot of hard work and determination. Richard comes from a completely different background, and he works hard too, but I never ever thought I'd live like this. So much of the time I take it for granted, but when I see your face, it becomes fresh again."

"So is this the biggest house of everyone you know?"

"Good gracious, no!" Amber laughs. "In fact, you'll find that most of these new houses look pretty much the same. Some are just a bit bigger and some a bit smaller. We can go and see some friends, maybe tomorrow, so you can compare."

"I'd love to," Vicky says dubiously, doubting that anyone could live in a house that's bigger.

"Let's go and see the kids," Amber says, pausing outside a doorway that leads to yet another wing of the house, where Vicky finds an entire nanny suite complete with kitchenette and living room, and of course the playroom.

"Mommy!" Jared looks up happily from his drum kit in the corner.

"Jar, honey, come and say hello to Miss Townsley," Amber says.

Vicky gets down on one knee so she's on the same level as Jared. "Nice to meet you," she says, shaking his hand solemnly. "As we were walking down the hallway I heard some excellent drum playing. Were you playing a tape?"

"No!" Jared shakes his head. "That was *me*."

"You?" Vicky looks puzzled. "It can't have been you. I heard some seriously good drumming. I think it was a drummer in a rock band. You must have been playing a CD."

"No!" Jared says, running back to the drum kit. "It was me. Listen," and he bangs the drums and cymbals, making a hell of a racket while Vicky opens her eyes wide and applauds.

"Wow!" she claps. "It was you. You're fantastic at that. Do you play anything else?"

"Yes," Jared says confidently. "I play the piano too. Do you want to hear?" And with that he takes Vicky's hand and leads her down the hallway toward the living room while Amber follows, astonished at how quickly Jared seems to have taken to Vicky, how good she clearly is with children.

"You said you don't have children of your own?" she asks Vicky as they're going downstairs.

"No, but nieces and a nephew whom I adore."

"You're obviously used to kids. It's very rare for Jared to take to people like that. Jar, where's Gracie?"

Jared shrugs as he opens the living-room door. "Don't know."

"Well, where's Lavinia?"

"Laundry room," he says, as he starts banging the keys of the piano.

"Vicky, will you excuse me just a minute?" Amber says. "I'm going to find Gracie."

As Jared bangs out his next song, the door of the living room opens and a vision in chocolate stands there. She's about three feet tall, bobbed hair with a giant pink bow in the side, a smocked dress that looks as if it is supposed to be pink, huge brown eyes that open wide when she sees Vicky, and she is almost entirely covered, from her nose to her knees, in smeared chocolate.

Behind her comes the overweight retriever, wagging his tail furiously as he licks the little girl's fingers, then attempts to eat her dress.

"Oh dear," Vicky says, unsure of what to do. "Um, has your mummy seen you?"

The little girl shakes her head.

"Grace!" Jared climbs down off the piano stool and stands sternly in front of his sister. "Where did you get chocolate from? And Ginger's not allowed chocolate. It's very dangerous."

"No!" Grace frowns, then dives into the very expensive-looking sofa, leaving streaks of brown all over it.

"Oh Christ," Vicky mutters. It's one thing to deal with family, but these children are not family, and she's really not sure what she should do. She thinks about picking Grace up to take her out of the room, but Grace doesn't know her.

"Come on, Grace," she says, holding out her hand, and Grace slides a sticky, chocolate-covered hand into hers. "Let's go and find your mummy."

Amber's hands fly up to her mouth. "Oh my goodness," she says. "Gracie, what have you been eating?"

"I ate the chocolate that is in the pantry," Grace announces seriously, pulling out a kitchen chair.

"Don't touch anything!" Amber shrieks, as Vicky stands by, feeling helpless.

"Do you want me to clean her up?" Vicky says.

"No, don't worry, I'll do it."

"Mom?" Jared comes running into the kitchen. "Grace fed chocolate to Ginger."

Amber's face falls. "You did?"

Grace shakes her head. "No, I did not feed Ginger. Ginger and I did eat the chocolate together."

"Oh God," Amber sighs. "How much chocolate? Where did you get it from?"

Grace leads her into the pantry where Amber discovers that Grace and Ginger have polished off almost the entire stash of chocolate on the top shelf. The evidence is still in the pantry—a box in the middle of the floor, that Grace had used to clamber up, then climbing the shelves like a ladder.

"Grace!" Amber admonishes sternly. "I've told you before, you are not allowed to help yourself to food in the pantry. And why did you let Ginger have chocolate?"

"Chocolate is very dangerous for dogs," Jared interjects sternly to Grace, whose lower lip starts wobbling. "Now Ginger's going to die and it's all your fault."

"Oh Jared, stop it!" Amber says, as Grace begins to cry, although he has a point. "Right." She wets some paper towel and cleans Grace's hands and face, then pulls her dress over her head.

"Lavinia!" she yells, and a middle-aged Jamaican woman comes into the room, nodding coolly at Vicky.

"Lavinia, I've got to take Ginger to the vet. Will you stay with the kids?"

"No, Mommy!" Gracie now starts wailing and attempting to cling to Amber's legs, and Lavinia attempts to pry her free. "No, Mommy! No, Mommy! Stay with me!" Grace's voice rises to a shriek, and Amber feels her patience coming to an end, particularly because Ginger is suddenly looking rather ill.

"Lavinia, get them out of here," she snaps, as Jared starts crying too.

"I'll stay with them," Vicky says. "Don't worry, you just take Ginger. We'll be fine."

"Oh my gosh, I'm so embarrassed," Amber says, as she bundles Ginger out the door. "I promise you they're not normally like this. They're normally the perfect children. I can't believe the impression we must be making."

"They're gorgeous," Vicky says. "Off you go. Don't worry about a thing."

"Mrs. . . ." Jared stops. "What's your name again?"

"It's Vicky." Vicky smiles. "My friends call me Vicky, so you can call me Vicky too."

"Oh." Jared looks worried. "But Mom and Dad say I have to call grown-ups Mr. and Mrs."

"Well, I understand that, but I like being called Vicky."

Jared still looks doubtful, and suddenly his face lights up. "I know!" he says. "I'll call you Mrs. Vicky!"

"Ah. Well, the thing is, I'm not married, so if you were going to call me anything it would be Miss Vicky, although," she leans forward and drops her voice to a whisper, "I'd still prefer it if you called me Vicky."

"If you're not married does that mean you haven't got kids?"

"Nope, no kids."

"And no Daddy?"

"Nope. Just me."

"Do you want kids?"

"Oh yes. I love kids."

"I have a Daddy."

"Yes I know. I'm looking forward to meeting him."

Jared studies Vicky. He likes her. He just can't figure out who she is. "Are you a friend of my mommy's?"

"Not exactly. But hopefully we'll become friends." Vicky hesitates, wondering whether to even try and explain that she may be coming to stay here for a little bit while their mother goes on holiday, but no, that's for Amber to explain.

"So, do you like basketball?" Jared says hopefully.

"Well, I've never played, but I've always wanted to learn. You look as if you're really good at basketball, do you want to take me outside and teach me?"

"Yeah! Cool!" Jared says, as he runs out to the mud room and puts on his shoes.

By the time Amber gets home with a two-week supply of charcoal tablets for Ginger, Vicky has shot hoops with Jared, has sat at the kitchen table with Jared and Gracie while they have their dinner—chicken nuggets and French fries followed by ice cream in a cone—has played with them in the garden, climbing to the top of the swing set with them and pushing Gracie high on the swing, and has helped Lavinia bathe both of them.

And the children are just as lovely as they had looked in the photograph. They are both sweet, well behaved, and thrilled to have a grown-up like Vicky be so interested in them. When Amber walks in Gracie is curled up on Vicky's lap, sucking her thumb and clutching Lambie, ready for bed.

Gracie looks up to see Amber, then closes her eyes and continues stroking Lambie's right leg, her comfort zone of choice.

"Wow!" Amber cannot believe how quickly the kids have taken to Vicky, although she can see why. Under different circumstances Vicky might have become a friend, and who knows, after this is done, maybe they will become friends. Because suddenly this seems far more of a reality than a dream. The fact of Vicky being here, the fact that Amber likes her, and, more important, that the children like her, enables Amber to breathe a sigh of relief.

Four weeks is a long time to be away from your family, particularly when the woman who will be replacing you is someone you don't know. But even in the few hours since Vicky has been here, Amber can see that they will all be fine. That Vicky will look after the children just as well as Amber. And possibly even better, she thinks with a pang of guilt that she quickly suppresses. Now it just remains to be seen what Richard thinks.

Richard, poor Richard, is dreading coming home to find The Journalist there. He knows her name is Vicky Townsley, but refuses to think of her by name, demonizing her instead by referring to her only as The Journalist, aka the woman who is destroying his life.

Okay, okay, so he knows that may be a bit dramatic, but if The Journalist hadn't written that piece in *Poise!* magazine, if he hadn't bought that damned magazine for Amber that day, if Amber hadn't written the letter, none of this would be happening.

And it's not as if there isn't enough stress going on in his life right now. God knows he wishes he could talk to Amber about work, but he doesn't want her to worry about what's going on in his life, and he figures it will all sort itself out pretty soon.

But then to add to all this stress The Journalist, that goddamned journalist, is going to be there when he gets home, which is the last thing he needs. He's so angry with Amber. He read her letter this morning on the train, but he still doesn't understand. If she's unhappy, then he must be the cause of that unhappiness, even though he doesn't think he's done anything wrong.

She may say it's not a trial separation, more of an experiment, but since when do happily married wives leave their husbands and children for four weeks? Four weeks! It's not like she's asking to go off to a spa with the girls for the weekend, that he would understand. But she's asking to go for four whole weeks, and to go and live the life of a single girl, which is the part he finds most worrying.

Why would she want to be single? Why does she want to live in a flat off Marylebone High Street, work on a magazine, hang out in bars and clubs in London of all places, when she has everything she could possibly want or need right here in Highfield?

It's not as if he doesn't understand where she's coming from—he also finds the competitiveness of Highfield living exhausting and stressful, particularly given the state of his work at the moment, but how on earth could leaving change anything? How does going to London—London!—for four weeks make a difference? She says she needs a break from her life, but what if, and this is the thought that terrifies him most of all, what if she likes it?

And therein lies his biggest fear. What if she's lying, if secretly she's been planning to leave him, is treating this as a test run for a single life? Because while Richard's life may not be perfect, the one thing he's absolutely sure of is Amber. She remains the best thing that's ever happened to him, the only woman he ever wanted to marry, and even though he is occasionally irritated by her lack of confidence, the lack of confidence that sends her running into Prada and spending thousands of unnecessary dollars without even thinking, the real Amber is still the greatest woman he has ever known, and he doesn't want their marriage to change.

Change is the single most terrifying aspect of Richard's life. It is fear of change that kept him at Godfrey Hamilton Saltz for ten years. Fear of change that has stopped him from leaving the trading floor altogether and utilizing the entrepreneurial skills he is convinced he has, buying a small, ailing company and building it into something large and profitable and wonderful.

Fear of change that has kept him in Highfield, dragged him down to the playground on Sunday mornings with the kids to talk shop with the other dads, made him put on his tux a few times a year to accompany Amber to the social gatherings of the season, be gracious and charming to women like Suzy Bartlow and Nadine Potts, women whose evil he could sense, whose ostentation made his stomach turn.

It is fear of change that has kept him exactly where he is, even when he knows he is not sure how much longer he can go on. Fear of change that has kept him on the death train at five-twenty in the morning three days a week, on his way to an office he cannot stand, with people looking over his shoulder at every move, waiting for him to recoup the enormous losses he has caused, judging him as somehow unworthy because he was not making as much money as the others. And we wonder why he is stressed.

Richard stands up when the train pulls into Highfield and takes a deep breath as he steps off the train and goes to find his car in its usual spot in the commuter parking lot—the spot that he had to wait four years for, the spot he's never going to give up, even if he found he was no longer working in the city . . .

Time to go home and meet The Journalist. He throws his briefcase in the back of the car and switches on the engine. Maybe she'll be awful, he thinks. Maybe Amber will hate her, will refuse to leave the children with her. Maybe this won't happen after all, and feeling slightly better with this thought, he starts the drive home.

Chapter Seventeen

The four days with Vicky Townsley are far better than Richard expects. Not that he sees her much, apart from the evenings, of course, but there is something very cute about her, and he can see how much the children take to her, and suddenly it doesn't seem quite so frightening. In fact, if anything, he is beginning to look at it in much the same way as Amber, as an adventure.

Amber is more excited than he's seen her in years. Amber is more excited than she's been in years. Within the first five minutes of seeing how Richard and Vicky get on, Amber knows that everything is going to be all right, that Richard is going to come around, and that Vicky is going to be absolutely fine stepping into her shoes. Now all she has to worry about is stepping into Vicky's.

Amber had been dreading Richard coming home, particularly after the cold front that has existed in their house. As charming as Richard is, he has the ability to be completely charmless when he wishes, and she has been terrified Richard will put Vicky off, that Vicky will decide not to choose her, based on the rudeness or truculence of her husband.

A less secure woman might be concerned at Richard's transformation. He left the house in such a bad mood,

comes home scowling, and then seems to become charm itself as Vicky talks to him.

And Vicky is attractive. Cute in a very English way.
Peaches and cream complexion, good figure although it
could be a lot better with some time in a gym, and surprisingly good teeth, although it shouldn't be a surprise, except
that Amber, like so many Americans, presumes that in England all the food is terrible and everyone has dreadful teeth.

"How do you do?" Vicky puts the knife down on the
chopping board where Amber has put her in charge of the
salad—Amber having decided to cook, trying to show Vicky
that she is the perfect wife and mother, that she does not, in
fact, delegate everything to Lavinia, but that she runs her
charity work, looks after the children, rushes the dog to the
vet in an emergency, and still has time to look great.

In other words, Amber is trying to prove she is Super-
woman. Although Vicky isn't to know that that is not the
case.

Vicky shakes Richard's hand warmly, with a genuine smile,
slightly taken aback by how attractive he is. Perhaps it is true,
she thinks, smiling into Richard's baby-blue eyes, noting how
tall he is, how broad his shoulders. Perhaps everything really
is bigger and better in America, because they certainly don't
make many men like this at home. It's not that Richard is
spectacularly good-looking, he just has that glow of All-
American health that Vicky finds so appealing, and although
Richard is not conscious of the effect he is having on Vicky,
he finds his own eyes twinkling back at hers, and his smile in
response far warmer than he expected, and maybe this won't
be so bad after all.

Not that he'd ever be unfaithful to Amber. Not that he

thinks he would be sleeping with this other woman, but she's so cute! With her little English accent and flushed cheeks.

How could he have possibly thought this woman had come to destroy his marriage? In her little flippy Boden skirt and layered vests, appliquéd flats on her feet, how would someone as adorable as this ever be a problem and, more to the point, how is she not married?

"You're The Journalist?" Richard asks, as Amber beams, seeing that he likes Vicky, that he's intrigued. "The single woman from London?"

"That would be me," Vicky grins. "The spinster with just my cat for company, who's desperate to get married."

"Who? You or the cat?" Richard grins back.

"Both!" Vicky laughs.

"But how are you not married?" Richard is genuinely bemused. "You're so cute!"

And Vicky, unused to compliments such as this, such open compliments from such an attractive man, flushes all the way up to her hairline as Amber laughs. "Oh Richard! You've embarrassed her." But Amber is delighted at Richard's openness, delighted that he thinks she's cute—perhaps now he'll be happy about the prospect of the swap.

Just in case you were wondering, Amber is not concerned about Richard's fidelity. Amber is not one of those women who has experienced hardships with men. Hardships in practically every other area of her life, but her natural coolness when she was younger always intrigued men, and she tended to be the dumper rather than the dumpee.

She had never understood girlfriends who put up with their men mistreating them, who allowed their men back after they had admitted to affairs. Amber was black and white about infidelity. Her life had been too hard as a child for her to put up with lies or problems as an adult. If Richard were to be unfaithful, their marriage would be over. That's it. No second chances, no room for discussion. Amber would simply move on and start again.

But still, she never expected it to happen. One of the reasons she had fallen in love with Richard, one of the qualities that still makes him stand out in her eyes, is his integrity, his knowledge of right from wrong, his strong moral core, and Amber knows that Richard is not a man who would have a flippant affair. Not just because he knows Amber would leave him in a heartbeat, but because he genuinely wouldn't be able to do it.

Richard is a family man through and through. He loves Amber, he loves his kids, he wouldn't jeopardize it for a quick fling. And perhaps this is why Amber doesn't mind the twinkle in his eye when he looks at Vicky. For she is cute. It's lovely that he thinks that, and that it would never occur to him to take it further.

"Does Vicky get to sleep on your side of the bed while you're in London?" Richard grins, looking at Amber, and Amber rolls her eyes.

"Only in your dreams, Richard," she says, turning to see the flush back on Vicky's face.

"Oh God," Vicky groans. "I'm completely embarrassing myself here. I'm supposed to be a professional journalist and the pair of you are making me blush like a teenager. I'm going to need to go outside and get some air in a minute."

"How about a drink instead?" Amber says. "Richard, darling, will you pour us some wine?"

"Yes, darling," Richard says, leaning over and giving Amber a kiss, and Amber knows that everything is going to be all right.

* * *

The evening is a delight. Vicky keeps them both laughing with stories about being single in London, and asks lots of questions about their life in Highfield. Richard goes very quiet when Amber explains why she doesn't feel entirely happy here, but ultimately he says he understands, that he feels the same pressures Amber does, but because he's removed from it for most of the day he doesn't feel it with quite the same intensity.

"But why don't you move if it's that competitive?" Vicky takes a sip of her third glass of wine.

Amber shrugs. "I'm not sure that it would be that different anywhere else, or at least, anywhere that's within commutable distance to Wall Street. Also the schools in Highfield are amazing, so we save vast amounts of money by not having to send our kids to private school; and in many ways this town is wonderful."

"The quality of life here is great," Richard agrees. "So you have this running battle with yourself, weighing up the pros and cons, asking yourself whether it's worth it, and the pros always seem to outweigh the cons."

Amber turns to Richard. "I didn't know you felt it as strongly as I do." The surprise is obvious in her face.

"I do, I just don't talk about it because I can't see it changing, but also, and don't get mad at me for saying this, but you come up against it every day because of the women you choose to mix with."

Amber visibly bristles. "Are you saying I choose to mix with Suzy . . . and Nadine?"

Richard sighs. "I knew you'd get mad. And no, I'm not saying you choose to mix with them, but you do choose to do all the work you do for the League, and while I know it's all for a good cause, you know just as well as I do that it's just a thin disguise for social climbing, and that you get sucked in to all that crap with everyone else."

Amber is silent for a while, and then she shrugs and looks at Vicky. "That's why I want to do this. Because Richard's right. Being head of the committee that runs the Summer Gala for the League, or the summer house tour, isn't about raising the most money for charity, it's about being queen bee, about having all the other women in town know that you're at the top of the ladder, and it's cliquey, and bitchy, and"—Amber takes a deep breath—"and I just need to get away for a while. To reevaluate."

Vicky swallows hard. "Wow. And it seems as if your life is so perfect."

"And you know what? It is pretty perfect." Amber gestures around her. "I have a wonderful husband and a wonderful marriage. I live in a big, beautiful house. On the outside I look as if I have everything I could possibly want, but there's just so much *stuff*. Sometimes I look at everything I have, the clothes in my closet, the staff we need to maintain this house, and I just want out. I want a simpler life. I want to live in a small house with a couple of pairs of jeans and some sneakers. I just don't want all this stuff anymore." Her voice is rising with passion and Richard looks at her in shock.

"Honey," he says, "I never knew you felt this way."

"But that's what I've been trying to tell you," she says. "That's why I had to respond to Vicky's article. Because I don't know if that feeling is real or not. Oh God," she says. "I sound like a madwoman. I feel like I'm on this pendulum, swinging back and forth. Some mornings I wake up and I love everything about my life. I go out for lunch and dress up in my designer clothes and have a meeting with Amberley Jacks, and it's fun and I love it, even though it feels like I'm playing a big game.

"And other days," she continues, "I get up and go out and feel overwhelmed by everything. I don't want to have to compete with other women to see who paid the most for their outfit, or who ran up a bigger account at Rakers last year. I don't care about having the latest Balenciaga bag. . . ."

Vicky opens her eyes wide in surprise. "I thought this was the country!" she says. "The women here have Balenciaga bags?"

Ambers laughs. "I thought it was the country too, but it's not. It's the suburbs, and that's a whole other ball game, especially in Highfield. Oh yes, they have Balenciaga bags, or Birkins if they're really lucky, but not during the day unless you're meeting the girls for lunch."

"So what do they wear during the day?"

"Generally workout gear—you're supposed to look as if you're just running some errands while on your way to the gym, but you have to have enormous diamond studs"— Amber gestures to her own diamond studs with a roll of her eyes and Vicky laughs—"the latest Pumas, some cute yoga/Pilates pants, and a great bag. Honey," she places a hand on Vicky's arm and looks into her eyes, "it's all in the accessories."

"Far be it from me to throw a wrench in the works," Richard says, "but isn't that exactly what you wear pretty much every day? Isn't this a case of the pot calling the kettle black?"

"But that's the point," Amber sighs. "Some days I can see that carrying the right bag is indeed a matter of life and death, but more and more I'm starting to think that none of this matters. That since when did the size of your earrings or the label on the inside of your bag demonstrate what kind of person you are? I'm fed up with this consumerism, this perfectionism, with constantly competing with everyone else. Jesus, I wasn't brought up like this. I don't even know how I got here."

"Wow, that's quite a speech." Richard shakes his head as he looks at his wife.

"I'm sorry, honey, but it's true. The only good stuff, the only things I would never ever change are my family, my husband and my kids."

"So this really isn't about me?" Richard says softly.

"Oh sweetie." Amber gets up from the table and puts her arms around Richard from behind, nuzzling his neck. "I adore you. You're the best thing that ever happened to me. How could this be about you?"

Richard looks up at Vicky. "So when are you thinking of doing this?"

Vicky smiles. "I'll get in touch with Hugh, the director, to see what works best for him, and then we're pretty much all set."

"Director?" Amber and Richard disengage and look at Vicky in confusion. "What director?"

"Ah yes." Vicky takes a deep breath. "I knew there was something else I meant to tell you."

It is the only wrench in the works. Richard point-blank refuses to be filmed for television. And in the end, Vicky concedes, knowing that it is the only way she will get them to agree, and as good as the publicity would have been for *Poise!*, there's no TV show without the swap, and the magazine comes first.

And she has to admit she is slightly disappointed. While she told Hugh Janus that she didn't want to be famous, since they had decided to do it she'd talked herself into quite enjoying the fame and potential fortune that would arise. Because don't stars automatically become friends with other stars? She and Julia Roberts might start hanging out, she could definitely see Julia becoming a friend of hers. Vicky might help her get through those first difficult couple of years with the twins, perhaps Julia and Danny could bring the kids down to Kate and Andy's for the weekend.

Or maybe Michael Douglas and Catherine Zeta-Jones. She could see them becoming friends. Could imagine the kids hanging out together while she and Jamie Donnelly sip cocktails with Michael and Cat—do her friends call her Cat, she wonders, or Cathy, perhaps, or Cath?—on the terrace of their house in Bermuda.

Oh yes. Being famous wouldn't be so bad at all, thank you very much, but Vicky files away her daydreams for another time. Clearly she is not going to be the reality star of this TV show after all. Now she just has to phone Hugh Janus and tell him, and after that find a way of breaking the news to Janelle.

By the time Amber and Richard clear up after dinner—Vicky offered to help but the poor girl was almost comatose with jet lag so they sent her to bed—the cold front between them has evaporated completely, and Richard looks at Amber and raises an eyebrow, the look that signals he's feeling frisky, he's up for it tonight.

Normally Amber would groan, would hurriedly think of an excuse, would claim to have her period, or gas, or something, but she's missed Richard these last few days, has missed chatting to him on the phone all day long—for Richard is one of those men who phone their wife several times during the day to touch base, has hated how cold he has been since she told him Vicky was coming, and this is the least she can do.

And so they go up to bed, Amber puts on her pajamas, climbs into bed and into Richard's arms. Fifteen minutes later she pecks him on the lips, says, "I love you," turns the bedside light back on and picks up her magazine as Richard goes to the bathroom to clean up.

"I like her," Richard says, climbing back into bed and taking Amber's hand, grateful to have his wife back, to have the status quo returned to their marriage.

"I can tell." Amber gives him a look and he laughs. "But she is cute. And smart, and the kids like her. I think you'll probably have an amazing time with her. God, you might not want me to come home."

"Don't say that," Richard admonishes. "But I agree that she's far better than I expected. And I love the way she speaks."

"Just don't love it too much." Amber smiles. "So you're really okay with this? With me going ahead and flying to London for four weeks?"

Richard shrugs. "I have to be, don't I? If I asked you not to go, would you not go?"

Amber pauses and looks Richard in the eye.

"Exactly," Richard says, not needing an answer. "I know your mind's made up so I have to accept it. I guess I'm just relieved that I'm not being left with some awful woman while you're gone. At least I know it will be kind of fun."

"Just as long as you were joking when you made that comment about her sleeping on my side of the bed . . ."

"Just as long as you don't think you're going to be picking up strange men in bars and bringing them home to your super-hip bachelorette pad in London . . ." Richard smiles.

Amber snorts. "God, as if anyone would want me. I'm thirty-five and the mother of two children. Nobody even looks at me anymore. All of a sudden I go into stores and I'm not Miss anymore, I'm Ma'am. How did that happen? Tell me the truth, does Vicky look much younger than me? Because I bet she still gets called Miss. How is it that I look middle-aged and she doesn't? Is it just having kids? The physical wear and tear on my body?"

"First of all," Richard strokes her thigh appreciatively, "as cute as Vicky is, you have a much better body, and that's despite having two children."

"I do?" Amber perks up.

"You do. But secondly, she doesn't have any responsibilities. I hate to say it, but she doesn't look like a mom."

"And I do?"

"You look like a woman who's had some experience in life, but I love that about you. I think you're far more beautiful now than when we met."

Amber's eyes light up. "You really do?"

"I do. I think you have a maturity now that I love."

"But what about these," Amber smoothes out the frown lines on her forehead, "and these?" She traces the lines from her nose to her mouth. "Vicky doesn't seem to have all these lines."

"She's probably Botoxed them out," Richard says.

"Do you think?"

Richard shrugs. "She does work on a women's magazine. She probably gets offered shots of Botox with her sandwich at lunchtime."

"God, I never thought of that. I think I should do it. I should go and get some. These lines make me feel so old."

"I love your lines," Richard says. "They're the marks of your life. I love that you have a few stretch marks on your stomach, they tell me the story of our children. And I love your frown lines," he leans forward and kisses them. "I love that whenever you're concentrating on something you frown. I don't want you to Botox anything. I love you exactly as you are."

Amber smiles at him and kisses him lovingly. "Do you know how lucky I am to have a man like you?"

"Yes," he says as he kisses her back. "Do you know how lucky you are to have a man like me?"

"Yes," she says happily. "But seriously, just a little bit of Botox?" She frowns as she pulls the skin between her eyebrows taut. "Just here?"

"Oh go to sleep," Richard laughs, and turns off the lamp on his side of the bed.

The rest of the trip is smooth. Vicky accompanies Amber to school to drop off Gracie, to a Little League game for Jared, to lunch with Deborah, with whom Vicky instantly feels a kinship, another English girl abroad.

"It's going to be a great piece," she tells Janelle, when she calls her for the second time, having already broken the bad news about the TV show. "I'm just sorry they won't agree to TV because it would have been great."

"I've got a conference call with Hugh Janus tomorrow,"

Janelle soothes. "We're going to see if there's anything else we can work on together. So is it very *Desperate Housewives*, darling?"

"There's nothing desperate about this life," Vicky laughs. "Wait until you see the house. It's like a bloody palace."

"Do you think she'll cope with your little flat, then?"

"You know what? I think she's a hell of a lot stronger than she appears. I think she's going to be absolutely fine."

Chapter Eighteen

"If I'd known how much work was involved," Vicky moans one evening when her sister-in-law phones to see how she's getting on, "I never would have done this."

"What kind of work? Still sorting out your flat?"

"How can a flat this small contain so much junk? How have I managed to accumulate this much crap in so short a time? I've only had this flat two years, and now it's stuffed to the gills. I never realized how much of this stuff is completely superfluous." Vicky is sitting on the floor of the tiny second bedroom that doubles as her office, sifting through yet another pile.

Thus far she has found four unpaid bills, all of which are a minimum of four months old; two invitations to parties, both of which she realizes she not only missed, but never even rsvp'd; a press release about a new method of laser vein removal that she'd brought home from work, not wanting anyone to know she was about to get the spider veins in her legs treated, and had been looking for for weeks; her driver's license—how in the hell did that get there? Wasn't it always in her bag?—and some readers' letters that she had brought home to respond to, but that had swiftly been eaten up by the pile.

"And what about the notes?" Kate says. "How are you getting on with telling Amber how you live your life?"

"So far I'm on page twenty-three," Vicky groans. "Does that answer your question?"

"Sounds like far too much work to me. So are we going to see you this weekend? The kids miss you, and frankly I'm not sure how much more of their whining I can take."

"Nothing like a bit of guilt to get me down to the country." Vicky rolls her eyes. "Thanks, Kate."

"I didn't mean it like that."

"Okay. Sorry. I'm just stressed. And yes, I'd love to come this weekend. I need a complete break from London, but you have to tell the kids I need a lie-in. The last thing I want to do is arrive in Connecticut next week with enormous bags under my eyes."

"God, it's next week. I can't believe you're actually going through with it. I can't believe it's happening, and so soon! Oh and before I forget," Kate smoothly changes the subject, "please please please bring me some tarama from Waitrose."

Vicky sighs. "How many packs this time?"

"Can you bring ten? That way I can stick them in the freezer until you get back, although if Amber is really being you for four weeks I suppose I can always get her to bring down a load too."

"Why not take advantage and get her to bring down fifty?"

Kate starts cackling. "Do you know what, that's a bloody good idea."

Vicky goes to the bathroom and sighs as she scrapes her hair back and examines her spotty chin and bleary eyes in the mirror.

"God," she mutters. "I'm thirty-five. I'm not supposed to still be getting bloody spots."

She is exhausted, had no idea quite how much she would have to do. First there were the notes: copious notes about all her friends, because Amber will have to step into the friendships as if she has always been there—what is the purpose of this swap after all, if not to fully inhabit the life of the swapee?

Ruth

The most important person at Poise!. *She's my extremely able, sparkly assistant (although sparkles are usually only on her T-shirts). She's very clever, horribly efficient and organized, and usually gets me to where I need to be. She's also a wonderful foil for Janelle's assistant, Caroline, who's bloody terrifying on a good day and monstrous on a bad (remember, Janelle's the editor). Caroline and Ruth are, bizarrely, friends, which keeps Caroline off my back. However, you shouldn't have to worry about Caroline as everyone knows you're my stand-in, so they won't expect too much, and I'm leaving everything in shape just so you don't get into trouble. Leona—more on her later—is going to pretty much do my job while I'm gone. You're going to be fine. Ruth completely adores Crunchie bars, so if you really want to get her on your side bring her a Crunchie when you come back from the canteen. She'll pretend to be upset because it ruins her diet, but she'll love you for it.*

Leona

I love her, she's my closest friend at work and will probably become yours. She's the features editor, which is much like the features director except she gets to do a bit more of the grunt work, and I get to go on snazzier lunches. But don't tell her I said that. She's always late for work—has two small kids at home—is funny and sarcastic, and usually wears fantastically expensive designer clothes that are covered with

stains, have unraveling hems, and look as though they cost a fiver at
Top Shop. She is my port in every storm, and is great for drinks after
work, although her nanny finishes at 8 p.m., so you have to get her
early. Which reminds me, I don't even know how much you drink. I always think that Americans don't drink or smoke at all, and I hope
that if that is the case you'll be able to change that for the four weeks
you're being me, because I have to say I do love a glass of wine, and after about three glasses I start hitting the cigarettes—Marlboro Light.

So, there are my biggest vices. Drinking and social smoking, but if
you really really hate smoking, then you won't have to do it.

Kate and Andy; Luke, Polly, and Sophie

Andy's my younger brother, Kate is his wife and the sister I always
wanted, and the three cheeky monkeys obviously my nephew and nieces.
Andy basically has the life I always wanted. They live in a fantastic
house in the country, and I know you'll love them because it will remind
you of home, although their house is much much smaller and much much
dirtier. They do however have big hairy dogs that may remind you of
Ginger, and lots of small children who are gorgeous and cuddly. They
also have chickens now, but don't know much about them. Am going to
see them before I go so if there's anything spectacular to report, will do so.

Suffice to say their home is my haven, and I try to go down at least
once a month, and preferably twice. I know I've written this somewhere
else, but I'm out so much during the week, usually to work things, that
I tend to be really quiet on the weekend, and if there's nothing going on
I just hop on the train (from Waterloo Station—I've left the schedule
pinned up on the noticeboard in the kitchen), and spend the weekend
with them. The children, by the way, are very easily manipulated by the
use of Smarties (the English equivalent of M&Ms). Oh God. I do
seem to use chocolate rather a lot to get people on my side, don't I? —
Am feeling very guilty and wondering what you think of me . . . Still, if
you go down laden with tubes of Smarties you'll definitely be the most

popular girl on the block. I have told Luke, Polly, and Sophie about this, but they don't quite understand that a lady with a funny accent will be coming to see them, wearing my clothes, and pretending to be me.

Kate is on hand for anything at all you need. She's immensely wise and sensible, and always at home—I know you'll love her.

Vicky continues writing about her friends who are likely to pop up—Deborah, the married one with three children in Hampstead; Jackie, the radio producer; and the rest of the people at work.

And then, of course, there is Jamie Donnelly. Should she write something about Jamie Donnelly? Because she has been seeing him these past few weeks, although mostly late at night, when he phones after a meeting, desperate to see her, but it's his busiest time, putting together a new comedy show, and she's hoping it will all change soon. He is so perfect for her; it is so very easy for her to see them together that she knows it is only a matter of time before he realizes the very same thing.

Because it's not as if he isn't keen. And when they are together, their chemistry is undeniable. And he was genuinely disappointed when Vicky told him about Swapping Lives, that she would be in America for four weeks, although she was slightly perturbed when he seemed to perk up after seeing pictures of Amber.

"She's a married woman!" Vicky had attempted a jokey voice. "And sleeping with you isn't part of the swap."

"But if you're going to swap lives, then surely it is?" Jamie had said, admiring Amber's long legs and flat stomach. "Christ, has she really had two children?"

"Yes she has. And meanwhile, you don't think I'm going to be sleeping with her husband, do you? How would you feel about that?"

"I wouldn't mind," Jamie had said. "It's all in the name of research." He'd looked up and seen Vicky's crestfallen face. "Oh come here." He had opened his arms and she had fallen gratefully into them. "I was only joking. The only woman I want to be with is you."

The only woman I want to be with is you.

The only woman I want to be with is you.

The only woman I want to be with is you.

See? Why on earth would he have said that if he hadn't meant it? Vicky takes those words and cherishes them, rolls them over and over in her mind, tastes them on her tongue, tastes the sweetness and longing when she hears them. This is surely meant to be, she thinks happily, remembering the way he held open his arms, trying not to think of how difficult it will be to be away from him for four weeks.

Jamie Donnelly

I've been seeing him for a little while, but he knows I'm going to be living your life for four weeks and I don't think you're going to be seeing him that much. But, *if he does call, get him to take you to Soho House as he knows everyone there and it will be fun for you. I don't think you would know him, but in England he's very famous, has a huge hit comedy series, and is Irish and very twinkly and sexy. It's very early days but I'm hoping it will become something more serious—he's definitely the kind of man I've been looking for.*

Daniel

Ah Daniel. How do I describe Daniel? He works in TV, lives round the corner, is a complete commitaphobe who has women falling all over him because they can somehow sense he's not for the taking so they view him as an enormous challenge. I seem to be the only woman who hasn't fallen head over heels, and as a consequence he likes me enormously and trusts me. I think he's fantastic, and the perfect neighborhood shag. Do you have that word in America? He's basically the man I call late at night when I'm feeling horny. Oh God. I've probably completely shocked you. I'm so sorry, but this is the life of a single girl, and I'm hoping you can remember when you must have done the same thing. So, if the phone starts ringing at midnight, it's probably going to be Daniel, and even though he also knows I'm gone for a while, he may just try his luck with you. Oh, and before you think I'm a complete slut, I have to say I haven't been sleeping with Daniel since I started seeing Jamie Donnelly, but every now and then we'll go out for a drink or dinner locally. It's not romantic, but it's fun, and he's a good guy, even though I'd hate to fall for him. Still, don't say I haven't warned you. . . .

And then there are the notes on her life, her routine, where she goes, what shops she uses, even her PIN for her ATM card, which she types through gritted teeth, having been trained never to give that number to anyone.

Oh God, she thinks. What if Amber's a psycho? What if she seems completely normal but in fact turns out to be a single white female who comes over here and takes over my life? What if she steals all my money, not that there's that much to steal, sleeps with Jamie Donnelly, fucks up my job, rips up my clothes . . . okay, okay, Vicky, take a deep breath. Now you're being ridiculous. And she goes ahead and writes down her PIN.

Meat comes from the butcher round the corner. Cheese from the cheese shop over the road. Anything else, go to Waitrose on the High Street (and look out for Madonna, I have spotted her in there a couple of times). I'm incredibly lazy about cooking, although every now and then I'll catch Nigella on the box and be inspired. Mostly in the evenings I'll just eat crackers and dips with some vegetables. Basically anything that doesn't need cooking, although to be honest I'm very rarely at home in the evenings. The only things that are always in my fridge are wine, Diet Coke, and chocolate if I get a craving.

Providores does fantastic coffee, and the Orrery is across the street, which is delicious but v. expensive—recommend it highly but only for work dinners that you can expense!

I know you'll have a fantastic time discovering the shops here. VV Rouleaux has amazing trim, although can't think why you'd need it. Nice place to browse, though. Kate sends me to Rachel Riley for the children's clothes—she'll probably put an order in with you as the sale starts while I'm away, and Kate can resist everything except a Rachel Riley sale. Oh, also Kate will be demanding you bring her taramasalata from Waitrose. Only do it if it's okay. She won't mind if you say no.

Selfridges is up the road, and any time I feel a bout of compulsive spending coming on, it's up to Selfridges I go—you'll definitely find your fill of Balenciaga bags in there, but remember, you're using my month's salary, and I definitely can't afford to buy designer stuff very often! (I, however, will thoroughly enjoy shopping in Highfield, although don't worry too much—I did listen when you said Richard wanted you to stop spending!)

And a tip at work: befriend Stella, the fashion editor. She's always got freebies lying around the fashion cupboard. I haven't bought makeup in years, and half my wardrobe is leftover from shoots that they've just forgotten about. Very unethical, I know, but if you won't tell anyone I won't. . . .

Speaking of clothes, I've been sorting out my wardrobe, because I'm completely embarrassed having been to your house and seen your palatial dressing room with color-coordinated clothes.

On a good note I've thrown away all my graying underwear—not that you'll be wearing my underwear, don't worry!—but it's forced me to finally get rid of it. I've also been ruthless and got rid of anything I haven't worn for a year, but unfortunately that's left me with not an awful lot.

I do tend to wear flat shoes for work, and heels in the evening. You'll notice I have a bit of a fetish for shoes and bags, but then again, what woman doesn't? Thankfully, I finally cleaned out all my handbags—I didn't want you to come over and find a pile of handbags all stuffed with rubbish, and I'm bloody pleased I did. I think I found enough crumpled tissues to stock a third-world country (why they'd need dirty crumpled tissues I don't know), seven lipsticks, three camera films that must be about a hundred years old because I've had a digital camera for three years, £67, and a bra. God knows. Don't ask. So now you have lots of super-clean, empty handbags from which to choose, although unfortunately no Birkins like yours! (That's what I'm most excited about—going out and actually carrying a real-live Hermès Birkin!)

I always oversleep, and it's always a rush to get into the office. The alarm clock next to the bed does work, but I always sleep through it; hopefully you'll be better. Sometimes I walk if I'm up early enough, or I get the Tube from Baker Street, and I'm leaving you my Travelcard. They never look at the picture, but if you feel guilty about it you can always get your own Travelcard and they'll reimburse you at the office.

I have breakfast at the office—a bagel, a yogurt, and some fruit. It sounds ridiculous saying you have to eat the same as me, but the sandwich bar on the corner has lots of different options if that sounds horrible. Although how horrible can a bagel, yogurt, and fruit be? Leona and Ruth have all my notes about work—I've left them separately at the office—and you'll be at the editorial meetings, but I don't think Janelle will expect you to contribute.

I do have a gym membership, but I haven't used it in six months. I started out with fantastic intentions, went five times a week for two months, then skipped a week because I was ill, and haven't managed to motivate myself to go back since. Still, I know that you exercise a lot, so it's there if you need it. The membership card is in my purse next to my driver's license.

Janelle says we're not allowed to talk during the swap, which I think is probably the right decision—it would be awful if you hated every-thing and were really unhappy, or vice versa. I'm sure the other one would then feel so guilty it would bring the swap to an end.

I hope I haven't overlooked anything although I'm sure I've forgotten loads. How do you put your whole life down on a few pieces of paper? But I know you'll be fine, and I so hope this is everything you expect it to be. I have this morbid fear that you'll find my flat tiny and grotty, and everything a bit small and pointless, while I live it up in your palace with your beautiful kids and nanny. Okay, I'll shut up now, just in case I'm making you miss them. So, remember to call Kate when you feel homesick, and good luck!

Vicky has finished all the piles in her office, filing papers that have been waiting to be filed for the best part of a year, cleaning the desk that hasn't seen Pledge since its long-gone days in the Ikea showroom, making sense of the mess of pa-per clips and elastic bands in the top drawer of her desk.

She has tackled her computer, defragmenting and cleaning the disk, wiping off any porn sites she may have visited—just out of curiosity, of course—over the past year, and cleaning off all the cookies.

She has rearranged her wardrobe, cleaned everything that needs to be cleaned, wiped down all the cupboards—no longer will Amber find any skeletons in there.

In short, Vicky will now be presenting her life as the quin-tessential single girl about town. With the exception of the number of Manolos in her closet (and yes, there are a few, but only a few), Vicky could now give Sarah Jessica a pretty good run for her money.

It just remains to be seen whether Amber can do the same thing.

Chapter **Nineteen**

Amber suppresses a giant yawn as she shuts the car door and heads over to the ballet school, clutching a Starbucks grande skim latte in her hand. Thank God Starbucks opens so early, she thinks, then stops in shock as she rounds the corner and sees a gaggle of women, all clutching similar cardboard coffee cups, waiting in line outside the ballet school.

Amber checks her watch. It's six twenty-three a.m. Jesus, she thinks, walking up to join the end of the line. Registration doesn't even start until eight a.m., and Amber was convinced she'd be the first woman there, although evidently twelve other women had exactly the same thought.

Amber hesitates for just a moment. In the line she can spot several women from the League, although this shouldn't surprise her, because Miss Cynthia's Ballet Academy is the one everyone wants to go to, and the competition is fierce.

There are two ballet schools in town. Miss Cynthia's Ballet Academy and the Highfield Academy of Ballet. Amber has never actually been to see the Highfield Academy of Ballet, but she knows that the girls who go there are generally the girls who didn't get into Miss Cynthia's.

For Miss Cynthia takes her ballet very seriously indeed.

The curriculum is that of the Royal Ballet School in England, and most of the mothers believe Miss Cynthia to be English, and rumor has it she is a distant cousin of the Queen. Deborah, however, being English herself, realized upon meeting Miss Cynthia that her accent, familiar though it was, had a distant ring to it that almost certainly wasn't English.

This was at one of Miss Cynthia's group meetings for prospective parents of prospective star ballerinas to come and see the school and meet Miss Cynthia. Unlike the Highfield Academy of Ballet, which will take anyone who phones up and registers their child, Miss Cynthia insists on vetting the parents first, followed by the children.

She holds these meetings at four p.m., serves English Breakfast tea, cucumber sandwiches with the crusts removed, and scones, and she speaks in upper-crust tones that would put Camilla Parker Bowles to shame.

Still, Deborah, clutching her cup of tea in one hand and her crustless cucumber sandwich in the other, concentrated fiercely as Miss Cynthia gave her speech, and suddenly, when Miss Cynthia was in the middle of describing the dress code for "her ballerinas"—the girls are never girls, always ballerinas—Deborah got it.

"Any questions?" Miss Cynthia asked at the end, with a gracious smile, her feet perfectly turned out in first position, her head cocked just so, the chic chignon at the base of her head just visible.

Deborah raised her hand. "Where are you from?" she asked pleasantly, in her much less grand, but distinctly English accent.

"I was trained at the Royal Academy of Ballet in Richmond," Miss Cynthia said, although the more perceptive among the audience noted the tension in her voice. "Any other questions?" She looked around the room, but Deborah wouldn't be put off.

"Sorry, I meant where were you born? It's just that someone told me you were English, but I definitely hear some kind of an accent and I can't figure it out."

"I spent most of my life in Richmond," Miss Cynthia said, through gritted teeth.

"But you sound ever so slightly Australian," Deborah said. "Or am I completely wrong?"

Miss Cynthia sighed. She'd never been publicly outed before, but now this irritating English girl had put her on the spot, and what was she supposed to say?

"My grandfather was English," she said. "But yes. I was born in Sydney."

"Ha! Knew it!" Deborah whispered to Amber. "Anyone who speaks with that many marbles in her mouth is definitely a fake. Cousin of the Queen indeed. Her grandfather was probably a burglar."

"So will you be sending Molly to Miss Cynthia?" Amber asked Deborah after the tea, noting the filthy looks that Miss Cynthia was shooting over at Deborah.

"Are you joking? So that pretentious old bitch can victimize her because I've got her number? No chance. I'm signing up for the Highfield Academy tomorrow. What about you?"

"I don't know." Amber frowned. "I think Gracie would love it here, and I do kind of like how seriously she takes it, how she refers to all her girls as 'ballerinas.' "

"It's up to you," Deborah shrugged, "but Molly is never going to be a ballerina anyway, not with that bottom of hers. Gets it from her mother, I'm afraid, nothing I can do, but the last thing I want is for her to feel inadequate at four years old because her ballet teacher makes her be a tree or something in the recital."

"A tree? What are you talking about?" Amber started laughing.

"Look at these thighs." Deborah gestured at her legs. "Even when I was four they were the same, only, obviously, smaller. I was about a foot taller than everyone else and chubby. I was desperate to be a fairy ballerina but my ballet teacher made me feel like a fairy elephant and, to make it worse, every year at the recital I had to be a tree. All the other girls got to wear pink sparkly tutus and tiaras and dance around prettily, and Harriet, who was also rather large, and I had to stand at the back dressed in green tutus, with crowns made of branches and tissue-paper leaves. It was a fucking nightmare."

"Oh my gosh, that's terrible," Amber said, wiping the tears of laughter away. "No really, I mean it's funny, but it's awful. What a horrible thing to do to a child. But honestly, I don't think Miss Cynthia would do that. I heard that everyone's in pink at their recitals."

"Okay, so maybe she wouldn't make Molly be a tree, but I'd still rather she went to the other one. I've heard it's much more creative, and they focus more on the kids having fun than on the serious ballet stuff. Gracie's little and delicate and Miss Cynthia will love her."

"I am probably going to put her into Miss Cynthia's," Amber nodded, "but I do agree Miss Cynthia seems like a bit of a cow. Maybe for Christmas I'll give her a jar of that disgusting Australian stuff that they all eat. What's it called? Marmite?"

"No, not Marmite, that's English. It's Vegemite!" Deborah

started laughing. "Oh God, would you, please? Give her a jar of Vegemite and a didgeridoo to remind her of home." And with that the two of them started shaking with laughter, until tears were streaming down their faces.

Meanwhile Gracie does love her ballet classes. And Molly does love hers. Amber has her reservations about Miss Cynthia, particularly after one of the little girls, Hannah Greenberg, disappeared in the middle of last term. She had been getting a little chubbier, and Suzy said she'd bumped into Hannah's mother, Rachel, who said Miss Cynthia had asked her to try and watch what Hannah was eating, and Rachel had been so horrified she'd pulled Hannah immediately from the class.

But who knows whether it was actually true or not, and until Miss Cynthia did or said something unforgivable to Amber, Gracie was going to continue going there, even if it did mean getting in line at the ungodly hour of six twenty-three in the morning at the beginning of every term to ensure her spot.

"Amber!" Amber looks up and spies Nadine from the League standing a few people in front of her.

"Hi, Nadine!" Amber says. "How are you?"

"I'm great," Nadine says. "How are you?"

"Incredibly busy," Amber laughs. "Life is going crazy."

Nadine smiles and there's a long silence that always makes Amber feel uncomfortable, and she does what she always does when people just stand and look at her silently, as if in expectation—she gets verbal diarrhea and starts talking, nineteen to the dozen, just to fill the silence.

"I'm off to London tomorrow," she says. "For four weeks, which is completely insane, but I'm doing this Swapping

Lives piece for this English magazine where I swap lives with a single girl and she comes and sees what it's like to be married with children, and now I can't believe how much I have to do and I haven't even packed although frankly I'm not even sure what I'm supposed to bring because I'm meant to wear all the other girl's clothes and she's supposed to wear mine, and now I just don't know what I've let myself in for." Amber takes a breath. Shit, she thinks. As usual, too much information.

"You're doing *what*?" Nadine says, as the other women in between them also turn round and look at Amber.

"Did you say you're 'swapping lives'?" one of the other women says, and suddenly they're all riveted.

"You're leaving your husband and children for four weeks?" says a blond woman in a green cable cashmere sweater who Amber doesn't know, and Amber suddenly has an incredibly strong temptation to turn around and run away.

"I am *so* jealous," continues the woman in the green sweater. "Oh my gosh, you are so brave! You get to go to London and pretend to be single for four weeks? Can I come with you?" And she laughs as Amber exhales in relief. For a moment there she was terrified they'd all start berating her: how can she leave her children; what kind of a mother must she be; what is she even thinking of, letting her husband share a house with a single woman, doesn't she know what kinds of things happen in situations like this?

Not that any of these women has ever had a situation like this, but Amber thinks she knows what they're thinking because she's been thinking all these things herself, and even now, now that Richard is driving her to Kennedy tomorrow lunchtime to get the flight to London, she still can't quite believe it is happening.

The line of women, who a couple of minutes before seemed to be half asleep, sipping at their Starbucks and trying not to catch one another's eye, now comes alive as they all turn to one another and repeat what they've heard, and soon they are all gathered around Amber, shooting questions at her, wanting to know what made her do it, what her husband thinks, whether she'll miss the children.

"Of course!" Amber says. "That's the hardest thing about all of this. I'm going to miss them enormously, but I just want to remember who I was before I had a husband and children. When I think back to before I met Richard, when I worked in the city and had an apartment, it's not even that it feels like a lifetime ago, it feels like it happened to someone else. I've always said I'd love, just once in a while, to be reminded of who the real Amber is, who she was before she was defined as solely a wife and mother, and now I have this great opportunity. Does that make sense?"

And everyone agrees. Everyone agrees, and is clearly envious, and for the first time Amber stops feeling guilty and starts to feel excited. This is finally going to happen.

"I've come to say good-bye." Deborah walks in the back door and comes straight into the kitchen carrying a box wrapped in Union Jack wrapping paper.

"What's that?" Amber asks, eyeing the box warily.

"This is your London Survival Kit," Deborah says gleefully. "Come on, open it now and I'll explain."

Amber opens the box and pulls out first an *A to Z*. "That's your map of London," Deborah says. "So you'll never get lost."

Next comes a phrase book of cockney rhyming slang. "Trust me, there's much more to it than just apples and pears, but this is for you to understand when the cabbies talk to you. Don't, whatever you do, try and incorporate any of it yourself because it's just unspeakably naff when Americans try and speak cockney rhyming slang."

"Naff?" Amber raises an eyebrow.

"Cheesy."

There are bags of cat treats, "so you can make friends with Vicky's cat because I know you're not a cat person and cats can sense that, so this will hopefully get you off on the right foot"; DVDs of *Little Britain* and *Coronation Street*, "even though it's Manchester, not London, it's a British institution and you ought to watch some of it"; and a red-and-white football scarf saying Gunners. "First, soccer is called football in England, and everyone in England has a team, and your team must be Arsenal," Deborah says very seriously.

"But shouldn't my team be whatever Vicky's team is?" Amber asks. "And she doesn't strike me as someone who would be interested in football."

"I don't care. You must support Arsenal or you can't be my friend, and when you're talking about them you can refer to them as the Gunners, pronounced 'Gooners.' Okay?"

Amber shrugs. "If you say so, although I can't imagine myself having conversations about soccer. Sorry, football."

"And finally," Deborah pulls a small black notebook out of the bottom of the box and gives it to Amber, "these are my very own English notes to help you fit in."

Amber flicks through the notes and starts laughing. "You're not serious?" she says.

"Which bit?" Deborah cranes to see which bit Amber is reading. "You mean, say 'fuck' a lot in everyday sentences whenever you can, unless of course you're talking to young children."

"Yes. That bit."

"No, I'm serious. I know it sounds weird but we swear a lot in England. Seriously. Nobody bats an eyelid over the word *fuck*. It's a great word. It can be an adjective: You're fucking bonkers. A noun: You old fucker. Or, obviously, a verb: I was fucking him—but hopefully you won't be using it in that sense. Although you can also say, I was completely fucked last night, which might mean you had sex, or might also mean you were very drunk, or very tired."

"Please tell me you're joking." Amber is no longer laughing, but looking very confused.

"Wish I fucking was." Deborah grins. "Just wait and see. But you don't have to read the whole thing now, just remember some of the key points. Don't ever say to anyone 'Have a nice day,' ever, because everyone in England thinks Americans are all mad, and they all take the piss out of them for saying 'have a nice day.' Also, do not tip, unless in a restaurant or a black cab, and ten to fifteen percent is the norm, never twenty, and don't talk to strangers."

"Can I ask you a question?"

"Sure."

"If everyone in England says fucking, fucked, or fucker all the time," Amber swallows, unused to using those words at all, let alone three times in one sentence, "how come I never hear you use those words ever?"

"Because, my darling, when I first started living in America I was effing and blinding with the best of them, and then I quickly realized that it was not going at all well, so I had to consciously cut it out of my language. Now I consider it offensive if someone says oh my God, rather than oh my gosh."

"Well . . ." Amber is dubious. "I'm not sure that I'm going

to be able to curse like that, but thank you for the warning. At least I won't be shocked if I hear it from other people."

"And the other thing is," Deborah walks over to the kettle and flicks it on, knowing that Amber won't mind if she makes herself a cup of tea, "you, Mrs. Winslow, are quite the talk of the town."

"What do you mean?"

"I ran into Erin Armitage at Stop and Shop and she was asking me all about Swapping Lives. Then I went to get some new underwear in town and Suzy Potts was there and she wanted to know all about it, and then I went to Hallmark to get you a going-away card, and the sales assistant in there asked if it was for the lady who was doing Swapping Lives."

"No!" Amber is horrified.

"I'm afraid so."

"Oh God," she groans. "Richard is going to hate being the talk of the town."

"Well, you'd better tell him not to go out for the next four weeks, then," Deborah says. "But you really trust him with having another woman in your house? I mean, I know you trust him and I'm not saying I wouldn't trust him or that I don't think he's trustworthy, but you're really okay with this?"

"Of course I'm okay," Amber snaps, a little too sharply. "The one thing about Richard and me is that we don't have any secrets, and he would never do that to me."

"You're right. I'm sorry, I shouldn't have said that. And what about you?" Deborah asks with a glint in her eye. "What if Vicky Townsley has some gorgeous man lined up who you could have a quick fling with and no one would ever know?"

"Absolutely not," Amber says sternly. "I can't believe you're even asking me that."

"But what if no one would ever find out? Richard would never know, and it's not something that would ever develop."

"But *I'd* know," Amber says primly. "And what kind of person do you think I am anyway? Would you have an affair with someone if Spencer would never find out?"

"No!" It's now Deborah's turn to look horrified. "Absolutely not. But you can't blame me for asking the question."

Later that evening Richard, Amber, Jared, and Gracie go out for an early dinner, the last dinner they have as a family.

Amber has already explained to the kids that Mommy is going on a vacation for four weeks—or twenty-eight wake-ups, which sounded, rather frighteningly, far longer—and that the nice lady called Vicky is going to come and stay to help look after them, and that Mommy loves them very much and that Mommy would write them letters every day and they could write letters to Mommy too.

Still, the atmosphere tonight is somber and sad. Richard is serious yet loving, and everyone seems slightly subdued. They go to Becconi's, the local pizza restaurant that has aspirations to something far grander with its wisteria-covered pergolas outside, and white paper tablecloths, and yet invariably the largest percentage of its customers are families with young children who spill their sippy cups on the tablecloths and draw all over the now soggy paper with the crayons Becconi's so thoughtfully provides.

Halfway through her chef's salad and pizza—Amber had wanted the pizza but was trying to be good, and now finds Gracie is insisting on eating most of her salad, so she is able to justify her additional slice of pizza—Amber's eyes fill with tears.

"Why are you sad, Mommy?" Gracie asks, reaching out her

little hand to stroke Amber's back, in a precise imitation of the way Amber strokes Gracie's back when Gracie is upset.

"Oh darling," Amber says, smiling even as her eyes well up. "I'm just going to miss you so much," and she reaches down and gives Gracie a tight squeeze, then turns and attempts to hug Jared on her other side, who shrugs her off, not wanting to appear uncool given that two boys from basketball camp are sitting in full view and are now laughing and pointing at him. "Get off, Mom," he says, wriggling away.

"I'm sorry," Amber says, first to Jared, and then again to Richard, who also looks as if he's going to cry.

"I didn't know it would be like this," she says quietly, taking Richard's hand across the table. "It seemed like a fun thing to do, and now I know that I shouldn't be doing it, and if there was a way to get out of it I would."

"Would you really?" Richard says.

"I really would," Amber says. And she means it. "But it's too late and you know that. But I'll miss you so much, Richard. You're my world, you know that. You and the kids."

"I know," Richard smiles sadly. "I just wish you weren't going."

"I know." Amber squeezes his hand. "Me too."

The children are in bed as Richard pours a glass of wine for Amber and they sit on the deck, watching the stars.

A patter of feet can be heard, and Gracie is in the doorway.

"Gracie, honey, what's the matter?" Amber says.

"Um. Um. Um." Gracie thinks hard before hitting on the perfect problem to explain her presence. "I need books on my bed," she says seriously.

"Okay. I'll come up with you," Amber says, walking Gracie back to bed and putting books on the bed. "No more getting out of bed," Amber says, kissing her good night.

A minute later another patter of feet can be heard. This time it's Jared. "Gracie's in my bedroom," he whines. "She threw all my books on the floor."

Amber gets up and goes upstairs to find Gracie grinning in the middle of Jared's bedroom.

"Gracie!" Her voice is stern. "What did I tell you? Get back into bed. You're both supposed to be in bed. No more getting out or there will be trouble."

She tucks them both in, goes downstairs, snuggles up to Richard, then hears screaming from both of them.

"No, Jared!" Gracie shouts. "Get out of my bedroom!"

"No!" Jared can be heard. "Make me."

"Right, that's it." Richard stands up and goes upstairs, and two minutes later both children are wailing as Richard tries to sternly order them back into their rooms.

Amber sighs as she walks up the stairs to make the peace. Maybe this break isn't such a bad thing after all.

Chapter Twenty

Vicky is extremely grateful that Richard has not picked her up at Kennedy Airport. If she were Amber, the probability is that he would, but as he dropped Amber off earlier today for her own flight to London, and Vicky wasn't due to arrive for another three hours, Richard apologized but said he had work commitments.

Still, this is far better, Vicky thinks, leaning back in the luxurious town car that she booked to drive her up to Highfield, Connecticut, to step into Amber's life. She starts reading through the notes that Amber has e-mailed her, wishing they were slightly more comprehensive, more like hers, but perhaps as a mother Amber simply didn't have time, and it isn't as if there aren't enough people around to help—there is Richard, evidently, Lavinia, the kids, the best friend Deborah.

If Vicky had left notes this sparse Amber would have been in big trouble, but the only source of help would have been Eartha, and a big furry cat jumping on a duvet in the middle of the night and demanding to have her throat rubbed isn't really all that much of a help.

Vicky discovers that they never use the front door in the house, always the side door that takes you into the mud room, and that it's pretty much always unlocked, crime being virtually nonexistent in Highfield. Shoes come off as soon as you come in the house (children's shoes, that is), and the children must hang up their coats themselves.

In fact the vast majority of Amber's notes focus on the children. Vicky has been looking forward to taking the children to the playground in the afternoons after camp has finished, and going to various farms she's looked up online. She's even discovered that a nearby town is running a children's theater program every Thursday afternoon, and has lined up tickets for various puppet shows and productions.

Vicky is determined to be a wonderful mother, not that Amber isn't a wonderful mother, but even in the short time she'd spent with her when she came over to do the recce, Vicky could see that Amber was a busy woman, and that although loving and attentive with the children when she was with them, she didn't seem to be with them nearly as much as, say, Kate was with Luke, Polly, and Sophie. Vicky is hoping that during her four weeks she'll spend every afternoon with the children, cook them the things that she ate as a child—fish fingers, cottage pie, meat loaf, jelly and ice cream—but looking through the schedules that Amber has e-mailed over, Vicky doesn't have a clue when she's supposed to spend this time with them.

Both children are in camp in the morning, and it would appear that with the exception of a scheduled playdate every Friday afternoon, both children have some kind of class every afternoon.

Jared's schedule is as follows:

Monday 3 p.m.: Basketball Camp
Tuesday 4 p.m.: Little League practice
Wednesday 3.30 p.m.: Swimming
Thursday 4 p.m.: Karate

Friday 3 p.m.: Playdate
Saturday 4 p.m.: Little League game

Vicky takes a deep breath before looking at Gracie's schedule.

Monday 2 p.m.: Ballet at Miss Cynthia's
Tuesday 3 p.m.: Art class
Wednesday 3 p.m.: Music class
Thursday 4 p.m.: Swimming
Friday 3 p.m.: Playdate
Saturday: Free time

Well, thank God for free time, thinks Vicky, and poor, poor Jared. All he gets is Sundays, and she thinks of Kate, and how Kate never does anything with the children. How Luke, Polly, and Sophie roam around the house and garden all day, occasionally torturing frogs they capture in the pond, but mostly building forts in the woods inside which Luke is forced to sit as Polly and Sophie serve him tea in acorn teacups and "delicious suppers" of pinecones and mud.

When it's raining the three of them race around the house, or lock themselves away suspiciously in closets planning duplicitous spy activities involving walkie-talkies and binoculars, while Kate, calmly oblivious to all of it, sits at the kitchen table with a friend, or potters round the garden collecting vegetables for supper.

Perhaps Vicky can bring a bit less structure to their lives, she thinks. After all, it wouldn't be the end of the world if Jared were to miss karate one week, or Gracie to miss swimming. Think how lovely it would be to take them to the theater. Or failing that, perhaps they could just stay at home one day and cook something, or go on a nature trail at the nature center Vicky has found. It's all very well stepping into Amber's life, but already Vicky can see there are things that she would do differently, and perhaps she could make a change for the better, perhaps she could introduce a new way of thinking that might make everyone happier.

Vicky's already planning on giving the nanny some free time. Lavinia wasn't too friendly when Vicky met her before, but this time Vicky is armed with a giant box of Quality Street that Amber has told her are Lavinia's favorite, and Vicky is hopeful it will be enough ammunition to garner her support.

And while she'd like Lavinia to be around, and certainly to carry on helping with the laundry and cleaning up, Vicky is certain that she doesn't want to send the children off with Lavinia all the time. After all, what's a mother for?

The house is oddly quiet as Vicky pushes open the door to the mud room and walks into the kitchen, placing her very light suitcase on the floor. She can't take it upstairs to Amber's room, because the one thing they were both very clear on was that there would be no sleeping with the husband. Not that Vicky would want to sleep with the husband, even though he was attractive, but it's best to clarify right from the beginning that they will have separate bedrooms.

There's a note on the kitchen counter, and Vicky wanders over and sees it's for her.

Dear Vicky,

Welcome! I just wanted to write you a note and wish you a wonderful visit to my life! I'm very nervous but very excited and am sure you feel the same way! Richard is going to give you the master bedroom and he'll sleep in the guest room downstairs, so go ahead

and put your stuff away (although what stuff? Given that you're going to be wearing my clothes, you probably, like me, have packed almost nothing. Isn't this the most bizarre way of traveling???). So, good luck, and Deborah said she's around today if there's anything at all that you need. And don't forget that Jared and Gracie have playdates this afternoon, although Lavinia can fill you in.
Fondly,
Amber

Fondly? thinks Vicky. Whoops. For of course she has left a very similar note, and has, perhaps inappropriately she now realizes, signed off with *lots of love,* and several kisses. Yet another sign of how they do things differently in America.

A whining outside the door alerts her to Ginger's face, peering in at the window, and as she opens the kitchen door Ginger bounds in and proceeds to jump excitedly all over Vicky, covering her outfit with huge muddy paw prints.

"Oh God." Vicky tries to push him away, but 114 pounds of golden retriever is not that easy to push away. "Ginger, get down!" she commands, at which point Ginger pants eagerly and jumps up again. "Ginger, sit!" she tries, in her best Joan Crawford voice. "Sit!" but Ginger then runs circles around the island in the kitchen, jumping up on Vicky again.

"Oh well," Vicky sighs, calming Ginger down by stroking him gently and crooning to him. "I'll just have to change clothes. What a shame, I'll have to put on some of your mummy's gorgeous designer wardrobe. Oh dear." And leaving Ginger in the mud room—thanks to Ginger she now realizes why it's called a mud room—she takes her suitcase upstairs to Amber's bedroom.

* * *

Now this, she thinks, is what it's all about. Amber is not one of the top customers at Rakers for nothing. Her wardrobe is packed with all the clothes Vicky dreams about but generally, apart from a very occasional blowout, can't afford. There are Michael Kors jackets, TSE sweaters, Oscar de la Renta dresses, and of course the obligatory Manolo Blahnik shoes. But not just the couple of pairs that are in Vicky's wardrobe, lines and lines and lines of them—enough to open a Manolo Blahnik store. And on the other side of the closet is the casual stuff. Lines of Pumas and Nikes in every conceivable color and style, shelves of workout gear, fleeces in lime green, orange, and hot-pink.

I don't wear all the good designer clothes every day. Generally the good stuff is for when we go out for dinner, for charity events, when I go to the city, and of course for the committee meetings of the League. Mostly during the day I run around in the workout gear, but obviously you do whatever makes you feel comfortable. And I know you're swooning over the Birkins, so treat them well, and make sure you never leave them unattended! Enjoy . . .

Oh God, groans Vicky, eyeing up the Birkins, and a Chloe dress that she'd lusted after in *Vogue* a couple of months ago. I'll just see what they look like. No one's home, no one will know. And in less time than it takes to say "Jimmy Choo," Vicky is standing in her underwear, pulling on the Chloe dress.

And it fits her perfectly. Originally a size larger than Amber, Vicky has been dieting furiously to get into Amber's wardrobe, and now she is thrilled that they are the same size, even though Vicky could never be quite as firm, as cellulite-free as Amber.

Vicky slips her feet into very high Gucci satin sandals that snake up her ankles and are quite possibly the sexiest things she's ever seen, and then slips a Chanel bag on her shoulder, throws a mink wrap around her neck, and sashays over to the huge mirror on the wall. "Hello, darling," she says, pretending to be holding a cigarette in a long, ebony cigarette holder. "Missed me?"

At that point Vicky knows not only is she being ridiculous, but this is the point at which the culprit is always caught, usually by a housekeeper or nanny, and feeling horribly guilty as she pictures Lavinia's disapproving face, she strips off the dress and pulls on some stretchy leggings and a fleece, slipping her feet into Nikes, even though she suspects that Amber never wears shoes inside the house—those wooden floors are just too shiny for that.

Looking at herself in the mirror, Vicky hardly recognizes herself. She would never, in a million years, wear these kinds of clothes unless she was going to an exercise class, and yet Amber insists this is her daily uniform. Admittedly she is incredibly comfortable, but she looks so . . . ordinary. So dowdy. Surely this look can be jazzed up somehow. And then she remembers. The Balenciaga or Prada bag. The diamond studs.

Ten minutes later Vicky reexamines herself in the mirror, and this time she smiles. Amber's four-carat diamond studs glitter in her ears, the black Birkin bag is casually looped over her arm, and she has reapplied some makeup, a similar amount to that which Amber was wearing when she and Vicky met.

"That's more like it," Vicky nods, with a grin. "Now I look

the part," and with a spring in her step that surely owes more to her mood than to the Nikes on her feet, Vicky heads downstairs.

An hour later she has looked inside every cupboard. She has located the teacups but not the tea bags, although the pantry has every kind of herbal tea you can imagine; but frankly, as far as Vicky is concerned, if it ain't Tetley it ain't tea. She has found the television sets (hidden away behind a built-in), located the few books in the house (in a room Amber referred to as the library, so-called because it houses the only bookshelves in the house, and the only books on the bookshelves are Richard's business books), and has moved a radio from the laundry room to the kitchen so she can have some noise to break up the silence. Well, now what? She drums her fingers on the kitchen table. What am I supposed to do with myself now?

Across the Atlantic Amber is lying happily on Vicky's bed, sighing with pleasure as she thinks about where she is and what she's doing. She got a black cab at Heathrow, even though Vicky had told her not to, warning her that it would be horrendously expensive, and then tipped him over twenty percent, even though Deborah had said nobody does that, but she would have felt horrible giving him anything else.

He was obviously delighted, and said giving a beautiful lady like herself a ride was pleasure enough in itself, and Amber smiled, wondering if all the men in England were quite so charming.

She loved driving up Marylebone High Street, found it to be everything she had dreamed of, and so much more besides. Was that an Aveda store she saw before her? Oh joy! To be single and living in shopping heaven. What more could a girl ask for?

Vicky's apartment was what Amber calls a walk-up. In a small apartment building just off the High Street, it was dark and had a rather peculiar smell when she walked up the narrow staircase, and for the first time since touching down Amber suddenly thought, what if this is awful? What if Vicky lives in a pigsty? Even though she had seen pictures, she was still clearly the one most disadvantaged, having not been able to give Vicky's life the once-over, the way Vicky had done hers.

But as soon as she managed to get the key to work and slid open the door, Amber was delighted. The flat—she had to get used to calling it a flat rather than an apartment—was light and airy, flooded with sunshine, which belied its rather small size. Decorated with enormous style in neutral colors, the flat's shots of color came from the books, of which there must have been thousands.

Floor-to-ceiling bookshelves lined each wall of the living room, stacks of books were piled artfully on the coffee table, among Indian trinkets and Balinese bowls. This was a true home, Amber thought happily, a flat filled with things the owner has collected over the years, beautiful and personal, a place where Amber could truly be happy, and she picked up a delicate silver dish and ran her fingers over the burnished edges.

"I love it here," she said, wanting to run around with glee, but instead she went to examine the rest of the flat.

Ah, she thought, seeing the kitchen. Perhaps it's not as perfect as I thought. The kitchen was a small, dark L-shape off the living room, with no natural light. No amount of cool maple cupboards or smart granite counters could disguise the fact that the kitchen was tiny, with an under-the-counter fridge that was barely big enough to hold a few sodas.

No wonder she never eats at home, Amber thought. You can't fit anything in that fridge, but then again Amber isn't exactly a chef, so it's no bad thing. If anything, this kitchen was bigger than the one she had in her apartment when she met Richard, and if she could cope with that, she can definitely cope with this. It's all a matter of relativity, she told herself, not to mention that she barely ever uses her Viking stove anyway.

The bedroom was sweet. Enormous windows led onto a lovely iron balcony, and she opened them so the sheer linen curtains billowed in the wind. The closets were far smaller than she was used to, and she tutted as she looked through the clothes. Not because she didn't like what she saw—she's looking forward to experimenting with that English boho style—but because everything was crammed so tightly together; how do the clothes not get horrendously wrinkled? Amber has learned that there ought to be an inch between the hangers, and she wondered if Vicky would mind if she sorted out her closets.

On opening the door of the bathroom, Eartha charged out. She'd been locked in there by mistake when Vicky left, and she was not a happy cat, although now someone was there she was very happy indeed, and she wound her way around and around Amber's ankles, purring enthusiastically as she rubbed her face on Amber's legs.

"Hello, you sweet kittie cat." Amber bent down on one knee to stroke her. Not that Amber was particularly a cat person, but she's never heard such a loud purr, and this cat seemed to like her, and who can resist being so obviously pursued?

"Hang on," Amber said, running into the living room for her suitcase and pulling out the bag of cat treats that Deborah had given her. She opened it and fed them to Eartha who then jumped onto Amber's lap for some more loving.

"You and I are going to get along just fine," Amber said, scooping her up and cradling her like a baby, which Eartha didn't seem to mind in the slightest, and then Amber went to inspect the bathroom.

Not that she should be surprised. She was used to a shower that is the mother of all showers. A shower that doesn't have just one showerhead, nor even two, but has eight. One giant one that hangs from the ceiling, and seven more that spout from the walls of her huge, oversized stall that is almost a room in itself. In fact, looking at Vicky's bathroom, Amber judged that it was ever so slightly smaller than her shower.

But what was worse was there was no shower. There was a bathtub with a hose, and dubiously Amber turned it on to see it produce a faint trickle of water. Damn. She'd heard about the British and their showers, but she didn't actually think it would still be so bad in this day and age.

It was like British food. For years Americans joked that the British had the worst food in the world, and then just recently *Gourmet* magazine had devoted an entire issue to how Britain now had the best food in the world.

So really, can you blame Amber for assuming that the showers would naturally follow suit?

She sighed with disappointment and resigned herself to getting used to baths. Ugh. Sitting in your own dirty water. Maybe she could have two baths. One to soap herself, and then one to rinse. Or maybe sponge baths. But standing there Amber made a decision. I am not going to let one silly thing like the lack of a decent shower ruin this trip for me. I am going to have a wonderful time.

And that is when she collapsed onto the bed with a huge grin on her face, followed swiftly by Eartha, who climbed straight onto her stomach, and that is where we first find her, on her first day in Vicky's life.

Chapter Twenty-one

Vicky didn't expect it to feel quite so strange. She keeps looking around to ask permission to do things: Is it okay if I drive the car? Can I help myself to food in the fridge? Should I be feeding Ginger or does he always beg like this? And most important, what am I supposed to do until the kids get home?

There is no Lavinia, presumably because she has gone to collect the children from their various activities, and the last thing Vicky wants is for Lavinia to walk in and find her doing something heinous and lazy like watching the *Oprah* show in the middle of the day, so in the end she makes herself a bagel—because of the jet lag she is starving, even though she's already had about eight meals today—and sits at the kitchen counter leafing through the pile of catalogs that are threatening to topple off the edge of the desk.

In the Neiman Marcus catalog she finds three pairs of shoes that she would kill for but couldn't afford; in J. Jill she admires a floaty chiffonlike skirt, and in Frontgate she spends a few minutes fantasizing over the various pool toys, and wondering whether Amber and Richard already have one of those glorious-looking rafts with a hole in the arm just the right size for a piña colada.

They do, after all, have the swimming pool, and Amber is

one of those women who have a permanent tan from April through to October. Vicky has seen those movies where the women lounge around the pool all morning, working on their tans and keeping up with celebrity gossip via the trashy magazines, and she is rather hopeful that she will find some time to do the same, even though Amber's typical schedule doesn't seem to have any sunbathing time worked into it.

Today is a glorious August day, and the water is starting to tempt. Vicky goes outside and dips a finger in, and she smiles widely. It's almost as warm as a bath—just the way Vicky likes it. Oh what the hell. She has time for a quick swim, and going to the pool house she finds that of course Amber and Richard have one of the rafts with a hole in the arm for a drink—what self-respecting McMansion owner wouldn't?—and pulling it out she places it carefully next to the edge of the pool before heading back in to double-check the timetable.

The timetable hasn't changed. Fridays are still playdate days, and given that it's only three-thirty, Lavinia and the kids won't be back for hours, so even though Vicky is determined to be the greatest mother in the whole wide world, it doesn't have to start until the children get home from their playdate. Admittedly, she did think about spending the afternoon cooking one of the meals remembered from her own child- hood, but she can always start the whole mother thing to- morrow, and a cursory glance at the freezer reveals it is stuffed to the gills with frozen pizzas and chicken nuggets, so it isn't as if the children are going to go hungry if she doesn't cook. Not that Amber ever cooks herself, and Vicky's had a long flight and is tired—hell, she deserves to spend a couple of hours trying to erase her white, pasty skin, the product of a typical English summer in London.

* * *

Now this is more like it. Vicky smiles as she floats around the pool, stretching out luxuriously as she enjoys the silence. Christ, she thinks, how does Amber ever get up and out? If I lived here all the time I'd be out here all day every day. This is like being on holiday, how could anyone ever motivate themselves to do anything other than this?

Her bathing suit is still squashed somewhere at the bottom of her suitcase, and the last thing she felt like doing was unpacking. And there's no one here, and no one to see, and she just wanted to see what it felt like, floating on this raft, and so what if she's in bra and knickers. It's not as if she's never done this before, although granted, if she were stripping off in a London park she probably wouldn't wear a black lacy push-up bra that she's practically spilling out of, teamed with a purple G-string, but she's only going to be a minute, and it was so much easier to just strip off and leave her clothes on a sunbed.

Vicky closes her eyes and thinks about her childhood, remembers begging her parents to put in a swimming pool, announcing very seriously that the only thing she ever wanted for her eighth birthday was a proper swimming pool, and if she didn't get one she might die.

Around the corner there was a family called the Simpsons, and they had a swimming pool. Vicky knew they must have been very rich, and even though she wasn't that friendly with the daughter, Cathy, every now and then the neighborhood gang of kids would be invited over for a swimming party.

Then Samantha Payne's parents bought a new house and they had a swimming pool too, and it was indoor, and when they went over there the pool was so hot there was steam rising up from it, clouding the glass roof.

"Please, please, please," Vicky remembers begging as her parents had laughed and said not only was it not worth it given the typical English summer, but did Vicky think they were made of money?

And now here she is, she thinks happily, finally with a swimming pool, even though it's only hers for a month; but she's definitely going to make the most of it, and if she misses a few of Amber's charity meetings, what the hell? Surely it's just as important to look the part as it is to play the part, and having a suntan suddenly seems like a top priority.

"Vicky! Vicky!"

The voice sounds as if it's coming from far away and reluctantly Vicky opens her eyes. She's so comfortable, drifting around the pool, fast asleep, in the middle of a wonderful dream where she's on a yacht with Jamie Donnelly who is just about to kiss her (even though he doesn't look like Jamie Donnelly, in fact he doesn't seem to have much of a face at all, which is the usual story with her dreams—one of these days she must remember to look that up and see what it means—but still, it feels delicious), and someone from shore is disturbing that kiss by shouting her name.

Except it's not someone from shore. It's Lavinia standing by the side of the swimming pool, holding Gracie on her hip as Jared dances from foot to foot announcing that he wants to go swimming too.

Vicky blinks her eyes in a bid to focus and wake up properly, and sees that over by the gate is another woman with three children, and as Vicky rouses herself she is mortified that she has fallen asleep in the swimming pool on her first day here, and there are guests, and what a terrible first impression. What kind of a mother would do this?

"Oh God, Lavinia, I'm so sorry!" Vicky paddles to the side of the pool and rather gracelessly clambers out. "I fell asleep. It must have been the jet lag. I'm so embarrassed!" And she becomes more so as she stands and remembers what she's wearing. A black lacy bra that is probably too small for her, and a purple G-string.

"You'd better put some cream on that white skin of yours," Lavinia sniffs. "You're the color of a lobster."

"Oh God," Vicky groans, willing herself not to cry, and it's only as she desperately tries to pull on her clothes that she hears hoots of laughter and whistles behind her.

Turning she sees a team of Mexican gardeners leaning on their hoes as they whistle and grin approvingly at her, speaking among themselves in Spanish.

"Oh, fuck off" she is tempted to shout, and manages not to, remembering that she is still trying to make a good impression, and there are five small children around who do not need to hear that.

"I'm so sorry," she says again to Lavinia, now dressed, with a flush of embarrassment still on her cheeks.

"I'm Vicky," she says to the other mother. "I'm staying here for a month."

"And making yourself at home, I see," says the other mother, but not unkindly, and there is a twinkle in her eye. "Just ignore the gardeners," she continues. "You've probably just made their summer. And I'm Nadine. We've had a playdate this afternoon and I needed to just come by and pick up the permission slip for the kids to go on a field trip next week. Amber was meant to have dropped it off but she must have forgotten. Do you know where it is?"

"Um, Lavinia? Do you know?"

"Nope."

"Well, let's go inside and have a look for it," Vicky says pleasantly. "I'm sure it's somewhere around. Hi, Gracie!" Vicky smiles up at Gracie, sitting on Lavinia's hip, sure that the child will remember her, will be pleased to see her given how well they got on last time, but without Amber here Gracie, suddenly shy, hides behind Lavinia's shoulder and refuses to look Vicky in the eye.

Well this is a great start, thinks Vicky. At least it's not going to get any worse.

The permission slip is nowhere to be found. Lavinia disappears to finish the laundry, leaving Vicky with the two children, Nadine, Nadine's children, and a lost permission slip.

Feeling like a spy, Vicky checks all the drawers of the desk, Jared and Gracie's backpacks, and various coat pockets. Nothing.

"Is there any chance I could get another one?" she asks. "Do you think if I came to camp early on Monday morning and got one it would be fine?"

"You can try," Nadine says. "Although they said the deadline was today, and anyone who didn't have a slip couldn't go."

"Go where?" Jared asks, skidding to a stop in the kitchen, followed by Nadine's son who goes crashing into him.

"To the Bronx Zoo," Nadine's son says. "You're not coming because you don't have a permission slip."

"I wanna go to the Bronx Zoo." Jared's little face crumples up.

"Don't worry," Vicky pleads. "I'll sort it out on Monday. You'll still go. I'll come in and talk to the camp on Monday."

"Can I go to the zoo too?" Gracie wanders in, looking hopefully up at Vicky, having decided that she will talk to her after all.

Vicky looks at Nadine.

"No, honey," Nadine says. "It's just for the big kids."

"But I wanna go to the zoo too!" Gracie starts wailing, and Nadine mouths an apology at Vicky, who suddenly thinks that perhaps Nadine isn't quite as nice as she seems.

"I'd better go," Nadine says, hustling her children together and taking them out the back door. "Say bye bye to Jared and Gracie, kids." Her kids say nothing.

"Say bye bye to Mrs.—? What was it again?"

"Oh I'm not Mrs." Vicky laughs. "It's Vicky."

"I'd prefer the children to call you Mrs. something, or Miss."

"Oh. Okay. Well, Miss Townsley, then, I suppose."

Nadine nods. "Say bye-bye to Miss Townsley."

And the kids say nothing as Nadine leaves and Vicky sinks onto a stool at the kitchen counter, wondering why the words *Miss Townsley* suddenly make her feel like the oldest spinster in the world.

"How does she seem?" Suzy is on the other end of Nadine's cell phone as she pulls out of the driveway of Amber's house.

"Completely disorganized. And slutty. I can't even tell you what she was wearing when we pulled in. She was fast asleep, floating in the swimming pool on a raft in black and purple lacy underwear. Can you believe it?"

"Nooooo!" Suzy is horrified, wants more information, is loving hearing that not everything about Amber's life is perfect. "I can't believe Amber would let someone slutty in her house! She wore underwear in the pool? That's outrageous! Do you think Richard is safe?"

"God no." Nadine laughs. "Not that she's anything special, but I wouldn't let someone like that in my house with my husband. Are you kidding? The only reason I can think that Amber is doing this has to be that her marriage is in trouble, don't you think?"

"I totally agree. Letting another woman come and pretend to be you for a month! I mean, I could understand it for, like, a week maybe. For a TV show or something, but a month! A whole month? That tells me that yes, there's definitely something up with the marriage."

"I know, and they always try and appear so perfect. Just goes to show you that you never know what goes on behind closed doors."

"So do you think she's going to be, you know, going after Richard?" Suzy is almost breathless in her excitement at this new, unexpected gossip. When Amber had been confronted about Swapping Lives by the women in the League, she hadn't said she was doing it because she was unhappy—God forbid any of those women should know her life is anything other than peachy-perfect—she had said she was doing it as an anthropological experiment, that a friend of hers worked on a British magazine and had begged her to do it, and she was curious to see whether she could still hack it as a single girl.

It was the greatest gift she had given the League since the complete set of Villeroy & Boch dinner service for last year's silent auction.

The phones in Highfield buzzed for days, and just as the brouhaha was dying down, here was this to set them all a-buzzing again. The girl that Amber said was just a nice girl, a single journalist from London, is actually a slut! A man-eating black-lace-wearing slut who has already had numerous affairs with married men! She has practically told Nadine that she will be sleeping in Amber's bed! She's implied that she finds Richard unbelievably attractive! What do we all think of Amber's perfect marriage now?

Oh my. And who thought life in suburbia was boring?

"So who wants pizza for dinner?" Vicky has already put the pizza under the grill, and has rounded up the children from the playroom, Lavinia still nowhere to be found.

"I don't like pizza," Gracie says, pouting as she stands next to her chair.

"And I had pizza for lunch," Jared says. "I don't want pizza again. I want something else."

"Oh." Bugger. What now? If she were at home, with her nieces and nephew, she'd be telling them that they get what they get and they don't get upset. As Kate always says, she's not running a restaurant, and Kate ought to know.

Polly and Sophie have always been fantastic eaters, but Luke never eats anything. In the beginning Kate would kill herself offering alternatives, and then each mealtime became a series of bribes. "Three more bites and you can have some ice cream; ten more bites and you can watch *Star Wars*."

After a while she got fed up with the constant battles, and decided to try a new tactic: She puts the meal on the table and after that it's up to them. If Luke doesn't want to eat, he doesn't have to, but he doesn't get anything else once he leaves the table.

Normally Vicky thinks Kate is a genius when it comes to child-rearing, and tends to emulate her when she's with Kate's kids. But these aren't Kate's kids. Nor are they hers, and she's not at home, and with a flash of guilt she realizes

she should have asked them before just making pizza thinking that it was a fail-safe.

"Okay, sorry, guys," she says. "What would you like?"

"Hot dogs," Jared says, getting up from the table, swiftly
followed by Gracie who announces she would like a grilled
cheese.

Ten minutes later Jared says he doesn't like the hot dog that
Vicky cooked in a pot of boiling water. "Mom always puts it
in the microwave," he whines. Funny, thinks Vicky, I don't
remember him being this whiny or difficult the last time I
was here.

"And I don't like this," Gracie says, pushing her grilled
cheese away. "This isn't the way Mom makes it."

Eventually Vicky finds a supper that makes them happy.
Unfortunately it consists of chocolate-chip cookies, muffins,
and ice cream.

At six o'clock she finally gives in and calls Lavinia to help
bathe them. It's now eleven o'clock at night in England, she's
had a hell of a long day, and her skin is starting to feel horribly tight from her unexpected nap in the swimming pool.

At seven o'clock Gracie is in bed, Vicky having read her
The Tiger Who Came to Tea, which Vicky brought with her
from London, thrilling Gracie who insists that she reads it
three times.

At seven-thirty Vicky manages to calm Jared down from
his sugar high and put him into bed, and it's all she can do to
drag her feet up the stairs into the master bedroom and unpack, when the phone rings.

"Hi, Vicky, it's Richard."

"Oh hi!"

"I'm just calling to let you know that I'm going to be late

tonight. I'm so sorry, I thought maybe we could have dinner and I could tell you a bit about how everything works, but I'm stuck in a meeting and probably won't be back before ten. How has your first day been?"

"Exhausting," she says. "And strange. I keep wanting to ask permission to do things, and then I remember that I'm supposed to be the mother here, and I'm the one who grants the permission, not asks it. And then I met Nadine, and I had fallen asleep in the swimming pool, and now I'm sunburned and it was incredibly embarrassing . . ." she trails off. Probably not appropriate to tell Richard she'd stripped off in his swimming pool.

"Don't worry about it. I'm glad someone's using the pool other than the kids. Amber begged me to put the pool in and never has time to use it. And you have to be careful with that sun. It's far stronger than you think."

"Thank you. I've realized that now. The kids wanted you to go and say good night to them."

Richard sighs. "I know. They always do. I'm definitely going to be home earlier next week. Will you be up when I get back?"

"I doubt it. It's all I can do to keep my eyes open tonight. I think I'm going to turn in now."

"Turn in?"

"Go to bed."

"Ah. Okay. So I'll see you in the morning. Sleep well."

"Thanks, Richard. See you in the morning." And as Vicky puts down the phone she realizes that for the first time she sounded, and felt, just like a wife, and she's not sure it's such a good thing after all.

Chapter Twenty-two

I feel like such a tourist, Amber thinks, striding along Gloucester Place on her way to the offices of *Poise!* on South Audley Street.

So many people, all different shapes and sizes, all walking briskly on their way to their respective offices. It's been years, Amber realizes, since she was part of the workforce, just another office worker striving to make it in on time, cup of coffee in a flimsy paper cup clutched firmly in hand. Years. A lifetime ago. When marriage and children weren't even possibilities, felt as if they were aeons away.

Do they know I'm a fake? Amber wonders, wanting to stop and gaze in every shop window, but not wanting to appear to be what she is—a tourist pretending to be a Londoner.

She has dressed carefully for her first day of work. Although she fell in love with Vicky's boho wardrobe, admiring it from a distance and actually wearing it were two different things entirely. Not to mention that once she took a closer look she realized the clothes in the wardrobe seemed to run a range of four sizes. Pulling on a skirt there was no telling whether it would fit like a glove, or immediately fall off and pool around her ankles.

Vicky's weight is clearly not consistent—anything from an

English size eight to a fourteen by the looks of things, and Amber is closer to a six than an eight, so three-quarters of Vicky's wardrobe is automatically ruled out.

Luckily their shoe size is the same, and this morning Amber has teamed a yellow silk sweater with an embroidered chocolate-brown skirt, gold beaded slip-ons on her feet, and a yellow coat that Vicky picked up at a designer sample sale and has never worn, had shoved to the back of her coat closet and completely forgotten about.

Amber admires herself in a shop window. She looks perfect. Hip, trendy, and certainly not a mother of two living in suburbia. With Vicky's Gucci sunglasses wrapped around her head, she is convinced she is the very picture of the features director of *Poise!* magazine—a style icon for thousands of women around the country.

Of course Amber isn't to know that Vicky bought the coat in a moment of panic, that anything in bright yellow is an aberration in London. She isn't to know that the skirt is from H&M, and has been bought by every other woman under the age of twenty-six in London, and just a few, like Vicky, over the age of thirty-five.

Not quite as trend-setting as she might think.

Still, she notices and appreciates the appreciative looks she gets from the British men. Good Lord, she thinks, a smile starting to spread on her face, I am still attractive! Who knew? Because back home in Highfield there are no men around to give her appreciative looks, even if they wanted to. At this time in the morning the men have taken the commuter train into the city, and are already firmly ensconced at their desks. When back home in Highfield, they are far too busy with their kids and wife to take the time to notice other women. And anyway, who's interested in looking at other wives?

And Amber is no one's wife today! Admittedly the weekend wasn't the best—there's only so much shopping in Marylebone High Street that can remove the tinge of loneliness, and this is the first weekend Amber has ever spent away from her kids.

Saturday was lovely. She slept in until midday—oh the joy of sleeping in again!—had a croissant and coffee at a pavement café, then wandered around window shopping for most of the afternoon.

Saturday night was spent in, watching television, struggling to understand the regional accents of the people in the U.K. version of *Big Brother*, flicking the channels, fascinated by the differences between U.K. and U.S. television, slightly horrified by the language—are people really allowed to say the f-word just on regular TV?—and the sex that seems to be accessible to all.

By Sunday lunchtime the reality of Swapping Lives started to kick in. Still tired from jet lag, and now lonely as well, Amber sat on Vicky's bed for a while looking at photographs of Richard and the kids, and allowed herself a few tears.

"I don't know if I can do this for a month," she whispered to herself, stroking Gracie's face in the picture. "What was I thinking?" And then she got up, grabbed the notes that Vicky had left on the kitchen counter, and picked up the phone to call Kate.

"Amber! Hello!" Kate's voice was warm down the phone, and Amber knew instantly she would like her, that they would get on. "Welcome to England, or should I say welcome to Vicky's world!" She chuckled. "How are you getting on?"

"Do you want to hear the truth, or the answer I'm supposed to say?"

"How about both? Start with the answer you're supposed to say, then tell me the truth."

"Well, yesterday was amazing. Just to have all this time to myself. I slept in, I went shopping, I didn't have to think about anyone other than myself, which I haven't had to do for years. I watched TV last night without having to worry about providing dinner for anyone, and without a husband moaning that he hates reality shows, and I sat in bed reading and eating chocolate Digestives, and got crumbs all over the sheets and there was no one to complain about it but Eartha, who couldn't have been happier."

"Sounds like heaven," Kate moaned.

"It was. And today I miss my kids, I miss my husband. I feel like I'm about to start crying all the time and I'm lonely as hell. And I don't know why I'm telling you this when I don't even know you, and I'm sorry, but I don't know what on earth I was thinking, and this is only day two. How am I going to survive a month?"

"Oh you poor love! I'd say come down and see us but by the time you got here you'd have to go home again, but I do feel for you. I always teased Vicky that I'd swap with her in a heartbeat, but I understand what you're saying. You want to swap but only for a day or so, just to remember who you were before you became a wife and a mother."

"Exactly! I just felt that I'd lost myself, and now I'm like, okay, now I remember, thanks a lot but I'll go back to my real life."

Kate laughed. "The thing is it is an opportunity of a lifetime. From what Vicky has told me you've been feeling stuck, so maybe you could use this time to figure out what you want to do, where you want to go."

"I know that makes sense, but right now I just feel scared. I don't know what I was thinking."

"Amber, everything happens for a reason. Vicky picked you for a reason, now you just have to figure out what that is. In the meantime, make some calls. Call some people in Vicky's life, ring her friends and make some arrangements. If you don't plan things, not only will the four weeks feel like four years, but you won't have achieved anything, and you're supposed to be living Vicky's life, aren't you? Walking in her shoes?"

"You're right, you're right. I will. I'll call some people now."

"And next weekend I want you to come and spend the weekend with us. Vicky's down here all the time and you can be mum to my lot while I have a lie-in. How does that sound?"

"Perfect!" Amber laughed, and as she put down the phone she knew she'd found a friend.

By Sunday evening she wasn't feeling quite so bad. She had plans to go to Deborah and Dick's for dinner on Tuesday, and a movie screening with Jackie on Thursday. She'd left messages for a couple of other people, and by the time she went to bed that evening she was starting to think that she could see the light at the end of the tunnel after all.

And now here she is, outside the offices of *Poise!*, pushing open the swing doors, standing before the man sitting behind reception, giving her name and being told to wait on one of the purple modern sofas off to one side.

And then she's directed up to the sixth floor, and as the lift zooms up, Amber feels as if she left her heart downstairs at reception, the nerves flooding in, apprehension and excitement causing a wave of nausea as the lift doors open and she finds herself staring into the friendly eyes of Ruth.

"You must be Amber!" Ruth says, shaking her hand warmly. "Come on. Let's go and get you a cup of tea and then we'll go and meet everyone. How's everything going? We're so excited you're here, everyone on the magazine is completely obsessed with *Desperate Housewives* and Vicky said it's just like that where you live, and we're all dying to hear about it."

"Oh." Amber has joked about being a Desperate Housewife but has never meant it to be taken seriously. But who else would answer an ad looking to swap lives? Who else would actually leave her beloved husband and children for four whole weeks to go and live the life of a single girl? No one other than a Desperate Housewife, that's who. And with a sigh of resignation Amber follows Ruth into the kitchen to get some tea.

When Amber goes to the loo, Leona comes running into the kitchen.

"Is she here? What's she like? What do you think? Is she like the Teri Hatcher one? Or Bree? Vicky said she was more like Bree but with Teri Hatcher's legs. What do you think?"

"Sssh. She seems really nice and she'll be back in a minute. She does look like a banana, though."

"What?"

"No seriously. She looks like a banana. She's wearing bright yellow and brown. It's making me hungry just looking at her."

"Oh don't be so horrible to the poor woman. She just got here. Anyway, isn't she supposed to be wearing Vicky's wardrobe? Vicky doesn't have anything bright yellow."

Amber rounds the corner, at which point Ruth introduces Leona.

"Anything you need, you just ask," Leona says. "We're sitting at the same desk and we work incredibly closely together, so I'm going to be helping you out. I've got to run in and see the editor a second, but I'll see you a bit later."

"What's she like?" Janelle is peering through the glass panels to the left of her door as Leona walks in.

"Seems nice. Looks like a banana."

"Darling, what do you mean?"

"I mean she looks like a banana. Wearing a very scary shade of yellow. Makes me want to put my sunglasses on."

"But is she a Desperate Housewife?"

"I'd say in that shade of yellow she's got to be pretty bloody desperate."

"Oh I see her!" Janelle claps her hands as she sees Ruth lead Amber in and start introducing her. "Oh I adore that color. Why is it that only the Americans can pull off those wonderful acid colors. Oh so smart," she muses to herself. "And the perfect colors to brighten up a dull winter day. Where's Stella? Can you be a darling and go and get Stella in here for me? I'm thinking fruit bowl for Christmas. Orange and yellow and purple. Gorgeous! And do bring Amber in to say hello." Janelle watches her admiringly as Amber shakes hands and waves to people sitting at banks of desks around the room, and Leona slips out of the office.

* * *

"Well?" Ruth has deposited both Amber and Stella with a besotted Janelle, and turns to find Leona standing there.

"Well what?" Ruth says.

"Well, Janelle clearly has one of her crushes." Leona rolls her eyes. "She was almost licking her shoe soles."

"I'll admit she's very pretty, but I still maintain she looks like a banana."

"Well, you'd better start thinking that's a good thing, because Janelle's decided to feature bananas, oranges, and plums for the Christmas issue."

"What are you talking about?"

"Look," and Leona gestures to Janelle's office where Janelle is clearly getting excited about something, pointing to Amber's sweater, as Stella nods, throwing in a few ideas of her own.

Janelle's door opens and Ruth and Leona immediately put their heads together, pretending to be busy.

". . . and you must come over for dinner one night with Stephen and me," Janelle says. "We'll host a dinner party for you, introduce you to some fabulous people. And if there's anything you need, just knock on the door, otherwise the girls will look after you, won't you, girls?" And the deputy editor, celebrity editor, and health editor all look up, all women in their thirties and forties, all married with children, all resigned to forever being "the Girls" in their editor's eyes. "Oh yes," they say in unison. "Absolutely."

"I thought she was supposed to be living Vicky's life?" Ruth whispers when Amber goes to get a coffee.

"She is. Why?"

"When was the last time Janelle offered to host a dinner party for Vicky?"

"Darling," Leona does a horrifyingly accurate impersonation of Janelle, "if Vicky were a Winslow, Stephen and I would have her over for dinner all the time. Don't take it personally, darling, but she's almost an equal, and were she not American, she might even be someone I'd want to be friends with."

"Well this is certainly going to be interesting," Ruth says. "Meanwhile what's she actually going to do while she's here?"

"Bloody good question," Leona says. "I have absolutely no idea."

Amber is not a young temp, and cannot be treated as such, so going through press clippings and offering tea to the desk is not something that can be asked of her. She is not a journalist and cannot be asked to write pieces for the forthcoming issues. She is a confident, fairly intimidating American wife and mother, and as such is proving to be something of a problem.

Because it was never the case that Amber was really ever going to step into Vicky's shoes at work. How could a novice come in and do the work of the features director when she doesn't know the first thing about magazines? There are, admittedly, a few things Amber could do, but none of them would be the types of things Vicky would do.

She can attend meetings with Janelle, even though everyone else at the meeting would know she was there as a courtesy rather than for what she could contribute. She could possibly write small editorial pieces, even though Vicky left those types of pieces behind many years ago.

Perhaps she could sift through the thousands of unsolicited articles that arrive on the features director's desk daily, and who knows, being inexperienced, she may even bother to read some of them before consigning them to the trash.

The last thing they want is for her to sit around bored, and in the end it is Leona who comes up with the perfect solution. "Let's send her out to do a story!" she says. "It gets her out of the office, it's something Vicky might do once in a blue moon—"

"Bollocks!" interjects Ruth. "Vicky only goes out to do stories if they're off to luxury spas in Thailand."

"Well, okay, you've got a point, but why not send her on a press trip? If her writing's crap we can just rewrite it for her. Now all we have to do is think up a piece and find somewhere for her to go. Ruth, you go through all the press releases that came in over the last week and pull anything that sounds interesting and put it on my desk."

"What should I do with Amber in the meantime?"

"Oh God," groans Leona. "I know! We're running that piece on taking time for ourselves when the kids get to be too much. I'll ask her to do a box on ten things that give us breathing space. She's a mum. I'm sure she can do that. And let me have those press releases this afternoon."

Amber hasn't written anything creative for around fifteen years, not since she was in college. She spends the morning reading through British newspapers and magazines to familiarize herself with them, grabs a sandwich from Pret à Manger to eat at her desk with the rest of the girls, then spends the afternoon struggling to come up with ten things that give mums breathing space.

When six o'clock comes she finds she hasn't thought about Jared, Gracie, or Richard all day. She's joined in the banter across the desk, including answering the many, many questions about life in America, and feels, for the first time in years, that she's actually used her brain somewhat.

At six Leona comes over and congratulates her.

"I've just read the piece and it's perfect!" she says. Truthfully. "We're going to run it as is. Looks like we'll have to find more pieces for you."

"Really?" Amber is thrilled. And surprised.

"Really. You're obviously a natural. Listen, I'm off to a screening tonight at the Charlotte Street Hotel. Do you want to come?"

"I'd love to," Amber says, "but I'm really tired. Can we do it another night?"

"Sure," Leona says. "There's one on Thursday in Soho. How does that sound?"

"I'm already going with Jackie," Amber says.

"My my!" Leona laughs. "You are busy already, aren't you? Tell you what, how about lunch tomorrow? We'll go somewhere nice."

"Great!" says Amber. "I'll put it in my book." And as Amber rides down in the lift, as she walks home past Selfridges, cutting through to Hinde Street, Amber finds that the smile never leaves her face.

Perhaps this wasn't such a mistake after all.

Chapter Twenty-three

"Ouch!"

Richard looks up at Vicky and winces in sympathy as she walks gingerly into the kitchen, trying not to let her thighs rub against each other, nor her arms touch her sides.

"I know." She tries a smile, her skin feeling hot and tight as she does. "I think I overdid it a bit yesterday."

"Oh my God," Richard jumps up and goes to the medicine cabinet on the other side of the kitchen. "You'd better put something on that immediately. I think this should help," and he hands her a bottle of calamine lotion.

"Vicky?" Gracie hasn't stopped staring at Vicky since she walked in.

"Yes, darling?" Vicky stops shaking the bottle to look at Gracie.

"Why is your face the color of my socks?" And she extends her legs to show off her purple socks.

"It's not the color of your socks, silly," Jared interrupts, "your socks are purple and Vicky's face is red. Red like a . . . fire truck."

"No!" Gracie's voice rises indignantly. "It *is* the color of my socks."

"Oh I hope it's not, darling, because that would be really

scary," Vicky says, leaning down and giving Gracie a painful squeeze. "But this is what happens when you don't put enough sun cream on."

"Is that sunburn, then?" Jared asks curiously.

"This isn't just sunburn," Vicky says, sighing with pleasure as she smooths the thick white liquid all over her face and the children watch her in fascination. "This is practically sun roast. In fact, I'm not Vicky anymore, I'm roasted Vicky. And it's very very painful."

Richard shakes his head. "I can't believe you didn't put any cream on. It was ninety-seven degrees yesterday."

"Well, first of all, I wasn't planning on falling asleep on that raft in the swimming pool, and second of all I thought my skin was fairly strong. You're talking to the girl who used to sunbathe with olive oil in the back garden."

"Olive oil?" Richard spits his coffee out with laughter. "That's the most dangerous thing I've ever heard. And you must have smelled terrible."

"Are you kidding? I smelled delicious. Bit of salt and pepper, sprinkling of lemon juice, and I was good enough to eat."

"Were you really good enough to eat?" Jared asks seriously. Jared is now at the age when he listens to everything. Even when he looks as if he's focusing fiercely on a television show, he will still manage to hear every morsel of interesting adult conversation going on in the next room, and will then ask inappropriate questions about it at inappropriate times.

"No, Jared," Richard says, "that's just a figure of speech. But seriously, Vicky, didn't you burn like crazy with olive oil?"

"No," she shrugs. "I just went a lovely golden brown, although I suppose the English sun isn't that strong. And worse, I used to lie on a sheet of tinfoil."

Richard starts laughing again. "And I thought you were joking about being roasted Vicky."

"Dad?" Jared taps him on the arm. "What's a figure of speech? Is that like an action figure?"

"No, Jar, it's just a way of saying something, so when . . ." he trails off and rolls his eyes at Vicky. "It's complicated, Jar. I'll explain when you're older. Vicky, there's coffee over there, and because it's Saturday I made French toast and eggs. Just help yourself."

And Vicky does, sitting down to an enormous plate of French toast, bacon, scrambled eggs, and maple syrup, reading the *New York Times* while Richard reads the business section and the children run into the family room to watch Saturday-morning television.

This, Vicky thinks, sipping her coffee and surreptitiously looking at Richard, dressed today in a polo shirt and khaki shorts, *this* I could get used to. Oh stop, she tells herself. The last thing you need right now is to be lusting after another woman's husband. And anyway, it's not particularly Richard she's lusting after, she realizes. It's the whole picture. It's eating French toast that your handsome husband has made on a Saturday morning. It's sipping fresh coffee at an antique breakfast table by the large French windows as sunlight streams in and glints on the glasses of orange juice. It's sitting in companionable silence with another person, able to read the papers separately, but together.

This is what I want with Jamie Donnelly, she thinks. This is exactly how I can see myself living with Jamie Donnelly, exactly the sort of feeling that I want to have, although it's hard when she only sees him late at night, when they're still in such early days, when passion is still the driving force behind their relationship.

Vicky would love to push the fast-forward button, take their relationship to exactly where she's sitting now, but she's trying hard to ignore that urge, because she's felt it many times before, and it's only ever got her into trouble. Never one to take things slowly, every time Vicky has thought that this time she may have met her Mr. Right, she has jumped in feet first, and her relationships have always followed the exact same pattern: They meet her and fall madly in love with her because of what she appears to be—independent, funny, slightly aloof. As soon as they fall hook, line, and sinker, Vicky feels she can trust them enough to let her true feelings show, at which point she becomes affectionate, warm, dependent. Convinced that this time it's real, she will drop hints about the kind of future she wants, tell them of her dreams to have children, and animals, to live in the country. She will stop going out for dinner, and will start cooking for them, proving what a wonderful wife she would make.

And if their laundry needs collecting, their spare room needs organizing, their letters need posting, then Vicky will do that too, all in the name of love and her future.

It may take three weeks. Sometimes three months, and occasionally we're talking longer, but at some point they always run away, always say they're not ready for what Vicky wants. They thought they were at the same stage, but clearly Vicky needs much more than they can give; and Vicky is then left alone again, convinced she has done something wrong, convinced that she will never find her Mr. Right.

But if she were to find her Mr. Right, if indeed Jamie Donnelly is her Mr. Right, then this is exactly how she would choose to spend her Saturday mornings. Reading the papers quietly, perhaps both reading out loud the occasional funny or interesting quote or story, taking the kids out to lunch, then perhaps a long walk in the park or on the heath with the dog.

Richard feels Vicky watching him and looks up to catch her eye. "I'm being rude, aren't I?" he says, putting the paper down. "I'm sorry. I just don't know quite how to behave. Amber kept saying I had to treat you like her, which is completely ridiculous, not to mention impossible given that I barely know you. So I'm torn between being incredibly polite and trying to explain our lives to you, or doing what I normally do on a Saturday morning, which is this. And now I realize that this is rude, and you probably have loads of questions, so go on. Shoot. Ask me anything."

"Whoa!" Vicky laughs and puts her arms up. "I don't have any questions. I was just thinking that this whole . . . experiment . . . is so strange. I didn't think I would be able to really feel what it would be like to be married and have kids, and what I was thinking while you were reading the paper was that right now I think I do know exactly what it must be like, and I didn't expect to have that feeling, and definitely not on my very first day."

"So what do you think it must be like?"

"Well, right now it feels very easy. Relaxed. Comfortable. I love that you're sitting there reading the paper and don't feel the need to entertain me. That's exactly what's supposed to happen, except I didn't think you'd be able to do it so quickly."

"You mean you didn't think I'd be able to be so rude so quickly." Richard grins.

"Exactly!" Vicky laughs.

"Well, I know what you're saying, but this isn't an accurate reflection of a typical Saturday morning."

"Oh no? What's the difference?"

"First, the kids are on their best behavior because you're here, but we'll see how long that lasts. Second, Saturday-morning television is a very occasional treat. Amber hates them watching TV, and only tends to use it as a last resort, so usually they're bored by this time and are pulling at our sleeves and begging to go out somewhere.

"And usually we're not nearly this organized. My confession today is that because you're here I got everything ready for breakfast last night so it was all incredibly easy this morning. Usually Amber and I are both running around preparing the food, getting drinks, making our own breakfasts, dealing with fights between Jared and Gracie. Let me tell you, today feels like a vacation."

"Maybe Swapping Lives will show you a different way of doing things?" Vicky grins.

"How so?"

"Maybe it will teach you to be a bit more organized." She laughs, as Richard shakes his head.

"It's a nice thought, but I can't see Amber and me keeping this up."

"So what's on the plan for the rest of the day?"

"I thought we could go up to the farmers' market in Weston. It's much easier to hit the grocery store for vegetables, but the farmers' market is a real experience, and I thought tonight we could do a barbecue, so we can get the salad stuff there. Plus you get to see what a country farmers' market is like."

"Sounds perfect!"

"We can take the kids out to lunch and then hang out here. I'll take Jared to his Little League game at four. You're welcome to come with us, or you can hang out here and swim with Gracie."

Vicky gestures to herself. "I think the last thing I'm going to be doing today is swimming," she laughs.

"You could wear a wet suit," Richard says.

"Ouch! Even the thought of rolling a wet suit onto my poor, sore skin is painful. Nope. I'm covering up today and staying out of the pool."

"Okay. So if you give me twenty minutes I just have to make a phone call and then we'll go."

"Sounds great," Vicky says, as Richard gets up and goes upstairs. Damn, she thinks. I wish I hadn't noticed how nice his legs are.

They go to the farmers' market, buy armfuls of fresh tomatoes, cucumbers, lettuce, and onions that came out of the ground that morning. They buy fresh honey and flowers, and homemade pecan slices that stick to their fingers, washing them down with sugary sweet lemonade.

Every single person at the farmers' market comments on Vicky's skin color. "Wow, that looks painful," they say, one after the other, all curious as to how someone could be so negligent, all understanding as soon as Vicky opens her mouth and reveals she's English.

It gets to the point that Vicky offers the explanation before they say anything, and soon Jared joins in, leading Vicky to stands they haven't yet been to, standing next to her and pointing at her face. "It's sunburn," Jared shouts, to get their attention. "This is Vicky and she's from England, and she fell asleep on a raft in the swimming pool yesterday because she's jet-lagged."

From the farmers' market they go to Gymini Stars for the children to run around on the play quad for a bit out of the sun, and from Gymini Stars they go to the diner for lunch.

And everything is just as perfect as Vicky had always imagined.

From the diner they go home, pick up Ginger, and take him to Lake Mohegan to exercise. Ginger is so excited he can hardly contain himself. The most exercise he usually gets is down to the bottom of the driveway and back when Lavinia picks up the mail. Amber had great ambitions to walk him at the dog park every morning when they first got him, but that was before Gracie came along, before her charity work, before life got in the way.

So Ginger doesn't just run around, he jumps in the lake and swims excitedly to bring back sticks that Richard throws out for him, while the children jump up and down on the shore and squeal with glee as Ginger comes out and shakes himself dry all over the four of them.

Vicky takes Ginger to the car and attempts to dry him with a jacket, as a woman loads her own golden retriever into the Ford Explorer parked next to them. The woman has been standing near them by the lake, and now she looks over at Vicky and smiles.

"You have a beautiful family," she says, and Vicky feels a surge of sadness, and joy.

"Thank you," she says, knowing that while this may not be hers, the possibility is now there. She's bonding with the kids, she's comfortable with Richard, and she can finally see that marriage isn't this impossible dream that has been, and will be, forever out of her reach. She could have this too. She is the sort of person other women—women like the one with the Ford Explorer—look at and envy.

And Vicky feels a surge of joy in her heart, because she never ever thought she was going to be this woman. She had always thought it was a dream, that anyone looking at her would know instantly that she was a single journalist with a terrible track record with men, but maybe she got it all wrong. Maybe this is the beginning of a whole new life, a way of attracting a whole new life. Maybe she should have done this years ago. Maybe this experiment isn't so strange after all.

And Richard? How does Richard feel about all this? Like Vicky, he is stunned by how normal it seems. Admittedly this isn't his typical Saturday, but where he thought he would have to stand on ceremony for this foreign journalist, he finds he feels far more comfortable with her than he ever imagined he would, and this doesn't feel nearly as strange as he expected.

He had liked her when he met her, but he hadn't expected to like her this much. And Richard realizes just how much he misses female friendship, the only females in his life being Amber and his mother.

The trading floor of Godfrey Hamilton Saltz was almost entirely male-dominated, the train journeys to and from work were spent either reading the paper or catching up with the other—male—commuters, and aside from the evenings spent with other couples at dinner, Richard realizes that he has no idea when he last spent this much time with a woman who was not family.

And more than that, he had no idea, before today, how much he missed it. When he was at the university his two best friends were female: Michelle and Cristina. They did everything together, and when Amber and he first met, he couldn't wait for her to meet the two of them, convinced they would get on like a house on fire.

But the fire never quite ignited, in part because of

Michelle's husband, Michael, and in part because Cristina had always been secretly in love with Richard and couldn't deal with him having first a serious girlfriend, and then a wife.

Cristina moved to San Diego, and for a few years she and Richard kept in touch with the odd e-mail, the even more rare phone call, and a very occasional lunch when she came to New York, but it's been two or three years since they exchanged anything other than a Christmas card, and it's only now, toward the end of this day that Richard is spending with Vicky, that he thinks about his old friends, and thinks how much he has missed female friendship.

He's never thought, before today, of how unlikely it is for a married man to be friends with a woman. If she's single, he thinks, everyone assumes they're having an affair, and if she's married, then they are still presumed to be having an affair. Why is it, he wonders, that it's so frowned upon, so impossible to have friends of the opposite sex once you are married?

Perhaps it would be different had Cristina and Michelle moved out to Highfield. Perhaps then they would all be friends, and it would be okay for him to go out occasionally with one of them, perhaps it wouldn't necessarily set tongues a-wagging, or be a red flag for Amber.

Although it's not as if Amber has male friends either, and were he to spot Amber in the window of the diner having lunch with another man, he knows he would immediately assume the worst.

But what a shame! How much he has missed! He has forgotten how much he had always enjoyed the company of women, and particularly this woman, who is quite unlike the women he has known.

He wonders if it is cultural, for Vicky is far sharper and funnier than most of the people he knows out here, and she has an openness and honesty he is not used to. She has already told him all about the man she is seeing—this Jamie Donnelly—and asked his opinion, although he didn't tell her what he thought.

And what he thought is this: When a man only rings you late at night, when he only wants to see you late at night, when he doesn't take you out for dinner, or introduce you to his friends, or spend any time or attention on you, then this is not a relationship. This is sex.

And then he can't help himself. He wonders what Vicky is like in bed, and almost as he thinks it he mentally kicks himself. Stop it! he says. You're a happily married man. And he tries very hard not to think about it for the rest of the day.

Which is much harder than he'd like to admit.

Chapter Twenty-four

By Friday afternoon Amber is exhausted. Once I am back home I will never complain again, she muses, thinking of all the times she tells Deborah she is exhausted, when all she has done is run around town doing errands.

This week, though, she has actually done some work. After the success of her box on ten things that give mums breathing space, Leona has given her more and more to do, without having to resort to sending her on a press trip just to get her out of the way.

From "How to Tell If Your Husband Is Having an Affair" (Amber found that one frighteningly easy, and thanks her lucky stars she's never had to deal with Richard suddenly joining a gym, or splashing himself with aftershave in the mornings . . .) to "Best New Self-tanners for Summer," Amber is having the time of her life.

Mostly, she realizes, she feels young again. Sitting in a busy, buzzing office, surrounded by younger girls all dressed in the latest fashions, all of whom see her as one of them, rather than just "a mum," has given Amber a shot of adrenaline and excitement that she hasn't felt since her days in the workplace, a feeling she had forgotten about entirely.

This is what I've been missing, she thinks, sometime around Thursday when the girls ask her to join them for lunch at Truc Vert, where they sit around a scrubbed wooden table and banter and laugh over delicious salads and glasses of white wine.

"So come on, Amber," Ruth says over lunch, "tell us what your life is like in America. Is it very different? What will Vicky be doing now?"

"Now?" Amber looks at her watch. "Now it's half past eight in the morning so she'll be showering while our nanny gets the kids dressed to take them to camp, although sometimes I take them, so Vicky may be getting them ready or packing their lunches."

Little does she know that Vicky, in her determination to be the greatest mother of all time, has now given Lavinia a later start in the mornings, wanting to do it all herself, to see what it's really like to be a full-time mother, and one without the advantages of middle-class wealth—that is, a full-time nanny.

At eight-thirty this morning Vicky is trying to persuade Gracie to drink from her sippy cup even though she is insisting on drinking from "a big girl cup," and just as Vicky suspects, Gracie goes on to pour milk all over her dress. She erupts in a storm of wails as Vicky carries her upstairs to change her, while Jared refuses to sit at the table and eat his muffin.

Once Gracie is changed she runs into the playroom and covers herself, and most of the playroom, with green paint, and when Vicky has packed their lunches and calls them for camp, already fifteen minutes late, Grace and Jared are fighting over the green paint, and both of them are now covered.

"Oh God," she groans, fighting back the tears of frustration, for Jared had three bad dreams last night and insisted on coming in to get her, and all she wants to do right now is crawl back under the covers and go to sleep. "God, please give me the strength to deal with this."

She drives Jared and Gracie to camp, and once she is all alone in the car she breathes a sigh of relief. This motherhood thing is definitely not all it's cracked up to be.

"Will your kids be behaving for her, do you think?" Leona grins.

"Oh yes," Amber says, unaware that her playroom has been redecorated in green, allegedly washable, paint. "My kids are very well behaved."

She goes on to tell them about her life. About the charities. The work she's done. The socializing.

"But what else do you do?" Ruth asks, confused.

"Isn't that enough?"

"I don't know," Leona says. "Aren't you doing this because you were feeling unfulfilled?"

Amber nods slowly. "It's true. I feel as though I fill my days running around doing things, but none of it seems to matter. Even though I'm supposed to be helping these charities, even I can see that that isn't the reason why we all get involved. No one cares about raising the money to build a new recovery center, or apartment building for the homeless. What they care about is who's got the most expensive outfit at the gala, and who has the biggest house. And what I hate most of all is that I buy into that. Even though I see it for what it is, and hate it, I do it all the same. I got this decorating firm, Amberley Jacks, to do our living room—"

"I know Amberley Jacks!" Leona interrupts. "I just read a piece about them in *W*. They're the firm to use right now."

"And that's the point. I used them because the other girls would be jealous, and you know what?"

"What?" The girls all lean in.

"The room looks like crap."

"Noooo!" They lean out again.

"Yes. It's lilac, for God's sake. Lilac and plum. Every time I walk into it I want to throw up."

"But at least you recognize it for what it is," Leona says seriously. "Doesn't that make you automatically different? Better?"

"Different, perhaps. Better? No. I would only be better if I stopped doing it. It's like that old saying: Three frogs were sitting on a log and two decided to jump off, so how many were left on the log?"

"One?" Ruth suggests.

"Nope. Three. That's the point. They only *decided* to jump off, they didn't actually do anything about it. It's not what you think about that matters in life, it's what you actually *do* about it."

Leona smiles as she orders more coffee. "Well, you're doing something about it, aren't you? You're here, living the life of a single girl."

"I know. I do feel that this is the first step to get me out of this rut."

"Do you actually like where you live?"

"No. Not really."

"So why can't you move?" asks Stella.

"It's complicated. My husband needs to commute to his job on Wall Street, and there aren't that many places that are within commuting distance. And I guess I've always been scared of change. I've worked so hard for everything I've got, and even though part of me hates it, part of me loves that I can live in a house like I do, buy the clothes I do, because I grew up with nothing. Not that I think any of it is real, or even matters particularly, but I came from nothing, and I still look around at all that we have and can't believe quite how far I've come."

"Even though it's not yours, it's your husband's job that provides it?"

"Ouch," Amber laughs.

"God, I'm sorry," Leona says. "That came out sounding far bitchier than I had anticipated."

"No, it's okay. And you're right. I don't contribute anything. Maybe that's what needs to change. Maybe I need to work, find a job, do something for me, something real. And I have to tell you, even though this is only the first week, I am loving every minute of it."

"Even writing about the shit farms?" Ruth laughs, referring to the article they had given her about the latest and greatest health farm, which provides five colonics a day.

"Even writing about the shit farms was fun," Amber said. "Although I'm not sure I'd feel the same way if I actually had to go there. Maybe I'd feel differently if I was from California, but as it is you can keep your shit to yourself, thank you very much."

After work on Friday she zips over to the blue bar at the Berkeley for a drink, and then, instead of joining the others at Hospital—Janelle is a member and had got the others in—she decides to go home for an early night.

Now this is what I've missed, she thinks, pulling on pajamas after a fairly pathetic, but nevertheless hot, shower, and sinking onto the sofa with an oversized bag of nacho chips for dinner.

She yawns her way through *Will & Grace*, and just as *Big Brother* is starting she gets up to go to bed, when the doorbell rings.

It's ten-fifteen. Who on earth would be at her door, or more to the point, Vicky's door, at ten-fifteen? And what should she do? Were she in Highfield, Richard would answer it, but then again were she in Highfield *no one* would ring her doorbell at this time of night. The whole of Highfield is sleeping at this time of night. Were she single and living in Manhattan she would just ignore it, but here? Of course she knows that Vicky would answer it, and so, hesitantly, finally, she picks up the intercom and says hello.

"Hi, Vix," comes a voice. "It's Dan."

"Um. It's not Vicky," Amber says, realizing this must be the Daniel that Vicky had mentioned. "This is Amber. Vicky's away in America for a few weeks. Can I give her a message?"

"Oh shit," comes a mumble, at which point Amber realizes that Dan is ever so slightly drunk. "Well, can I come in anyway?"

"Oh." Amber looks down at herself. She can't possibly let a strange man in while wearing pajamas so late at night. Never mind what the neighbors would think, what would Richard think? How would she feel if Richard were letting a strange woman in late at night while she was away?

But this isn't about Richard. This is about Vicky. Walking in her shoes. Living her life. Doing what she would do, and there is no doubt about it. If Vicky were here right now she would let Daniel in. That's all she has to do. Let him in, perhaps make him a cup of tea, be friendly, and then send him on his way. She's willing to befriend him, no benefits required.

* * *

Daniel struggles to focus on this sexy, lithe redhead standing in Vicky's doorway. She's slightly taller than Vicky, almost the same height as him, and despite the pajamas and robe, he can see her body is as taut as an athlete's. Well, well, well. This is an unexpected surprise.

"Hel-lo!" Daniel grins, leaning against the doorjamb in a bid to appear somewhat less drunk—and wobbly—than he is.

"Hello." Amber smiles politely but stiffly, extending her hand, which Daniel shakes warmly, and for what feels like several minutes, staring into Amber's eyes, clutching her hand firmly while she tries to extricate it. "Do you want a cup of tea?" Amber asks eventually, whisking her hand away with all her might, praying that he'll say no but knowing that, being British, he'll say yes.

Amber is discovering that a cup of tea is the British panacea for just about anything. She has caught the odd soap opera with delight, noting that however distressed the characters are, whether they have just discovered their husbands are dying, their daughters are drug addicts, they only have twenty-four hours to live, someone somewhere will say, "Go on, have a nice cuppa tea. That'll make you feel better."

"Love a cup of tea," Daniel says, following a reluctant Amber into the kitchen, admiring the delicate bones of her ankles as she walks.

"I've got to be honest, I'd completely forgotten about you." He grins while Amber fills the kettle. "Not to mention the fact that Vicky didn't tell me you were, well, you know . . ."

"No, I don't know. What?" He may be drunk, and she may be unavailable but here is a man, and an attractive one at that, who appears to be somewhat taken with her. Amber doesn't remember the last time someone actively flirted with her, and so what if he's a little sozzled. She's still going to enjoy it and take her compliments where she can.

"Well, you're rather saucy, aren't you?" Daniel says, and Amber can't help herself. She cracks up with laughter.

"Saucy?" she finally manages to splutter. "Saucy? What on earth does saucy mean?"

"You know," Daniel says. "Sexy. Nice. Attractive."

"Well thank you for the compliment, but just so you know, I'm also married."

Daniel's ears prick up. For a commitaphobe such as he is, what could be more perfect, what could be more attractive, than a glamorous redhead who's not only married but whose husband is on the other side of the Atlantic? Who would ever know? Who would ever tell? Did ever a situation present itself that was as perfect as this?

"Even better," Daniel says lasciviously. "Married women are just my cup of tea."

"Speaking of which," Amber tries to hide her flush, not because she's attracted to Daniel but because she's so unused to being in a situation like this, "milk and sugar?"

"Yes, please. So you're the swapper."

"Careful. People might talk."

Daniel raises an eyebrow. "Well, let's give them something to talk about, then . . ."

Amber splutters with laughter. "Goodness. You just don't stop, do you?"

"Not when I see something I want."

Amber decides to try another tack. She is, after all, a mother, and here is a man acting much like a willful child. "Come along, Daniel," she says sternly. "Come and sit in the living room. After you've finished your tea I think you ought to have some strong coffee to sober you up, and then I'll send you home."

"Oooh, yes, teacher." Daniel grins, and Amber shakes her head and sighs. "So how come your husband let you come over to England for a month?"

"I thought you'd forgotten all about this swap?"

"It's all coming back to me now. But seriously, what kind of man would let a woman as delicious as you out of his sight for that long?"

"Well, truth be told, he didn't want to. This was something I did without his knowledge, and once Vicky picked me I felt it was something I had to go through with, but trust me, he wasn't happy about it at all."

"And how do you think Vicky will be getting on with him?"

"Despite your inference, my husband is as faithful as I am. It's not like either of us to have an affair."

"Who's suggesting an affair? I was thinking about one joyful night of passion."

"With you and your beery breath?" Daniel's flirting is making Amber more forward than she is used to, and for a moment she feels just like a single woman, a powerful woman used to using her sexuality to get what she wants, or doesn't want. In fact, for the first time since she arrived Amber suddenly has a flash of what it really means to be Vicky, what being a single woman living in the city is really all about, and it is just as heady and empowering and exciting as it was all those years ago when Amber herself was single.

"I would brush my teeth for you."

"Oh please!" Amber laughs. "Will you just grow up?"

"Okay, okay." Daniel holds his hands up in defeat and laughs. "So should I assume I won't be staying the night?"

"Not unless you're comfortable staying on the sofa."

"Sounds fine to me," Daniel says. "Is there room for both of us?"

"Oh very funny. Look, it's very late and I'm very tired, and in the morning I'm catching a train down to Vicky's brother and sister-in-law in the country. I really think you ought to go home."

"Okay, okay. Point taken. I know when I'm not wanted. But how about this: Dinner on Sunday night? I bet you haven't seen the neighborhood at all."

"Actually I think I know it pretty well. I've been shopping at Waitrose, had lunch at Giraffe, been to Selfridges, had coffee at Providores . . ."

"Ah. Well, how about other neighborhoods, then? Why don't we go out for dinner so I can introduce you to some proper British food?"

"Do you mean steak and kidney pie and trifle?" Amber asks dubiously.

"No. Well, I mean maybe there's steak and kidney pie on the menu, but I could just take you to a great restaurant. We could get to know each other a little bit. Come on. How about it?" Amber hesitates and Daniel finally utters the words to make her change her mind: "If you were Vicky you'd say yes without a second thought."

"If I were Vicky I wouldn't be sending you home now," Amber bats back quickly.

"Ah yes. Good point. Does that mean I can stay?"

"No it does not. Good night, Daniel."

"How about dinner on Sunday?" he pleads as she ushers him to the front door.

"I don't know," Amber says. "Let me think about it."

"Oh God," groans Daniel just as Amber is shutting the

front door on him. "Nothing I love more than a woman who plays hard to get. Do you know, I could fall in love with you?"

"Oh behave," Amber echoes Austin Powers as she closes the door, and is then surprised to find herself grinning as she walks down the hallway and goes into the bathroom to brush her teeth.

"Amber!" Kate folds her arms around Amber, who, unused to this display of warmth, particularly from the English, whom she had always thought of as extraordinarily reserved, attempts to hug her back. "Oh so lovely that you're here! And look how glamorous and gorgeous you are. Our little town won't know what to make of you! Kids! Come and say hello to Amber."

Luke, Polly, and Sophie, who had been hanging back behind Kate, now step forward sheepishly and say hello.

"Oh my gosh!" Amber can't help herself. "They speak in perfect little British accents! How adorable!"

"I can speak in an American accent too," Luke says.

"Go on," Amber encourages. "What can you say?"

"May the Force be with you," Luke says, in a hybrid mid-Atlantic accent, and Amber applauds.

"Good job!" she says. "That was perfect."

"Come on." Kate links her arm through Amber's and leads her to the car. "Andy's at home dealing with the chickens. Unfortunately the coop isn't as secure as we thought and a fox got in last night and got three of the chickens before the dogs scared him off."

"Miss Martha and Dottie and Darth Vader are all in heaven now," says Sophie, slipping her hand into Amber's as they walk along.

"Darth Vader?" Amber raises an eyebrow.

"Ah yes. I think it's clear that Darth Vader, or Miss Vader as she is—sorry, was—sometimes known, was Luke's."

"That's an interesting name." Amber grins at Luke.

"I know. She was my first, but it's okay because I'm going to get another chicken and this one's going to be called Melman."

"Melman?"

"Yes. From *Madagascar*."

Kate shrugs and rolls her eyes as they reach the beaten-up old Saab. "It's his latest obsession, just out on DVD."

They drive along country roads and Kate points out country pubs, local farms, and where she does her shopping.

"That's our school!" The kids bounce up and down in the backseat, leaning forward to stretch an arm across Amber to point out something else. "That's our playground! That's where I do ballet!"

"Is this making you feel more at home now?" Kate laughs, turning to look at Amber as they sit at a traffic light.

"Apart from the English accents, absolutely." Amber grins, and it's true. Now she feels like she belongs again. Back in a family, albeit not her own.

Andy is waiting outside the house as they pull up, hooting for the dogs to get out of the way.

"Hello!" he says, shaking her hand warmly, and smiling down at her. "Should I be calling you Amber or Vicky?"

"I think Amber is perfect," Amber says.

"Good. So, Amber, why don't you come into the kitchen and sit down for a nice cup of tea?"

* * *

Amber is pulled upstairs midway through her cup of tea to go and see Polly and Sophie's bedroom, and then the children insist she come with them to the vegetable patch at the back of the garden to help them pick peas for lunch, and Luke wants to show her where Darth Vader will be buried.

"Buried?" Amber whispers to Kate. "Aren't you going to eat the chicken?"

"Unfortunately not. These chickens were layers rather than roasters, plus none of them would have been plump enough, but I do rather fancy being entirely self-sufficient. I think Melman and her two companions will be roasters, although God knows what the kids will say when Melman suddenly appears on the supper table surrounded by roast potatoes and garlic."

"Come on!" Luke's head appears round the kitchen door. "Amber, hurry up!"

The four of them pick the peas, then come back in to find Kate preparing a huge salad.

"What can I do to help?" Amber asks, standing helplessly behind Kate.

"The kids like shelling the peas and the salmon's all ready to go in the poacher. I think we're all done. Andy's going to do drinks, but maybe you could set the table outside? Would that be okay?"

"Of course," and Kate points out where Amber will find everything.

"What kind of help do you have during the week?" Amber asks when the six of them have finished lunch, the kids having run off down to the stream at the bottom of the garden to throw stones, the grown-ups still drinking wine, and talking about coffee, although all of them are far too comfortable lazing in the sun to get up and go inside to put the kettle on.

"Help? I have Mrs. Reilly who comes twice a week to clean the house and help with the laundry."

"And for the kids?"

"Well, she's wonderful with the kids, but she's not a nanny, if that's what you mean. She's my lady who does."

"Does? Does what?"

"You know. Clean."

"So who helps with the kids?"

"You're looking at her," Andy laughs. "Kate is wife, mum, nanny, gardener, chief washer-upper, decorator."

Kate laughs at the expression on Amber's face. "Don't look so horrified, Amber. I'd love to have help, but we couldn't afford it."

Andy looks stricken for an instant. "Would you really love to have help with the kids?"

"No, not really, darling. Only when they're tired and whiny. The truth is I did have a maternity nurse for Sophie and I couldn't stand having someone else look after my baby. I know it must be a complete luxury to have an au pair or a nanny, and it's not that I think there's anything wrong with it, I just don't think I would feel in control of my life if other people were looking after it instead of me."

"That's it!" Amber says suddenly. "That's how I feel! Kate, you've just put your finger on it."

"What do you mean?"

"I mean that I'm not in control of my life. I have a full-time nanny, a cleaning team that comes three times a week to thoroughly clean my house, a gardening team, a swimming pool man. Other people decorate my house, the nanny does the cooking. Oh my gosh," and she goes quiet as she thinks about the reality of her life. "I'm living my life but I'm not involved in it. That's exactly what's wrong with me."

"But if you're not involved in it, how are you really living it?" Kate asks gently.

"That's the point." Amber shakes her head, the weight of the realization sitting firmly on her shoulders. "I'm not living. I'm just existing, I guess, as though I'm caught in limbo, watching my life play out in front of me like a movie! Oh my God, do you have any idea how huge this is? I mean, look at you. You look after your own kids, you made this delicious lunch yourself, you're in charge of your life."

"I think you'll find *I'm* the one in charge," Andy jokes as Kate rolls her eyes.

"It's not always this perfect," Kate laughs. "You happen to have come down on a glorious English summer's day when the children are behaving perfectly. On days like this anyone could do it all. It's when it's raining and we're all stuck inside and everyone's miserable and all I want is someone to come and take the children away to give me some peace and quiet."

"I guess it's all about balance," Amber says quietly. "And right now the balance in my life is completely off."

"Well, here's to balance," and Andy pours everyone another glass of wine.

"And to more glorious summer days." Kate smiles and they toast one another again.

Chapter Twenty-five

Is it really possible to walk in another woman's shoes? Vicky types on her laptop as she sits at the desk in the kitchen on Friday morning while Lavinia clatters around behind her, tidying up the kitchen after the daily bomb has hit during breakfast.

The children are in camp, and while Amber would normally be at the gym at this time, Vicky has decided that given her now-healing-but-still-painful sunburn, the gym will have to wait until Monday, and given how quiet the house is—the Brazilian cleaning team isn't due to arrive for another half-hour—it's the perfect time to start writing the diary of her time here.

The whole experience is quite different from what Vicky expected. She hadn't realized how difficult it would be to step into someone else's life, although she imagines Amber is having an easier time, having already lived a single girl's life, knowing fairly well what it entails.

But this, pretending to be married, feels just that. A pretense. Most of the time Vicky feels as if she's watching a movie, except she happens to be playing the starring role. It isn't helped by the fact that she is in America, where everything is foreign, and exciting, and that much more glamorous than it would be in, say, Penge, or Surbiton. No, the English suburbs could learn a lesson or two from the American suburbs, particularly here in Connecticut.

Vicky has never seen such perfection in her life. From the way the women dress—their perfect pink-and-green floral Lily Pulitzer pants with oh-so-cute Jack Rogers sandals—to the home-baked pies and tarts they bring along to dinner parties, although this much is hearsay from Deborah, Vicky not having yet been invited to any dinner parties, although she's hoping for an invitation soon.

And thank God for Deborah, who has felt like the port in the storm, who has already been over more times than Vicky would like to think about to help Vicky out when she gets stuck.

On Monday the oil company came to refill the tank, and Vicky had no idea where to direct them, and couldn't get hold of Richard. Deborah came to the rescue. On Tuesday the cleaning team stood in the kitchen waiting patiently and smilingly for their money. Vicky had no idea where it was, so Deborah dashed over with some money for which Richard promptly reimbursed her, showing the faintest sign of irritation that Vicky hadn't known where to look. (Didn't Amber tell you, for heaven's sake? he said, gesturing to a drawer in the desk of the kitchen, at the back of which was a large envelope stuffed with bills, labeled "House Cash." Well, no.) Now Vicky realizes why Amber's notes were so short. Because she had forgotten almost everything. Vicky had no idea the tick-control people were coming to spray the garden, and no one could play outside. That happened on the day she had promised Jared and Gracie a picnic for supper, and then had to renege when the giant truck pulled up and a big burly man warned her not to go outside for the rest of the day.

And ticks? Who ever heard of ticks being such a problem? But everywhere she goes people are clucking and discussing the terrible Lyme disease that's passed to humans from deer ticks. Amber hadn't mentioned anything about checking the children at bathtime every night, looking for teeny tiny ticks that Deborah says are about the size of a freckle, which terrified Vicky because how on earth is she supposed to differentiate between a tick and a freckle when she's never even seen a tick, and is convinced she wouldn't know a tick from a freckle if her life depended on it. . . .

It's only after a few days that Vicky realizes why Amber doesn't mention anything about checking for ticks at bathtime, or only giving Jared butter sandwiches because he won't eat anything else, not even egg mayonnaise (which surely all children adore), and she doesn't tell Vicky not to give Gracie peanut butter sandwiches—a lesson she learned the hard way after the chief counselor of Gracie's camp called her in and sternly admonished her, announcing that the camp is a nut-free zone due to several children having severe nut allergies.

Vicky realizes that Amber doesn't mention this because Amber doesn't *know*. Lavinia, the nanny, is having more free time this week than she's had in years, and as a result she's decided that Vicky is not the enemy after all, and has slowly opened up to her, informing her of quite how little time Amber spends with the children.

Who makes the kids' lunches in the morning? Lavinia. Who bathes them every night and checks for ticks? Lavinia. Who drives them to most of their activities, other than the ones at which friends of Amber's will be? Why, Lavinia of course.

And yet the children are lovely, far better behaved than

Vicky had expected, and she can't understand why Amber, who also seems so nice, and professes to love her children so much, doesn't spend more time with them.

"Oh she's very busy," says Lavinia, who, despite being overworked and underpaid, is loyal and likes her bosses. "All that charity work. Raising money for the church. She's a busy lady."

And therein lies the problem. No matter how hard Vicky tries to emulate Amber, she can't quite see how Amber is so busy. There has been plenty of time for Vicky to dream of drifting around the swimming pool—she's hoping that next week her skin will be tough enough for her to put that particular plan in motion, with factor 30 sun cream in future. There has been plenty of time, period. Time in which Vicky ambles around the enormous house, wondering whether she should perhaps do some dusting, before remembering that a cleaning team takes care of that. Maybe she should do the children's laundry, but Lavinia wouldn't hear of it.

So she has cooked the children, and Richard, lavish meals. Not known for her cooking skills, even Vicky knows how to follow a recipe, and she has produced all the nursery classics she loved so much when she was a child.

Richard is delirious with joy. He's far more used to cold pizza or take-outs from various restaurants around town, and this past week he's been sitting down to proper home-cooked meals.

The children on the other hand are not quite so happy. In fact they are downright suspicious of this foreign food. Toad in the hole was the biggest success thus far, and only because they had huge fun playing with it, trying to put the sausages back perfectly in the batter, both of them refusing to take a single bite. Even macaroni and cheese, which Vicky was convinced they would love, was a disaster. She made it with three different cheeses, a hint of mustard, a sprinkling of nutmeg, and even Vicky was astounded by how delicious it was.

"This isn't macaroni and cheese," Jared announced, staring suspiciously at the dish Vicky had put on the table.

"Yes it is, Jar. I made it myself."

"But it's the wrong *color*," he said, pushing his plate away.

"Just take one bite. It's absolutely delicious," Vicky said, demonstrating by gobbling up two mouthfuls herself, and making ecstatic noises of joy when she finished. "Mmmm. Mmmm. Yummy. That is so yummy."

But Jared refused to even taste it. Gracie on the other hand took an enthusiastic forkful, then spat it out all over the table.

Nope. The cooking hasn't been a success, and feeling somewhat guilty Vicky is resorting to the stockpile of pizza and chicken nuggets in the freezer.

This mother game, she realizes, isn't quite as much fun as it looks when she's the beloved aunt down at Kate and Andy's. There are the constant fights she has to break up between Jared and Gracie, the whining and crying that seem to start soon after they wake up, until roughly just before they go to bed.

The first three days they were perfect. Vicky thought she had landed in a commercial for bizarro children—the children from another planet who looked like normal children but were far better behaved. Unfortunately the thrill of having a new mother wore off by day four, and the bad behavior and fighting started, not to mention the constant asking when their real mommy would be coming home.

Gracie took it hardest, and Vicky made an extra special effort to do things with her, try and distract her from the fact that Amber wasn't there, and as she was sitting in the kitchen making a dollhouse out of one of the stack of Manolo Blahnik shoe boxes piled in Amber's closet—surely she wouldn't mind . . . what could she be keeping them for anyway?—Vicky realized what a sacrifice Amber had made. It was so easy for Vicky to give up her single life, so easy for her to walk toward what she knew, with absolute certainty, would be better.

But how could Amber have done the same thing? How could she have left her children and husband so easily? Even though temporary, Vicky is surprised that Amber was able to do the swap. Surprised that any woman would be able to do it, particularly when the husband is as nice as Richard, the kids as sweet as these, the lifestyle as wonderful as this.

Vicky can see how easy it would be to lose yourself in this seemingly perfect world. Whether immersed in the children or doing nothing, without a job, or something to keep her busy, Vicky can't imagine how Amber doesn't go out of her mind with boredom.

Which is why, she supposes, she does so much charity work. Ah yes. Speaking of charity work, Vicky goes to check the charity schedule, the one area in which Amber was meticulous. Knowing that she doesn't have any events until next week, she hasn't bothered to look at it before now, aside from the cursory glance on the plane, and now when she looks, she gasps in horror.

Friday, August 17, noon, jewelry lunch at our house. Sonia Parkinson is the jewelry designer, and she should be coming here to set up at around eleven. I've ordered food from Rosemary & Thyme in town; you should pick it up in the morning, although you'll need to make a big salad, and get fresh bread from the bakery. Also, usually I do a fruit plate with some magic bars and lemon squares afterward—you can get the fruit and bars at Heywood Farms. Often I make a couple of pitchers of iced tea, and set out a selection of sodas. Sonia will come and set up her displays, then the women from the League will come at noon, and will probably browse as they eat lunch. I'm sorry to land this on you but I planned it before we knew we were going to swap! But I know you'll be fine . . .

Fine? Vicky's heart starts pounding. Fine? How can this be fine when it's ten o'clock and she's sitting at the desk in the kitchen typing, still in her pajamas, and God knows how many women are going to be coming for lunch in two hours. Oh shit. Oh shit shit shit.

"Lavinia!" Vicky shrieks from the bottom of the stairs.

"I'm upstairs doing laundry," comes a distant voice.

"Okay, I'll come upstairs. It's an emergency." And Vicky runs upstairs to rope Lavinia in to help.

Lavinia goes to pick up the food while Vicky brews up some tea and pours it into pitchers with thousands of ice cubes, praying it will be cold by the time the women arrive.

She starts a salad with what's in the fridge—some slightly wilted lettuce that is probably still good for another three hours if she's lucky, two small baskets of baby tomatoes, and lots and lots of sliced red onion. With any luck Lavinia will have been able to buy lots more salad stuff while she's out.

Scurrying round the pantry she finds some paper plates—God knows how Amber entertains, but given that Vicky has no idea how many people are coming, it will have to be paper today—paper napkins, half of them a lovely blue toile, and the other half clearly left over from Gracie's third birthday as they have Barbie pictures all over them. "Oh fuck it," Vicky mutters, balancing the toile napkins on top of the Barbie ones, hoping that perhaps there won't be that many people and they won't ever get to Barbie.

And then the doorbell rings.

"Hi, I'm Sonia." A woman stands on the doorstep surrounded by boxes, looking slightly puzzled at the door being opened at eleven a.m. by someone still in pajamas. "Is Amber home?"

"Um, no. She's in England. I'm Vicky. I'm her temporary replacement."

"Ah ha!" Sonia grins. "You're the swapper?"

"Careful," Vicky says. "I don't want people to get the wrong idea."

"In this town? Are you kidding? People have already got the wrong idea. You're the scarlet woman come to steal Amber's husband."

"Oh my God. You're not serious?"

"Yes," Sonia laughs. "But don't worry about it. Everyone's just madly excited they've got something to gossip about, and it's great for me, means we're going to have a huge turnout today because everyone's dying to see what you look like."

"This is horrific," Vicky groans. "I can't believe everyone's talking about me. Look at me, for Christ's sake. Do I look like a scarlet woman to you?"

"No, but please tell me you're not planning on wearing pajamas to lunch? Although who knows, it might start a new trend."

"I have to take a shower but I haven't had time. I didn't know about this lunch until an hour ago, and now I've got to get everything ready, and I've done nothing."

"No flowers? No candles? No room spray?" Sonia looks horrified, and Vicky isn't sure whether she's joking or not.

"All I can say is thank God Amber's not here to see what a horrible job I'm doing." The sound of keys from the kitchen captures Vicky's attention, and Sonia follows Vicky into the kitchen to find Lavinia unpacking bags.

"Oh thank God!" Vicky says. "The food."

"They'd mislaid the order," Lavinia says, "and they were out of most of it, so I had to go to the supermarket and choose a couple of things. Figured I couldn't leave you empty-handed."

"So what did you get?"

"Macaroni and cheese and meat loaf."

"What? Oh God. What about the salad? Did you get salad stuff?"

"Oh no!" Lavinia groans. "I *knew* there was something I forgot. But I bought your fruit and magic bars. I have to go and pick up Gracie from school now. I'll see you later." And Lavinia leaves Vicky to unpack the bags, almost in tears as she surveys tin trays of congealing macaroni and cheese and an unappetizing meat loaf.

"Well, this will certainly be . . . *different*," Sonia says, as she starts unpacking her boxes and laying necklaces and earrings out on the kitchen counter. "I doubt any of this crowd has eaten macaroni and cheese or meat loaf since they were seven."

"Never mind that, it even looks horrible. I know this isn't what Amber would do, but on the bright side at least they'll be happy to see her come back. This is probably the most revolting lunch they've ever been to. Skanky old salad, Barbie napkins, and yucky-looking mac and cheese and meat loaf."

"I shouldn't worry about it too much," Sonia laughs. "Most of these women aren't going to eat that anyway. Red meat in the meat loaf and macaroni and cheese way too carby. Shame you don't have more salad, but they're not here for the food, they're here to see what they're wearing, and hopefully to buy my jewelry."

"Oh shit!" Vicky yelps, looking at the clock. "I've got fifteen minutes. If the doorbell rings, will you get it?" and without waiting for an answer she runs upstairs.

No time for a shower, barely time for makeup, her hair, which is in dire need of a wash, is scraped back in a ponytail while she rifles through Amber's wardrobe. "What to wear, what to wear?"

And today is not a day that is kind to her. Vicky is used to these days at home. She can put on her favorite jeans on a Saturday and feel like a goddess—sexy, skinny, gorgeous, and Sunday, just one day later, she will pull on the same jeans and feel like an ogre—ugly, fat, disgusting.

Today is that Sunday, except it's not even her own wardrobe. She had thought that she and Amber were the same size, except now she realizes that in the week she's been here she's clearly been overeating to mask her discomfort, and now everything feels uncomfortably tight, and as for Amber's Chip & Pepper jeans, they barely make it over her knees.

And Amber said the women dress up for one another, and didn't that Sonia just say the same thing? But what does that mean? Does that mean jeans and high-heeled boots, or a cocktail dress?

In the end, in the four minutes remaining, Vicky settles on a knee-length Audrey Hepburn–style black cotton dress, with a black silk bow just under the bust. It fits, it's comfortable, and in line with this Holly Golightly moment, Vicky throws on several strands of large costume pearls, slips her feet into black satin slingbacks, and twists her hair up in a beehive. No time for makeup other than a slick of lipstick, and no time to check herself in the mirror as the doorbell rings. She will just have to do.

"Are you going to a party?" Deborah grins on the doorstep as she kisses Vicky hello and deposits a giant cake box on the table.

"Oh God, you mean this is completely wrong, isn't it?" Vicky looks at Deborah's outfit of chinos and a pink linen shirt, and turns to run upstairs and change.

"No, don't worry, I was just teasing. Anyway, I wouldn't judge my outfit as what you should wear—I'm always either coming back from the stables or about to go to the stables, and I'm always the worst-dressed one here, although frankly I couldn't care less. Anyway, love that dress. I've always told Amber it's very Audrey."

"Well, that was the look I was going for."

"You pulled it off. And don't worry about what everyone else is wearing. Half of them will be in brand-new designer outfits from Rakers that they bought just for today, and frankly who can be bothered to compete with that? So how did you manage everything today? Amber said she was doing food from my favorite place, Rosemary and Thyme."

"Ah yes. I'm afraid there's been a bit of a disaster on that front," Vicky says. "They misplaced the order and I'd put Lavinia in charge, so she took herself off to Stop and Shop and came back with macaroni and cheese and meat loaf."

"Say that again?"

"Unfortunately you heard it right the first time."

"Oh well. Most of these women don't eat anyway. And I don't mind. I love macaroni and cheese."

"Not sure you'll like this one. It's a rather frightening shade of orange."

"Mmm. Plastic macaroni and cheese. Even better." And Vicky laughs. "Honestly," Deborah continues, "Amber always gets herself into such a state when she does these things. Far better to be laid back about it, plus you shouldn't care anyway. You're a journalist, not a Stepford wife."

"I know," Vicky groans, "but I'm a journalist pretending to be a Stepford wife just for a little while. I was hoping to do a better job than I seem to be doing."

"Well, no one's here yet. Let's go in the kitchen and I'll help finish the setting up, and just in case you were wondering, I think you're doing a great job."

"You do? Really?"

"I do, really, and I mean that in the English sense of the word."

"As opposed to?"

"The American sense of the word. Not that I dislike living here, because I absolutely love it, but I do think most of the women here are completely bonkers. They praise their children for absolutely everything. Their children breathe and they're clapping saying, 'Good job! Great job!' I'm much more English about my parenting. As far as I'm concerned criticism is essential to give them a healthy dose of low self-worth."

Vicky laughs.

"Anyway, the point is you are doing a good job. It's bloody difficult to step into someone's life, and it's not as if you've ever been married. The very fact that Jared and Gracie seem to adore you is testament to how well you're doing. Trust me, they don't take to everyone like that, and I hear you're getting on with Richard too."

"Oh God," Vicky groans, "I suppose you've heard the rumors too?"

"What rumors? The ones that have you seducing Richard and sleeping with him in the marital bed?"

"Yes, those would be the ones."

"No. I haven't heard those. But if I had," Deborah peers at her closely, "tell me they wouldn't be true, because right now I really like you, but if I discovered you were having an affair with my best friend's husband, I'd have to start hating you, and I really don't want to have to do that."

"Hand on heart, I am not having an affair with Richard," Vicky says, thanking her lucky stars that just then the doorbell rings, because this is not a conversation she is comfortable taking further. It's not a thought she's comfortable taking further either, so why does the thought keep creeping into her head?

It's not as if she isn't quite happy with Jamie Donnelly. Okay, it might be a little early to start thinking of herself as being entirely committed, especially given that she's phoned him a couple of times (yes, she knows that under the terms of Swapping Lives she isn't really allowed to do that, but if you won't tell, she won't), and he hasn't been in and hasn't called her back.

And it's not as if she's the type to get involved with a married man, it's just that living so closely with someone, sharing his house, sharing his children, sharing his life, affords an intimacy between them that is difficult to ignore, and while Vicky honestly has no intention of taking it further, it's easy to see how it could happen.

Not that it will, but it's not outside the realm of possibility, that's all.

The evenings Vicky spends with Richard are quite unlike the majority of evenings he spends with Amber. Although they do occasionally still have baths together, Amber has normally eaten before he comes home, and when he does get home they have cursory chitchat about their respective days before Amber disappears into the family room to watch television—reality shows like *The Bachelor* that he abhors—and he goes into his office to deal with household bills. Sometimes he'll join her in the family room for a nine o'clock *Law & Order* or *CSI*, but on the whole Amber will go to bed first and read, and by the time he goes up there she's asleep, or about to be.

Sunday night is their "date night." The night when they get a baby-sitter, go out for dinner, and make love, although often these days that feels a little cursory as well. Richard would love them to experiment more, would love Amber to, well, even *move* a little more would be a welcome change, but he accepts that this is the best he's going to get right now.

But since Vicky has been here, Richard has been coming home to find that Vicky has waited for him to have dinner—Vicky's parents always having had dinner together at night, and thus Vicky assuming that this is a normal thing to do.

They have sat and lingered over dinner, sharing stories, a couple of glasses of wine, and Richard has been reminded of the early days with Amber, the excitement of getting to know someone new, the thrill of not knowing all of their stories, gradually peeling back the layers to find the person who lies beneath.

And as he gets to know her, he can't deny that he finds her attractive. Not that Richard is thinking of doing anything about it—he isn't that sort of man; will look but would never touch—but how lovely to have something to look forward to at the end of every day. It's the one bright spot in his days that feel crazier and crazier. Home is the one place where he feels in control: strong, the patriarch, the man who makes everything better. And even though he's not planning on anything happening with Vicky Townsley, he is enjoying the touch of light relief she provides when he walks in the door. So much easier to think about than to walk through the mud-room door worrying about just how much money his wife would have spent that day.

"Hello, I'm Vicky. I'm the swapping-lives journalist you've all heard about, and no, I'm not sleeping with Richard, nor have any intention to, and yes, I realize I'm dressed completely inappropriately." Vicky has had it with the whispered glances and frosty pretense at politeness.

"Actually I think your dress is so pretty," Suzy says, lifting the fabric and fingering it lightly.

"Oh thank you! Well you must be the first. Clearly I got

the dress code wrong," Vicky notes Suzy's own Seven for all Mankind jeans, Manolo boots, and pink beaded djellaba, "but I'm stuck now, and I'm fed up with everyone talking about me."

"Oh just ignore them," Suzy says, linking her arm through Vicky's as she walks through to the kitchen, stopping short when she sees the still untouched food on the kitchen table. "Not everyone has to get this perfect, and it's very hard. When I did my first luncheon for the girls I got the flowers from Heywood Farms—can you imagine? They were the most horrible carnations you've ever seen, but I didn't know any better. I hope Amber told you to go to Blossom."

"Actually no, she didn't mention anything about flowers. I haven't got flowers. It was all I could do to get food, and that, as you can see, was a bit of a disaster."

"You mean that's for our lunch?" Suzy eyes the meat loaf and mac and cheese, which, despite having been transferred to Amber's best majolica, still doesn't look any more appetizing. "Oh my! I thought it was for the children!"

"Ah no. I'm sure it tastes better than it looks."

"Oh, don't worry," Suzy pats her arm reassuringly. "You can't be expected to get everything right first time. Now come into the family room with me and tell me how you're getting on with Richard."

Chapter Twenty-six

"Darling husband?" Kate asks as they're going into the house for lemonade after lying around on the sun loungers all afternoon, watching the kids play in the garden, chatting, and reading the papers. "Did you manage to fix the chicken coop, and have you spoken to Bill-the-chicken-man about replacements?"

"Surprising as it may be," Andy laughs, "I *have* fixed the coop, and Bill is bringing over a few more birds later this afternoon, plus he's going to check the coop to make sure it's fox-proof."

"Bill-the-chicken-man?" Amber raises an eyebrow.

Andy shrugs. "It's a habit of ours. Few people are ever referred to by their given names alone. There's Robert-the-gardener, Jake-the-spark—"

"Spark?"

"Our electrician," Kate explains with a laugh. "And rather a delicious one at that."

"Yes," Andy sighs. "The other prerequisite of working in our house seems to be that my darling wife has to have a crush on you."

"But not serious crushes," Kate pouts, "only little pretend ones, and I can't help it if I feel protected by all these big strong men taking care of me."

"Jake doesn't take care of you, Katie, he takes care of the wires."

"But they all make me feel safe, which is much the same thing."

"What about me?" Andy laughs as he steps up behind Kate, puts his arms around her and starts nuzzling her neck. "Do I make you feel safe?"

"Oh get off, you big lump," she says affectionately. "Go back to your chickens and leave me alone."

"I can't believe you talk about crushes in front of your husband," Amber says, once Andy has indeed taken Kate's advice and gone back to his chickens.

"Why? I'm only being silly. He knows I wouldn't ever do anything about it, although I have to say I did see Jake once without his shirt and his abs are rather yummy." She gives a little shiver, then grins.

"But does he trust you?"

"Of course!" Kate laughs. "I wouldn't ever do anything. It's just fun to look. Don't you do the same with your husband?"

"Goodness, no! My husband would be devastated if I talked about having a crush on someone. He wouldn't find it funny at all."

"Oh. He sounds very serious."

"No, he's not serious," and then Amber stops, because she realizes that while Richard per se is not serious, both of them certainly take themselves far more seriously than Kate and Andy seem to. In fact, Amber can't remember the last time they teased each other in the way Kate and Andy did over lunch, laughing affectionately together over a shared joke.

"Maybe we are too serious," Amber ventures, thinking out

loud. "Maybe that's part of this dissatisfaction. Maybe we've forgotten how to have fun."

Kate puts down her tea towel and turns to look at Amber. "Marriage should be about fun," she says gently. "It's about friendship, and laughter, and trust, and fun. If it's not fun, if you take it all too seriously, what's the point? You know I've been with Andy for fifteen years, and the reason it still works is because he's my best friend and he still makes me laugh. Admittedly, not all the time, and often we get completely bogged down in work, and the kids, and life, but he's still the person I most want to phone when anything happens in life, and he's still the person who makes me laugh the most."

Amber listens intently, her eyes fixed on Kate, her mind over the Atlantic Ocean with her family in Connecticut. They used to laugh as well, she thinks. In the early days before life got so crazy with children, and charities, and, well, just life.

And suddenly it seems that middle-age has set in. Richard is permanently exhausted from his commute, barely sees the children, and Amber is so busy keeping up with the Joneses she doesn't have time to stop and relax, enjoy her kids, enjoy her husband, have fun in the way that Kate and Andy seem to have fun here.

Today is the perfect example. They haven't actually done anything today. Nothing other than shell peas, play in the garden, lie on sun loungers, pop down to the local supermarket for some brie and cheese crackers for tonight. And yet today has been the most idyllic Saturday Amber can imagine. Granted, it helps that they are in the heart of the English countryside, that the sun is beaming and the bees and butterflies are buzzing around the lavender that's spilling over the old brick terrace where they've been lying, that the only sounds, other than the children laughing and occasionally fighting, have been the birds and the odd plane flying high overhead.

But couldn't she do this back at home? It's not as if they live in the city anymore. In fact, if Amber remembers correctly, the only sounds in their backyard are birds and the odd plane flying overhead.

Amber never seems to have time to enjoy it the way she has today. Saturdays are filled with breakfasts at the diner, trips to the bookstore, playdates, lunch at the deli, and only if they have time can they squeeze in swimming in their own pool, and even then Amber rarely goes in, not wanting to get her hair wet, so Richard splashes about with the kids for a bit while Amber reads the papers.

When they first moved in, when Amber couldn't sleep with excitement over the swimming pool, she dreamed of long lazy days, just like the one she has had today, playing with the kids in the pool, floating around on a raft with a drink in hand, even sensual midnight swims with Richard, maybe even making love under the wisteria-draped pergola on a hot summer night.

The truth is they barely use the pool. The truth is she isn't living the life she always wanted to live. The truth is, Amber realizes as she listens to Kate, that she and Richard are so busy running, constantly striving to reach some goal in the future, they never take time to stop and just enjoy where they are.

And where they are is really not so bad, Amber realizes. Not that Highfield is necessarily her town of choice, not anymore, but if she were to pull out of the charities, spend more time with her children, focus on her family and friends, in that order, wouldn't she start to enjoy what she has more?

"Richard is a wonderful man," Amber says eventually to Kate. "And he is my best friend. I think that the two of us have got so caught up in life, in the busyness and the stress, that we've stopped enjoying each other. It's not that we don't love each other—heaven knows we do—but I don't honestly remember the last time we had fun."

Amber takes a deep breath. "I know I've only been here a week, but I feel as though I'm having one epiphany after another. I was so nervous about coming, so convinced I had done the wrong thing, I almost thought about backing out, but now I see why I'm here."

Kate raises an eyebrow questioningly.

"I needed to get away from my life for a while to really see it properly. I knew I wasn't happy, but I love my husband and love my kids, and couldn't figure out what it was that was wrong.

"During the past week I've seen that I miss doing something for *me*, something that engages my brain, makes me feel useful; and the other thing that I now see so clearly is that I haven't been engaged in my life. I see you here, with your adorable children, and no help, and you manage fine. I've been so terrified about being overwhelmed by looking after my children myself, that instead I run away and spend my life being overwhelmed by this stupid charity work.

"Oh my gosh, Kate. I'm so glad I came down to see you this weekend. I can so see where I've been going wrong, and what needs to be done to make it right."

"You see?" Kate says cheerfully. "Everything happens for a reason. I just wonder how Vicky's getting on, what epiphanies she may have had, and whether she's had any huge realizations while she's living your life."

Amber shrugs her shoulders sadly. "I've been desperate to call home to find out, but it's against the rules."

"Aren't rules made to be broken?" Kate grins.

"Do you think I should phone?"

"I absolutely do," Kate says, handing her the cordless phone. "And after you speak, let me have a word with Vicky. Although I have to say you're a wonderful substitute and I'm having a lovely time with you, I do miss her."

Amber picks up the phone and dials, quietly putting down the phone when the answering machine picks up, and she looks at her watch.

"Should have known," she says. "Saturday means the kids will probably be on their way to the Little League game, and Richard's the stand-in coach this week so his cell will be turned off. I guess it serves me right for trying to break the rules."

"I know you must miss your children horribly, but isn't it wonderful to be free?"

Amber frowns. "Yes and no. I think that a week swapping lives would have been perfect. Now I don't know what I was thinking, agreeing to leave everyone for a month. The only thing that keeps me going is that this week has flown by, so hopefully the next three will go just as fast. The novelty of being able to do whatever I want whenever I want was amazing for the first three days, and now I just miss my family, I miss my life, but I'm still glad I did it."

"Well, I must say I'm glad you did it too. I've loved having you around today. Are you going to stay all weekend?"

"I'm staying tonight and then I think I'm going to get

back tomorrow. This friend of Vicky's wants to take me out to dinner."

"Which friend?"

"Daniel."

"Ah. Friend in the broader sense of the word." Kate grins.

"Yes, precisely. Not that I have to do what Vicky would do on this occasion," Amber smiles, "but he turned up the other night very late and very drunk, and seemed a bit taken with me. I hope he doesn't think I'm a date."

"He knows you're married?" Kate asks.

"Yes. Very much so. If anything I think that piqued his interest even more. He mentioned something like a joyful night of passion."

Kate whoops with laughter. "And there you were saying your life was boring."

"I didn't say that!" Amber laughs back. "But I do want to get to know Vicky's friends, so I think I should say yes."

"Absolutely you should say yes." Kate nods. "And there's nothing nicer than having an attractive man flirt with you, especially when you feel like an old married woman that no one would ever even look at."

"True," Amber says. "And he is attractive."

"See?" Kate says delightedly. "Maybe we can get you to develop an innocent crush after all."

Amber gives Kate a huge hug when she leaves. She kisses the children, gives Andy a smaller hug, and thanks them profusely for one of the nicest weekends of her life.

"Please come down again," Kate whispers into her ear. "It's been so lovely having you here, and the kids loved you too."

"I'm sure I will," Amber says. "Vicky's so lucky, having a family like you."

"And your family's so lucky," Kate smiles, "having a mummy and wife like you."

Daniel turns up to collect Amber at six o'clock, a bunch of full-blown peonies in hand.

"These are by way of apology," he says sheepishly when she opens the door. "I'm appalled at my behavior the other night. Turning up on your doorstep drunk was hardly the best way to introduce myself, but hopefully I'll prove to you this evening that I'm not so bad after all."

"The flowers are lovely," Amber says. "Come in while I put them in water, then shall we go?"

"Great," says Daniel, thinking that Amber is even more lovely than he remembered from the other night. She has a coolness and reserve that he has always found stunningly attractive, not to mention that exotic sophistication that a certain kind of American woman seems to hold.

"Where are we going?" Amber's voice comes from the kitchen.

"It's a surprise," Daniel calls back.

Amber appears in the doorway, the peonies now in a glass bowl that she sets carefully on the coffee table. "I don't like surprises," she says.

"You'll like this one," he says. "Look, please try and relax. I'm not going to flirt with you or make a pass at you. I'm just here having a friendly dinner, just as I would with Vicky."

"Except you'd go to bed with Vicky afterward, no?"

"True." Daniel shrugs. "But still, it's not a love thing with Vicky and me. It's friends with benefits, and I certainly don't expect you to go to bed with me afterward." Although, he thinks, if you'd like to that would be perfectly fine with me.

"Okay," Amber smiles. "This just feels very strange. You

have to remember I'm married with children, I don't have dinner with men I don't know, haven't done anything like this for years, and even though I know it's not a date, it just feels . . . well . . . like a date, I guess."

"It's not a date," Daniel says, opening the front door and ushering her downstairs to the car. "It's just an evening."

Daniel hadn't booked a restaurant. Instead he had bought out the local deli: fresh slices of prosciutto and Parma ham, exotic cheeses, crusty baguettes, pâtés, olives, roasted peppers with nutty olive oil and sprinklings of chili, two bottles of Pinot chilling in the cooler.

"Oh my gosh!" Amber says in delight when they park on the outskirts of Regent's Park, and Daniel produces the hamper and ice boxes from the boot of the car. "A picnic! How perfect!"

Daniel grins in delight. "I thought a quintessentially English picnic would be the perfect introduction to London for an American visitor. Unfortunately the food is mostly Mediterranean, but rather that than bangers and mash, I thought."

"No, it's perfect. And on such a lovely night. Did you organize the weather too?"

"Absolutely." Daniel nods seriously as they stroll through the park, avoiding the softball games being played, picking their way through other picnickers dotted around. "Had a word with the man upstairs this morning."

"Okay, I'm relaxed now." Amber grins. "This isn't a date. This is just a lovely thing to do on a summer's evening."

"And they say I don't know how to make a woman happy . . ." Daniel rolls his eyes.

"Well, right now I'd say you're making this woman very happy indeed," Amber says innocently, and Daniel resists the temptation to come back with a flirtatious wisecrack. Not now. Not yet. But God, she is gorgeous, and who knows what might happen after a few glasses of wine. . . .

Chapter Twenty-seven

The jewelry sale was a huge success. Despite the food, about which Sonia was right, no one really ate anything anyway, they sold nearly everything. For a while at the beginning Sonia was worried, but once Heidi snapped up a gold necklace for $1,200, it seemed that everyone rushed in to buy something for themselves.

Every good party must have a drama, and sure enough Vicky's jewelry party even had a little drama of its own when Nadine showed up, Suzy's alleged best friend. The two of them, Nadine and Suzy, kissed each other hello, told each other they looked fabulous, and then spent the rest of the afternoon ignoring each other and whispering amongst the cliques that had formed on either side of the room.

"What's going on?" a bemused Vicky had asked Deborah after she'd walked in on Nadine, almost in tears in the kitchen, being comforted by two of the other girls, all of them whispering furiously, all of them silent as soon as Vicky entered, resuming their conversation when they saw it was only Vicky.

Deborah had rolled her eyes when Vicky asked her. Nadine had apparently confessed to one of the other girls, when slightly drunk and in a situation where she didn't think anything would be repeated, that she secretly thought of Suzy's husband as Muttley, because of his unfortunate underbite.

It seems that one of the girls had immediately told Suzy, and a war had begun. But this being a grown-up war among supposed adult women, there was no fighting, no direct confrontation, Suzy had just icily frozen her out, and Nadine didn't know what she had done.

Nadine was ringing Suzy and leaving messages, and Suzy would just fail to call her back, had blocked all private calls so her callers were forced to reveal their caller ID, and if she saw Nadine's number, she wouldn't answer. And these were girls who had spoken five times a day, so after a couple of days of radio silence, Nadine figured something was up.

But she couldn't think of what she had done. Didn't remember her confession about Muttley, and so she left a few messages pleading with Suzy to let her know if she had done something to upset her, telling Suzy that she was such a wonderful friend, Nadine would never knowingly do anything to hurt her.

And Suzy didn't respond. Instead she drew the battle lines and set about recruiting her army, ensuring that the coolest, prettiest, richest women were on her side. "What a B-I-T-C-H," she would say about Nadine, and the others, delighted to have an opportunity to be one of the queen bee's workers, would shake their heads in professed bewilderment at how Nadine could have been so awful.

Nadine only knew for sure that she had been completely snubbed when she drove past Suzy's house two days ago to see the driveway full of cars, each of which belonged to one of Suzy's friends, and where Nadine's Escalade was supposed to have been—right in the front as she would normally have been the first to arrive, to help Suzy organize what Nadine knew must have been one of Suzy's infamous coffee mornings—was Heidi's Lincoln Navigator, mocking her in all its champagne glory.

Nadine had been tempted to stop the car. To walk in as if nothing were wrong, as if she hadn't been deliberately excluded from an event at which she would usually be number two bee, but of course she didn't have the courage, would never do something like that, so instead she drove home through a sea of tears and left messages for three of her friends, including the girl who had passed the Muttley message on to Suzy, and asked them what she might have done, why Suzy was now ignoring her.

Suzy would never be so obvious as to ignore Nadine in person. Her torture is far more subtle than that. To Nadine's face she will always be charm itself, it is only when her back is turned that Suzy's knives will be drawn.

"God," Vicky says after Deborah has told her the whole story, Deborah refusing to take sides, although well aware that she is neither cool enough, pretty enough, nor rich enough for either side to have made much of an effort to recruit her. "It sounds like they're all still twelve years old."

"I'm not sure that women ever change that much," Deborah says the next day, the two of them standing waist-deep in the pool while the kids splash around, screaming with laughter. "Maybe it's an American thing, or maybe it's a suburban thing, but the cliques here are pretty much exactly the same as when we were all at school."

"Suzy's obviously the queen bee," Vicky says, remembering back to her own schooldays when Catherine Enderley had been the queen bee. The prettiest—and bitchiest—girl in the class, who would one day grant you the gift of her friendship as if it were the most precious pearl, and the next day would treat you as something distasteful she had found on the sole of her shoe.

"And everyone wants to be around the queen bee," Deborah says. "Which gives her far more power than she deserves, so she can get away with being bitchy and two-faced, because she's still the one everyone wants to be friends with."

"But why?" Vicky asks, not understanding. "Why would they want to be friends with someone so awful?"

"I think maybe some of them just have incredibly low self-esteem. Nadine, for example. She's not a bad girl, but she has no self-worth at all."

"You're joking!" Vicky says. "But she seems to have so much. She's pretty, she seems bright, funny. Nice husband, kids. Why would she have no self-worth?"

Deborah shrugs. "Why do any of us? But I think she attached herself to Suzy because that's what gives her a sense of worth, intertwining herself so deeply with someone who has what she wants, who is what she wants to be. If that person deigns to be friends with Nadine, then some of that sparkle will inevitably rub off on Nadine too, and then she will be good enough."

"And what about Amber?" Vicky asks curiously. "Where does she fit in?"

Deborah smiles. "Ah yes. What about Amber? Bloody good question because Amber is Suzy's number one rival, even though Amber's completely torn about whether she wants to be."

"What do you mean?"

"Well, Amber is a Winslow, which over here counts for a hell of a lot, and however much money Suzy's husband makes, he'll never be 'old money,' he'll never come from one of those grand patrician families like the Winslows, whose forefathers came over on the *Mayflower*, so that's something she can't compete against, which immediately gives Amber a head start.

"And then Richard is hugely successful, and they're about the only people who live in a house that truly compares to Suzy's, and even though Amber is much lower key than Suzy, doesn't feel the need to impress quite as much except when she's feeling hugely insecure or there's a committee meeting, Amber is the only other one who can basically afford the same lifestyle."

"But it's only money," Vicky says, bemused. "Is Suzy really so shallow that she's judging everyone by money, by what they have, what size house, what designer clothes?"

"Um, yes!" Deborah laughs. "It's the American class system. Instead of judging people by their accents like we do in good old Blighty, they judge you by money, and how much money you have basically determines what class you are, regardless of where you came from. Look at Amber, she's Suzy's number one rival and she grew up in a trailer park."

"Does Suzy know?"

"Suzy wouldn't care. That's the point. Wherever you came from is irrelevant, it's what you have that matters and where you are now, and I have to say, as awful as it sometimes feels, it's one of the things I love most about America. That you can start with nothing and achieve anything you want as long as you have a dream and you're prepared to work hard."

"Just tough when you're a Desperate Housewife living in the suburbs trying to keep up with the queen bee."

"It can be, but I don't bother. I'd never be fully accepted anyway given that I'm English," Deborah says. "The best thing you can do is sit on the sidelines and watch. Bloody good material for a book, I always think."

"You're the second person to suggest that." Vicky pauses, remembering Hugh Janus saying something about a book, as Gracie comes swimming over to her and clambers onto her back, urging Vicky to swim to the deep end while Gracie clings on, shrieking with joy.

"Well, if you do it before me just make sure you give me an acknowledgment." Deborah grins as Vicky disappears off to join the splashing children gathered around the step at the deep end.

The next week Vicky starts to find her stride. She may not have walked a mile in Amber's shoes, but she is definitely starting to feel she is on the way. The children are more comfortable with her, and Lavinia is now far more friendly and helpful given the amount of free time Vicky is giving her as part of her continuing quest to find out what being a mother and wife is really about.

Now that Lavinia is no longer chauffeuring the children about from class to class, and she herself is sitting outside Gracie's ballet class attempting to make small talk with the other nannies and mothers, Vicky finds that the relaxation, her perceived boredom during the first week, was deceptive: Now the days fly by, and there seems to be little, if any, time to herself.

Gone are the mornings spent floating around the pool while the children are in camp. Now Vicky spends her mornings at Stop and Shop, or the garden center—she has decided to tackle Amber's flower beds behind the pool, which are a curious mix of pachysandra and weeds—or the hardware store, or the post office, or any one of a million places that she has to squeeze in between dropping Gracie off at camp and picking her up and taking her home for a nap.

Now, by the end of the evening, she is always tired. By the end of the afternoon today she couldn't wait to get the kids in bed so she could put some Diana Krall on the stereo in the kitchen and putter around making supper for her and Richard with a large glass of a delicious Chardonnay.

But Richard has just phoned to say he will be home late, has a business meeting and not to worry about cooking him anything.

At seven-thirty, as Vicky is throwing together a salad for herself, Gracie appears at the bottom of the stairs in the mud room.

"Gracie, darling," Vicky rushes over to her, "what are you doing out of bed? What's the matter?"

Gracie's little face crumples as she squeezes her Lambie tightly. "I miss my mommy," she sobs, as Vicky attempts to cradle her in her arms.

"Mummy will be home soon," she croons. "Mummy misses you very much too, and she'll be home very soon, I promise."

"But I want her now!" Gracie sobs, fighting Vicky off, and thumping her little fists on the stairs. "I want my mommy now! I want her to come home!" And she dissolves into a fresh round of sobs.

I want her too, Vicky thinks. I don't know how to comfort this child, and I know what it feels like to want your mother and she's not there. And more to the point, what the hell was I thinking, doing Swapping Lives for a month? A month! Much too long. A week would have been fine, and just as the novelty has evidently worn off for Gracie, so has the novelty worn off for Vicky.

And oh God, help me comfort this little girl, help me make her feel better, but mostly help her to stop crying, because I just don't know what to do.

It takes Vicky half an hour to calm Gracie down. Eventually she manages to get Gracie into bed where she hiccups into her pillow, still crying until she falls asleep, her cheeks still tear-stained, her pajamas soaking wet from her tears.

Vicky goes back downstairs, exhausted, then she hears a noise coming from the main stairs. On investigation she finds Jared, also sitting on the bottom step of the stairs—clearly this is a family trait—and while he's not quite crying, it's clear he's on the verge of tears.

"Jared, darling," Vicky says, "are you okay? What's the matter?"

"I miss my mom too," Jared says, trying very hard to be a man and not to cry.

"I know," Vicky sits next to him on the step and nods her head. "I know, Jared, and I miss her too. She will be home very soon, though, I promise."

"But why did she go for so long?" Jared says. "It's been so long already, and why did she have to go?"

"I don't actually know," Vicky says, and this time she really doesn't.

When Richard arrives home at ten o'clock, he's expecting the house to be quiet. Vicky had said she was exhausted, that she was thrilled he was going to have a business meeting this evening because she needed an early night.

The house may be quiet, but the lights are still on in the

kitchen and when he weaves in to turn them off—he's had rather more alcohol than he would normally have—he notices that the lights are on in the pool, and there, swimming a leisurely lap, is Vicky.

How odd, he thinks. He and Amber always used to say that they would have midnight swims. When they built the house they even put a balcony with a staircase down to the pool outside the master bedroom for precisely that purpose, and yet, aside from a handful of times the first summer they moved in, they haven't used it since.

He'd love to go swimming at night, but Amber is always in bed by nine. The few times he suggests a late-night swim, Amber has rolled her eyes or laughed as if he had suggested they take a quick trip to the moon and back before the kids wake up in the morning.

He's used to it now. Amber gives him a perfunctory kiss while they watch television in the family room, and disappears up to bed where she'll put on her cotton pajamas and climb under the covers with her books or magazines.

It is so strange seeing someone swimming in the pool at night, which has always been Richard's favorite time to be out there. When he was a child he and his brothers and sisters would swim in the pond at night. They'd light torches and troop out there, jumping off the jetty into the cool water when the nights were hot and humid, when the only noises were the cicadas chirping in the bushes, when the sky was like a blanket of black velvet, sprinkled with pinpoints of light, thousands of stars, and occasionally the warm glow of a full moon.

Night swimming has always comforted him, reminded him of his childhood, particularly here, when again the only noises are the cicadas, the steam rises gently off the surface of the pool, where again on a clear night you can see the moon reflected in the blackness of the water.

Richard opens the French door in the kitchen, walks down the deck, and calls out to Vicky as she approaches the end of the pool. The light from the deck is just enough that he is able to see her towel is there with a glass of wine and a half-empty bottle.

"Having fun?" he asks, crouching down as she swims toward the end.

"I am in heaven," she grins. "This is the most beautiful night, and I've now decided that when I marry I've got to marry rich because I'm not sure I'm going to be able to live without a swimming pool."

"What about that man you were telling me about—Jimmy? Would he keep you in the style to which you're rapidly becoming accustomed?"

"It's Jamie, and yes, he probably would. Depending on how famous you are, if you're lucky and you're in the big league you get to have a big old mansion in the country with a swimming pool. Of course the only problem is you can only use it for about three days a year because the weather's so bloody awful, but still, three days of heaven would be better than none."

"So you want to marry rich?" Richard winces ever so slightly.

"No, not really," Vicky laughs. "Quite frankly, at this point I can't afford to be picky. Beggars can't be choosy and all that . . ."

"You're lovely," Richard says, not meaning the words to sound quite as meaningful as they do.

"Um. Well. Thank you," Vicky says awkwardly, not knowing quite how to respond, thankful that the light on the deck is not strong enough to reflect her blush. "So are you coming in?" she shouts back as she swims away from Richard to diffuse the way his words made her feel, to allow the blush to disappear in the darkness of the night. Oh shit, she thinks. Why did I just say that? I didn't mean that. I don't want you to come swimming. Please say no.

"Sure!" Richard grins. And he starts undressing. And even though it's night and the pool lights are not on, Vicky's eyes have adjusted enough that she can see everything, and even though she knows this is another woman's husband, there's surely no harm in looking, is there? But it's a shiver of lust that runs through her as she watches him pull his shirt off, and she wants to get out of the pool and go running inside, to safety, to where she knows she won't do something she may regret, but her legs seem to have turned to stone, and she finds that she doesn't go anywhere. Just holds on to the side of the pool as Richard slips in wearing just his boxer shorts.

"Wow," he says. "This is gorgeous. I don't remember the last time I went swimming at night."

"You're joking! If this were my house I'd be doing this every night."

They swim past one another in opposite directions for a few lazy laps, not talking, just listening to the noises of the night, and then Vicky stops to catch her breath, not used to this much exercise, and the night is so still as she crouches in the water, leaning back against the wall, listening to just the sound of her breathing, when she becomes aware of Richard's breath, next to hers.

Neither of them says anything. Vicky feels frozen, timeless, and weightless in the dark, and she is not thinking as she turns to where she can just make out Richard's silhouette, and she is not thinking as she feels his hands alight softly on her shoulders, and she is not thinking as she moves closer to him, close enough to feel his breath on her lips, closer still, closer . . .

"Daddy!" A voice from the deck makes both of them jump, split apart, guilty, and Richard clambers out of the pool immediately.

"Honey?" he says to Gracie who is standing there clutching Lambie. "What's the matter, honey? Don't worry, Daddy's here. Daddy won't let anything happen to you," and with that he picks her up and carries her inside.

Chapter Twenty-eight

"I'm warning you now," Amber shakes a finger at Daniel. "This is not a date, and you are not allowed to flirt with me."

"But I have to flirt with you." Daniel grins as he shakes the blanket out on the grass underneath a large old maple tree. "It's my job."

"Well try and think of this as less work, more . . ."

". . . play?" he finishes off for her with another grin.

"No, that's not what I meant at all," Amber says, unable to keep the smile from her face. Of course she's not interested. Of course she's not going to do anything about it, but when was the last time someone actually dared to flirt with her? When was the last time, for that matter, she had been on her own with a man other than her husband for an entire evening?

It's not that I miss being single, she muses, as she helps Daniel open the containers and set them out on the blanket, it's that I miss excitement. How lovely to do something different, to have some attention paid to you, to really feel like a woman again.

Because that is precisely how Amber hasn't been feeling. Does she feel like a wife? Of course. And a mother? Without a doubt. But a woman? Very rarely these days. Rarely does she feel seductive, feminine, sensual. Rarely is she aware of her own, once powerful, sexuality.

As a mother she has become desexualized, she realizes with a shock. All the passion that she once poured onto her husband, she now pours into her children, leaving her with the comfortable feeling of an old pair of slippers: She adores Richard, feels safe and cozy and warm with him, and would never question the validity of their marriage, but she has quite forgotten the heady feeling of being made to feel sexy, of having someone so clearly lust after you.

And Daniel? What had Vicky said in her notes about Daniel? Her neighborhood "shag"—Amber remembers that unfamiliar word with a smile. But of course she would start thinking about sex when with him, if only because she knows that is his role in Vicky's life.

How convenient, she thinks. But how difficult to just leave it be at that. How is it possible to sleep with someone on a regular basis, someone who is a friend, and not have it turn into something more, not become emotionally involved?

Daniel sits down opposite her and pours the wine into a plastic cup, handing it to her with a rueful smile.

"Cheers," he says. "Sorry about the cups. The crystal was in the dishwasher."

"Now I know you're lying," Amber shoots back. "Crystal never *ever* goes into a dishwasher. But cheers. To . . . what? To swapping lives!" she says finally.

"Wife-swapping, did you say?" Daniel says deliberately. "I'll drink to that. Hear, hear. To wife-swapping. And all who indulge in it."

Amber shakes her head. "Are you this incorrigible all the time? And if so, how does Vicky put up with you?"

"The answer to your question is no, I'm not this incorrigible all the time, only when I'm around feisty Americans with great legs," he eyes her legs approvingly, "and the reason Vix is able to put up with me is because we're friends first, and I would say lovers second, although since Jamie Donnelly came into the equation she won't shag me anymore anyway."

"And are you upset about that?"

"Upset? That she's been refusing me or that she's with Donnelly?"

Amber shrugs. "Either? Both?"

"Well obviously I'm slightly disappointed when I feel like, well, you know, and she fobs me off with some chitchat and a chaste good-night kiss, but I think you're asking me if I'm jealous, and the answer to that is a definite no."

"Okay. So now I have to ask you something. Would you and Vicky ever be more than friends?"

"Nope," Daniel says, without even having to think about it.

"But how can you be so sure? If you're friends and you like each other and you get on and you sleep together, how could you not have a relationship together?" Amber's confusion is obvious. "I mean, what else is there?"

"What else? Chemistry of course."

"But you must have chemistry, otherwise why would you be sleeping together on an ongoing basis?"

"Well yes, we do have chemistry in bed, I suppose," Daniel says, "but whatever else is supposed to be there, passion, being in love, that certain *je ne sais quoi,* is missing, and without that what would be the point?"

Amber laughs as Daniel refills her glass; he is thrilled at how quickly she downed that first glass, loving nothing more than a tipsy redhead on a hot summer's night.

"You're laughing, why?" he queries.

"Because you're so naive!" she says. "That *je ne sais quoi* isn't real. It isn't what real relationships are based on. Real relationships are based on being best friends, on honesty, and laughter, and conversation, and integrity, not the *je ne sais quoi* that lasts all of five minutes once you're married and have children."

"You sound like you've been sent here to try and talk me into something." Daniel narrows his eyes at her suspiciously.

"Hand on my heart I haven't," Amber swears seriously. "It's just that I'm always hearing single people talk about this passion and lust, and I think that that shouldn't be the foundation for a relationship. What you have with Vicky is friendship and a great sex life, and frankly I'm not sure it gets any better than that."

"So are you telling me you don't have any passion with your husband?" This is getting better and better, thinks Daniel.

"No, I didn't say that." Amber is slightly flustered by such a direct question from such a relative stranger. "I do, but it's a different kind of passion. It's one that comes from being together for years, from raising children together, from liking doing the same things, from a deep understanding of what makes another person tick." And as she says these things Amber thinks about Richard, pictures him waking up next to her in the morning, his hair mussed up, his eyes bleary with sleep, and thinks about how, still, after all these years, he will reach out to her and spoon behind her for a few minutes every morning, nuzzling into her hair as she falls back to sleep, whispering "I love you" just before he gets out of bed and goes to have a shower.

She thinks of Richard with the children. What a wonderful father he is. How she is filled with a sense of pride when she watches him gently pick Gracie up and carry her on his hip, turning to give her an "Eskimo kiss," his large nose and Gracie's tiny one rubbing together as Gracie giggles.

She thinks of him walking past her as she's getting dressed, examining herself in the mirror dressed in a T-shirt and underpants, how he will stop and give her a squeeze, a kiss, a gentle rub on her back, how he is always showing her how much he loves her.

And Amber? Does she reciprocate these gestures? In the beginning she didn't, unused to such a demonstrative man, used instead to men who would refuse to acknowledge a relationship by anything so crass as public displays of affection, but now she responds in kind. Tousles his hair as she walks past him in the kitchen on a Saturday morning, as he eats a bagel at the counter and reads the *Wall Street Journal.* Sidles up next to him and gives him a hug as he makes French toast and pancakes for the kids on a Sunday, delighting and embarrassing the kids at the same time while they stand in the kitchen hugging and kissing.

A sob threatens to escape her throat. Oh God. She misses him. She misses her children. She misses her family. And now she realizes why Richard was so upset about her leaving. What the hell was she thinking by leaving them for a month? *A month!* What planet was she on?

Daniel sits and watches the expression change on her face, from sincere, to thoughtful, to pensive, to sadness. Oh shit, he thinks, that was a question that went horribly wrong.

"Drink up," he says quickly in a forced cheery tone. "Still lots of wine to finish off. I can't have you sitting here looking as if you're about to burst into tears. Here, have some pâté and tell me what's going on in the offices of *Poise!* this week."

It does the trick. Amber tells him about her time there, about being given some writing assignments, about Leona being thrilled with what she's doing. She tells him how she feels, using her mind again after so many years, how it may be that she's discovering a talent she never knew she had, and all the time Daniel nods and listens attentively, laughing in the right places and making her feel as if she is the most fascinating woman in the world.

And then it's Daniel's turn. He tells her about television producing, keeps her laughing with tales of shows he has done, and things that have gone wrong. He is well versed in this, in seducing pretty women with charm and humor, and his stories are well rehearsed and have the desired effect. In no time the sadness has all but disappeared from Amber's eyes, and she is sputtering her wine out with laughter at one of his stories.

They are into their second bottle of wine now, and Daniel is wondering whether he might dare try anything. She is definitely responding to him, her body now more relaxed, the stiffness and coolness far less thanks to the stories and the alcohol. I wonder, he thinks, looking at her lips, I wonder if I should take the chance.

Not yet, he thinks, although she is irresistible. No point in blowing it before he's absolutely sure he's in with a chance.

"Daniel?" A voice interrupts his reverie and he and Amber both look up to see a man standing there in T-shirt and shorts, baseball cap on head and softball bat in hand. The man takes off his cap and grins. It's Hugh.

"Hugh!" Daniel scrambles to his feet and shakes hands heartily. "How are you, mate? What are you doing here?"

"Company softball game," Hugh says. "Just finished."

"I haven't seen you in ages. How's the world of documentaries?"

"Bit slow at the moment but can't complain," Hugh says,

looking down and smiling at Amber, waiting to be introduced, suddenly realizing she is familiar but he can't quite
place her until she speaks.

"We've spoken on the phone," she says, in her distinctive
American accent, having recognized Hugh's voice immediately. "I'm Amber Winslow. I'm afraid I'm the one responsible for things being a bit slow. You called me while I was at
home in America."

"Of course!" Hugh Janus leans down and shakes her hand.
"I understand why you didn't want to be involved in a documentary. It's not everyone's cup of tea. Andy Warhol may
have said everyone would be famous for fifteen minutes . . ."

". . . but not everyone *wants* to be famous for fifteen minutes?" Amber finishes off for him, as he laughs.

"Or in your case even one minute, I suspect," Hugh says.

"You're right about that. I hope it didn't mess up your
plans too much."

"Actually, we're still going to do it," Hugh says. "We've had
a couple of meetings with Janelle Salinger at *Poise!*, and when
they run the piece about how the swap actually was, they're
going to recruit more people to do it, and at that point we're
going to step in and hopefully make the documentary."

"You mean Vicky's going to do it again?" Amber looks
horrified.

"No," Hugh laughs. "Not Vicky. But we're going to look
for single career women and Desperate Housewives and
swap them for a month."

"Are you trying to imply that I'm a Desperate Housewife?" Amber says.

"Not in the slightest. I've seen photos of your house, remember? There's nothing desperate about that mansion you

live in. Jesus. I'd give my eyeteeth to have a house like that, not to mention the pool in the back garden. And anyway, the company wasn't comfortable with sending a crew out to the States, cost-cutting and all that, and this way we'll be able to do the whole thing over here."

"So it's a good thing we refused?"

"It's a bloody good thing. So how's Vicky? I know she's not supposed to have got in touch with anyone, but you must know something?"

"She speaks to Janelle but she hasn't passed anything on really. I think she's worried that if she brings it up I'll get so homesick I'll jump on the first plane out of here."

"And would you?"

"Yes. I'm loving being here, and loving working again, even though I realize I'm not so much working as playing at working, but I just miss my family so much. I think what it's made me realize is that at this point in my life it would be a good thing for me to find something else to do outside of my roles within the family, and outside of the charity stuff."

"So you want to work again?"

"I do. I'd love to. I just don't know what I'd like to do, but I'm loving writing, so who knows, maybe I'll find myself writing the great American novel."

"Or maybe you and Vicky could get a book deal out of this," Hugh says.

"Now that," Amber grins, "sounds like the best idea I've heard all day."

"I thought *this* was the best idea you'd heard all day," Daniel grumbles, gesturing to the picnic, rather wishing Hugh would now disappear, although he doesn't seem to be going anywhere.

"Am I not allowed to hear more than two good ideas a day?" Amber smiles. "Hugh, why don't you sit down and join us for a glass of wine?"

"I'd love to." Hugh smiles, dropping down onto the blanket and grinning at Daniel. "I would say I hope I'm not interrupting anything, because this does look like a romantic picnic for two, but Dan, mate, Vicky showed me pictures of Amber's husband, and he looks like an Olympic god."

"Oh please!" Amber laughs, as Daniel curses Hugh in silence, wishing he would just disappear.

"So how come there are all these gorgeous single men in London?" Amber asks after a while, as the three of them come to the end of the second bottle of wine. "And more to the point, given that there are so many single men in London, how in the hell has Vicky managed not to land one of them?"

"She's seeing Jamie Donnelly," Daniel reminds her.

"No!" Hugh says. "I knew there was something going on. We had a business lunch and Jamie Donnelly came over—he's an old mate from a show we used to work on together—and all of a sudden there was all this chemistry flying around. Jamie Donnelly, eh? Well, she'd better be careful. He's not exactly a one-woman man."

"You can say that again," Daniel laughs as Amber frowns.

"What do you mean?" she says.

"He's got a reputation for being a serious womanizer," Hugh says. "He's got a different woman on his arm pretty much every night."

Amber is horrified. "But I think Vicky really likes him. Does she know this?"

"Well, if she reads the paper, which I assume she does, she'd know. It's not exactly a secret."

"But I think she really thinks this could turn into something serious," Amber persists. "Honestly, I've talked to her about him, she's seriously in love with the guy."

Hugh raises his eyebrows, as does Daniel, because even he hasn't realized quite how serious Vicky is about Jamie.

"She is?" Hugh says. "God, well, maybe I've got it wrong. Maybe he's finally met the woman who's going to be able to tame him. I hope so. Vicky's a nice girl, deserves to meet someone. What about you, Dan? When are you going to settle down?"

"Not in the foreseeable future," Daniel says. "So many women, so little time. So how's Lara? Are you married yet?"

Hugh's face falls. "No. Not married yet, actually. Things aren't going too well at the moment. It's the first time we've really hit a rough spot, and we're just taking it a day at a time right now."

"Oh that's terrible." Amber places a hand on Hugh's arm. "I hope it works out for you."

"Thanks," says Hugh. "I suppose whatever's meant to be will be." He looks at his watch. "Look, I'd better be going. I've already far outstayed my welcome, but thanks for the wine. Great to actually meet you, Amber. Good luck with everything."

"Thanks, Hugh." She stands up and, instead of taking his outstretched hand, spontaneously gives him a hug, a maternal, reassuring hug, patting him on the back as if to say everything's going to be okay. After all, isn't that exactly what Vicky would do?

*   *   *

Daniel is not happy. The evening was going so well before Hugh Janus arrived. Momentum was gathering, he definitely thought he was in with a chance, and then Hugh arrived and any frissons disappeared, leaving Amber lost in thought once again, and himself without a hope in hell.

They reach the flat and Amber turns to him and gives him a hug. As he stands there in her arms, wondering if now might be the time to lift her hair and place a soft kiss on her bare shoulder, he feels her pat him on the back in exactly the same maternal, reassuring way she did to Hugh Janus, and he knows that if ever he was right, if ever at some point that evening there was a moment when something might have happened, when Amber might have put aside her other life and welcomed him in instead, that moment has well and truly gone.

And he's not sure he'll ever get it back.

"I've had a wonderful evening," Amber says, pulling away from him with a smile, then reaching up and placing a kiss on his cheek. "I think you're a lovely man, and if I weren't married I would have been more than a little flattered by all the attention you've paid me this evening, although I have a feeling that if I weren't married, you might have treated me differently." The words are harsh, but softened by Amber's gentle smile.

"What do you mean?"

"I mean that I think you like what isn't yours. That what really turns you on is the thrill of the chase, the thrill of the unattainable, and that the minute it's yours you probably don't want it anymore."

Daniel starts to protest, but the wine has fogged his brain, and he can't quite get the words out, so instead he shrugs with a smile. "I think," he says finally, "that I would have paid you the same attention whatever your situation."

"Well, that's lovely to hear," she says, and opens the front door, pausing for a moment to look at Daniel. "Thank you for a perfect evening," she says. "Can we do it again? As friends?"

"Sure," says Daniel. "I'll call you," and he waves and turns away, feeling fairly certain that he won't see Amber again, or if he does, his chance has come and gone.

Amber sits cross-legged on Vicky's bed and places the photographs of her family on the cover in front of her, and she starts to cry, the pain of missing them just too much for her to bear any longer.

"Oh bugger," she says out loud, in true English fashion, and reaches for the phone, not caring that she's not supposed to call home, nor that it is around five o'clock in the afternoon, which is dinnertime and commonly referred to in her house as the witching hour. I want Richard, she thinks. I'm far away from home and I'm lonely, and I need to hear my husband's voice. I need to hear that everything's okay, because I don't want to do this anymore. I don't want to be here. I want to be home, where I belong.

The phone rings and rings, and then Amber hears the machine pick up and, bizarrely, she hears Vicky's clipped English tones on her answering machine. "You've reached the Winslow residence," she hears. "There's no one available to take your call, but please leave your name and number after the tone and someone will get back to you." "Oh God," Amber whispers, putting down the receiver without leaving a message, taking a big gulp of breath. "I know I signed up for this but why do I feel that I'm in danger? Why are my antennae suddenly going up?" Amber hadn't expected to hear Vicky's voice on her machine, and hadn't expected to feel what she is suddenly, and unaccountably, feeling.

Fear.

Amber shivers as a thought comes to her. What do I do if another woman is trying to take over my life?

Chapter Twenty-nine

"Vicky had a boo-boo last night but Daddy kissed it and made it better," Gracie announces at the breakfast table and Vicky winces.

"It was on her face," Gracie continues as Vicky starts to flush, despite there not being anyone other than the children present, Richard having—thank God—gone to work, and Lavinia sleeping in.

Shit, Vicky muttered to herself last night as she wrapped a terry-cloth robe around herself and walked into the house. She glided quietly past Gracie's bedroom door, hearing Richard talk softly to Grace as he put her back to bed. She hesitated, wondering whether to go in, but didn't want to face Richard, didn't want to be reminded of what had just almost happened, because this was not part of the equation. Having an affair with a married man was the last thing she wanted to happen.

And even though she knew she hadn't imagined the chemistry between them, it wasn't something she had any intention of acting upon. Even last night, she hadn't planned for anything to happen, hadn't expected Richard to strip off and jump in the pool.

It wasn't as if Richard had married the wrong woman and

had suddenly found his soul mate. It was clear that if something had happened, it would have been because Richard was lonely, because he felt abandoned by his wife, because he was seeking comfort, not because he had suddenly decided he was crazy about Vicky.

Vicky sat on the huge bed in the master bedroom, wrapped in her robe, and waited with pounding heart for Richard to come in so they could at least talk about it. I'll tell him it's a mistake, she thought. Tell him that we ought to probably avoid one another for the next couple of weeks until it's time for me to go home, and as she thought about home she felt a wave of homesickness.

This life was wonderful, there was no doubt about it, but it was not her life, and all of a sudden she missed her flat off Marylebone High Street. Missed her local butcher, coffee at Providores, lunch at the Japanese café.

She missed work. Missed Leona, and Ruth, and even Janelle. She missed being surrounded by people all the time: even on the weekends, even those days when she chose not to socialize, holed up in her little flat watching television for hours and hours, DVDs of her favorite films, she still knew she was surrounded by people, and if she ever felt lonely, all she had to do was walk out her front door.

As quiet and peaceful as it was here, if she wanted to go anywhere, to see people, to do anything, she had to climb into Amber's huge SUV and drive into town. Nobody ever dropped in, nobody seemed to walk anywhere. She had even tried a couple of impromptu playdates with friends of Jared's, but their mothers were horrified at the very idea of their children coming back to Jared's after camp that day—although they'd happily schedule something in the Thursday three p.m. window in three weeks' time.

Her brief experience with the League had shown her that it was not something she wanted to be a part of, even as research, for the cliquishness and bitchiness reminded her overwhelmingly of her schooldays, and that was something she tried very hard not to remember most of the time.

For all its superficial perfection, Vicky could see that this life was exactly that: superficial. Her single life, with her eclectic group of friends, her disorganized wardrobe that was a combination of high street and the odd designer discount item, her beloved cat, Eartha—oh God, how she missed Eartha—her single life may be nothing compared to this, it may be something that all these women were thrilled to have left behind, but sitting on Amber's bed, her arms wrapped around her knees, trying not to shiver in the air-conditioned coolness of the room, Vicky suddenly realized that she wouldn't swap her life for anything in the world.

Amber's children were delicious, but they were not hers. And Richard was delicious, she thought sadly, but he was not hers either. It was an experiment that may not have gone horribly wrong, but has definitely taught her to appreciate what she has. The grass may look greener on the other side, but that doesn't necessarily mean that it is.

And perhaps because of what happened, perhaps because Vicky was embarrassed, and humiliated, and didn't know how to face Richard in the morning, all she wanted was to go back home.

The next morning Richard has left for work by the time Vicky gets up, for which she is enormously grateful. Of course they will have to talk about it somehow, and she wishes he had told her what he had said to Gracie, for he must have said something, she obviously saw something that had to be explained, but Vicky will deal with it later, or so she thinks until Gracie drops the bombshell about her boo-boo.

Oh well, thinks Vicky, as she turns away from the table, busying herself making the coffee, at least I know what he said.

"Where's the boo-boo?" Jared asks suspiciously.

"It was on my nose," Vicky says, walking over to the table and crouching down. "I was swimming so fast I bumped my nose on the wall, can you believe that? Is it cut? Is it bruised? Do you see anything?"

Jared examines her nose carefully before shaking his head. "Nothing," he says, before turning his attention back to his bowl of Cheerios. Thank God. Vicky finally manages to exhale as Jared and Gracie start fighting over who gets to read the back of the cereal box.

When Vicky gets back from dropping the kids at camp, there's a message from Richard on the machine. "Hi, Vicky, I'm just letting you know that I have a crazy day at work today, and won't be back until late tonight, so don't worry about dinner. Have a great day and say hi to the kids for me. Bye."

Nothing. No indication that anything has happened, that there is anything to talk about, and the cloud that has been weighing down heavily on Vicky's shoulders starts to rise. Perhaps she is making far too big a deal out of it. Hell, these moments happen, and maybe they don't mean anything. What's important is not what did happen, but what didn't, and judging from Richard's ordinary-sounding message, nothing will again.

I'm not going to think about it anymore, Vicky decides,

picking up the phone and calling Deborah. I'm just going to pretend it never happened.

"Hey, I was just thinking about you," Deborah says. "You know that Irish comedian Jamie Donnelly?"

"Um . . . yes," Vicky says, sure that she hasn't told Deborah about Jamie Donnelly.

"Did you see the British papers?"

Vicky's heart starts beating fast. "No, what? What's happened?"

"He's only bloody shagging Nicollette Sheridan. Can you believe it? What would a gorgeous woman like Nicollette Sheridan see in a two-bit Irish playboy comedian like Jamie Donnelly?" There's a long silence. "Vicky? Vicky? Are you there?"

"Yes," Vicky says as the tears start to well up.

"Oh God, you probably think I'm pathetic," Deborah says. "But I'm completely addicted to showbiz gossip. Sorry, but it's my secret shame. I go online every morning to read the British tabloids, and Spencer brings me back *US* and *People* every time he goes to the chemist for anything. Am I pathetic? Should I just shut up?"

"No, no," Vicky manages. "It's fine. Listen, I've got to go. I'll call you back, okay?"

"Sure," says Deborah, wondering how she could possibly have offended Vicky. "Look, are you okay? Did I say something wrong?"

"No, no, but there's someone at the door. I'll call you back. Promise." And Vicky puts down the phone, goes to Amber's computer and goes online to the *Sun* where she sees the story for herself. And while Vicky never normally believes what she reads in the papers, the photograph of Jamie and Nicollette is there, in mid-snog, taken at the Soho House on Friday night. This time there are no explanations that could justify this. No "Nicollette and I are old friends" rubbish. He's a liar and a cheat.

"Fucker!" she yells at the computer screen, banging the table in anger. "You fucking fucker!"

"Vicky?" A frightened Lavinia pops her head around the door of the office. "Is everything okay?"

"No!" Vicky bursts into tears as Lavinia rushes over to put an arm around her in a bid to comfort her. "No it bloody isn't. I want to go home."

An hour later Vicky is sipping from a cup of tea, her tears finally having subsided. Great, she thinks. My period's coming and I'm having the worst PMS I've ever had in my life, I almost jumped into bed with a married man, and the man I thought I was going to spend the rest of my life with is now sleeping with Nicollette Sheridan. Nicollette Sheridan, for God's sake. Who the hell can compete with Nicollette Sheridan? I don't want to be here anymore, work or no work, and I'm tired, and pissed off, and fed up, and if I wasn't thirty-five years old I'd add that I want my mum.

Oh Christ, she mutters, as she dunks a biscuit into her tea. At least my day can't get any worse . . .

"Guess what?" she says to the kids when she picks them up from camp. "I've decided that today is a no-classes day, so instead we're going for a special treat. We're going to go to the aquarium and we're going to eat ice cream all afternoon!"

"Yay!" chorus Jared and Gracie from the backseat. "Ice cream, ice cream, ice cream!"

It is for purely selfish reasons that Vicky has decided to go to the aquarium. She has opted out of all practices, all classes, all lessons today because she's fed up with the routine. And after only two weeks, she thinks wryly. God alone knows how Amber puts up with it. And Vicky has always loved aquariums, finds something incredibly soothing about wandering around darkened rooms looking at fish. Even now she regularly goes to the London Aquarium by herself, and happily spends a few hours centering herself, always feeling infinitely better by the time she leaves.

They drive over to the Maritime Center in Norwalk, stopping at Mr. Chubby's en route for the first ice cream of the afternoon, then park in the parking lot where they join the masses of people all with the same idea—cooling off in the air-conditioned aquarium on a blisteringly hot day.

Gracie puts her little hand in Vicky's, her other thumb firmly in her mouth as they wander around looking at the sea horses, stroking the stingrays, the kids bouncing with excitement when they find the tank full of the same fish as in *Finding Nemo*.

The turtles are enormous and majestic, the sharks eerily graceful, and as they step behind the jellyfish tank to sit and watch the jellyfish float up and down in their phosphorescent splendor, the children let out shouts of joy.

"Daddy!" they both yell, and run over to where Richard is sitting on a bench, gazing at the jellyfish, in his suit and tie, his briefcase by his feet, looking completely shell-shocked.

"Richard?" Now it is Vicky's turn to be shell-shocked. "What are you doing here?"

And Richard, confident, gregarious, friendly Richard, for once seems entirely lost for words.

"Let's take the children for ice cream," he says eventually. "And I'll explain."

"Ice cream! Ice cream!" the children clamor, and even though they've just polished off a Mr. Chubby's special, Vicky concurs, because clearly Richard has some explaining to do, and if a little ice cream will help keep the children quiet, give Richard the time and space to say his piece, then so be it.

And the events of last night are well and truly forgotten. When Vicky does finally remember what so nearly happened, for a few seconds she wonders whether she did in fact dream it.

"You what?" Vicky says, the shock apparent on her face.

"I lost my job," Richard says again, looking at the table, unable to look her in the eye.

"But what do you mean, you lost your job? When? Why are you at the aquarium? I don't understand. How could you have lost your job?"

"I lost it six months ago," Richard says quietly as Vicky takes a sharp inhalation of breath and her mouth drops open in shock.

"Six months?" she repeats.

"Yes. Six months ago. They're downsizing. Last year wasn't a great year, and they let a few of us go."

"But why doesn't Amber know? I don't understand how you cannot tell her something like this. Six months? What, you leave for 'work' every morning in your suit and it's all a great big pretense? You spend your days here? That's the craziest thing I've ever heard."

"You've never been in my situation so don't judge me," Richard says harshly and Vicky sits back and apologizes.

"I have a wife and two children to support, not to mention

living in Highfield, which isn't quite as taxing on my pocket as Greenwich, but it's getting there."

"But how do you . . . I mean, what about money? Do you have—"

"The answer is not much. I got severance pay, sure, but not nearly as much as I expected, and not nearly enough to support our life here. We're pretty much out of money now, and I haven't been able to find another job, and I don't know what I'm going to do."

The fear suddenly shows on his face, and Vicky finds that she is no longer looking at Richard the man but at Richard the boy, and as she sits there her heart goes out to him.

"I'm so sorry," she whispers. "But I can't believe you haven't told Amber. You've got to tell her."

"I know," he says. "But I don't know how. She loves her life here, and she spends money like it's water and there's just nothing left. I'm putting more and more debt on the credit card and the stress I'm under is enormous. That's why I go to the aquarium. It's about the only place I can relax and not think about anything, just turn off and gaze at the jellyfish."

Vicky smiles gently. "I know what you mean. But Amber loves you, she'll understand."

"Of course she loves me, but we have to make big changes, and I'm not sure Amber is ready for that, I'm not sure that's what she bargained for when she married me."

"I disagree," Vicky says. "She married you for better or worse, and anyway, Amber told me she didn't come from money, so it isn't as if she isn't used to struggling a little bit."

"But that's why she doesn't want to go back there. She thought she'd be safe marrying a Winslow."

"And she is safe because you love her and isn't that what really matters?"

"Only in fairy tales. In real life what matters is that you love each other and you're able to send your kids to private school, and if you choose public school, then you're able to supplement it with ballet and judo and Suzuki music classes and God knows what else. In real life you have to make sure your wife is dressed in the latest Pucci dress to keep up with the Suzys or Nadines," he says bitterly, "and you have to pay a fortune to the hottest interior designers of the moment just so everyone can come in and see that you were the idiots who paid a fortune for a heinous lilac living room."

Vicky splutters with laughter. "Oh God, I'm sorry," she says, crestfallen. "I mean, what you're saying is true, and it's not funny, but your living room is rather heinous. I didn't want to say anything . . ."

"I know," Richard says, managing a small smile. "And all of that stuff means so much to Amber. I don't know how to tell her we can't afford it anymore."

"What are you frightened of?" Vicky asks gently. "What's your worst fear?"

There's a long silence. "I don't know," he says eventually. "Maybe that she'll leave."

"But you can't carry on without her knowing. You have to tell her."

"And how do I do that during this Swapping Lives craziness? This isn't the kind of thing that you can do over the phone."

Vicky nods in agreement. "You know what?" she says. "I think I'm done."

"What do you mean?"

"I mean that we've been doing this for two weeks and I

think it's long enough. It's a great experiment, and it's taught me a couple of things. First, that it isn't possible to really live another person's life. Even if you're wearing their clothes and doing all the things they do, you're never really going to have a sense of how they live their lives; and second, it's made me appreciate what I have. I always thought this was what I wanted, but now that I'm here I just want to go home. God knows how Amber is doing, but I'd be very surprised if she isn't feeling the same thing. She's left you and the children, for God's sake; she's probably ill with homesickness.

"I'm going to call my editor in the morning," Vicky says firmly. "And tell her it's enough. You need to tell Amber face-to-face and I need to go home."

"You would do that?" Richard's face is a combination of relief and fear.

"I will do that. Just remember that old expression: There's nothing to fear but fear itself. I promise you it won't be as bad as you expect. You think Amber is happy in Highfield, but from everything she told me, she's not as satisfied in her life as you think. God, no! Not you!" Vicky says quickly, seeing Richard's face fall. "Just this whole keeping up with the Joneses. It doesn't make her as happy as you think. To be honest, my impression was she just doesn't know how to extricate herself from it. Maybe this will be just what you need, both of you. Maybe you can start again somewhere else. Amber told me that the only reason she stayed in Highfield was because you needed to commute to the city."

"She did? I thought the only reason we stayed in Highfield was because she really loved it."

"Well at least this proves one thing." Vicky smiles. "The two of you really do need to talk."

* * *

"Darling!" Janelle's voice on the phone brings up a wave of affection in Vicky. "How is everything? And naughty you, phoning. You're not supposed to be in touch with anyone here!"

"I know, Janelle, and I'm sorry, but something's come up," and Vicky proceeds to tell Janelle the story, only leaving out the part with her and Richard in the swimming pool.

When Janelle has stopped shivering with excitement— "Oh darling, what a fabulous story this is going to be!"—she sighs. "Well I would prefer you to stay another couple of weeks but if you really think you've got enough for the story, then I suppose I could talk to Amber and see how she feels. Such a shame, though, if she leaves. Stephen and I were planning on throwing a wonderful dinner party for her, although I suppose you could come instead and tell us all about it."

Over in America Vicky rolls her eyes and grins. Nothing ever changes. "Would you talk to Amber and see if she'd come home?" Vicky asks.

"I've got a better idea," Janelle says. "I can see her at your desk. Why don't you ask her yourself?"

"Amber Winslow," Amber picks up the phone sounding briskly professional.

"Amber! It's Vicky!"

There's a pause. "I'm sorry. Vicky who?"

Vicky widens her eyes slightly. Two bloody weeks, she thinks, and now I'm Vicky who?

"Vicky Townsley?" she says, her voice slightly colder. "You know, your Swapping Lives partner?"

"Oh Vicky!" Amber gushes. "Oh my gosh! I'm so sorry. I

thought you were a PR! Your phone never stops ringing with people calling from PR agencies. They're driving me mad. How are you? And how are my children? And Richard? What are you doing calling me? I thought we weren't allowed to make personal phone calls . . ."

"I know all that," Vicky says. "And everyone is wonderful, they just miss you enormously. I think it's been really hard on Gracie especially . . ." Vicky hears Amber catch her breath.

"The thing is," she continues, "I think I've really got enough. I mean, I've been here two weeks living your life, and while it's been wonderful, I can't see what's going to happen in the next two weeks that will make the story any different or any better."

"So what are you trying to say?"

"Well, what I suppose I'm trying to say is, if you agree, could we cut it short and swap back now?"

"How now?" Amber asks. "You mean like tomorrow?"

"Well, yes. Not necessarily tomorrow, but sooner rather than later. To be honest, I just desperately miss my life, and I can't see what either of us is going to get by doing this any longer. But obviously, if you disagree then we'll stay."

"Disagree?" Amber resists the urge to whoop for joy. "Are you crazy? I'm dying of homesickness and all I want to do is get back to my family. This is the best news ever! I'm coming home! Yahoo!"

"Does that mean you haven't had a good time?" Vicky asks.

"I've had a great time," Amber says. "But I honestly don't know what I was thinking, writing in to you and then actually doing it. Although I have discovered that I adore working again."

"Are you writing?"

"A lot more than I expected to be, and it seems I'm pretty good at it. I was thinking about maybe looking for a job when I get back, maybe something like a junior writer on a local paper or something."

"So you have found out things about yourself, then? It hasn't been a wasted opportunity?"

"Oh my gosh, no! I feel like I've had a dose of reality, being here. And I've learned that I need something more in my life other than the League. I need to be useful and needed, to be defined by something other than being a wife, mother, or charity member."

"So should I start looking into flights?" Vicky says.

"Absolutely!" Amber grins. "And does this mean I can talk to my kids now?"

"I don't see why not," Vicky says. "Hang on. Jared! Gracie!" she yells up the stairs to the kids, who are in the playroom. "Pick up the phone. Someone wants to say hello!"

Chapter Thirty

Despite Richard's fear at having to admit to his wife that he is not the successful hunter that she thinks he is, that he has failed at being the breadwinner, that for the past six months when he has looked in the mirror every morning he has seen failure written all over his face, there is something of a relief in finally coming clean.

The pressure of living a lie has taken its toll, his fear of not being the man his wife thinks he is causing him far more stress than he had realized. As angry as he was at Amber's leaving, as much as he didn't understand it, he couldn't help but feel this was God's way of punishing him for not living up to the Highfield husband standard.

The truth was that although he didn't like not having a job, was ashamed at being laid off and not being able to walk into something else immediately, he couldn't honestly say that he loved his job. Not anymore. Not for years.

In the beginning, when he first started trading, he loved the buzz of making money, the rollercoaster of emotions that came with each huge win and loss, the wins generally far outweighing the losses.

He wasn't a kid anymore, yet he found himself surrounded by kids, getting younger and younger every year, all of them with the same hunger, passion, and drive that he vaguely remembered having when he first came into the business.

He doesn't remember when the drive started to disappear, but suspects it may have been around the time they moved to Highfield. Not that there was anything wrong with Highfield, but it had been one hell of a shock moving from the city to the suburbs, the commute was a killer, and Amber, who had wanted to move out to the suburbs to raise her children in a "more simple way," seemed to be constantly stressed about how she was going to continue to impress the circles in which she moved.

Despite its first impressions, Highfield was far more sinister than Manhattan. At least Manhattan was obvious about what it was. You knew what you were getting in Manhattan. You knew your kids were going to be going through murder to get into one of the handful of private schools that anyone who was anyone had to go to; you knew you would have to pull every string you had to ensure they got the best start in life, and if that meant bringing in private tutors to ensure your three-year-old had a basic understanding of the French language to impress at the interview, then so be it.

But Highfield wasn't supposed to be like that. Everyone who'd moved out here from the city said they'd chosen Highfield precisely because it wasn't like that. Because it was in the country, and there were fields and trees. Because they wanted their children to grow up in nature, and go to the "unbelievably good" public schools, and because they all said they wanted to get out of the rat race.

They said they loved Highfield because it had New England charm with just enough city sophistication for the ex-Manhattanites to feel at home. They loved that it had an enormous arts festival every year, bringing people from near and far, all flocking to revel in the town that had been built up by artists and actors and writers in the twenties.

On paper Highfield had seemed perfect, but the more city people who have moved out there, the more city values they brought with them, and Richard only has to look at Amber to see how little has actually changed since moving out here.

He loves Amber precisely because she's not from that world. Because she came from nothing. Because she didn't expect anything from him. But her humble beginnings gave her a chameleon quality—Amber was able to make herself into whoever she thought she needed to be to fit in—and although Richard knows that the Amber who goes to the League gala in Oscar de la Renta is not the Amber he married, he also knows that as long as they stay here this is who she is going to be.

Up until six months ago he didn't mind. He was more than able to provide her with her wardrobe of beautiful clothes, her Amberley Jacks living room, her McMansion that puts all others to shame, but now he's going to have to tell her it's all over, and although he is relieved that he can finally share his own shame, share his secret with the most important woman in his life, everything has to change, and he feels sick with fear at what Amber will say.

He had prayed it wouldn't come to this. Had spent the first couple of months phoning everyone he knew, asking if there was anything available, calling headhunters he'd employed himself to find other team members, said members, ironically enough, still employed.

Everyone had been happy to meet with him, some buying lunch, some giving him flattering amounts of "face-time" in their offices, but none had led to anything. "It's a terrible market," he'd heard over and over again. "Even for someone in your position," and this had inevitably led to sob stories of valued employees of the bank, men far more senior, employed for far longer, who had been let go.

"If there's ever anything I can do," they'd all said as they shook his hand and pressed their business card upon him, but the one thing he wanted them to do they weren't able to do: provide him with a job.

And the more time that had elapsed, the more he had taken to daydreaming, going to the aquarium for hours, losing himself in the hypnotic throbbing of the jellyfish, conjuring up elaborate fantasies of what he would really love to do.

Because the truth was, he didn't really want to be back in the city. He'd had enough of Wall Street, was burned out, and money just didn't mean as much to him as it did to his younger, hungrier counterparts who lived for the thrill of the deal, for the ridiculous, enormous bonuses they took home at the end of every year, and that was despite the "terrible market."

His family never had any money, and it didn't do him any harm. In fact his memories of his childhood are all good, all happy, and when times were really bad it was turned into an adventure. The Christmas they couldn't afford decorations or even a tree, they cut down a small white pine from the yard and made their own decorations, his brothers and sisters concentrating fiercely as they cut out paper lanterns by the fire, his mother making it into a big game as she sat in the shabby wing chair by the fireplace, stringing popcorn with his sisters.

Richard knew that money didn't buy happiness, and he also knew that, deep down, Amber knew it too. And his dream? To buy a small business somewhere, something small and local, maybe a family-run operation. To have an office close to home, somewhere where he could come home for lunch, spend time with the kids, get to know his family again.

What Richard really wanted was the simpler life he thought they'd be getting when they moved out to Highfield. He wanted to re-create his childhood, wanted his children to be happy playing Pooh sticks in a little river somewhere, wanted them to know the joy of playing hide and seek in a hayfield, not being constantly ferried by a nanny from class to class, nor losing themselves for mindless hours in an Xbox or PlayStation.

He doesn't want Gracie growing up to be like the nine-year-olds he sees around town on the weekends. Tiny little versions of their mothers, in glittery navel-baring T-shirts, mini Louis Vuitton purses slung over their shoulders, the expressions on their faces already jaded as they borrow their mothers' phones at the nail salon, and sit chatting to friends, splaying their fingers expertly and nonchalantly as a small Korean woman bends over and paints their nails carefully with Ballet Slippers. The girls chew gum and cross their legs, ignore their manicurists in a bid to be more sophisticated. More like their mothers.

He doesn't want Jared demanding the latest Nike trainers because those are the only ones that are cool, walking around town with a sense of entitlement that comes from being one of the children of the wealthy but uninvolved: children of parents who are rarely around, the fathers working on Wall Street, the mothers coping as best they can with Wall Street widowhood by throwing themselves into their committees, their Leagues, their PTAs, all determined to be the best they can, to have the best children they can; to be, or to have, the cleverest, the prettiest, the sportiest, the thinnest, the most—and even when they do, it doesn't seem to be enough.

But Amber does seem to want it. There are times when she doesn't, but how will she cope when he tells her they can't keep up anymore? The market isn't getting any better, the hope he had for the first few weeks after he was laid off is well and truly gone, and all the time he is meeting men who are in the same situation as him, only they've been out of work for months, and some of them for years.

How will Amber be able to hold her head up when he tells her they can't afford their lifestyle? That the only asset they have is the house—his financial adviser had always told him it wasn't really necessary to have savings until they hit forty, and he still had a couple of years to go, had never worried about their future, assumed his income would keep them safe—and now the house is going to have to be sold.

It's the last resort, but unless he finds a job tomorrow, he can't see another way out. If they sold the house they'd have enough equity to buy something much smaller and live perfectly comfortably, although they wouldn't be shopping at Rakers anymore, wouldn't be on Amberley Jacks's Christmas card list this year, would definitely become the source of the town's gossip—women like Suzy and Nadine would have a field day.

Which is perhaps what he's most scared of. Not that he gives a damn about them, but he knows how humiliating it's going to be for Amber. He'd be quite happy in an unassuming cape, and Amber has enough style to make it beautiful, but how does Amber explain their change of lifestyle away? Is she strong enough to withstand being talked about and whispered about, being the object of pity among her so-called friends in the League?

But Amber is strong, he tells himself. She has come from far worse than this, and had the ability to re-create herself from nothing then. If she did it then, she can do it again. It will be hard for her to accept at first, he knows, but once she does, they will be okay.

Please, God, let them be okay.

Amber passes through customs and out into the crowds of expectant faces in the arrivals lounge at Kennedy Airport. Richard is sending a car for her, and she starts to scan the signs looking for her name, wanting to get into the car and get home as quickly as possible.

And then she sees them. Richard, so tall, so handsome, so familiar, with Gracie in one arm, his other hand resting on Jared's head. As a smile spreads on her face and she starts to run toward them, Jared and Gracie see her, and Jared runs toward her, his arms outstretched, his face pure joy.

"Mommy!" he shrieks as he jumps into her arms, followed by Gracie and Richard.

Amber doesn't say anything. Just hugs her children tightly as the tears stream down her face. Oh God, she thinks. How could I leave them? And then she stands up, the children still clinging to her legs, and kisses Richard, feeling suddenly awkward and slightly shy.

"Hey, stranger," she whispers as they pull apart and smile at each other.

"Hey, yourself," he says. "Happy to be home?"

"You have no idea!" she says, and she links arms with him as they walk to the parking lot, and by the time they reach the car all the awkwardness has disappeared, and Amber cannot wipe the grin off her face, so overjoyed is she to be finally back where she belongs.

"We missed you, Mommy!" Jared says as they hit the highway.

"Yes, Mommy. Why did you go for such a long, long time?" Gracie's little voice comes from the backseat.

"Don't worry, kids," Amber says. "I'm never going away again. Mommy's going to stay in Highfield forever," and she turns to smile at Richard as she puts her hand on his, and is it her imagination or does he look ever so slightly pale?

"Is everything okay, Rich?" she asks.

He turns to her and smiles. "Everything's great," he says. "I thought we could give the kids supper and then go out ourselves later. I've booked a table at La Plage for eight o'clock. Can you manage that or are you too tired?" La Plage is their favorite restaurant in Highfield, and one they don't go to often enough. It's the perfect place for Richard to make his confession, not least because it would be impossible to create a scene in La Plage's quiet sophisticated atmosphere, when there will undoubtedly be at least three other tables of people they know having dinner there, La Plage being one of the few places to "be seen" in Highfield.

"Oh honey, I'm exhausted. It's now . . ." she checks her watch, "eleven o'clock in England, and I'd really just love to be with you and the kids. Can we do La Plage tomorrow night instead? Can we maybe just have an early night tonight?"

"But there's so much to talk about," Richard says, knowing that he can't put this off another night, the pressure of the secret becoming almost too much for him to bear. "I want to hear all about London."

"I just can't face getting dressed up and going out," Amber says.

"Stay home, Mommy!" chorus Jared and Gracie from the back seat. "Don't go out. Stay home."

"See?" Amber grins. "Looks like you're outvoted. But I tell you what. When the kids are in bed why don't we get take-out and you and I will eat on the porch? We'll have a couple of glasses of wine and I can tell you a bit about London, and meanwhile you can tell me what it was like having Vicky here. How was it, having Vicky here? Promise me you didn't sleep with her?" She's half joking. And half not.

Richard turns to her and smiles, so grateful that the moment he had shared with Vicky never materialized into something else, knowing that he has always been a hopeless liar, that if anything had happened Amber would know, has always been able to read him like a book.

"Hand on my heart," he puts his hand on his heart, and does his best Clinton impersonation. "I did not have sex with that woman."

"And no blow jobs either?" she whispers.

He grins, and whispers back. "No blow jobs either."

"Good," Amber says. "But you know I just had to ask."

"I know. And I missed you. I really, really missed you."

"I really, really missed you too."

The children take a while to settle, the excitement at having Amber home sending them into giggling fits as they keep appearing at the bottom of the stairs long after they've, repeatedly, been put to bed.

Amber and Richard sit outside, and Amber bubbles over with excitement as she tells him about London. About how invigorating it was, being around "real" people again, about feeling that she was contributing something by actually writing pieces for the magazine, that it's made her realize that she wants to go back to work. No, she *needs* to go back to work. Not full-time, never full-time, but she has to do something that occupies her brain.

"And the League doesn't?" Richard grins.

"Oh God," she says. "That's one thing I haven't missed in the slightest. How did Vicky cope with the League? How was the jewelry show? Did she survive the hell of Suzy?"

"Actually she did great. She and Deborah became buddies and she did a good job, although it wasn't you."

"Did you like her? Did you get on with her? Come on, admit it, didn't you find her attractive?"

"Oh will you stop? Why do you keep asking me this? Have you got something to tell me?"

"Actually I have," Amber says playfully, reaching over the table and helping herself to more Szechuan vegetables. "I had a date, and he thought I was the most gorgeous woman in the world."

"You're not serious?" Richard is horrified. "You had a date and you're telling me about it, why?"

Amber shrugs with a naughty grin. "Oh don't be silly. I didn't do anything. I'd never do anything, it was just really weird that this friend of Vicky's, Daniel, insisted on taking me out and I thought it was just as friends but he had this whole romantic picnic planned and he flirted outrageously with me."

"I still don't understand why you're telling me."

"Because you're my best friend, and I tell you everything, and because it made me realize that I never want to be single again, and I never want to be dating again, or flirting with anyone other than you, darling husband. Although I'll admit, it's damn nice to be flirted with after all these years."

"Well I'm glad he made you happy." Richard swallows hard. "Now there's something I have to tell you. Oh shit." He takes a deep breath and looks away, unable to look Amber in the eye, and Amber starts to shake as a vise of fear grips her heart.

"Oh God," she whispers. "You did do something with Vicky, didn't you? You slept with her. Oh my God."

"No!" Richard meets her eye. "I did not. It's something else. I . . ."

"What?" There's a silence as Richard tries to figure out how to say it. "What?" she ends up shrieking at him, terrified of what she's going to hear.

"I lost my job," Richard says finally, exhaling and looking her in the eye.

"Is that it? You lost your job?" Amber starts to laugh with relief. "Oh Jesus. I thought you were going to say you have cancer, or someone has died, or something really terrible. You lost your job? Oh you poor baby. But you'll get another one." She gets up and sits in Richard's lap, crooning to him as she kisses his cheek. "My talented, clever, handsome husband will get another job in no time. It's no big deal. Don't worry."

"No, you don't understand." Richard sits back and clears his throat. "I lost my job a while ago. I haven't been able to get another one, and, well, we're kind of out of money."

"What?" Amber gets off his lap and stands in front of him. "What do you mean, a while ago? How long ago?"

"Six months."

There's a silence that seems to stretch on forever before the shriek. "Six months? Six months?" Amber's voice rises to near-hysteria. "You lost your job six months ago and you didn't tell me. What the hell were you thinking? How could you not tell me? Six months? Six months?"

"Sssshhh. You'll wake the children."

"I don't care about the children. I care that my husband has lied to me for six months. So all these mornings when you've been leaving for work in your suit and tie, you've been lying to me? Oh my God. Who are you? I don't even know you." And Amber starts to cry.

"I didn't tell you because I couldn't," Richard says. "At first I thought I'd just walk into another one, and then I'd just tell you after the fact, and in the beginning I was going to lots of interviews but nothing came of them and so now I have to tell you."

"Did you say we're out of money?" Amber says quietly.

"Yes."

"What about severance pay?"

"It's gone. We've been living on it for six months."

"You stupid fucking irresponsible idiot," Amber screams. "If you'd told me we could have figured something out, and instead you lie to me, your wife, the person you're supposed to be closest to in the world, and now we're all out of money. So now what? What happens now? What am I supposed to say? What are we supposed to do?"

Richard takes a deep breath. "We have to sell the house."

"Oh my Lord," Amber shakes her head and looks up at the sky, "what have I done to deserve this?"

Chapter Thirty-one

"Hi, this is Daniel phoning to see if you want to go to the theater on Saturday—"

"Daniel!" Vicky rushes over to the phone and picks up, interrupting Daniel's message on the machine.

"Amber?" Daniel's voice is hopeful.

"No! It's me! Vicky! I'm home!"

"Oh." Daniel tries, but fails, to hide the disappointment in his voice.

"Well thanks a lot," Vicky snorts with laughter. "Don't get too excited I'm home, you might fall off your chair."

"Sorry, Vix," Daniel recovers. "But I thought you were still in America for another week or so. Did I get it wrong?"

"Nah. You're right, but we decided to cut it short. I missed you too much."

"Oh ha ha. Now I know you're joking. Missed Jamie Donnelly, more like."

Vicky is silenced for a second, thinking about the time she wasted missing Jamie Donnelly, then pulls herself together. "Jamie Donnelly's shagging Nicollette Sheridan apparently," she says. "So that's all over. Lying bloody bastard."

"But you knew he was a womanizer," Daniel protests.

"Yes, but naively I thought I might be the one to change his wicked ways."

"You women. All the same." Daniel laughs. "You all think you'll be the one to reform us."

"Actually I beg to differ," Vicky says. "As far as you're concerned I know you're a lost cause, and not only do I not think I would ever stand a chance of reforming you, I wouldn't even want to try."

"Thanks a lot," Daniel pretends to be hurt. "But your American counterpart could have reformed me. She was gorgeous. Seriously. A heartbreaker."

"Bollocks!" Vicky snorts. "I mean yes, she's gorgeous, but the only reason you fancied her so much is because she's married, happily so, and didn't give you a second glance. It's the thrill of the chase, Dan my man. If Amber ever turned round and said, why Daniel, I do believe I made a mistake in marrying Richard, and you are in fact the man I've been looking for my entire life, you'd run a bloody mile."

"Oh all right, maybe you're right," Daniel grumbles. "But not before shagging her."

"God, you never change, do you?"

"No. Speaking of shagging, what's her husband like, and did you do the dirty deed?"

"No I did not! Married men are not my speed, thank you," Vicky says indignantly, grateful Daniel can't see the near-guilty flush on her cheeks.

"So," Daniel settles into his sofa with a grin. "Now that Amber has left and you're home, how about a welcome-home get-together this evening? My place or yours?"

Vicky hesitates, and then shakes her head. "No, Dan," she says eventually. "I think we have to stop this sleeping together business. I really love you as a friend, but I think it would be best if we stopped sleeping together. It just . . .

doesn't feel right anymore. I don't quite know how to explain it, but I'd rather just be friends, proper friends."

"Oh." Daniel's ego slaps his disappointment down as he mentally scrolls down a list of other women he can call. "Don't worry, Vicky. Sounds great."

"So do you still want to get together this evening?" she says. "We could have a drink, or dinner or something."

"You know what?" Daniel remembers a curvaceous brunette named Rachel that he met a month or so ago and never got around to calling. Perhaps he'll give her a call tonight. And if Rachel is busy there's that eager new researcher at work who's desperate to please, and if he can't get hold of her he could always try Poppy, who's usually up for a late-night tryst. "I'm going to have an early night instead."

"Liar!" Vicky laughs. "You're just going to flick through your little black book until you find someone who will have sex with you tonight."

"I'm not that kind of man!" Daniel protests.

"Don't worry, Dan. I'm not judging you. It's one of the reasons I love you, and one of the reasons I won't be sleeping with you anymore. Have a great evening and call me if ever you want to go to the movies, okay?"

"You're the best, Vix," Daniel says, and with a sigh of pity he says good-bye, wishing he could actually fall for someone like her, settle down with a good girl, someone who makes him laugh, who loves him for who he is, who would ensure he would never be lonely again.

But then again, so many women, so little time. And Daniel picks up his BlackBerry and scrolls down, looking for the one among the hundreds who may be available tonight.

*　*　*

Daniel doesn't think about why Vicky said no, but Vicky does. She hadn't thought about Daniel while she was away, but now that she's back she knows that she can't continue because she deserves better.

She deserves more than someone who calls her up every now and then late at night when he's feeling horny. Deserves better than someone to whom she is just another number in the BlackBerry, an easy one at that because she lives so close—hell, possibly for Daniel she's even a last resort: No other women available tonight? Then I'll call good old Vix.

She doesn't want to be good old Vix anymore. Spending the two weeks with Richard, living the life of a married woman, has given her a glimpse of what a true marriage can be like.

Not that she would ever admit she had fallen for Richard, but she did find him attractive; and more than that, for the first time ever she had an idea of the intimacy that came with marriage, the friendship, the sharing.

And it wasn't as if she didn't want it anymore—God knows, at her age she was still just as keen to find a Richard of her own—but she could see that it had to be right, that she wouldn't settle for just anyone, that sex without strings had been just fine before, when she didn't know what else she was missing, but now that she knew she would never settle for sex with no strings again, not even while she was waiting for her Richard to appear on the horizon.

I do deserve better than a Daniel, she thinks, or a Jamie Donnelly. I deserve better than a good-looking Lothario, or a man who claims to be my friend just to get me between the sheets. But if he doesn't come along, she realizes, lying in her bed and stroking Eartha, who purrs delightedly, thrilled to have her mistress home at last (the other woman had been perfectly fine, but she hadn't stroked her in quite the right way, and Eartha could definitely smell dog . . .), if he doesn't come along I am quite happy.

Perhaps I did need to go away to appreciate what I have, thinks Vicky, feeling safe and cozy in her small flat, knowing that tomorrow morning she will wake up at whatever time she wakes up, and will have the rest of the day in which to do whatever she feels like doing. She will make herself coffee in her little kitchen, and will drink it curled up on the sofa reading the stack of magazines she bought at the airport and didn't have a chance to read because she slept the entire way home.

She will wander down the High Street to get a croissant at Patisserie Valerie, and will then come home and phone her friends, tell them about her experiences of swapping lives.

This afternoon she will jump on the train and go down to Somerset to see Kate and Andy. She has presents for everyone—sweatshirts, baseball caps, and of course bags of M&M's for the kids, snowglobes of New York, an antique map of New England for the adults.

She is desperate to see her family, has missed them enormously, and she realizes now that she is home how unsettling the past few weeks have been. It is enormous fun pretending to be someone else, but it would have been more fun for about three days. Long enough to see what it was like, not long enough to miss her life so much.

Although perhaps she wouldn't have learned to appreciate what she has if she had only stayed a handful of days.

Admittedly there are things she will miss about being Amber. She will miss her fantastic wardrobe, even though she didn't have a chance to wear half the things Amber owns, not least because half of them didn't fit her.

She will miss pretending to be mistress of an enormous house, even though the house wasn't hers, wasn't decorated the way she would decorate, but it was fun to pretend.

She will miss the children, because they were adorable, particularly that little Gracie, and she will miss Richard, will miss hearing his stories over dinner, going out to the diner with him and the kids, loving the pretense of being a real family.

But she also had no time for herself, not once the routine had kicked in, not once she had decided to be supermom and had basically waved good-bye to Lavinia. When the children were crying, or whining, or fighting, Vicky was the only one who could step in. When Gracie came in crying at five o'clock in the morning, Vicky had to get up and soothe her, put her back to bed. When Jared arrived at camp and burst into tears because he'd forgotten his Hulk fist for show-and-tell, Vicky was the one who had to schlep back home to get it.

When Richard was around, on the weekends, Vicky could indulge in her perfect fantasy of what it was to be married, but during the week, the humdrum existence of life in the suburbs, with the husbands at work and the über-wives running the show, sent Vicky's fantasies disappearing out the window.

I would love to be married, she thinks, gazing into space and allowing herself a gentle memory of Richard's near-kiss in the pool before shaking her head and sending it on its way, but only if I found someone wonderful, and right now I'm just going to enjoy being by myself.

Look at this, she thinks, stepping out of bed and shuffling into the living room with a wide grin on her face, so thankful for everything she has. Look how lucky I am to be living in this gorgeous flat, to have my wonderful job, to be exactly where I am right now.

And she picks up the phone and calls Kate and Andy to tell them what train she'll be on.

"I missed you!" Kate wraps Vicky in a giant hug, disengages for a second, then hugs her again, squeezing her tight.

"Oh God, I missed you too!" Vicky says. "Where are the kids?"

"At home boxing up eggs."

"Eggs? I thought you only had five chickens. How many eggs have you got?"

Kate rolls her eyes. "It's a long story. We lost some chickens to the fox—you missed a terribly sad funeral," Kate tries, and fails, to keep a straight face, "and then Bill-the-chicken-man said he knew of someone who wanted to get rid of their chickens, so we said we'd take them, and now we have twenty chickens, and more eggs than we know what to do with, so the kids are boxing them up and selling them at the village shop."

"Oh the dramas of living in the country." Vicky grins, linking her arm through Kate's as they walk to the car. "So tell me about Amber. Did she come to see you? Did you like her? Please tell me the kids didn't like her as much as me."

"Of course the kids didn't like her as much as you—you're their auntie, for heaven's sake—but she did come down and she was very nice, although I think she was a bit overwhelmed by the chaos in our house."

"Ah yes," Vicky laughs. "I imagine she would have been."

"Is her house as grand and quiet as I imagine?"

"I want to say no, but," Vicky winces, "yes. It's all very perfect, apart from the playroom which is the only room in the house where there's ever any mess, and even that has to be cleaned up by the nanny every night."

"I know. She was saying that she has a team of people running her life, and I think we made her miss doing things herself."

"Well that's good," Vicky says, "because I'm pretty sure the teams of people are going to be disappearing."

"She did say she wanted more control of her life."

"She's going to get it," Vicky bursts out. "And don't tell anyone I told you because we're saving it for the piece, but her husband lost his job six months ago and hadn't told anyone, and I'm pretty sure she's going to get her wish because I don't think there's any money left."

"Oh gracious!" Kate says in alarm. "I suppose they do say be careful what you wish for. And what about you, young lady? And your wish to have this life and be an old married lady? Is that still going strong since Swapping Lives?"

"Yes and no. It's made me realize that I do actually love my life, and although of course I'd give it up, it would have to be for the right person. I know this sounds odd, but I don't feel desperate anymore. If it happens, then lovely, and if not, well that's lovely too."

"Well, I think that's the healthiest way of all to feel." Kate smiles as they reach the car. "Now let's go home and crack open some champagne."

"Auntie Vicky!" Luke and Polly place their egg cartons carefully on the floor, while Sophie just lets hers drop, thereby smashing all the eggs, as they run into Vicky's arms.

"There was an American lady who was staying in your flat," Luke says, "and she was really nice and she came to stay here and Dad was joking that we should call her Auntie Vicky but we didn't and she's not as fun as you because she didn't come up to our bedrooms and play with us on the floor like you do . . ."

"But she did play with me," Sophie says. "And Bill-the-chicken-man said she had a serious pair of legs on her . . ."

"I did not!" an indignant voice comes over from the other side of the garden where Andy and Bill-the-chicken-man emerge from the kitchen, bottles of beer in hand.

"Yes you did!" the three children chorus.

"You said you wished you were in with a chance!" Luke says with a grin.

"Did I really? I must have been very drunk to say that out loud. Hello!" he says, extending a hand to Vicky. "I'm Bill. I think we met once before."

"Vicky. Hello," and she shakes his hand and smiles, turning to give Andy a big hug.

"Bill's right," Andy says as he gets the barbecue ready for supper. "She did have a serious pair of legs, but still, she wasn't you, and that's all that matters."

"Will you all stop going on about me saying she had a serious pair of legs. You make me sound like an old lech." Bill rolls his eyes.

"What's a lech?" Luke asks.

"Never you mind," Bill says. "Have you finished those boxes yet? I told the shop I'd deliver them by six."

"Oh, but Bill, you've got to stay for supper!" Kate insists, coming out of the kitchen with a fresh jug of Pimms. "I've got tons of food. Delicious roast lamb and salad, and yummy gazpacho that we made this morning."

"Roast lamb," Bill says dreamily. "Well . . ."

"Do stay. Doesn't your ex have the kids this weekend?"

"Yes, but . . ."

"But nothing. You're staying for supper. I won't take no for an answer."

"Kate," Vicky hisses in a whisper as she runs back into the kitchen on the pretense of helping Kate prepare the marinade. "I hope this isn't a setup."

"What do you mean?" Kate says innocently.

"You know what I mean. I hope you're not playing matchmaker."

"Vicky!" Kate says, disgruntled. "How can you accuse me of such a thing? I haven't invited him to stay for a romantic dinner, it's us and all the kids. I wouldn't dream of fixing you up with Bill."

"Okay, good."

Kate sidles up to Vicky at the sink and bumps her hip gently against Vicky's. "But did you see his bum?"

"What?" Vicky turns to her in horror.

"No, seriously. He has the sexiest bum I've ever seen. You look at it when we go back out. I bet he looks delicious naked."

"Kate Townsley! How old are you?"

"Old enough to indulge in chaste fantasies about men with sexy bums, especially in faded Levis," she shivers. "Good Lord, I should have a cold shower."

"Not that I'm interested," Vicky says slowly, "but how come he's divorced?"

"Wife ran off with the builder. All rather awful, although now he says he realizes it's a good thing, although very hard on the kids. They weren't that happy, he says now, but he would have stayed, just assumed that that was the way his life was going to be."

"And no girlfriend?" Vicky says, because he is quite attractive, even though she hadn't ever really thought about it before, had assumed he was unavailable.

"Nope." Kate grins at her. "Are you interested?"

"Oh don't be ridiculous!" Vicky says. "I don't even know the man."

"Okay, okay. Just make sure you check out his bum," she whispers, as the men walk back into the kitchen.

Kate takes the kids up to bathe them, Andy disappears over to the neighbor to take back the saw he'd borrowed earlier, and Vicky and Bill clear the dishes.

"You've got to be careful about accepting dinner invitations here," Vicky says. "Delicious food but you have to do the washing-up."

"Wash or dry?" Bill says.

"I'll wash."

"I was hoping you'd say that. I'm a hopeless washer. My ex-wife used to ban me from doing any washing-up. Can't say I minded desperately."

"Does she still live locally?"

"Yes, we still live in the same house actually."

"You do?"

"Well, it's divided into two, but it's great for the children. They're eight and ten, and we wanted to cause them as little disruption as possible, so Melanie and Des live on one side, and I live on the other with my chickens."

"You got the raw end of the deal, then."

"Why, because of the chickens?" Vicky nods as Bill bursts into laughter. "Actually she hates the chickens, and I'd far rather have the chickens than Des."

"He was your builder?"

"Yup. Actually he's not bad. He can't be that bad for putting up with Mel." Bill grins.

"But isn't it weird, living in the same house as them?"

"I know others think so, but it works for us. Speaking of weird, isn't it weird to swap lives with a married woman?"

"Fair enough," Vicky laughs. "You win. Although that was for work rather than by choice."

"Are you glad you did it?"

"Yes, I really am. I think it really changed the way I think, made me much happier with what I've got."

"I bet the husband must have been happy when you showed up."

Vicky almost drops the plate she's washing in shock. "Why, Bill! Was that a compliment?"

"A very heavy-handed one," he says sheepishly, "but yes."

"Well thank you," she grins. "Flattery will get you everywhere. Even though," she gives him a sideways glance, "I don't have a serious pair of legs."

"Oh I don't know." Bill raises an eyebrow. "They didn't look too bad to me," and embarrassed at how forward he is, he looks away and pretends to be busy with the tea towel. "There. Done." He finishes drying the last dish and hangs the damp cloth on the hook.

"I should go and help Kate with the kids," Vicky says during the awkward silence.

"Absolutely not," Bill says. "You can't leave a guest here all by himself. Come and sit with me outside and tell me everything about Swapping Lives."

And so Vicky does.

"Well?" Kate says as Bill finally leaves at the end of the evening. "I saw the two of you through the window while I was bathing the kids. Laughing and flirting away, Miss 'I'm not interested'!"

"I was not flirting!" Vicky says, with a blush. "Okay, well, maybe just a tiny bit."

"So?"

"So?"

"So did anything happen?"

"Yes. We had sex on the sun lounger while you were upstairs."

Kate's mouth falls open as Vicky starts to laugh.

"Oh, you ridiculous thing! Of course we didn't have sex. But he asked me if I'd like to come over for dinner next time I'm up. He says he's a wonderful cook."

"And will you?"

"I said I'd love to."

"Oh goodness!" Kate says excitedly, her cheeks flushed with alcohol and promise. "Imagine if you married him! You'd live two minutes away! We'd see you all the time. Vicky Arlington! Mrs. Arlington! Mrs. Bill Arlington!"

"Andy!" Vicky calls her brother in from the other room. "Will you shut your wife up?"

"Absolutely," he grins. "Kate? Mrs. Arlington would very much like it if you shut up. How's that?" He turns to Vicky who rolls her eyes.

"You're as bad as one another. It's dinner, for God's sake. And it's at his house, not even a date. And who knows what will happen? We'll probably just be friends."

"Okay, but just tell me one thing, and then I'll shut up forever," Kate pleads. "Did you notice his bum?"

"Yes," Vicky grins. "And yes, you're right. It is as sexy as you described."

Chapter **Thirty-two**

Amber doesn't speak to Richard for three days.

"What a welcome home," she mutters to him over the breakfast table the next morning, trying not to let the kids see that she is furious with him, that he has spent last night in the same place he has spent the previous two and a half weeks—the guest room.

"How could you not tell me?" she hisses, slamming the plate of toast on the table in front of him. Then later, as she clears up, "No money left. Jesus Christ. How could you not have told me?"

The questions are rhetorical. Richard says nothing. As awful as it is, having this hissing, spurting, simmering version of his wife home, he has to admit he feels a hell of a lot better having told her. There are no pretenses these last three days. No "Bye, darling, see you after work." No leaving the house in his suit and wondering how to fill his day and where to go so he won't be caught, won't be seen by any of Amber's friends or nannies who happen to spy him somewhere.

These last few days he has slept better than he has in the past six months. Admittedly he is vaguely concerned about Amber, wishes that he could lie next to her in their huge bed, wishes more that he could make love to her—it's been three weeks, for God's sake—but he knows she will need to vent, and once she has got all the anger out, they will figure out what to do.

In the meantime he disappears into his home office during the day. Sits online for hours, checking out the job Web sites, halfheartedly applying for other trading positions, knowing even as he e-mails his résumé that he doesn't really want this. At the same time he looks at businesses for sale, starts to read up on running small businesses, orders books from Amazon about successful businessmen who started small, turning their mom-and-pop shops into multimillion-dollar worldwide organizations.

On day three Amber knocks on the door of his office.

"Okay," she says, her expression still stern, but the steam no longer pouring out of her ears. "Now we have to talk."

"We could leave," Amber says after they've talked about selling the house, what it would be worth, how much they could put away and what would then be left to buy. They've talked about what Richard really wants to do, how he doesn't have the energy to go into the city anymore, how he wants to spend more time with them. And they've talked about Highfield. About how it isn't what Richard expected, isn't what he wants for their children, although he knows how much Amber loves it, how settled she is, and for her sake they should start looking for a smaller house.

"What do you mean, 'we could leave'?"

"I mean we could *leave*. The kids are young enough, we could start again somewhere else. Somewhere that isn't a microcosm of Manhattan. Somewhere quiet, and simple, where nobody judges you based on which season's Luella bag you're carrying, or who," she smiles wryly, "decorated your living room."

"You would leave Highfield?"

Amber looks at Richard for a long time, then takes a deep breath. "In a heartbeat," she says finally.

"Are you serious?"

"Yes." She nods. "I think I needed to get away to see it for what it is. I'm tired of trying to keep up, and I agree with you, I don't want Jared and Gracie becoming the children I see around town."

"But where would we go?"

"I don't know," Amber says. "And you need to know that I'm still upset that you didn't tell me. I understand that you didn't want to hurt me unnecessarily, but I need some more time to get over that betrayal. Having said that," she takes a deep breath, "I would support you buying a small business. I think you'd be great at it. I've always thought you should be your own boss, and I know you haven't been happy on Wall Street for a long time. So I think we should base where we go on what you end up buying, and maybe we could even find something that you and I could do together."

"Come here," Richard says, holding out his arms.

"No," Amber stands up and heads for the door. "This doesn't mean you're forgiven. It doesn't mean that everything's suddenly okay. I still need some time, but I've pulled myself up from far worse situations, and I can do it again; and who knows, maybe this will be the best thing that ever happened to us. But I can't pretend that I'm fine with it. Not yet."

Amber drops the children off at Deborah's the next day, and sends Lavinia out to do the grocery shopping.

"You're not coming in?" Deborah asks after giving Amber a huge welcome-back hug. "But I need to talk to you, I have to fill you in on League gossip, not to mention hear everything about London. You look great! I love that skirt." Deborah fingers Amber's suspiciously trendy skirt. "Whistles?"

"Nope. Jigsaw!" Amber laughs and shakes her head. "I've got a million things to do," she says. "Life is crazy busy, but I'll come and pick the kids up and I promise we can have a glass of wine then and I'll fill you in on what's going on."

"What do you mean?" Deborah calls out after her as Amber climbs back into her car. "Stop! You can't leave me hanging like this. What do you mean, 'what's going on'? What *is* going on?"

"Tell you later," Amber calls back through the window as she drives off with a wave, heading back home to continue her research on the Internet.

The way Amber thinks is this: If she can't trust her husband to tell her he's lost his job so they can figure out what the next step should be, instead of saying nothing and letting her blow his severance pay on ridiculous frivolities because she had no idea they were about to be broke, how can she possibly trust him to find a business?

And so Amber has taken it upon herself to find a business. No. More than a business. A new life. She has dived into this new project with a vigor and enthusiasm that she hasn't felt since, well, since she was sitting behind the features director's desk at *Poise!* magazine.

Already she has found a few businesses that would have suited Richard perfectly, but a closer investigation of the towns in which they're based has ruled them out. She's found a few towns that she's fallen in love with, but a closer investigation of the businesses has ruled them out.

Just for the hell of it, she's taken to going to realtor.com to see what they could get for their money, just in case they would move to any of these towns, and she is shocked when she sees what their money will buy.

In Highfield, a starter home now runs at close to a million dollars. In Portland, Oregon, a starter condo runs at around a hundred and fifty thousand. In Tucson, Arizona, they could buy a luxury house for a million and a half, and in Charlottesville, Virginia, a small farm would be just under a million.

And then she stumbles upon an apple orchard for sale just outside Albany, New York. It's a pick-your-own orchard, a successful family business that has a farm shop selling homemade pies, apple butter, apple desserts. They have their own Web site, and with rising excitement Amber scans the pictures of the house: an eighteenth-century farmhouse, picture-perfect, surrounded by a picket fence with clouds of lavender and catmint, the farm shop across the road next to the orchards, a playground, and a barnyard complete with chickens, geese, sheep, goats, three (little) pigs, two cows, and a pony.

"The local schools regularly bring classes to Appletree Orchard for field trips," Amber reads, "where the children learn how to look after animals, including hand-rearing our lambs in the spring."

And best of all, it's well within their price range. Laughably cheap. A house and a business in one. Plus four outbuildings including a barn that would make a perfect office, because as it stands the orchard is pretty but seasonal. If it were ever to become something substantial, they would have to figure out how to make money in winter. She prints out the pages from the Web site and takes them down to Richard's office.

"Have a look at this," she says, placing the pages in front

of him. "I'm going to get the kids from Deborah's and she wants to hear about London, so I'll probably be back in a couple of hours."

"Okay," Richard says, calling out after her as she goes, "I love you!"

"I love you too!" she yells back absentmindedly, her mind already in Sommersby, New York, picturing the children collecting fresh eggs from the chickens, concentrating on what you would do with an apple orchard in winter.

But Richard smiles. Now he knows he's on the way to being forgiven.

"Mail order!" Amber announces, rushing into his office, the children behind her.

Richard grins. "Great minds think alike," he says, swiveling his computer screen so Amber can see the Web site he's looking at: "Baked and unbaked, fresh and frozen apple pies delivered to your door," she reads. "Twenty-eight different varieties of pie. All delicious, all 100 percent organic and natural."

"Is that Appletree Orchard's Web site?" she asks, not remembering seeing it before.

"No. I've been looking at orchard Web sites in general and what they offer, and mail order and Internet do seem to be where it's at. We could combine pies, pastries, and cakes with gift baskets. Look at this." He clicks again and Amber perches on the arm of his chair to look at harry anddavid.com, admire their hampers filled with fresh apples, gourmet cheeses, nuts, crackers, and delicious jams.

"We could do all of this," Richard says happily. "And more. We could really make this work."

"And children's parties," Amber says excitedly. "We could

offer children's parties at the farm, petting, playground, food and drink included." Amber smiles. "You know, I'm not sure we're ever going to become millionaires with something like this."

"No, but we'd be happy," Richard says. "It would be our own business, and seeing as you're now the star writer in the family you could write all the copy in the catalogs."

"Oh thanks a lot," Amber sniffs. "But before you get your knickers in a twist . . ."

"What?" Richard starts to laugh.

"What?"

"What did you just say?"

"I said 'before you get your knickers in a twist.' It's an English expression." Amber smiles. "One of my favorites actually. That, and cor blimey."

Richard reaches out and pulls Amber onto his lap. "I do love you, you know," he says, nuzzling her neck. "And I'm sorry. I know I was wrong. I really am so sorry for being so stupid."

"Dad!" Jared pipes up from the corner of the room where he and Gracie are decorating Richard's now defunct business cards. "You did say a bad word!" His eyes are wide with horror.

"Oh. You're right, Jar. Sorry. I didn't mean to say the s-word and I won't say it again."

"You have to say sorry to Mommy," Gracie adds.

"Okay." Richard grins, so thankful that he has Amber home, that she is supporting him, that they will find a way out of this mess, and that there is a light at the end of the tunnel, and all of a sudden it seems to be burning bright. "I'm sorry, Mommy."

"That's okay." Amber lets out a reluctant smile as she finds herself relaxing involuntarily into his arms. "But as I was saying, before you get all excited, let's check out the town, okay? There's no point doing all this research if it's a horrible town with crappy schools."

Richard reaches behind Amber to his desk and hands her a stack of papers.

"What's this?"

"Schools report. Town information. Ranked number nine in best small towns in America." He looks at his watch. "And in about half an hour Ted Riley is faxing over the business report."

"Ted Riley?"

Richard grins. "The owner of Appletree Orchard. I spent an hour on the phone with him. We're driving up there to see it on Tuesday."

Amber's mouth drops open. "How did you manage all this while I was out?"

"Honestly? I'm excited. I'm really excited about this change. I'm excited about the prospect of starting my own business . . ."

"Our own business," Amber corrects him.

"Oh yes?" Richard raises an eyebrow.

"Yes," Amber says firmly. "Never mind just writing the copy. It's a family business, which means it needs a family to run it."

"You're right. So Gracie can write the copy for the catalogs, and Jared can be in charge of inventory."

"Be serious."

"I'm sorry, darling. But yes, you're right. Part of not wanting to be on Wall Street anymore is to spend more time with my family, and a family business could be perfect. But we shouldn't get too excited until we see it."

"I know. But if this isn't the one for us, at least we've made a firm decision that we're going to move, and if Appletree Orchard is awful, something better will come along."

"Will you phone our Realtor tomorrow morning and get her to come over to value this?"

"Yup, but I have to tell you, a girl in the League just sold her house on Edgetree Road for $3.6 million, and it's not as nice as this, not as big, and in a far worse location."

"That's what I was hoping," Richard says. "Let's get her over and see what she says."

"I'll call her first thing," says Amber. "Wouldn't it be so weird if this all worked out? If doing Swapping Lives turns out to be the best thing that ever happened to us?"

"How so?"

"Well, I didn't realize how much I missed working, and I didn't realize how trapped I felt here, and if I hadn't gone, yes, you would still have lost your job, but the chances are we would have stayed in Highfield and you would have just found another job in the city. I just feel this is such a fresh start for us. This is exactly what we need."

"I hope you're right," says Richard. "And I guess it's what you've recently been saying: everything happens for a reason."

"That's right." Amber smiles, remembering how she picked up the phrase from Kate. "And now we just have to wait and see what the future has in store."

Chapter **Thirty-three**

"Amber was very nice," Leona says, when Vicky is firmly ensconced back at her desk, so happy to be back at work, to be with her colleagues who are more like family than even her friends. "But I have to be honest, she wasn't you, and she was a bit like a fish out of water."

They all huddle around her, all dying to know whether being in Highfield was like the television show, whether she was still desperate to get married, what the American housewives thought of her.

"It was great," Vicky laughs, as a crowd gathers. "Sexy husband, gorgeous huge McMansion, sweet children, and a wardrobe you'd kill for. Three Birkin bags," she turns to Stella with a grin.

"Three?" Stella attempts to hide her envy. "God, how gauche. Those Americans, can't do anything by halves."

"Jealous? *Moi?*" Leona puts a hand to her chest in affected fashion and shakes her head at Stella. "You fashion editors. You're all the same. So come on, Vicky," she turns back to her, "we're all dying to know if you shagged the husband."

"You're a married woman, Leona! How can you ask with such glee?"

"Basically because it's not my husband, although frankly

you're welcome to have sex with my husband if you want, would take some of the pressure off me." She rolls her eyes as the others laugh. "I'm not joking," she adds, with a serious expression as she looks around the room hopefully. "Anyone?"

"As it happens, no, I did not have sex with her husband, and why is that the first question everyone wants to ask?"

"Because he's gorgeous?" Leona says. "We've all seen the pictures."

"Well, he is gorgeous, but no, we didn't have sex."

"Not even a kiss?" Leona persists, and Vicky colors.

"You did! You brazen hussy! You snogged him!" But Leona's eyes are wide with shock.

"No, I didn't!" Vicky says.

"So why are you blushing?"

"Because I did quite fancy him, but trust me, he wasn't interested in me. This is a man who loves his wife, and you've met her, she's gorgeous, why would he even look at me?"

"Darling," Janelle is standing on the outskirts of the group, listening with amusement, "just because a man has filet mignon at home, doesn't mean he doesn't fancy a McDonald's every now and then."

The group laughs, and immediately disperses to appear busy. Vicky whispers to a giggling Ruth, "Am I going completely crazy or did our editor just liken me to McDonald's?"

"I know. I can't actually believe she said that." Ruth's shoulders are shaking with laughter. "I'd never say you were a McDonald's. Roast chicken, perhaps, but not McDonald's."

"Roast bloody chicken indeed. I'd forgotten what it was like here. Should have stayed in Highfield."

* * *

But Vicky couldn't be happier to be back. Her week is a whirlwind of catching up, meeting with journalists, checking the copy for the next issue. The following week, when she's caught her breath and America is already beginning to feel like a distant memory, she picks up the phone and calls Amber, and is nevertheless surprised when Richard picks up the phone.

"Hi, Richard," Vicky says. "It's Vicky."

"Vicky! How are you?" Richard's voice is as jovial and warm as it has always been.

"I'm great. Happy to be home. How are you? I've been thinking about all of you so much. I miss the kids!" She wants to ask if he's told Amber yet, but doesn't dare.

"They miss you too, although they're pretty happy to have their mom back."

"How is Amber?"

"She's doing great, although I have to tell you it's been crazy since she got back. We're listing the house, and we've found a new house to buy, and a business, and everything's insanely busy."

"You've found a house? And a business?" Vicky is in shock. "Already?"

"You know what? I'll let Amber tell you all about it," Richard says. "Hang on, I'll just get her."

"But that's unbelievable!" Vicky says, as Amber finishes telling the story, of how they went to Appletree Orchard and it's a little disorganized, needs quite a lot of work, but could be amazing. "Your life will be completely changed."

"I know," Amber smiles. "And I have to thank you for it. I'm obviously resigning from the League, and you know what? I can't wait! I can't wait to spend more time with my husband, with my kids, and get involved in a business again."

"How is it, having Richard at home?"

Amber sighs. "Right now he's driving me a bit crazy. He keeps coming in asking what's for lunch, or asking where I'm going, or why is Deborah phoning again when I've already spoken to her three times today."

Vicky laughs. "Are you sure you're ready to go into business with him?"

"You know what? If it doesn't work we can always do something else. Working at *Poise!* just made me miss working. It made me miss doing something other than organizing fashion shows and galas. And Vicky, you should see this place. We flew up there to see it, and even though it's kind of overgrown and messy, it could be so beautiful, and I honestly don't think I would have had the courage to change my life like this if I hadn't done the piece, so thank you."

"Oh God, you don't have to thank me. I'm just glad it all worked out, although I'm also glad that it's been so life-changing for you—it will make wonderful copy. Speaking of the copy, do you have anything ready yet for me to read?"

"I do," Amber smiles. "I just have to do one more read-through, but I did as you asked: a thousand words."

"And you've put in the stuff about Richard losing his job, and buying a business and everything?"

"Well, I said he left his job. I didn't want to put in about him being laid off six months ago. Do you mind? I just know his ego couldn't take that, and in the future if he ever does decide to go back to Wall Street it would be terrible to have that in print. I haven't lied, I just haven't told the whole truth."

"Okay, don't worry. It will be fine, just get it over to me as soon as possible," Vicky says, realizing she'll have to adjust her own copy somewhat, remove the paragraphs about finding Richard at the aquarium, but it's fine; it isn't the crux of the story. "Give your delicious kids a big hug and kiss from me," Vicky says. "And tell Jared I haven't forgotten about the dalek. I've already sent one to him and he should get it any day."

"A what?"

"It's a British thing," Vicky laughs. "I got him hooked on stories about a TV show called *Dr. Who*. It's not quite as sophisticated as *Star Wars*, but close."

"Is this why he keeps walking around jerkily saying, 'Exterminate. Exterminate'?" Amber asks with a laugh.

"I'm afraid I'm guilty," Vicky says. "Now get back to finishing the piece and I'll put an advance copy in the post as soon as I have it."

"Vicky?" Ruth calls out from her desk. "Huge Anus on the phone for you. Do you want to call him back?"

"What?" Leona splutters from the other side of the desk.

"I know. Poor bloke. He'll tell you his name is Hugh Janus, but everyone calls him Huge Anus. Thanks, Ruth. I'll take it."

"So the queen of swapping lives returns," Hugh's voice comes down the phone. "How was it?"

"Lonely," Vicky says, realizing that it was. That she missed this far more than she even knew at the time. "And it's good to be home."

"Has Janelle filled you in? That we're going ahead with the documentary, but we're doing another ad when your piece goes in, looking for two more people to swap lives, but this time both in England to keep the budget down."

"That's great, Hugh. And kind of a relief not to have my fifteen minutes of fame. Not sure I could deal with that."

"Well, the reason I'm calling is to see if I can make a lunch date with you. I've got a meeting with the head of documentaries next week, and I need to make a presentation about the show, and for that I need to know more about your experience. I've already left a message for Amber in the States, and I'd love to meet up with you sooner rather than later."

"Sounds great." Vicky flicks through her diary, surprised to see how busy this week is. "Oh shit," she says. "It looks like they've saved everything up for when I got back. This week looks crazy. I'm just not going to be able to do it. When's your meeting? Maybe I could do next week."

"Tuesday."

Vicky shakes her head. "It's not going to work."

"Okay. Dinner, then? What about dinner?"

"Sure. Dinner would be fine."

"Okay. How about Thursday?"

"Can't. Got a preview I have to cover on Thursday."

"Wednesday?"

"Nope." Vicky is beginning to realize dinner doesn't look quite so good either. "Actually, dinner isn't that easy either, although . . ." she hesitates. "I know it's short notice but I could do tonight . . ."

"Great!" Hugh enthuses. "Locanda Locatelli at eight o'clock?"

"You can get a table at Locanda Locatelli at eight o'clock on a few hours' notice?" Vicky's impressed.

"It's not about what you know, it's who you know."

"And presumably, Hugh they know too," Vicky quips.

"Exactly. I'll see you there."

"Great," says Vicky, and puts down the phone.

Hugh stands up from the table and gives Vicky the obligatory double kiss. "You look great," he tells her, and she shakes her head in denial, having come straight from the office and not having had time to change or even freshen up.

This morning she decided she was going for cute, mostly because she didn't have time to wash her hair, so she pulled it into pigtails, which she knows women her age shouldn't really do but Kylie Minogue does it and gets away with it, and frankly if it's good enough for Kylie Minogue it's good enough for her. She's in a gray ruffled-edge cardigan with a soft pink gypsy skirt and tan ballet pumps. The perfect office uniform. Admittedly, had she known she'd be at such a smart restaurant this evening, she would have worn something more sophisticated, something more Amber-like, but the lovely thing about living in London is that she knows it doesn't matter, that one table might be filled with men in suits, and another with people in jeans, no one caring that much what anyone else looks like.

"I keep expecting everyone in the restaurant to turn around and look me up and down to check out what I'm wearing." She grins at Hugh as she sits down.

"Why would they do that?"

"That's what they do in Highfield. When you walk into a restaurant for lunch, all the women turn around just to make sure they're wearing more expensive clothes."

"But I thought Highfield was in the country."

"No. It's the suburbs," Vicky emphasizes the word. "It's limbo-land, neither the city nor the country. Very strange."

"Not like the suburbs here?"

"No, not at all. Everyone's very stressed and busy and rushing their children around to make sure they fulfill their genius potential . . ."

"I take it all the children have genius potential?" Hugh grins.

"But of course. There are no average children in the suburbs." Vicky grins back. "Who ever heard of anything so ridiculous! So it ought to be peaceful and countrylike, because there are trees and meadows, and lovely winding country lanes, but everyone's always rushing and honking their horns and trying to keep up with everyone else, so it's all rather exhausting."

"Sounds like a nightmare. Actually, it sounds like London."

"No. Not like London. Probably more like Manhattan."

"I love Manhattan," Hugh says. "Haven't been there for years. One of the reasons why I was hoping we'd be able to do Swapping Lives with you was to go back to Manhattan."

"Have you spent much time there?"

Hugh nods. "I had an American girlfriend when I was at university. She was a true New Yorker, from the Village, went to Stuyvesant High School, and I used to fly out and see her all the time."

"What happened to her?"

"We lost touch," he says sadly. "I do Google her from time to time, but Lara was incredibly jealous of previous girlfriends, couldn't handle me being friends with them, so I lost touch with all of them, which was a shame because some of them became real friends."

"I've never understood that," Vicky says.

"What?"

"That whole jealousy insecurity thing. I mean, if you didn't want to be with them, you wouldn't be. How can someone in the past threaten what you have now?"

"I agree," Hugh says. "Just one of the many reasons why it wasn't meant to be."

"This is your long-term girlfriend?"

"Was," Hugh corrects her.

"So when did you break up?"

"I moved out about three weeks ago. Probably just about the time you went off to America. We're still supposed to be seeing each other, trying to make it work, but I can't see the point. Maybe this is naive, but when it's right it's right, and after seven years together if it isn't right, why keep trying?"

"I'm sorry," Vicky says. "It must be hard after seven years."

"It is hard, but I've known for a while we were never going to get married. I knew she wanted to, and she was desperate for a child, but I could never see myself having a child with her. I still don't know exactly why, because I did love her. I suppose a part of me will always love her, but I just could never see us spending the rest of our lives together, and I couldn't bring a child into this world knowing that. Oh God, will you listen to me? I should just shut up. Tell me about you. What's going on in your love life?"

Vicky smiles ruefully. "Nothing to tell," she says. "The guy I was seeing who I thought I really liked is now shagging a major Hollywood star and I had to find out from a girl while I was in America. Bastard didn't even have the decency to tell me himself."

"Jamie Donnelly," Hugh says.

Vicky stares at him, her mouth open. "How did you know?"

"I saw all that chemistry between the two of you when we ran into him that day we were having lunch, remember?"

"Yes, well, said chemistry didn't amount to very much. Other than that I have a hot date coming up with Bill-the-chicken-man, and that's it."

"Bill-the-chicken-man?" Hugh cracks up.

"Yes. Bill-the-chicken-man, and I don't see why *you're* laughing, Huge An—"

"Oh all right, all right." Hugh raises his hands in defeat. "No need to get nasty. But who on earth is Bill-the-chicken-man?"

"He's a divorced father of two who lives in Somerset near my brother and sister-in-law."

"Are you interested?"

Vicky shrugs and blushes slightly. "He's got a sexy bum," she says eventually with a grin. "And he seems like a nice guy. He's got a great smile," she adds, wondering what else to say.

"Well, that's a good start," says Hugh, smiling, and Vicky suddenly notices that Hugh's smile is not so bad either. In fact, why had she not noticed before how attractive Hugh is? She sits a little straighter, and brushes her hair behind her ears. Not that he's interested. He's just split up with his girlfriend of seven years. Stop it, she tells herself. He's got to have a rebound relationship first, and he's not even ready for that.

"What are you having?" Hugh asks, as the waiter hovers over them.

"Hmmm? Oh, sorry." Vicky blushes, lost in thought as she gazes at Hugh Janus. "Can you give me a couple more minutes? I was miles away."

* * *

Two bottles of wine later Hugh and Vicky are still talking animatedly, each one constantly interrupting the other, each with a funnier story to tell. Neither of them is able to stop smiling, and Vicky realizes that she hasn't had this nice a time in months.

Hugh walks Vicky home, weaving their way through the back streets toward her flat, both of them still talking until the awkward silence descends as they reach Vicky's front door.

I fancy him, she thinks with a start, as they stand there, both ever so slightly drunk, both smiling at the other, but I shouldn't ask him in. It's too soon. He's just come out of a relationship. I'm not going to do this. And I'm definitely not going to sleep with him. I'm going to play hard to get.

"Do you want to come in?" Vicky hears the words come out of her mouth before she can stop them.

There's a silence. "I'd love to," Hugh says eventually. "But I'd better not."

Vicky starts fumbling awkwardly in her bag for her key to hide her disappointment, and Hugh places a hand on her arm to still her.

"I really would love to," he says, looking into her eyes with a smile. "I've had a fantastic time tonight. Look, I'm going to be up to my eyes this weekend doing the presentation, but can we do this again?"

"Sure," Vicky says, still embarrassed by her perceived rejection, turning to go inside. "Call me."

"Wait. How about next Thursday night? I'll pick you up here? Eight o'clock?"

"Sounds great!" The smile on her face is both relieved and real.

"Thank you for a wonderful evening," Hugh says, and he leans forward and gives her a quick, but soft, kiss on the lips, and pulling back with a regretful smile he waves and walks away.

"Guess what?" Kate is on the phone first thing the next morning, her voice full of excitement.

"What? More chickens laying more eggs? You've added a cow so the children can get their own milk?"

"Hmm, not a bad idea, but no, that's not why I'm calling. Guess who I bumped into just now at the post office."

"Bill-the-chicken-man?"

"Yes! How did you know?"

"Oh Kate, don't be so silly. Who else would it be?"

"Well anyway, he was asking after you, and whether you were coming down this weekend, and I said I didn't know, so he asked for your number. Do you mind that I gave it to him? It's just that he seemed really interested, and I had to tell you."

"I don't mind at all. And yes, I probably will come down this weekend. But . . . I also had kind of a date last night." Vicky smiles at the memory.

"You can't have a date!" Kate says firmly. "You have to marry Bill-the-chicken-man."

"First of all I don't have to marry anyone," Vicky laughs. "And second, it wasn't exactly a date, but he kissed me good-bye on the lips, and we're going out next Thursday."

"With or without tongues?" Kate asks suspiciously.

"Without!" Vicky exclaims in horror. "What kind of girl do you think I am?"

"I know exactly what kind of girl you are," Kate laughs. "That's why I asked."

"Well anyway. He's really nice."

"Oh but please don't fall in love with him. I bet his bum's not nearly as sexy as Bill's."

"Actually it's not, but I'm not in love with anyone at the moment. I'm just having fun, and it's lovely to have so much attention, particularly given that I've wasted the last few months with that bastard Jamie Donnelly."

"Oh you're making me miss being single," Kate moans. "It's so exciting, having all these lovely men."

"You don't know that they're all lovely. The bastard Jamie Donnelly definitely wasn't. But I agree," Vicky smiles, "right now I love being single, and I wouldn't change places with anyone for all the money in the world."

"The piece is wonderful!" Janelle calls Vicky into her office and pushes a preview issue of the magazine at her.

"Swapping Lives: Could you step into another person's life? Wear her clothes, live with her husband, go out with her friends? We sent single Vicky Townsley, features editor of *Poise!*, over to the country that spawned the hit show *Desperate Housewives* to see if she could live the life of a married woman. And Desperate Housewife Amber Winslow flew over to Vicky's hip London flat to try and live the life of a single girl. Who was happier? Is the grass greener on the other side? Read on and find out."

On one side is a photograph of Vicky, Eartha on her lap, glass of wine in hand, curled up on the sofa in her stylish flat. On the other side is Amber sitting next to the swimming pool, Richard grinning behind her, Gracie and Jared on her lap, Ginger lying at her feet, all of them looking like the perfect American family.

Looking at the picture, Vicky feels a pang. Even now, even

knowing what she knows, the grass still looks just a little bit greener, but as she starts to read the article, she realizes that just because the grass looks greener doesn't necessarily mean that it is, and although her garden may be small, her flowers not yet blooming, her lawn just getting ready to renew itself after a drought, her grass isn't so bad.

And who knows, with a little bit of fertilizer and some tender loving care, from Bill-the-chicken-man or Hugh Janus, or perhaps someone entirely new she has yet to meet, her grass may turn out to be on the very best side of all.